Two Brothers

Praise for
The Maniac Responsible:

"First rate … extraordinary … a work of art. … Brilliant!"

- Newsweek

"Real and Powerful."

- Dallas Times Herald

Praise for
On the Run with Dick and Jane

"A literary Halley's comet!"

- Gore Vidal

"Not likely to be forgotten."

- Thomas E. Kennedy

Praise for
Time and Money: The Economy and the Planets:

"Robert Gover's challenging and fascinating new book is both massive in its scope and startling in its vision. It truly offers something for everyone."

- FinancialCyclesWeekly.com

"Gover's experience as a social commentator makes *Time and Money* worth a read, regardless of one's views about astrology."

- Euromoney Magazine

"Using the art of astrology, Robert Gover predicts fundamental changes, even revolutions around the world, from 2008 all the way to 2020. I agree with many of his forecasts."

- Dr. Ravi Batra, Southern Methodist University

Books by Robert Gover

One Hundred Dollar Misunderstanding
Here Goes Kitten
J.C. Saves
The JC and Kitten Trilogy
The Maniac Responsible
Poorboy at the Party
Getting Pretty on the Table
Going for Mr. Big
Tomorrow Now Occurs Again
On the Run with Dick and Jane
Two Brothers

Nonfiction

Voodoo Contra:
Contradictory Meanings of the Word

Time & Money:
The Economy and the Planets

www.RobertGover.com

Two Brothers

Robert Gover

Hopewell Publications

Published by Hopewell
Publications, LLC
PO Box 11, Titusville, NJ
08560-0011 (609) 818-1049

info@HopePubs.com
www.HopePubs.com

International Standard Book Number: 9781933435251

Library of Congress Control Number: 2008934388

First Edition

Printed in the United States of America

For my two sons Bryant and Damian.

*Thanks to Matt Ryan, Chrissy Coleman and
Norman Gover for their editorial input.*

*Special thanks to my wife Carolyn for her love,
encouragement and support,
and to stepdaughter Nicole for her raw,
spontaneous reading of the manuscript.*

Chapter 1

Shortly before I brought home my long lost, politically radical, derelict and psychotic brother Robert, I was lonely. Shortly after bringing him home, I was madly in love with a girl 34 years younger than myself and my personal security guard was trying to kill me. Meanwhile, it seemed that brother Robert had emerged from his dungeon of tragedy into the bright sunshine of good fortune. I am not a superstitious man but it had me wondering if this was some kind of transmigration of souls. Had my brother and I somehow exchanged personal destinies?

These changes in my life began on a Friday afternoon in February of 2008 when I got a call from a private psychiatric facility in Camarillo. A female voice identifying herself as Dr. Mary Grace said they planned to discharge my brother Robert this Monday morning, "If you will agree to pick him up here and provide him a place to live while he gets back on his feet."

I told the lady psychiatrist that the last I'd known, my brother was diagnosed incurable and expected to spend the rest of his life incarcerated. "It comes as quite a shock to get word that you're discharging him. Is he all right? Is he any danger to himself or others?"

"As long as he takes his daily medications," the lady doctor said, "he's no threat to himself or others."

"Will I need to hire someone to supervise him?"

"No, he's quite capable of taking care of himself. We just need a place for him to live. We can send someone out once a week, if you'd like, to check on his progress and give you whatever back-up you need. The trust fund his father established to pay for his care covers everything."

"I think you should know, Dr. Grace, that my brother and I have been estranged for four decades."

"Yes, Robert has told us as much."

"Has the fund to pay for his care run low? If it's depleted, I will replenish it."

"No," she said, "there is no need for that. The fund is more than sufficient to cover all costs."

Growing up, my big brother Bob had been my hero, so when his life disintegrated and he wound up a homeless wretch, addicted and insane, it ate a hole in my psyche—yet ironically, at the same time, it freed me to become my true self. We had grown up in a family that argued politics morning, noon and night, and Bob's collapse was at once a heart aching loss and an ideological victory. He and our mother were liberal while our father and I were conservative.

In the last four decades, the only encounter I'd had with brother Bob was back in the eighties. I was strolling up State Street in Santa Barbara one morning when I passed a homeless person sitting with his back against a building, holding out a begging cup. He had a blanket over his head and shoulders so that only his gaunt, filthy face was partially visible. As I walked past him, I was distracted by a police car pulling to a stop at the curb to my right. A few steps onward I realized that peering out through those blue eyes under that moldy blanket was brother Robert. I wheeled around, just in time to see him being handcuffed and put into the police car. It pulled away before I could get their attention.

I went to the police station and got Bob released into my custody and took him home. I tried to converse with him but he seemed co-matose, struck dumb, a walking zombie. When I asked him questions, he stared past me with a vacant look in his eyes. He fit the phrase, "The lights were on but nobody was home." I helped him shower and shave, and gave him clean clothes. In the middle of the afternoon I left him to do some business and when I came back that evening, he was flat on the living room floor, dead drunk. I got him a pillow and blanket, and the next morning he was gone. With him went about a dozen bottles from my living room bar. On his way out the door, he'd dropped a few, leaving a trail of broken glass and spilled liquor.

Back in the sixties and seventies, while I earned degrees from the University of Southern California and then Harvard, Bob became a political radical and college dropout, speaking at antiwar rallies, getting arrested numerous times, hiding out in various friends' apartments, dodging the police, and finally about seven years ago, landing in San Quentin. Our father, shortly before he passed away, had called in a political favor to get Bob transferred from San Quentin to this private facility in Camarillo called Covington, and set up a fund to pay for his care. We were told Bob would live there the rest of his life. Mom and Dad drove down to visit him only once. They said his mind was so far gone, they decided another visit was pointless. They'd rather remember him the way he'd been before his illness.

Our lives had diverged forty-three years ago when I was sixteen and he'd left for Stanford on a swimming scholarship. Everyone expected big things from Bob, an Olympic contender in the butterfly event and straight A student with a talent for writing. Two years later I left for the University of Southern California fearful that I, the little brother, could never measure up.

What surprises life had in store.

I had a plane to catch Monday afternoon but I agreed to pick Bob up at 9 AM and bring him here to my beach house. I'd then be gone for three or four days, staying at the Metropolitan Club in Manhattan. I was transitioning into retirement. The board wanted me to supervise my replacement till everyone was confident that the regulators would not hit us. Or, if it became necessary, we'd be bailed out the way Bear Stearns had been. About six months ago, in the summer of 2007, I'd told the board the real threat was that we'd not yet gotten the full ripple effect of the mortgage collapse. Real estate prices would continue to drop, I said, while inflation spiked. We were looking at the worst credit bubble in American history and worse "stagflation" then we'd had in the late seventies. They listened politely but didn't believe it. One member went so far as to suggest that I needed a night on the town to get me out of my pessimistic mood. It was the collective national mood that had become pessimistic, not me. I'm retiring with a package that adds up to around $34 million.

Between Friday and Monday morning, I thought a lot about how close Bob and I had been growing up, and then how totally estranged we'd been for the past forty-three years. How do you relate to a brother who has spent so much of his life in and out of jails, rehabs and insane asylums, then San Quentin and this upscale psych ward? Would it be possible to renew those childhood bonds? We were, after all, the only immediate family either of us had left, for our parents have passed on and I am twice divorced. I have four children from those two marriages, but they are grown now, out in the world on their own, and I rarely, if ever, hear from any of them.

I was feeling the kind of loneliness I felt years ago when, on a solo sail to Hawaii—something I attempted on a dare—my boat was damaged in a storm and I was adrift in the middle of the Pacific Ocean, with nothing but the vast sea and sky and endless hours to review my life and ponder my death—until I was spotted by an Air Force plane and picked up by a Japanese fishing trawler. After that experience, I vowed to concentrate on building the company. It was the one thing I was uniquely suited to do. I was an entrepreneurial warrior. That was my forte. I became so obsessed with my work that weekends with the family were an irritating distraction. Now, facing retirement after an incredibly busy life, I was again adrift.

I'd broken up with my second wife Laura five or six years ago. She was now living three thousand miles away on the East Coast, in Rehoboth Beach, Delaware, near her parents, providing our two children access to their maternal grandparents. Laura said she had loved living in the Padero Lane beach house here on the West Coast, but that my long absences, harried weekend visits, and the ubiquitous presence of the security people made it impossible.

She didn't understand the company's need for security. Three of our management people had been kidnapped during the past five years. We'd paid millions to get two of them back and never did recover our man in Karachi, Pakistan. It cost a lot less to have our key people protected by a topnotch security agency. Protecting our key people also means protecting whatever family members are living with them.

My first wife Kelly and two children by her—I had not seen or heard from them since I'd married Laura in the late eighties. Not even a Christmas card. I was no longer sure where Kelly lived. My personal financial manager makes sure the needs of both ex-wives and all four children are met. Since they want nothing to do with me, I do not try to contact them. It's enough to know they are all doing well. The older two both have lucrative careers in corporate law and the youngest two are university students, one at Penn State, the other at Georgetown.

So here I am, semi-retired and living alone, with only our maid Alicia, a dour Hispanic woman in her forties who cooks and cleans, and otherwise keeps to herself. My loneliness is occasionally relieved by a visit from one retired colleague or another, and I am routinely invited to various social affairs in nearby Montecito where Bob and I grew up. But I was decompressing from a very busy business life that had required I be in far-flung cities of the world for research or negotiations, spending hours above the clouds in the company plane, working, always working. Now I faced the common lament of the newly retired: "Is this all there is?"

Bob's presence, I decided, would at least relieve the loneliness, if he is well enough to be released. If not, I can return him to the hospital. Was it possible that we might even recapture the togetherness we had as children and teenagers? Was that too much to hope for?

Bright and early Monday morning, I suited up for the trip to New York and, before departing for LAX, diverted to Camarillo to pick up brother Bob.

Chapter 2

I was sitting on a bench outside the entrance with my backpack between my feet when I got my first glimpse of John, peering at me through the windshield of his car. We hadn't seen each other in so many years, maybe he wasn't sure it was me. I stood up and waved. He smiled and bounced out of his car and came around to give me a bear hug. He smelled of expensive cologne and new clothing. I must have smelled to him of toxic pharmaceuticals and the vapors of the nut house.

He was dressed in a dark blue suit, crisp white shirt and shiny silk necktie. It reminded me of how Dad used to say you should dress to make a statement. A well-tailored suit, tasteful necktie and shoes that say to your workers, "I cost more than you make in a month." I was wearing a work shirt, jeans and sneakers bought at the nearby Salvation Army Thrift Store. But I'd never put much attention into clothes. Dad used to say to me, "Why do you wear the same clothes day after day? Was your mother frightened by a monk?" I'd protest that I changed underwear and socks every day but spent so much time in a Speedo swimming laps, I didn't need to change my other clothes.

John held the hug for longer than I'd expected, the successful organization man embracing the failed individualist. After the hug, he held me by the shoulders, looked intently into my eyes and said, "How are you feeling, Bob?"

"Much better, Jack," I said. I didn't specify better than what. I certainly felt better than when I arrived at this hospital seven years ago in a straight jacket. It was going to take me some time to adjust to the outside, for I'd grown so accustomed to being ostracized that returning to normal society had me trembling with apprehension.

He said, "It's good to see you, brother, after all these years. You look fit."

"Thanks, Jack. I feel pretty good, all things considered." His words helped ease my jitters. I might have commented on his looks, but held my tongue. He looked to be in pretty good shape physically. What surprised me, though, was an attitude I'd never seen in my little brother—supreme confidence. He'd become the kind of man people automatically defer to.

"Wait here," he said, "I'll go inside and complete the paperwork."

"Thanks for doing this, Jack," I said to his back as he pushed through the front door into the lobby. He lifted his right arm in a backward wave without turning around.

As kids we'd called each other Jack and Bob when we were feeling light-hearted, and John and Robert when we were serious or argumentative. We got that from our mother. She'd call us Jack and Bob when she was happy with us, and John and Robert when she had, as she liked to say, "a bone to pick."

I wondered what brand of car he was driving. In Covington, television viewing was restricted, so I was unfamiliar with new car models. I walked to the back of the car to see the brand name. Mercedes. I should have guessed. It was silver, looked brand spanking new, like he'd just driven it off the showroom floor this morning. Jack took after our father, maintained his material possessions in tiptop shape. I took after our mother—her energies went into protesting injustices and supporting socially beneficial causes. Dad sometimes called her a weak-kneed liberal. When aroused, she called him a brain-dead fascist. Dad's company was in Ventura and he often overnighted there, or somewhere other than the bedroom he shared with Mom. They maintained their marriage, they said, "for the sake of the children," my brother and me. Every four years, Dad bought two new Mercedes, a sedan for himself and a station wagon for Mom, and despite their politically contentious relationship, they stayed married till they passed on.

I tossed my bag on the back seat and sat in the front passenger seat, noting the contrasting textures of our very different lives. Brother John had won the ongoing political debates we'd had as teenagers, for the world now operates on the free-market, unrestrained capitalism he and Dad so passionately espoused. My brother had found extraordinary success. I've lived in very different circumstances. Now here we were—me age 60 and him 58—turning that corner on life's journey when you are expected to retire, relax, leave behind everything that had brought joy and magic into your life. The Golden Years, they're called.

I had been 20 years old when I dropped out of Stanford, became involved in the Movement to end the war in Vietnam, extend full citizenship to African Americans, create an alternative culture. I became so involved in the movement that I'd stopped going to classes or showing up for swimming practice. I'd never been steadily employed by a company, university or government. Rarely filed with the IRS, so the Social Security check I'd soon collect would be pitiful. Push come to shove, I could live on leftovers thrown out the back doors of restaurants. Brother John, on the other hand, had become a multimillionaire. I'd heard rumors that his net worth was pushing upwards toward a billion.

I had long ago lost my fear of poverty and in recent years I'd developed certain mental capacities. I'd become part of a healing group in the Bay Area which met once a week to use the psychic healing techniques of Jose Silva. We worked on a list of people in critical condition in area hospitals and got results that astounded the few doctors who took an interest. I had also developed the ability to project my mind and view people at a distance. For the past decade or so, I'd been mentally looking in on brother John, and knew he was now going through a change, suffering feelings of abandonment. I knew too that this had roots in our childhood when I, the big brother, was lavishly showered by our parents with loving admiration, leaving little Jack feeling he had to out-do himself to win their affections. This he had certainly done. I had become incapacitated and they had left everything to him. Now they were dead and he was twice divorced, living alone. He needed me and I needed to be needed, and the best service I could give at this point in our lives, I figured, was to restore his sense of self-esteem. I knew that he'd given the best of himself to a huge corporation, and now it was done with him.

He emerged from the lobby about fifteen minutes later, slid behind the wheel and said, "I'm divorced, you know, living in the Padero house. There's plenty of room for you."

Our father had bought a beach house back in the middle sixties when it was a deteriorating shack on a lonely promontory overlooking a vacant stretch of beach south of Santa Barbara. He'd bought it shortly after I left for Stanford, with money he'd put aside for my higher education. In my most resentful moments, I'd viewed this house as bought by my athletic scholarship.

John had become the kind of man people notice and talk about, so I knew the particulars of his life. I knew he'd lived on the East Coast for a couple of decades after graduating from Harvard, but had also maintained the beach house on Padero Lane. I knew that both our parents had lived out their last years in the guesthouse there. His business demanded he travel the world, so he had houses and townhouses from Manhattan to Beijing, but the Padero house has special meaning for him. He'd called it home his last year in high school and while he was going to college, during the years when his star was rising and I was sinking into ruin.

One rainy night in the middle nineties when I had a part-time job as a taxi driver in Santa Barbara, I'd seen him being picked up by a limo. I'd driven to the beach house that night in a rainstorm with the intention of knocking on the door and presenting myself as the long lost brother. I stopped short of knocking when I heard loud male and female voices arguing behind the door and children crying. It would have been very bad timing for the derelict brother to inject himself into this family squabble, so I got back in the taxi and drove away. This was a period when I was sleeping in the taxi, in a free municipal parking lot.

"We've refurbished the guest cottage," said Jack as he drove. "You can stay there till you get back on your feet."

"Thanks. That's very generous of you." I sounded to myself like a mechanical answering machine and hoped my sincere gratitude came through. Jack didn't have to do this—take me out of the nuthouse and give me a place to live.

"It's nothing. I rebuilt the Padero house with the money from the sale of our old house," he said, meaning our parents' house on Picacho Lane in Montecito, the Bel Air of Santa Barbara, where we'd grown up together. Our father's small company had been part of the vast military-industrial complex I came to despise. After he died, the company was leased. Now Dad's company was making brother John some of the billions spent on wars in Iraq and Afghanistan.

"Is the old homestead on Picacho Lane still there?" I asked. I knew the answer. Just making conversation.

"The new owners tore it down and built a new house on the property. Eight bedrooms, four-car garage, stand-alone guesthouse, and a gorgeous swimming pool."

In high school, I used to complain that our backyard pool was too small to swim laps. My family had attended my swimming meets, although that sport is, for non-participants, like watching paint dry. They had stoked my self-esteem with congratulations and prideful smiles. There were moments in my teens when I'd felt sorry for Jack—so much admiration was directed at me while he was ignored.

"I don't suppose you'd like your old job back," said Jack with a grin as he drove the 101 past Ventura. "I'm sure you can find something better than driving a taxi."

I was slightly surprised that he knew I'd driven a taxi. It had been a temporary, on and off job, during a time when I'd drifted back to the old hometown. We'd lived within walking distance—me in a room on Gutierrez Street, him in a townhouse on the beach—but had no contact. I remember seeing him a few times as I was driving the taxi past the outdoor café on the Mesa where he sometimes stopped for morning coffee. I might have stopped and approached him but I was in bad shape back then, couldn't hold a steady job, and would sometimes resort to panhandling.

Once he took me out of the county jail and brought me to a townhouse he was living in then—he was between wives and the Padero house was being rebuilt. I was drinking heavily at the time and don't remember much, only that I stole two big paper shopping bags full of whiskey before I fled. Why did I flee? I was trapped in John Barleycorn's dungeon, feeling deep and helpless shame. I carried those two big bags full of bottles to The Fig Tree, at the corner of Chapala Street and the 101, where the homeless hung out. Every bottle was empty by dawn.

"Have anything in mind?" he asked. "About what you'd like to do?"

"I'd like to open a bookstore," I said. I don't know where that came from. It just popped out.

I saw Jack heave a sigh and guessed he wanted to say that my running a bookstore was totally unrealistic. Instead, he said, "Well, there's a lot of detail work connected with owning a business. You up for that?"

"Better than working for someone else," I said.

"You'd have to work longer hours and you'd have to deal with licensing authorities, keep your own books, inventory, many other details. Very stressful. You'd be in competition with the big chains, you know. It wouldn't be an eight-hour shift and go home."

"I have no home to go to."

"Bob, you have a home with me. I want to do whatever it takes to restore you to full health. You look good. I have no reason to think you're not totally healed. So how about this: I need help with my properties. It's not easy maintaining so many far-flung properties, you know. You wouldn't have to do the maintenance work yourself. Just make sure the work gets done. Think you could handle that?"

"Yeah, I think so."

"In some strange way, I feel that we've come full circle, back to where we were when we were little kids with our lives ahead of us."

"Back then, it seemed such a long, long road," I said.

"Remember the trip to New Mexico with Mom and Dad? We were eight and ten years old, I think. We drove north out of Albuquerque and it seemed like the distant mountains were so far away, so high, such an impossible barrier, we both thought we'd never get over them."

"I remember. We were in the back seat of Mom's station wagon, peering past Mom and Dad, staring at those mountains in the distance. We complained to Dad that it looked like we'd be driving forever up that long, long hill toward those impossible mountain tops, and we wanted to stop and eat, get out of the car and play."

"Yeah, and I remember what Dad said. That this feeling was like contemplating the road of life when you're a kid, but that as you continue on the road of life, things that seemed impossible, turn out to have been easy."

"Yeah, and he also said that it's the unexpected that becomes difficult. Dad gave us a full-blown philosophy-of-life lecture as we drove toward those mountain peaks."

"Do you remember that leaving Albuquerque, it was warm and sunny? I think this was during our mid-year school break in early January. And by the time we got up the mountain, it was snowing and we had to overnight in a motel in Flagstaff because the snow was so deep we couldn't drive on safely."

"Safety was the word," I said. "Dad was obsessed with safety. We wanted to drive through that blizzard but he insisted we stop."

"You and Mom wanted to drive on," said John. "I was happy to stop. You were the one who was reckless."

"You're right. Mom said she trusted to providence and we kept asking her what providence was. Once, when I was flat broke, I made some money driving that same route out of Albuquerque and hitting another blizzard around Flagstaff and driving on through it, trusting to providence, hauling a load of Mexican marijuana."

John looked like he didn't know whether to scowl or laugh. "By yourself?" he asked.

"With a girlfriend. Her name was Jenny. She was upset because I insisted on driving on through that snowstorm. You couldn't see twenty feet ahead. She was sure we'd wind up either dead or in jail."

"What became of Jenny?"

"She left me when we got back to LA. I woke up the next morning in a motel on Sunset and she was gone. Never heard from her again."

"You were never short of girlfriends, were you. I envied you, you had so many."

"After high school, they were mostly the kind who come for the cocaine and marijuana, not the kind who married dear old dad."

"Those were the years I was at Harvard, cold and lonely on the East Coast. While you were enjoying real flesh and blood sex, I was jacking off to Playboy centerfolds."

"And getting the education that would lead to the successful life you have."

"Had," said Jack. "I'm easing into retirement."

It occurred to me at that moment that my bother's life and mine have, in a sense, paralleled the nation's growing estrangement between rich and poor. My friend Jorge Hernandez says his astrological studies indicate the nation is in for the most profound changes in its history, during another great depression due to begin this year, 2008, and last a decade or more. It may not get called a great depression, Jorge says, but it's likely to be worse than the nineteen thirties. Jorge predicted the housing price collapse and how it would impact the world economy, as it's doing now. Jorge can be found any sunny afternoon sitting in the courtyard at Covington, his laptop on his knees, printer beside his feet, downloading historical passages about previous great depressions and astrological charts he says show that they all occurred under the same planetary pattern. I take his word for it because his economic predictions are right on.

Strange that brother Jack and I are coming together now, on the cusp of unprecedented times.

Chapter 3

It didn't take long to see that brother Bob, no matter what he'd been through before, was clear minded and physically fit now. I was delighted to note the sparkle of intelligence in his eyes, his easy way of speaking, and that he still carried himself with that straight-backed posture he'd had as a youth. Except for his drab clothing, a stranger meeting him would never imagine he'd been in and out of jails and psych wards for so much of his life. Just seven years ago, he'd been declared incurably insane, a terminal case, and now here he was, looking and sounding as good as new. That I was taking him out of that hospital and giving him a place to live made me feel so much better about myself.

And there was so much I wanted to tell him. My life, for all its success, had not prepared me for the loneliness I felt as I faced my retirement years. I had a busy social life before I eased out of the company. Now, I attend parties, but rarely, thrown by Montecito divorcees, usually, on the prowl for new husbands. I have no intention of becoming their prey. Nor, for that matter, a sex partner to any of them. I have my young, pretty rendezvous girls. I meet one or two discreetly at the Biltmore whenever I get the urge. I pay cash—dollars, euros or yen—and they're always upbeat and trouble-free. There are times when I envy my colleagues who have retired with life mates they love profoundly and will be with till death parts them. And surrounded by their children and grandchildren through their declining years.

My two youngest children came here during summers but now that they're both in college, they've let it be known they have better things to do. My two oldest also stopped coming here when they went to college. This loss of my children baffles and disturbs me but I know it's my own fault. I put my energy into parenting the corporation and neglected my children. I looked forward to telling my brother all this and more. But later, after we become reacquainted.

I turned off the 101 at Santa Claus Lane, then right onto Padero Lane. The house is about midway along this stretch of beachfront, flanked on one side by the 101 and railroad tracks, and on the other side, the ocean. At Santa Claus Lane, there is a small amusement park where Bob and I had spent some happy childhood hours. It was vacant now, in February.

As we turned onto the lane leading to the beach house, Bob stiffened, sat up in his seat and said, "Wow." I'd momentarily forgotten that he'd never seen the newest restoration. It had been professionally designed, made out of redwood, stone and glass. Two stories of glass with a double-door entrance facing front, and on the ocean side, two stories of insulated glass. Five bedrooms and a three-bedroom guesthouse. Swimming pool between the main house and the beach. This property was probably the best investment our Dad ever made. It's a wonderful home and has increased in price dramatically. I think Dad paid around a quarter of a million back in sixty-five, and now it was worth mega-millions.

"A feat of architecture," said Bob. "It takes my breath away."

"You'll be staying in the guest cottage. See it? It's tucked away in those pine trees to the left of the main house."

"This is so generous of you, Jack. Thank you!"

"Don't mention it."

If Bob had stayed at Stanford instead of taking to the streets to protest the established order, he'd feel no need to thank me, for he'd own fifty percent of this property and everything else Dad had left.

"Bob, I've got to call the limo service now, and get ready to be picked up and taken to LAX for a trip to New York. I'll be gone a few days. Make yourself at home. The front door to the guest cottage is unlocked. The key is inside on the dining room table." As we were getting out of the car, I said, "And I want you to know how wonderful it is to be with you again after all these years."

He shot me a serious look and said, "That means a lot to me, John."

"One more thing. If you feel eyes on you, it's the security people. A gentleman named Jake Valance and his crew protect this place. I'll introduce you to him next time he stops by."

Bob stared at me a moment with a look of incomprehension, like he was waiting for me to say more. He picked up his backpack as I drove the car into the garage, and strolled toward the guest cottage. He'd lost muscle mass over the years but still had the broad-shoulders and slim-waist I'd envied. "I'll see you when I get back tomorrow," I called after him. He waved a hand without turning around. When I get back, I'll buy him some decent clothes. His blue jeans look ready to disintegrate.

Here I am with more money than God, as my first wife Kelly used to say. My annual income is more than enough to take care of the various properties, two exes, and four children. I sometimes marvel that profits and interest grow faster than the whole clan could spend it. Not that they would do that—they are happy with their trust funds and busy with their own careers.

And there is brother Bob, dressed like a homeless panhandler as he comes out of years of confinement. Am I ready to confess that I feel guilty? That I wish our parents had tracked him down years ago and saved him from spiraling out of control? Instead, Dad had said that he'd had every advantage I'd had and there was nothing we could do to prevent his self-destructive behavior. Even our mother was so baffled she finally gave up on him. They declared Bob lost and focused all their love on me.

I've long been aware that someone like me could amass a fortune and wind up an old Scrooge with no personal life, no loving wife and children and grandchildren. I prepared a large corporation for the future but not myself. I did everything according to the book while Bob became a renegade. He's a failure and I'm a success, yet there is a huge hole in my life where the joys of family might have been, if I'd been differently constituted. Bob has no family either. Nor friends that I know of. Yet he has a twinkle in his eye and radiates a quiet, calm kind of joy.

I sat down in the living room and autodialed the limo service, told customer service I'm ready for the ride to LAX, and she assured me it would be there within twenty minutes. I've made this trip so many times over the years, the limo routine is on automatic.

While I was waiting, I flipped open the laptop I keep in the living-room and checked out the Wall Street Journal and Financial Times of London. Nothing startling in either so I went to my personal accounts and checked out my four hedge funds, which each give a running net. All were doing exceedingly well, especially the currency exchange, short the dollar against the euro and the yen. No logical reason the dollar should be falling but Herby Stein, my personal financial manager, advised I short the dollar and it is paying off week by week. Herby is convinced the dollar is destined to fall much farther. I am not convinced, and keep a tight stop-loss. Herby thinks I should put more money into the falling dollar. I'm not convinced it will continue to fall, and would rather buy more foreign stocks, and American healthcare related stocks. Our way of delivering health care is a bottomless well of wealth into the foreseeable future. Even the Democratic Party candidates, Hillary Clinton and Barack Obama, don't utter a peep about scrapping the present system in favor of a government-run single-payer socialist model. Their "universal" plans promise new profits to the big insurance and pharmaceutical companies.

In this moment of silent contemplation I was transported back to when I was sixteen, watching Bob pack up his old junker Corolla to leave for Stanford. This memory triggered a bereft feeling, and suddenly my eyes had tears. Why?

When brother Bob left for Stanford, I could not imagine how I would function. I'd relied on him, my big brother, to tell me the important things, like who to hang out with in high school, what teachers to avoid, how to comb my hair, what clothes to wear. I was an overweight roly-poly kid with glasses. I'd started swimming when I was seven, the same as Bob, but had no talent for it, only wanted to get those practice sessions over with so I could dry off, get back in my clothes and be warm. I didn't want to be at those swim sessions, wanted to be home reading, or following Dad around, or hanging on my big brother's tales of bad girls. To his senior prom he took the girl with the worst reputation in high school. "Why deny myself?" he said. Instead of cutting a figure at a post-prom party, he and this girl locked themselves in his bedroom and screwed till dawn. When Dad expressed outrage, Bob said, "Why go to those damn parties and drink and smoke cigarettes? Sex is so much healthier." Mom kept quiet but smirked. A couple years later, I took Kelly Corey, whose father was a top exec at IBM. Sex was out of the question—we drank and smoked till we turned green and puked. Dad was happy that I was dating a girl "from a good family," exceptionally affluent. Mom looked bored and busied herself with paperwork. I wondered what Bob would say, by then he was away at Stanford and spending weekends hanging out with Berkeley radicals. He'd stopped coming home for weekends and holidays. The Christmas of my senior year was lonely. Bob called and spoke to each of us by turns, and after that very long telephone call, Dad was adamant that I would go south, to Southern Cal, and not get mixed up in the craziness that Berkeley was becoming. Even if I'd gone to Berkeley I would not have gotten mixed up in it. It made no sense to me. I never wanted to overthrow the establishment as Bob did—all I wanted was to be accepted into the establishment.

Kelly, my first wife, had great social skills but became an embarrassment because she couldn't keep her panties on. We married in the early seventies while I was at Harvard. Five years later as my career was taking off, I knew I had to jettison her or I'd limit my upward mobility.

This flow of memories ended when I saw the limo drive up outside. I was ready, readjusted, wearing the right attitude for my meeting in New York tomorrow, followed by a dinner for a retiring mid-management guy whose name eludes me. I'll go through the motions at the dinner to honor him but my main purpose is to go over the accounts with my replacement, Dan. He called two days ago to say he was baffled by some of these, and no wonder. They are baffling. That's their glory. They baffle the IRS. I maintain the proper demeanor as I patiently explain them to Dan. They avoid taxes and maximize profits, albeit paper profits, imaginary equity, until the end of the process when they become convertible to real cash. That's the be all and end all of it. Most of these accounts are denominated in euros or yen or Swiss francs, but we convert to dollars, finally, for the dollar is golden. Has been since the Nixon years. We keep three different books using two different accounting systems—that's another thing Dan is having trouble with. We keep it legal, although it does complicate dealings with our accounting firm.

I shook off my woolgathering, grabbed my briefcase and was off. As the limo turned onto Padero Lane, Jake Valance's big black van cruised past us to lead the way. He gave me the thumbs up, meaning all is well with his operation. One of the security people will be on the flight to New York—I'm not supposed to know who, but I can figure it out by scanning the people around me in first class for the one who looks like a retired cop in plain clothes.

On this trip, I knew it was a guy sitting across the aisle reading the New York *Times*. I was tempted to buy him a drink and chat, ask him how in the world he could do such a boring job without going bonkers. I didn't feel the least bit threatened. On my last trip, I told our current CEO Jim Hurly that I'm husky enough to discourage muggers so I figure my size also discourages kidnappers, to which he returned a diminished smile and said, "We live in a dangerous world." Before nine-eleven, it seemed that the government was protecting us. Now it seems we are protecting the government, and all because of those top-secret contracts, which—I must not forget—constitute a sizeable portion of our net profits.

I feel the presence of my security escort like a light breeze on my left cheek, but whenever I glance his way, he averts his eyes. Which is fine with me. We really don't have anything to say to each other.

Chapter 4

In the guesthouse, I looked for traces of my parents, whose last home had been here, this cottage. I found none. That was strange, I thought, for our mother was a collector of family memorabilia. Surely when she and Dad lived out their final days here, she must have hung enlarged photos of John and me on these walls. In the master bedroom I found a cedar trunk and opened it expecting to find scrapbooks and photo albums, but found only blankets and towels. I wandered back to the living room, sat in an easy chair with a view through an opened front window, and put myself into the alpha brainwave state.

After meditating for about half an hour, I opened my eyes to see a limo pull up to the main house and John get into it. It whispered down the tidy blacktop lane toward Padero and the freeway to LA, leaving me with the soothing sounds of wind whispering through the pines, rhythmic surf pounding onto the beach, birds calling to each other. I wondered what I'd do if, God forbid, something terrible happened to Jack and he never returned. Who would own all this? Would they remove me like old trash? I wiped that image from my mind and replaced it with John and me restoring the brotherly love we had as children.

I still struggle, at times, to break the old habit of catastrophic thinking. He'll return. But maybe he will want to settle on some time frame for my staying here, this halfway house he's providing, and then what? Back to the streets? At age 60 and sober? Maybe I can get hold of a camera and make some money as a photographer. Oh, but the new cameras are digital and I know nothing of those. Well, I can learn. Meanwhile, I must discipline myself to banish catastrophic thoughts and entertain only images of the life I want. But what life is that? I'm thankful every day for all the wonderful things that found me in the past, the joy I have in the present, and whatever happy moments may find me in the future. My ambition is to stay sober and sane.

Then I remembered that my brother had mentioned managing his far-flung properties. Was he serious? I need to turn off this babbling brook of thoughts. Like jetlag, a large part of me is still back in Covington and can't quite believe the new environment my eyes reveal.

Sitting on the coffee table in front of the couch was a laptop. I opened it and went to an opening menu. Whose was it? I opened some files, hoping to find out, but all were empty of personal data. It was, apparently, brand new. Well, it was here and so was I. I'll use it, unless or until I am informed it has an owner.

I'd been learning computers in San Quentin—I was there only for a few months before I'd been transferred to the psych ward—and after seven years inside the nut house, I was back to start with computers, especially the likes of this one, which emitted barely an audible hum. I found I could go online with it, though, and that was enough for now. Jorge has been permitted to have his laptop in Covington. Later, I'll call him. He has a cell phone. Cell phones, ipods, Blackberries and other such devices barely existed when I went into Covington. All this instant communication would take some getting used to. I remembered Henry David Thoreau's comment when the telegraph was new back in his day and he wondered if people had anything worthwhile to communicate, or if the telegraph would merely become a distraction and add to environmental degradation. "Well," I said aloud to the Thoreau I carry in my mind, "you had the wonders of Walden Pond. I have the remains of what's called life on the outside."

I wandered through the guesthouse and stood gazing out the dining area's picture window at a gray, overcast sea, the horizon lost in a pea-soup-thick fog, the kind of mornings I remembered surfing at

Jalama Beach when the current coming around Point Conception delivered long, easy curlers. Little brother Jack had begged my friends and I to come with us, and we'd let him. Once he got slammed on the bottom and knocked unconscious. I wanted to take him home but he'd insisted on going back out to catch another wave—to show my friends and I that he had guts.

This morning for breakfast I'd had only a couple of pancakes, the frozen kind you pop into a toaster. Now, feeling hungry--from imaginary surfing?—I went out the back door and walked about fifty yards over a carpet of pine needles to a door opening into the main house kitchen. A very large kitchen with a chopping block planted in its middle, and before I reached the refrigerator to see what I might find, a female voice sounded behind me.

"I dial nine one one," it screeched in panic.

I turned to find a woman standing in a doorway to what turned out to be the maid's quarters, holding a cordless phone, poised to dial.

"I'm John's brother," I said, trying for a pleasant smile.

"John no here," she said. "You go away or I call police."

I held up my hands as though the phone were a gun she had pointed at me and eased out the back door, and returned over the pine needles to the guest cottage. Before I went in, I glanced back to see her staring daggers at me as she spoke into her phone. I figured she was John's cook or maid and wondered why he hadn't told her about me. Maybe she senses where I'm coming from, smells the vapors of the nuthouse.

The guesthouse refrigerator had some frozen dinners. I chose a meatloaf and mashed potatoes package, and popped it in the microwave.

I gazed out at the moody seascape as I ate and just as I'd finished the last bite, a doorbell chimed. At the front door stood a large black man in uniform. Something about his flat nose and deep-set eyes seemed familiar. "I'm responding to a call about a prowler here," he said. His voice and face played with my memory. "I'm Al Hansen with the Sheriff's Department."

"I'm Bob Bradford, John Bradford's brother." Then it came back to me. "Are you the same Al Hansen who played football for Santa Barbara High School?"

Deputy Al Hansen stepped back and looked me up and down with a frown that slowly morphed into a grin. "Are you the same Bob Bradford that was a champion swimmer in high school?"

I laughed and said, "So you found a career in law enforcement."

"Yeah, this is what old jocks do—the ones who didn't get scholarships."

"Come on in, Al. Good to see you after all these years."

He sauntered in and sat on the coach. "You got a scholarship to Stanford, didn't you?"

"Yes, but I dropped out."

"Where you been? I heard rumors about you over the years."

Al had played right guard on our high school team. He was big, solidly built and surprisingly light on his feet. He still had the flat stomach of a man who takes care of himself, but the weary attitude of a man who was not challenged by his job.

We stared at each other for a moment. We'd both aged and could pass on a city sidewalk without recognizing each other. But now, with a name for this ebony face, memories returned.

There was no point fibbing. "I've just been released from a psychiatric facility in Camarillo."

"I heard you became a hippie," said Al with a sly grin.

That word had different connotations today than it had back in the sixties. "Not exactly," I said. "I was part of the sixties counter-culture, but I never became a hippie"—or what I imagined to be his idea of a hippie. "I became a writer."

"How long you gonna be here?"

"I'm not sure. Would you like a cup of coffee? I was just about to make some."

"I'll go for a cup."

Walking into the kitchen, Al had to duck to avoid hitting his head on the doorframe.

"I'm surprised you never got any scholarship offers," I said. "Of all the football players around our age, I thought you were the only one with the potential to become a pro."

"I thought so, too," he said. "How did you do at Stanford?"

"I set a few records in my freshman year and then...well, kind of faded."

"What happened?"

"The Vietnam War."

"But you got a deferment for being in college, didn't you?"

"I was against the war. I went to demonstrations, got busted, landed in jail. What did you do during the sixties?"

"Got drafted, went to Nam, survived. Came home, joined the department, due to retire soon. Wife, three kids, seven grandkids. You married?"

"Divorced," I said by way of a misleading summary. If marriage is living with a woman for a couple of years or more, I'd been married multiple times. Never felt obliged to obtain the permission of church or state. While in Las Vegas for a couple of years, I fathered a son with a beautiful "café-au-lay" girl, but we never lived together and she didn't want anything more out of me than that kid, or so she'd said. I may have fathered other kids I don't know about, before I corkscrewed down and out.

"What landed you in that psych hospital? What kind of mental problems you have?"

I gave him the abbreviated version. "Depression, made worse by trying to medicate myself with drugs and booze." I didn't make the distinction between big D Depression and small d depression, or how I'd found many of the pharmaceuticals pushed by doctors far worse than most street drugs, or how astounding it is to see all those TV commercials pushing hypochondria to sell drugs.

"I remember you as a clean liver, always in training, no truck with drugs or booze."

"That was me in high school."

"You look clean now."

"I am."

"That's good. My oldest son developed a drug problem."

"Is he okay now?"

"He's improving. It pretty much wrecked his marriage, though. You go to Narcotics Anonymous?"

"Alcoholics Anonymous. I went from drugs to booze."

While we chatted I ground coffee beans and brewed a couple of cups. I poured two mugs full and we helped ourselves to milk and sweetener. As we stood side by side at the counter, staring out at the sea shrouded under a layer of mist, Al said, "You lost some weight, haven't you?"

"Yeah." I suddenly felt small and slight standing beside his bulk.

"How much you weigh?"

"Around one sixty-five, I guess."

"You used to weigh about twenty pounds more, right?"

"Yeah, back in high school."

"And you was fast, for a white boy. You scored a few times, didn't you?"

"Only once, Al. I wasn't good enough to make the team but in my senior year, when three running backs were injured, the football coach asked me to suit up for the final game. He had to clear this with the swimming coach."

"Oh yes, now I remember."

"You threw the key block when I scored my only TD. That was the beginning and end of my football career."

"I remember watching you compete—you swam the butterfly. I used to go to swimming meets to cheer on my cousin, Joe. Nice place your brother got here."

"My brother said this place is protected by private security."

"That's right, it is."

"I'm wondering why the maid didn't call them instead of the County Sheriff."

"They come and go on their own."

"You know who they are?"

"I play poker with Jake Valance once a week. He's in charge of their unit here in Santa Barbara County."

"Has this house ever been robbed?"

"No! Definitely not."

"Then why two layers of security?"

"It's not the material possessions they're worried about, it's what your brother carries around in his head."

"What does that mean?"

"Something to do with government contracts, I don't know. I don't even think Valance knows. He's felt me out about coming to work for him when I retire."

"Think you'll do it?"

"Well," said Al, evading my question, "don't be a stranger. Stop by my place and let's relive the high school days."

"I'm without wheels, Al. But if you'll leave your address and phone number, I'll be in touch."

"Your brother got more than one car. Check out his garage. I expect he'll lend you a set of wheels."

He pulled out a business card and left it on the kitchen table. As he was going out the front door, I said, "Would you check in with the maid before you leave, let her know I'm harmless?"

"Are you?" he said with a look that could be read as either a grin or a grimace.

"I sure am, my brother by another mother." That's a line I'd picked up from an African American woman at Covington.

He gave me a look of faux cynicism. Then grinned, snorted a laugh, and said, "It's good to reconnect with an old teammate."

He got back into his cruiser and talked on his cell phone—I assumed he was calling the maid—then was on his way out the lane, turning left on Padero.

I suddenly recalled that the single black kid on our high school swimming team, Joe Gerrity, was Al Hansen's cousin. He'd anchored our medley relay team that won the state championship. I remember Joe telling me he was thinking of going to the University of Texas and me wondering if it was a good idea for a black guy to go South, and him telling me the South couldn't be any more racist than rich-bitch Santa Barbara. That got my attention because I came from a wealthy family. During the following months, every day after practice Joe and I went together for smoothies at the local health food store, and he opened my mind to the capture and re-enslavement of black men between the Civil War and World War II—how thousands of black men were arrested on the flimsiest of charges and sold or rented to corporations, giving me the horrible meaning behind the words, "Jim Crow." I later realized Joe had taken me into his confidence because my liberal mother was a member of the NAACP. What I'd learned from Joe became the catalyst for my involvement in the Movement, which in turn started me on my brief career as a radical journalist, my descent into drugs and booze and skid-row hell.

What had become of Joe Gerrity? I made a mental note to ask Al next time I saw him.

Jake Valance

In 1967 when Jacob Valance was four years old, his father drop kicked him out of the barn's haymow and he flew two stories to land in the barnyard, mangling both ankles and breaking his right femur. His mother drove him to Beebe Hospital in Lewes, Delaware, about eight miles from the farm. The broken femur was reset and encased in a cast. Surgery was needed to reattach a torn tibia tendon in his right ankle and foot.

His parents were members of an offbeat Christian church that believed in total abstinence from alcohol, tobacco, dancing and card playing. Jesus would forgive sinners who repented, they believed, and both his parents repented weekly. His father drank heavily, was usually blind drunk by midnight Saturdays, and his mother strayed from her matrimonial bed almost as frequently, disappearing from their favorite tavern Friday nights with whatever man took her fancy. His father usually delivered a beating to his mother Saturday evenings for these transgressions. Jacob and his two sisters and two brothers were required by their father to witness the beatings, which got underway around sundown Saturdays, and consisted of pounding her body with his fists, beating her bare ass with his belt as she stood propped against the living room wall, and then raping her. Jacob was the youngest and he would later recall that the children were required to be as silent during these ritualistic punishments as they were during Sunday morning sermons in church. In fact they were more silent for the beatings than for the sermons—the beatings were far more awesome.

When he was ten years old, his father delivered a beating to his fourteen-year-old sister Marjorie, who'd been caught having sex with her boyfriend the night before in a car. That was the one time Jacob cried while witnessing such punishments, for Marjorie was his "little mother." His father, Alexander Valance, believed in toughening up his male offspring, which translated into making them rise at dawn to milk the two family cows and attend to other farm chores, milk the cows again before dinner, and make sure the milk containers were rolled down to the roadside for pickup by the local creamery every morning. Sometimes Alexander slapped the head of one son or another, "just because," he said. Sometimes he delivered a sudden punch to the solar plexus of this son or that. Being the youngest, Jacob eventually became the only son left on the farm, the sole object of his father's belief that to spare the rod was to spoil the child.

By the time Jacob was sixteen, in 1977, he was six feet tall and wiry-muscled, obliged to milk both cows morning and night, and suffer his father's outbursts alone. His father worked various jobs during the days, but was often laid off for one reason or another. By this time, all his brothers and sisters had moved away and were scattered, one as close as Ocean City, a 30 minute drive down Route 1 from the farm, another as far away as California.

As Jacob would later remember it, one cold winter morning while he was preparing to milk the two cows, his father came into the barn and, "just because," swung a punch toward Jacob's head, which Jacob ducked under and reflexively swung back, his fist connecting with his father's right eyebrow. Enraged, Alexander picked up an ax handle and came at Jacob intending to deliver serious punishment. Alexander gripped the ax handle like a baseball bat and raised it over his head, and Jacob rushed in to catch it at the top of its arc, then twist it out of his father's grip and commence to beat his father with all the pent up rage he'd accumulated over his growing-up years. When his father, overwhelmed by his youngest son's strength and quickness, tried to flee the barn, Jacob connected with the back of his head, knocking him to the barn floor, where he commenced to beat on his father's head. Alexander covered his head with his hands and rolled around on the barn floor trying to escape the blows, as Jacob continued to pound. He pounded till both of Alexander's hands were bloody and useless as protection, then pounded his unprotected head like it was a rotten melon. Even after Alexander lay motionless in a pool of blood, Jacob continued to beat his head with the ax handle. It wasn't until his mother appeared in the barn door and yelled that he stopped pounding.

His mother was in her forties by this time and walked with a limp. Some said her mind wasn't right either, after all the beatings she'd taken. She limped over to her fallen husband's body and bent down, lifted a wrist and felt for a pulse. "He's dead," she said to Jacob in a monotone. "What are we gonna do now?"

Do now? Without a word, Jacob walked out of the barn and into the house, upstairs to the bathroom and showered, then dressed and caught the school bus. It was October and football season, and Jacob loved football, would not miss a practice, would not miss a game. When he got home that evening, his mother was asleep on the barn floor beside her dead husband, her clothes soaked in his blood. Jacob lifted her up and helped her back to the house, then started the tractor, attached the snowplow to its front end, and drove it to the middle of a field covered with dried corn stalks. He lowered the blade and scraped the ground to get a hole started. Then he drove back to the barn and got a pickax and shovel, and finished digging the hole by hand. It came out more round than vertical but that was okay with Jacob. Finally, he lifted the cash from his father's wallet, then tied a rope around his father's torso and towed his carcass, dragged his father to the hole, rolled his body into it, and used the snowplow blade to shovel dirt into this rude grave, then spread and flatten the earth so no mound showed.

About a month later, a State Trooper showed up at their front door, asking for Alexander Valance. It was a Saturday and Jacob was fixing the fence that enclosed the cornfield. Seeing the patrol car parked in the barnyard, the trooper standing on the porch at the front door, his mother staring at him with a blank expression, Jacob hurried there.

"I'm Officer Andrew Gorman," the man said.

"I'm Jacob Valance."

"Son," said Trooper Gorman, "where is your father?"

"Who wants to know?" said Jacob.

The trooper took a deep breath and said, "Seems quite a few people want to know. We've gotten a lot of calls, asking us to find out what happened to Mr. Alexander Valance. He's not reported to his job and they have a paycheck waiting for him. He doesn't respond to phone calls, and people have stopped by to inquire but gotten no response from your mother."

"He moved away," said Jacob.

"Yeah," said his mother, "he just up and left us."

"Isn't that his car?" said Trooper Gorman, pointing to the old Ford pickup his father had driven for a decade or more.

"He left it with us," said Jacob. "He rode the bus to Wilmington and caught the train."

"Train to where?"

"We don't know. He hasn't called or written to tell us."

The trooper, a stout young man in his early thirties with an auburn mustache, looked deeply into Jacob's eyes for what seemed a long time, before saying, "Are you and your mother all right, son? She seems..."

"She doesn't talk much any more," said Jacob. "She hurt her leg and hip, too, and can't walk much either."

"What about you? Are you in school?"

"Sure, I'm in school."

"Going to graduate?"

"Of course. I play football, gonna get a free ride to college," said Jacob. "I'm also a pretty good basketball player, sir."

Trooper Gorman patted Jacob's shoulder and smiled. "Good. Here's hoping you get that scholarship. But we do need to find out where your father went. A lot of people are curious, including his former employer, who's sitting on an unclaimed paycheck."

"Sir, all I know is one day I woke up and he was gone. Mom said he told her he was going to Wilmington and catch a train and he never came back. We don't know where the hell he is, sir."

"Watch your language, son. Well, in that case, we'll have to take a look around. When someone just disappears this way, we need to do an investigation."

"Sure. Look around. I'll be right here if you need me."

His mother went into the house and sat in her rocking chair, watching an afternoon TV show. Jacob sat on the porch steps watching the trooper, who inspected the pickup, then the chicken house, and then went into the barn. Jacob had hosed down the bloody mess on the barn's wooden floor weeks ago, and had covered the area with two inches of fresh straw. He laughed silently to himself as he watched the trooper through the barn door. The trooper wandered about inside the barn, occasionally stopping for a closer look at this or that. He emerged after a few minutes and walked back to Jacob. "The thing is," he said, "Alexander rarely ever went anywhere, from what we've been told. He never even drove down to Ocean City because it's in another state. He stuck close to home, from all we've been told."

Jacob stared up at the trooper with a blank expression.

"Did you know your father to do much traveling?"

"No, sir. He did stick close to home. I don't know why he suddenly took off. But he did talk about leaving. He used to say that one day he was going to get the hell out of here and leave all this behind, go someplace where it's easier to find work."

"How old is your father?"

"I'm not sure. Don't even remember when his birthday is."

"He must be in his forties, maybe his fifties, right?"

"I guess."

"A lot of men leave home to find work in their twenties or thirties, but not their forties or fifties."

Jacob shook his head and made a helpless gesture with his hands.

"Well, I'll file a missing person report and we'll send a team out here to do a more thorough investigation." Trooper Gorman turned to leave and walked a few steps toward his patrol car, then turned back. Jacob had risen from the steps and had his hand on the doorknob. "One more thing. A lot of people tell us that your father beat your mother. With some regularity. Can you corroborate that?"

"What do you mean?" Jacob didn't know what corroborate meant.

"Did your father abuse your mother?"

"Abuse? As in give her beatings?"

"Yes."

"Yeah, he did, now and then. He beat us kids, too. Didn't want to spoil us."

Early in January, Jacob cut basketball practice because he had a swollen ankle. As soon as he got off the school bus he saw several State Police patrol cars and a van parked in the barnyard. Uniformed and plainclothesmen were wandering in and out of the house and barn, and crawling around the pickup. They'd collected baskets full of Alexander's clothing and were sorting through it. Jacob had burned the blood-stained clothes he and his mother had been wearing when he killed his father. His mother was inside rocking and watching her late afternoon TV shows. She was so absorbed it was like she didn't even know these men were here.

"Ma, what are the cops doing here?"

"I don't know. Ask them."

Jacob dropped his books on the couch and went back outside. He stood a moment watching two policemen sorting through his father's clothing. One looked up questioningly. "What you looking for?" said Jacob.

"Anything that will tell us what became of your father."

"He moved away."

"So you've said. We need to corroborate that. Seems he left a lot of things behind. What did he take with him?"

Jacob shrugged. He had dumped his father's stuff into a trash bag and hauled the bag in the pickup to a spot in the woods along the seldom-traveled road to Love Beach. Having no driver's license yet, he'd done this at night. But he wasn't fearful. If they searched the cornfield and found the body, he would plead self-defense and knew, push come to shove, that his age would save him from the death penalty. He'd go into juvie till he was eighteen, then be out in time to go to college on a free ride. His best friend Eric was in juvie now, so he'd have company, if it came to that. Anyhow, Jacob did not believe the investigators would find anything. Jacob had plowed the corn stalks under a few weeks ago, so when they'd gazed out at the cornfield, they saw nothing suspicious. They'd given up trying to question his mother. She'd responded with a blank stare, then burst into tears and ran upstairs and locked herself in the bedroom.

Occasionally, someone at school would point a finger at him and laughingly accuse him of running his old man out of town. Now and then he'd catch others staring at him with darker suspicions. Mostly, his peers viewed him with a new sense of danger. He'd grown some, too, and put on more muscle. He hung out with the jocks. He had status as co-captain of the football team. Guys knew he had a temper and would lash out viciously if provoked, and were deferential. Girls viewed him as a hunk, with the added allure that he was unpredictable and bad. He took Sally Wells to the senior prom, and almost got into serious trouble with the law for punching her senseless when she refused to have sex with him. He was arrested, jailed over night, hauled before a Justice of the Peace the next day, and ordered to pay Sally's doctor bills and two hundred dollars in damages.

His football coach said he was sure to get a scholarship, and some scouts did show up to watch him play, but when they learned he'd managed only a D average and barely qualified to graduate high school, none approached him with an offer. Jacob was shocked and very disappointed. He'd never thought poor grades would prevent him from getting athletic scholarship offers. He'd played three different positions during his high school career, and been a standout in all three, and believed that would certainly qualify him to make it to a university. He'd been working out with weights at home, was pumped, bulging with knotty muscles, and he was fast—the only white boy to qualify for the state finals in the hundred yard dash. Graduation from high school felt like being sentenced to an undetermined stretch in a prison without walls.

He got a summer job on the Rehoboth Beach police force, writing parking tickets and sticking them under the windshields of tourists' cars in front of meters that had run out. He felt humiliated, a lowly meter maid. He discovered he could occasionally exchange a ticket for a tip of five to twenty dollars. This plus his regular pay enabled him to trade his father's old pickup in on a used Mustang. When he heard that a larger city in New Jersey was hiring law enforcement recruits and sending them through police academy training, he took the ferryboat across Delaware Bay to Cape May and drove up to Atlantic City to apply. He was accepted, and launched on a career in law enforcement.

He got a job in a New Jersey suburb of Philadelphia and shared the rental of a house with another young officer, Ronnie Wallinski. He and Ronnie became cunt hounds. Weekend nights were busy but weekday nights became orgies in their rented house. The booze, pot and cocaine flowed, and a seemingly endless stream of new girls showed up to party. He got into trouble with the law again when one girl ran naked out of the house and down the suburban street screaming. Both he and Ronnie were fired, even though they'd pleaded they had no idea what set this girl off. Jake, as he'd come to be called by this time, was especially angered by the firing. Before he moved on to another police job, he waylaid this girl, "arrested" her as she walked home from work, drove her out of town in his Mustang to a wooded area between the suburbs and farmland. When he was done with her that first night, he wrapped her in a tarpaulin and tied her to a tree and returned the next day to continue, for three days. When he dropped her outside the local hospital's emergency entrance, he told her that if she ever spoke his name again, he'd come back and kill her. He later read a newspaper account of how the girl described being abducted and brutalized by a masked assailant.

Newark in the eighties was his kind of town, Jake thought. He was accepted onto the SWAT team and found joy in breaking down doors and bursting into African American crack houses, or suspected apartments, and often finding out later the police had been misinformed, or had broken into the wrong address. He got a thrill out of dragging *screaming young black girls out of bed and clapping handcuffs on them, then standing them against apartment walls to be "searched," especially when their fathers, brothers or boyfriends were forced to watch. During one such bust, the occupants had not been able to pay their electric bill and the apartment's interior was pitch black dark. As police flashlights roamed other rooms, he had a teenage girl give him a blowjob while he held his gun on her father, then blew her father away when he came. The sound of the shot brought other members of the SWAT team running, their flashlight beams dancing crazily, finally focusing on the dead father and grieving daughter. Jake explained that the man had tried to assault him and he'd had no choice but to defend himself. There was an investigation, during which it was found that the bullet had taken a trajectory upwards through the father's jaw and out the top of his skull, supporting Jake's story that the man had been leaping at him when he fired. He said he'd been on his knees because the father had kicked him in the private parts. The daughter later claimed she'd been raped by the cop who killed her father but no one was inclined to believe a female criminal doing time as a drug offender.*

In 2002 when he was thirty-five, Jake took a job with a security agency headquartered in New York City. He'd not been promoted on the Newark force and was resentful. The other officers tended to blame him whenever any complaint of police brutality was filed, whether he'd been guilty or not. They'd stopped inviting him to card games and other social events. Jake invested in an expensive new suit and showed up for the interview looking "extremely professional," as his interviewer put it. He had a Dick Tracy face, square jaw, narrow eyes, dark hair trimmed close to his scalp, and spoke in a nicely modulated baritone. He was broad shouldered, stood six feet two inches, and kept himself in tiptop shape.

After five years working various assignments in the New York metro area, he'd been sent to Santa Barbara to head up the unit there.

The agency had five clients in the Santa Barbara area, and Jake was seasoned enough to be perceived as doing an outstanding job. He'd gone around to each client and introduced himself personally. John

Bradford was just one among the five at first, but as time went by, Jake came to view Mr. Bradford with some curiosity. For one thing, Bradford had a no-nonsense, commanding presence. He peered up at Jake from his five feet ten inches with a frown that told Jake he had no fear, nor any interest in personal friendship. He did not give the security crew Christmas presents, as other clients did. He did not ask special favors. He was lax about informing the unit when and where he was going when he traveled, and until recently, he traveled more often than he stayed home. Until Bradford went into semi-retirement, Jake often had to call his company's main office in Manhattan to find out where Bradford was going after he'd left for the trip. He eventually became the only client Jake had ever had that he feared and loathed. Bradford had recently divorced his second wife and she'd moved away with their two children, and he was in no mood to make small talk with anyone, especially Jake. On those rare occasions when they spoke, Bradford's words were formally polite, while his eyes radiated contempt.

He learned from another Santa Barbara client that John Bradford was considered intelligent and a topnotch executive. This gentleman had grown up with John and related how, even as a teenager, Bradford was driven by ambition to succeed, and how his older brother had been an Olympic hopeful who had fallen on some sort of unspecified misfortune, while John had gone on to graduate with honors from Harvard with a Ph D in economics, then rise up through various corporations to become Chief Financial Officer of one international company, the job he was now semi-retired from. Jake had no idea what a CFO did, but he got the impression from Bradford's stern persona that his job involved cracking the whip over company inferiors. And that he might, if Jake tempted him to, punch him in the face, for there was something pugnacious about Bradford, some spark radiating from him that said, "Cross me and you'll suffer." Whereas Jake felt comfortable going into the homes of his other clients to chat now and then,

Bradford let him know he did not have time for small talk. Bradford was formal and distant, never rude. Jake believed the man treated his Mexican maid with more respect than he showed his security guard.

Chapter 5

Trips to New York were a lot easier before I semi-retired. I used the company's Gulfstream then. During the nineties, we executives had some camaraderie on those flights. That changed after the dotcom crash, Enron, World Com, and the terrorist attack of 911. An old spark of trust left our company. We became suspicious of each other, fearful that if some wild-haired Eliot Spitzer came after us, we might save our own butts by implicating each other. All this was complicated by the fact that we did top-secret work for other branches of this multi-headed creature, the government, whose one head doesn't know what its other heads are up to. A few years ago, in New York, I had a very pleasant lunch with a gentleman from an intelligence agency only to return to the office to find a frowning prick from the S.E.C. demanding I sit down for a long interview with him to explore certain transactions we'd done with the intelligence people, including the one I'd just had lunch with. Those transactions were classified. I finally got rid of the S.E.C. guy by referring him to Human Resources, who wined and dined him and bought him a date with a girl from an escort service, then loaded him on the commuter flight back to DC.

I was in New York for Tuesday, Wednesday and Thursday, and caught the midnight redeye out of Kennedy. The limo delivered me to my house by dawn's early light Friday.

As I came into the house, I realized I'd left brother Robert here without a car. It's a long walk to the nearest supermarket. I suppose Alicia took good care of him. She does the food shopping in her Toyota pickup.

I slept till around noon, then got up and, through my bedroom window, saw Bob down on the beach, walking slowly with his head down, as though looking for something he'd lost—maybe the worldly success a Stanford degree would have promised. He was wearing the same drab clothes he'd had on when I picked him up Monday. His thick hair, now turned snow white, glistened in the sunshine. I made a note to get him to go out and buy some decent clothes. In those drab rags, the police might pick him up as a vagrant. Dress him up in fresh clothes and that gorgeous white hair of his will make him distinguished. I'll admit to a little envy as I'm developing a V-shaped widow's peak, like our father had. My personal barber in New York has been tinting out the gray but now that I'm rarely in the Big Apple, I may let the gray grow in.

I opened my window and yelled, "Hey, Bob." He glanced around left and right, then up and saw me, and waved. "Let's go into town and get you some clothes."

He made a gesture with his hands that I took to mean he was agreeable. I pulled on a casual outfit and by the time I got down to the kitchen, he was seated at the table with Alicia pouring him a cup of coffee.

"How was your trip?" he asked.

"Boring. I am not enchanted by being semi-retired, don't feel ready for full retirement. I'm in a kind of limbo."

Actually, the trip had been frustrating, too, because Dan O'Brien could not get up to speed with all the idiosyncratic instruments the company files under more conventional items. Dan wanted to footnote these so he could keep track of them but that would defeat the purpose of the system I'd developed. We finally settled on him keeping an encrypted file in a bank vault. There were a couple hundred such accounts. I kept the list encrypted on my own personal computer, with two backups on two detachable hard drives in two different safes. I didn't even trust information storage companies with these.

Alicia had a cup of green tea ready for me. She set it before me with a look that told me she'd made peace with Bob's presence.

"I bet you think opening a bookstore is unrealistic?" said Bob.

That stopped me momentarily. I did think it was unrealistic but I was fighting my tendency to be impatient with other people's shortcomings. I also thought Bob would do much better taking me up on my offer to oversee the maintenance of my properties.

I said, "Probably unrealistic, considering how many bookstores there already are in Santa Barbara. Let's think about it. Where would you get the capital? Where would you rent the space? State Street rents are sky high, you know. Even in the less pricey areas, landlords would want to know your qualifications and experience. Where would you get the stock?"

"It wouldn't have to be in downtown Santa Barbara, it could be anywhere, even out in Santa Ynez, or down in Carpinteria."

"I see. That would make it easier." I stood up and said, "First, let's take a run into town and buy you some clothes. In those rags, the police are liable to stop you."

"It's important to wear the right costume," said Bob as he followed me out. His emphasis on the word costume was the kind of remark that, in our teenage years, might have instigated hours of argument. I ignored it.

We took the Jaguar two-seater, easy to maneuver through traffic and park. Downtown would fill up with tourists from L.A. by Saturday. I was glad we were going shopping today but I noticed Bob, after we parked the car in a municipal garage and were walking up State Street, was frowning. "Are you okay?" I asked.

"So many people, where did they come from?"

I thought he meant the foot traffic on State Street. "We've had a housing boom, people moved here by the droves."

"I mean where we parked. So many homeless people camping out in the municipal parking garage."

"Oh? I hadn't noticed."

"You parked next to an old Honda with a woman asleep in the back seat. I used to sleep in that same spot. Looks like there are dozens of homeless people living there now. Didn't you see them, John?"

"I didn't notice."

"They were camped out all over the place In that municipal parking garage."

"Maybe they are people who got hit by the mortgage crisis."

"Where will they all go when..."

"When what?"

"When the coming great depression hits."

"There isn't any coming great depression, Robert. Depressions are a thing of the past. A prolonged stagflation, but no great depresssion. Here's Brooks Brothers. Let's get you into some decent clothes. It'll change your thinking."

After we bought him some clothes, we cruised the business district, supposedly looking for a likely site for his bookstore. This gave me a chance to ask the question that had festered for forty-three years: "Bob, why did you drop out of Stanford back in the late sixties?"

"That's a long and gory story, Jack."

"We have time."

"To begin with," he said, "I wanted to participate in the creation of an alternative culture and write about it. I went to every demonstration within driving distance and wrote articles for underground newspapers. Remember those? The Berkeley Barb and others in the Bay Area, the L.A. Free Press, and the East Village Other in New York City."

"I never read those papers, Bob. I was concentrating on my education. "

"Back in the late sixties, there was so much going on, a whole new reality was struggling to be born, and I was cutting classes to check it out and write about it—the new music groups, the acid proselytizers, the free love groups, the free food people, Haight Ashbury. I was making trips to communes out in the boondocks, which meant I'd sleep over, cutting more classes."

"Seems to me," I said, "you could have done that without dropping out of Stanford."

"There's something else. To make a long story short, I was asked to speak at a rally in Berkeley and as I was about to climb up on the platform, the cops raided and one hit me on head with his club, knocked me out cold. I was rushed to a hospital where I was told I'd probably suffered a concussion—this was before imaging devices so they were guessing. They dismissed me a day or so later. After that, I couldn't get myself up in the morning to go to classes, wasn't motivated to do my daily workouts. A doctor at the university checked me out and said there was nothing wrong, and I was told that if I didn't get busy, they'd have to flunk me out. I tried but I couldn't get up to speed. So I drove to a commune in the mountains near Santa Cruz to recuperate. Took me a couple of months before I felt back to normal."

"Why didn't you come home?" I asked him.

"You know Dad would have chewed me out for my involvement in the Movement. He'd have told me I was just lazy and should get it in gear. Besides, I was embarrassed. How could I tell Dad that I'd lost my motivation to go to classes and train?"

"What puzzled me back then, Bob, was why you thought demonstrating against the established order would change anything."

"It wasn't only the demonstrations, Jack, it was the whole counter culture movement. Full citizenship for African Americans, stop the war in Vietnam, teach a realistic version of this country's history in our schools and universities, make sure women have equal rights with men, etcetera and so forth. It was a whole universe of positive change that I saw happening, and I wanted to be part of it, experience it, write about it, celebrate it. And, I'll admit, the sex was great too. Those were the days of free love. And you know me, I had an outrageous libido. How could I resist the great grass and gorgeous girls? I had lost my desire to stay in Stanford, but not my desire to enjoy the ladies—they healed me."

"In other words, Bob, you quit college to fuck around."

"That's how you and Dad would see it."

"How could a concussion take away your desire to stay in school yet not take away your desire to fuck around?"

"Back then, I didn't understand it either. It was years later—actually in Covington with Dr. Mary Grace—that I began to appreciate the peculiar effects a brain trauma can have. The brain is so complex, Jack. You can stimulate one tiny part of it and watch behaviors change. Pro football players who suffer concussions sometimes go through major personality changes. But there's no known way, yet, to predict exactly what the after-effects of anyone's concussion will be. Each brain is unique. Each bang on the head is unique."

"You want to know what your family thought? We thought you'd just dropped out and turned on and become a hippie drug addict, and we could not understand why you made it impossible for us to locate you."

"I did get addicted. First to cocaine and heroin. But they weren't that hard to kick, once I put my mind to it. It was the legal stuff, the hard liquor that really wrecked me. That and what I now know was a crippling disorientation caused by the head trauma. Some people can be what's called 'functioning alcoholics' and hold down jobs. There were weeks when I couldn't get myself out of bed to do anything except a hair of the dog. I was self-medicating with booze.

"When I finally moved all my stuff out of the dorm at Stanford, I got a room in a big house in Berkeley, all students. Well, I got kicked out of there when I couldn't pay the rent. I couldn't get out of bed because I was too broke to afford more booze or drugs. My car got towed and impounded. I sold all my clothes except what I was wearing. I used to hitchhike back to Stanford to pick up the monthly checks Dad was sending for pocket money, until I looked so ragged, no one would pick me up. I wound up sleeping in cardboard boxes or homeless shelters, spending my days trying to get a fix of smack, or enough alcohol to numb the pain and humiliation. I was dealing with cops, thieves, rapists, lice, toothless old geezers who'd kill you for a pint of whiskey. There were no rehabs back then, remember. You know what would have happened if I'd called home. Dad would have ordered me to return to Stanford and resume my studies and fulfill my scholarship obligations, period, end of discussion."

"He would have gotten you reinstated."

"You don't understand, Jack. I couldn't function. I was so out of it, I couldn't even stay at rural communes that had loved hosting me before the head trauma, the depression, the drugs and booze. After a few days at one commune, they called me on the carpet and asked why I was drinking so much. I couldn't give them a sensible answer—I couldn't tell them what I didn't yet know. They drove me back to skid row where life was busy, nasty, dangerous. It took me years to recover."

"But you did recover?"

"Yes, eventually, I was able to do a kind of cognitive therapy on myself and reason my way back to normal life. I borrowed a typewriter at a homeless shelter and began writing magazine articles. Usually paid about what it took to support myself for a month, so if I could sell one article a month, I was okay. Then I sold one to the New Yorker that became talked about, and soon I was knocking out a couple of pieces a month and making some get-ahead money. I got an apartment in San Francisco overlooking the marina. I had friends who admired me for my writing. I got lucky and landed a book contract."

"No kidding. You wrote a book?"

"Had a three-book contract but when I brought in the first book, the publisher who signed me was being merged with another publisher and my editor was handed his head and a new boss took over, and he canceled my contract. I said, 'You can't do that, it's illegal.' He smiled and said, 'So sue.' My agent said, 'They have your life insured by a Canadian company—for eight million. If they don't have you an accident, the justice system will have your ass you can't win against a big corporation.' This marked the end of the Sixties— the ruling class didn't want the inmates running the asylum any longer. So this new boss first cancelled publication of my book— review copies had already gone out so they sent out a notice not to review. But that same week, the book was featured on the cover of Publishers Weekly Magazine, indicating it was expected to top the bestseller list. So a couple of months later, the new boss said, 'Oh, we didn't cancel, we postponed.' The plan had been to bring out a first edition of fifty thousand copies and run it up to the bestseller list. The new boss brought out a first edition of five thousand, eliminated the promo, and told me, 'Your book didn't sell.' That justified canceling my contract. But it was really all about the Sixties. In the new boss' eyes, I was a counter-culture, West Coast crazy. Part of his job was to rewrite the history of the Sixties."

"Tough break! How did you handle it?"

"Not very well. I soothed my wounds with drugs and sex. That's what I was doing when I got my second bang on the head."

"What do you mean?"

"I bought a Mercedes sports car, a 1968 280 SL convertible with a detachable hardtop. Remember those? One afternoon, rushing to the airport, I rolled it. I hadn't buckled the seat belt and as the car was flipping I dove to the floor and wound up wrapped around the gearshift with the hardtop pressed against my head. Bleeding profusely. Got rushed to another hospital where I was told I'd probably suffered a concussion. That was the second one."

"And you still didn't call home. Why?"

"After that second hit, Jack, I was so disoriented I couldn't remember where I lived. Someone retrieved my suitcase from my wrecked car and put it into the ambulance that rushed me to the hospital. It had my checkbook. That's how I found my address and where I banked. When they released me from the hospital, I took a cab to my apartment but had lost my key and the property manager was nowhere to be found. I wandered into downtown and, well, just sat on a curb, trying to piece my life back together. The next thing I knew I was in a state psychiatric hospital, zonked out on Thorazine. When I got out of the state hospital, I went back to my apartment but the landlord had moved someone else in, sold my things to cover back rent, and claimed I owed him another couple of thou. I didn't have a cent in my pockets. Before my contract was cut, I'd been paid a hundred and fifty thou as the first third of the advance, but I had blown that money away. Nowhere to go but the streets, no way to ease the pain but booze and drugs.

"I was determined to make money to get back on my feet. Fell in with a rough crowd, imported marijuana, cocaine, heroin. Traveled the world, did drug deals for tens of thousands. It was a good living. But I couldn't write. Couldn't string two sentences together. And I did weird things. It was like I'd become a Dr. Jekyll and Mr. Hyde, taken on another personality that I had no control over."

"What weird things did you do?"

"Jack, I'm so ashamed of those acts I can't talk about them, not even to you, only to God. Eventually I got busted—this takes us into the early eighties when there were rehabs. I went in and out of prisons and rehabs, but the result was always the same—I'd come out broke and the only way I could make a living was dealing, and the only medicine I knew would help the depression was booze, which helped temporarily but over time made it much, much worse. Finally, the system gave up on me and sent me to San Quentin. I wasn't there long before someone recognized my name, connected me to Dad and called him. You know the rest."

"When you were going in and out of jails and rehabs, didn't they ask for your vital stats, like where you were born, the names of your parents?"

"I said I didn't know where I was born and my parents were both dead. I had a driver's license with a San Francisco address. Most of the people I hung out with had grown up in the system—juvenile detention, group homes, orphanages, foster care. I had become one of them."

"If you'd told the truth, Dad would have come to your rescue years sooner and saved you a lot of suffering."

"Dad would have blamed me for the mess I'd made of my life, and I'd have agreed with him. Remember the time we sailed over to Catalina Island and lost our rudder? We called home for help and

Mom wanted to rent a plane to fly us home but Dad told us to get our butts back to the mainland any way we could, then take a bus home."

"I remember it well," I said. "We mopped floors and washed dishes and begged money for two days to buy two tickets on the boat to San Pedro, then hitchhiked home. Dad believed in tough love."

"And tough love was not the answer for a brain damaged, drug addicted, psycho street person, sometimes flush with drug money, sometimes living in a cardboard box."

"Forgive me for persisting, Bob, but if you could find your way to homeless shelters, I don't understand why you couldn't find your way to a pay phone to call Mom. Dad was always working, you know. I was on the East Coast by then, and she was home alone all day."

"I did think of calling Mom, knew she would respond, but she would have caught hell from Dad. Besides, I was out of it, busy doing the next thing I needed to do to survive. I sensed there was a connection between what I had become and those bangs on the head, but exactly what that connection was, I had no clue. If I'd called Mom, it would have involved Dad and I could not tell them what I did not know. All I knew for sure is that I had become a psycho and was barely surviving. As for homeless shelters, I didn't so much find my way to them, I was guided, or just swept up with the crowd. Sometimes a Good Samaritan would take me by the arm, sometimes I'd just follow other homeless people who looked like they knew where they were going.

"That was before the late seventies when I'd recovered enough to get into the drug trade and make money. Through the eighties I lived in that blurry space between sanity and insanity. Sometimes I was zonked out on drugs. Sometimes I was traveling—driving down to Mexico, flying to Thailand, Brazil, Jamaica, you name it. It was like I'd started out in the university maze, gotten stuck in the skid row maze and then the drug trade maze.

"But I have to admit that I also loved the excitement of the big deals, the bags of cash, the happy pills, and the sex—there were always lots of hot babes hanging around. During the height of my drug dealing days, I lived in a threesome with a couple of young beauties. I'd wake up between these two and start the day with coffee laced with Yohimbe, a Mexican steroid called Diana Bol, a joint, maybe a dash of LSD and a couple lines of cocaine. Spent days on end having sex, doping, eating, sleeping and having sex. If some other chick took my fancy, my two lovelies would fetch her to me and help seduce her."

"Shades of Charles Manson."

"No, more like Charles Bukowski. We were just sensual, playful porpoises, worshipers of the highest and mightiest cums. And we loved to dress up and go out dining at the finest restaurants. That's when we became high profile. If I'd been right in the head, I'd have set up a respectable cover business, capitalized it with the drug money, put on the business suit and gone legit. Well, I did do an escort business in the eighties, but I was too scatterbrained, blew the cash away faster than it came in. I think it was an escort customer who dimed me, landing me in my first prison stretch. When I got out, it was back to the streets and start over. By the nineties, I had a pretty long rap sheet, a record of multiple arrests, and several aliases."

"What occurs to me as I listen to you," I said, "is that Dad raised a couple of obsessive-compulsives. The difference is that I put my energy into building a corporation while you —what did you do? You put your obsessive-compulsive energy into exploring the lower depths of society."

"I put a lot of energy into becoming a record-breaking swimmer, too, don't forget. This period we're talking about now, I was adrift with a busted compass. No one was more mystified by how I'd gone from Stanford to skid row then me. If you'd met me back then and asked me how it happened, I would have said I'd become a drug addict and drunk. I thought it was that simple. How the me who was so disciplined as a competitive swimmer had become the me curled up in a cardboard box on skid row, I had no clue. But in my mind, I'd also shown I could get off skid row—first by writing, then by drug dealing. By the nineties, I was using four AKA's and living in a four-bedroom apartment with a view of the Golden Gate. That's where I was living when I pulled the long sentence to San Quentin."

"And Dad got you out of San Quentin and established a fund to pay for your stay in Covington."

"For which I am eternally grateful."

"You seem fine now."

"Covington saved my life. I learned a lot from Dr. Mary Grace and my friend Jorge Hernandez. Brain science arose. We're now learning things about the brain we never knew before. Or had been wrong about. When I went into Covington, it was believed that brain damage was irreversible. Since then it's been proven that brains can be healed and reshaped. Brains aren't hard-wired, as previously believed, they're more like silly putty. You can remake neurological connections. We have the ability to willfully reformat our brains."

"Amazing! Are you in danger of any kind of relapse?"

"Dr. Grace says a relapse into severe depression is possible, but that if I take my meds faithfully and do my daily meditations, she believes I'll be able to live among normal people. Like you, brother."

I smiled at that and said, "When you get to know me better, Bob, I don't think you'll include me with normal people. I put all of myself into my career. I was away from home so much, I had more sex with prostitutes around the world than with my two wives. But now that I'm retiring, I'm determined to change. I need to build a personal life for myself."

"And I need to help you do that," said Bob. "You're the only family I have."

He's the only family I have, too, since both my ex-wives and their children have become estranged. I had no idea how Bob could help me, but it was exciting to be reunited with him.

Chapter 6

Thursday afternoon, John drove me into town and took me shopping like he was my daddy and I was a six year old. I hate to shop for anything, especially clothes. Would rather buy from the nearest thrift store than walk the floor at a Brooks Brothers. But I dutifully went along with Jack's wishes. Pushed his buttons wrong when I noticed homeless people living in the parking garage and mentioned the coming great depression, so I dropped that subject and just went with his view of things.

He bought me two suits, one black, the other an indeterminate blue, a dozen neckties, a camel hair sports jacket with leather elbow patches, four sports shirts, belts and suspenders, and three informal slacks. I changed into the sports jacket and a pair of slacks, and was ready to leave when he decided I also needed a few pairs of shoes. Finally, wearing this new sports outfit with expensive Italian shoes, we left the store loaded with boxes and bags and returned to the parking lot where his sports car was parked, and stuffed everything into the trunk.

"Now," said John, "let's drive around and see if we can spot an empty store or two that might be good for your bookstore."

We drove State Street from below the freeway to past Route 134 up into the mountains that protect Santa Barbara from the northern winds, stopping a few times to check possibilities, but found nothing. As we drove, he asked about my life and I tried to tell him a quick version of it, leaving out a lot. I didn't go into the details of my salad days as a fairly affluent writer, nor did I go into the details of living on skid row. Maybe someday I will write a memoir. One man's adventures through the extremes of society, from wealthy home to prestigious college to penniless bum to penthouse to prison to cutting-edge psychiatry and back home.

By the time we got done hashing over my past, it was pushing six o'clock so Jack said we should quit for today and call a realtor tomorrow. I think he sensed, by this time, that I wasn't hot to own and operate a bookstore, that I'd just blurted out the notion off the top of my head, and thought of it as an honest way to buy food and pay rent. He'd mentioned that he'd like me to become his property manager, and frankly that idea appealed to me a lot more.

When I noticed the dramatic increase in the number of homeless and mentioned the coming great depression, it caused brother John a snappish moment. He said depressions were a thing of the past. I replied that we were living through a collapse of the environment and a disintegrating society, and that the core of our economic woes was the Federal Reserve System—a group of private bankers masquerading as a government agency, who sell money to politicians who stick taxpayers with the bill at ever-compounding interest, the current prime example being the war in Iraq. John laughed heartily and chided me by saying, "So you're an economist now, eh?"

I let it go. We'd reversed roles. He was now the big brother, expert on all matters, and I put myself into his previous role as little brother, accepting whatever he said without comment.

Having searched for a store space and come up empty, Jack announced we were eating out tonight. He called Alicia and told her, then drove us to a posh restaurant in Montecito, the Four Seasons at the Biltmore Hotel, not far from a beach club where I'd life guarded during high school summers. There had been times when this kind of dining out was routine for me but now, after so many years removed from society, it was a strange new surrealism.

"Have a gin martini with me," Jack said after we'd been seated.

"Can't do that, Jack."

"Yes you can. How long has it been since you've had a drink?"

"Seven years and two months."

"Come on, one drink won't hurt you. I'll order us two Beefeaters straight up."

"No, please, not for me."

"Look, Bob, I know you've gotten in trouble with booze before but you've been dry for seven years. One can't hurt, can it?"

"If I have that one, there's no telling when I'd stop. I hate using terms like 'sober' and 'dry,' much prefer to say I'm in recovery. Some drunks can have one or two a year, but for me, one martini could land me back in the nut house."

"Okay, all right, forget it. Here's the waiter. What would you like to drink? I'll have my regular."

I ordered freshly squeezed orange juice.

Before the food arrived, Jack had two martinis and had ordered a bottle of wine. As I dug into my filet mignon I said, "I'm glad you didn't inherit the gene for alcoholism."

"There's a gene for it?"

"That's what some medical people say."

"How could you have different genes than me?"

"The alcoholism gene skips some. You don't know you have it till you realize you've become a drunk."

"Speaking of booze and drugs, what was it like in San Quentin?"

"Insane. A lot crazier than any nuthouse I've been in."

"How did you survive in there?"

"Meditated. Read a lot of books, wrote a lot of letters, researched our genealogy."

"What did you find out about our genealogy? We're Scotch-Irish, right?"

"We're much more than that. We're mixed."

"What do you mean, mixed?"

"I connected with a distant relative in Arizona who'd done a lot of research and I retraced much of her work. Our original immigrant ancestor came to the Virginia Colony in the sixteen twenties or thirties. It was his lineage that migrated to Kentucky at the end of the Revolutionary War. Johnny and Jane Bradford with two slave couples and their four kids. They went by three Conestoga wagons pulled by six oxen. Johnny and Jane kept a diary or journal."

John stared at me, astounded. "Where did you come up with all this?"

"Some of it I got from old records. Some from a booklet put together by the distant relative who now lives in Tucson. Our Kentucky forebears grew tobacco and made whiskey. They'd take bales of tobacco and barrels of whiskey to Cincinnati to sell or barter, and if they couldn't get a good price there, they'd raft down the Ohio to the Mississippi, to St. Louis, Memphis, sometimes all the way to New Orleans. They'd then buy horses and ride home. Once when they went to New Orleans—it was the crime capital of the country back then, the early eighteen hundreds—they lost two of their party. A slave named George and a young Bradford boy named Fontaine. Seems they disappeared in the bars and brothels of New Orleans."

"Wasn't there an event called the Whiskey Rebellion?"

"Yes, in seventeen ninety-one, about the time or our forebears were arriving in Kentucky, which was then a territory of Virginia. After the Constitution was written and passed, Alexander Hamilton thought he'd crack down on farmers who made whiskey for sale or barter, but that fracas was confined to Western Pennsylvania. The Kentucky Bradfords weren't touched. They were so remote, they may not even have known there was a rebellion happening in Western Pennsylvania. They made and sold whiskey for generations."

"These are our forefathers you're talking about? Moonshiners?"

"Yes."

"Amazing. I never knew any of this. Tell me more."

"After I eat my steak, Jack. I'm hungry."

He drank half the bottle of wine with his dinner and was feeling no pain by eight o'clock. "Let's go home and have a brandy," he said. I eyed the bottle of wine he' d abandoned, remembering times when I'd never do such a thing. I'd gulp down the half-empty glasses of others before I'd leave any booze behind.

Outside, when the valet delivered the car, John said, "Here, you drive." He tossed me the keys. "And be careful. This machine is a collector's item."

He seemed to have forgotten that I hadn't been behind the wheel of a car in about a decade. But my body remembered what my mind had forgotten and, after an uncertain start, I cruised down the freeway like I'd been doing it every day. The drive momentarily transported me back to the seventies when, flush with cash, I bought that new Mercedes two-seater, and lost it when one girlfriend interrupted me while I was balling another—a detail about my second concussion that I had not told John. I'd promised the first I'd take her somewhere when I drove to the airport, and she was holding me to my promise. So coitus interruptus and off I went in a rage. I tried to weave my way through a tie-up on the freeway and rolled that car four times. She wound up a ball on the floor. I wrapped myself around the gearshift and suffered the bang to the head. I had pretty much recovered from the first concussion when this second one knocked me clear out of my rightful mind.

"If you notice someone following us," said John, "don't worry. It's the security."

A pair of headlights followed us onto Padero Lane, but did not follow us back down the lane to the beach house. "Are you comfortable with them eyeballing you all the time?" I asked.

"I'm so used to it, I barely notice."

Alicia had left the living room and dining area in candlelight. A couple dozen candles. John went to his bar and poured two hefty portions of expensive French brandy into two huge snifters, long stems under large bulb-shaped glasses that fit in the palm of your hand. He'd apparently forgotten what I'd told him about my recovery. We sat back in easy chairs and stared out the two-story picture window at the sea under a full moon. John swirled his bandy around in his snifter. I imitated him. He sniffed and sipped. I sniffed and pondered the sensation in my nostrils.

Years ago in Brazil, I was told by an elderly macumbeiro, Afro-Brazilian pantheistic priestess, that derelict souls of the dead cling to the spiritual bodies of drunks, eager to partake of every drink. I've had horrible visions of ugly, threatening faces and figures, while asleep or on the edge of sleep. It took years of sobriety to get rid of those visions. I'm not about to invite them back. I knew from past experience that one sip of this brandy—especially on top of the meds I'm taking—and I'd be gone, back into madness, probably dead within a year. With the help of Alcoholics Anonymous I'd quit, and with the help of Dr. Grace, I'd reformatted my brain. Now, with John, I had a new lease on life. I'm flowing with an entirely different stream of the collective unconscious now, far from the realm of those thirsty, haunting visages.

"Tell me more about our forefathers," John said. "I'm fascinated."

"Well, in the early eighteen hundreds when they felt the need for a church, one Alexander Bradford and his slave Elijah built one, just the two of them, out of stone and oak. They used wooden pegs instead of nails. Only thing they had to buy for this church was stained glass. They sent all the way to Philadelphia for the stained glass windows. They called it Alexander's Chapel. It was shown in the movie 'Raintree County.' They also built a ferryboat, powered by a mule walking along one bank of the Cumberland River. That ferry was still working in the nineteen thirties."

"Why didn't our father tell us about all this?"

"Maybe he didn't know. His father moved to New York City where he was a wagon maker. Dad grew up in New York City and went to Harvard, as you well know, and became...well, I guess the term entrepreneur fits him. I'm not sure exactly what his company in Ventura made. Just that he filled government contracts that had to do with military hardware."

"His Ventura factory made artillery parts," said John. "That much I know. For both the Navy and the Army. He was forever having to retool as improvements in artillery were made."

"So we come from a long line of tobacco and alcohol dealers, who became gun makers."

"If it's worth doing," said John, holding a forefinger in the air, "it's worth doing for money."

"Not everything that needs doing makes money," I replied.

We stared at each other a beat, realizing we were about to regress to our teenage political arguments. "Let's not go there."

"Agreed."

"Where did our people come from before they went to Kentucky?"

"England. Back in the sixteen thirties, Robert Bradford and his son Andrew found their way to the Virginia Colony and ran a ferryboat service on the Chesapeake Bay, and lived in what is now Annapolis. Their children migrated north to Baltimore and south to fertile farmland in Virginia. I'm not absolutely sure about all the details—the records aren't clear. The Baltimore clan became quite prosperous. I think it was the Virginia line that spawned Johnny and Jane, who migrated to Kentucky. Johnny was the second-born son so he would not inherit the land, his older brother would. So he and his new bride decided to move west, and were given two slave couples by her father."

"Brother Bob, you're blowing my mind! I'm fascinated."

"Among the photos I have stored in Santa Monica are some of Alexander's Chapel and the surrounding graveyard. Before the Civil War, both blacks and whites buried their dead in that graveyard. After the Civil War, the blacks built their own church and graveyard. Segregation of corpses."

"I never knew our ancestors owned slaves. Makes me cringe with shame."

"Well, the slave owners of the Appalachians were not the same as the slave owners of the big plantations in the Deep South. When they first arrived in Kentucky, along the Cumberland River, winter was upon them so all three couples lived in a cave to survive. Being that close, I imagine they got well acquainted, especially under such stress—they all got sick. Jane lost her firstborn and the two slave couples lost three of their four kids. Indians came along and saved them from worse."

"They were attacked by Indians?"

Drinkers aren't good listeners. "No, Jack, they were healed by Indians. And that was strange because the Indians were being driven west by settlers, who often carried diseases the Indians had no immunity to. They called this area of Kentucky 'the dark and bloody ground'—it's where they came to hunt each autumn to stock up on meat for the winter. After that first winter, our people would have hightailed it back to Virginia if they could have, but four of their six oxen had died, so they had no choice but to hook up the other two to a plow and get busy planting and building cabins."

John looked at me skeptically. "Are you sure you didn't see all this in a movie?"

I laughed. "Sounds like a movie, but no, I've done a lot of research. As for our mixed ethnicity, on their last trip to New Orleans, our great-great grandfather returned with a wife who was said to be Chickasaw Indian, although she was accepted as White. Rumor has it that she may also have been mixed with French and African."

"You've got to be kidding. Dad told us we're Scotch-Irish."

"When I visited the lady in Arizona who did most of the research into the Bradford's, I saw an old photo of this matriarch. Her maiden name was Sally White and she looked Puerto Rican. The Chickasaw began mixing with white people back in the fifteen forties when they hosted the De Soto exploration group. They sent young girls to entertain the White explorers so it's a good bet some of those girls got pregnant. A century or so later, some Chickasaw became plantation owners. Want to have our genes analyzed and find out all the races and ethnicities we carry in us?"

"Not tonight," he said, standing and swaying slightly. "I live for the future. What does it matter what our ancestry is?"

"We bring our ancestors with us, whether we like it or not."

"Interesting perspective. Can't say I believe it."

"Knowing our past is the key to our future," I said. "Take all those assassinations in the sixties. We really have no idea who killed the two Kennedys, or Martin Luther King, or Malcolm X, or others, or what motivated the killers. There's a passage in the I Ching that says that if a beloved leader is assassinated, the society will suffer growing chaos until the assassin and his motives are known."

"Well," said John, "I can't believe I'm anything but Scotch-Irish, and despite a thousand and one conspiracy theories, our society isn't in chaos. Things aren't ideal here but they're better than anywhere else in the world I've been, and I've been to a lot of countries." He stretched and added, "I'm turning in. I'm content being Scotch-Irish. And I'm content living in the present and planning for the future. All I know for sure is this," he said, slapping the end table beside his favorite chair. "The material world."

John stood a moment staring out at the moonlit ocean before heading for the stairs. "I've had it for today." I was tempted to get up and help him navigate—he was unsteady on his feet. But I knew he would not appreciate my help—he sees himself as proud and independent, and once he got hold of the banister, he was okay.

Alone in the living room, I poured my brandy down the sink and went about inspecting the décor hung on the walls. The French Impressionists were prominent. There wasn't a single picture of either of his two wives or his children. Nor any photos of our parents or of us growing up. The room was like a gigantic and expensive motel room in its lack of personally meaningful objects. A stranger would deduce that the owner of this house had no family, no personal history. It was obvious that an interior decorator had put this room together. Oh, but I'd forgotten that brother John has other houses. I'd like to know where he keeps our childhood memorabilia. Surely he would not have thrown away all the scrapbooks and photos and trophies Mom so diligently collected.

As I left through the kitchen door for the guesthouse, a movement down on the beach caught my eye. A figure in dark clothes was walking north near the water line. When I stopped to gawk, he waved. Judging by what I could see of his clothes, he was a security guard on his appointed rounds.

Since earliest recollection, Jack and I had different ways of deciding who to trust. He checked their records. I checked my feelings. There was something about these security guys that raised the hair on the back of my neck. I'd been snooped by a variety of guards, especially during the past decade, but they were low-wage prison and hospital guards, not the kind who are hired to protect the wealthy. I felt a need to find out more about these guys. That gave me an excuse to call Al Hansen.

Chapter 7

At seven o'clock the next morning my cell phone went off and I rolled out of bed to retrieve it from my jacket pocket. I figured it was someone from the company's New York office calling at this hour but was surprised to find it was my ex-wife Laura, calling from Rehoboth Beach, Delaware.

"I know this is early for you, John, but I've got a very busy day. The reason I'm calling is to tell you about our house here—the roof's leaking and we've been told by an electrician that we need to get the whole house rewired. We really need a whole new roof, so it's going to come to thousands of dollars. Way over my budget."

Those who didn't know her would hear her as pleasantly calm and modulated, often pausing briefly before uttering a word she wants to emphasize, like, "...we need to get the whole house (pause) rewired." But I detected a familiar edge—she was seething beneath her placid surface. For years I'd been aware of that edge. It used to infect me like a contagious disease. It would raise my volume and we'd be off on another argument, all the more frustrating to me because she would strive to maintain her placid demeanor.

"How are you, Laura? I haven't spoken to you in a long, long time. How are the children?"

"I'm fine. Jack Junior is home from Penn State for a week and getting his car fixed. Lana is keeping her perfect GPA at Georgetown."

"That's wonderful. Please give them my love. As for the work on the house, my brother Robert is here and—"

"The one you never expected to see again?"

"The same. I would like to send him to Rehoboth Beach to oversee this work, and also check out what else may need to be done to the house."

"When did your brother get out of prison?"

"He was in a psychiatric facility. They released him into my care a few days ago."

"You want to send your (pause) psychotic brother here to (pause) fix this house? John, just tell your financial manager the problem here so he'll (pause) release the money. That's all I (pause) need from you."

"Laura, brother Bob is no longer psychotic. He's on medications that make him as normal as you and me."

"That's no consolation, considering how crazed we are. All I need is for you to tell your manager to release the money. I don't want some nut prowling around here."

"Laura, Robert is not some nut. And I'm planning to send him around to inspect all the properties anyway. This will be his first such trip. If that plan changes, give me a number where I can call you. If Robert will agree, I'm going to arrange to have him fly there and oversee whatever work needs to be done."

"He's not going to (pause) stay in my house."

"No, he'll get a motel room."

"You trust your crazy brother over me?"

"No, Laura, I know you could handle this but Robert needs to get back into the swing of things, and this will be an opportunity to do that. And I need someone to keep all the properties up to snuff."

There was silence on the line while she digested this. I took a few deep breaths to ease the anxiety this call had set off. I was suffering a slight hangover.

"All right," said Laura. "But I'm warning you. If your brother does or says anything...crazy, I'm going to call the police and have him...shipped back to you."

"His doctor says he's fine as long as he takes his meds, and since he's been here with me, I've found no reason to doubt the doctor's word. He's as pacific as a Buddhist monk. Now, the number that came up on my caller ID, is this the best one to reach you? I'll call later to let you know when to expect him."

She complained that I was twisting her arm, being overbearing, complicating what was really a simple thing to do. I reminded her that the house was in both our names, so I had every right to make sure the work was necessary, and that it was done correctly. She relented. Her only other option was to pay for the work herself.

I needed to have a sit-down with Herby Stein soon anyhow. And it would be a good idea to introduce Robert to Herby and get Robert busy inspecting the properties and overseeing whatever needed done to each.

I showered and shaved, dressed and called Herby, and set up an appointment for two o'clock this afternoon. Then I went downstairs to find brother Bob chatting with Alicia in the kitchen.

Bob was not overjoyed to learn that I wanted him to fly to the East Coast. I guess the idea of such a trip after being incarcerated for so many years frightened him, for he gazed at me with a downcast look and furrowed brow. I said, "I had no idea this would come up, but since it has, I'd really like you to handle this. If you will."

"Sure, I'll handle it. It's just that I have never done roofing or rewired a house."

"Oh no, you won't be doing the labor. You'll be picking the people to do the labor and making sure they do it right. Does making this trip...frighten you?"

"Not frighten, exactly, just... well, I haven't done much traveling for...what? A decade or two. I hear things are very different now. You get inspected before boarding a plane and you can't take certain things with you. Is that so?"

"Yes, because of nine-eleven. They're screening for terrorists."

"Oh. I thought they were clamping down harder on population control. I hear they make grandmothers remove their shoes."

"The Islamic terrorists are clever, Bob. There's no telling who they might use to do their dirty work."

"Assuming they are as clever as all that, why would they even think of repeating nine-eleven? They must have other surprises in mind now, don't you think?"

"It's part of the routine of air travel now. Accept it and let's get on with life."

"I'm all for getting on with life, Jack, but I can't say I'll ever accept what these fascist monkeys are doing. What they're doing is equating American citizens with the Islamic terrorists, guilty until proven innocent. Don't you think it would make more sense to enlist the allegiance of the American people?"

I heaved a deep sigh and massaged my temples, and thought of the old saying, that fish and houseguests begin to stink after three days. I got up from the table and found aspirin in the cabinet, took four with a swallow of water.

"Sorry," said Bob. "You're right. I need to make peace with America as it now is."

"I'll help you pack so you get through the inspection without incident. Meanwhile, we need to drive down to L.A. to see my personal financial manager. I want to introduce you to each other. I want you to be able to communicate directly with him concerning how much money he needs to send to cover whatever work is done. I'd like you to use a certified house inspector to go over the place and give you a report. Before and after the work is done. Do you think you can handle this?"

When he was slow to reply, I added, "If not, I'll have to hire a stranger. I'd much rather you do it, brother. After all, if things had worked out differently, you'd have inherited half of everything Dad left. What I'm doing, you see, is trying to work you in. Understand?"

"I'm grateful, John. I'll do it. Give me a few minutes to get used to the idea. I've been away so long, the idea of flying from Los Angeles to...where, exactly?"

"Philadelphia or Baltimore, take your pick. Then rent a car and drive to Rehoboth Beach. I'll get you set up with directions, addresses, credit cards, cell phone, everything. And after you meet

Herby Stein, you can call on him for anything else you might need. Okay?"

"Makes my mouth dry, John, but I'll get with the program, don't worry."

"If you really want to open a bookstore, we'll get to that, it's just not something we can do in a hurry. While you're away, I'll tell my favorite real estate gal to be searching for the right spot. By the time you get back, maybe we'll have found it. Then you can do both. Run your bookstore and manage the properties."

"No need for that, Jack. Forget the bookstore. It was just an off-the-cuff idea. I'd rather manage your properties."

It was a relief to hear him say that. I really do want to keep him around. Despite our differences, we are family.

I had Alicia make me a Bloody Mary to ease the hangover, then fix me a breakfast of scrambled eggs and bacon. Bob ate a melon.

By ten o'clock I'd set up an appointment with my personal financial manager and we were on our way. I had Bob drive the Jag again. If he needed to be prodded and pushed to get back into the swing of things, that's what I'd do.

As we drove he told me more about the years we'd been estranged. I was surprised to learn that he'd traveled through Mexico, Brazil, Thailand and other countries. My big brother had been a world traveler back in his thirties, the late seventies and early eighties. I was doing quite a bit of traveling then, too. He said a lot of his traveling was to arrange drug buys, but that he had also taken the time to explore various countries with the idea of one day moving out of the USA. That stimulated the fear of loneliness I'd been feeling lately. Was it ever going to be possible, I wondered, for we two brothers— such opposites in so many ways —to recover the bond we'd felt as children? Where else in the world can one live as well as we live in the USA?

One story he told me, as we drove the freeway, was about getting stuck in Dutch Guiana without an American Express card, which is the only credit card the hotel there would take back in the seventies, and how they told him they would throw him in jail if he didn't find a way to pay cash because they would not accept Visa or MasterCard. He'd been flying home from Brazil, had to change planes in Dutch Guiana, which in those days meant an overnight stay. "What did you do?" I asked.

"I asked around and found there was a guy stationed at the American Embassy who would lend you cash, if he trusted you to repay it when you got home. Seems I wasn't the only American who'd gotten stuck there. I had long hair and counter-culture clothes so I had to conjure up a degree from Stanford to convince the guy. He was from California, too, and talked about how much he loved to go back there to ski once a year. We talked skiing over a couple of drinks and he finally handed me the greenbacks I needed to be on my way, with his business card so I could send him a check when I got home."

"Did you repay him?"

"Oh yes, with an extra fifty bucks for his trouble."

"Seems to me, Bob, that if you were traveling as a drug dealer, you'd want to wear very conventional clothes."

"You think I was reckless? If I'd looked like a cop, it could have gotten me killed. You ever get stuck in a foreign country, Jack?"

"In Jakarta, I once had to drop my luggage and catch a military plane to Japan because of some social unrest of some kind."

"By unrest, do you mean revolution?"

"There were a lot of people out in the streets, but it was about wages and prices controls, I think. In any case, they seemed prone to blame us, as usual. They'd surrounded the American Embassy and were chanting and raising a ruckus. They were also protesting the World Trade Organization, which was like protesting the sunrise. I mean, progress happens as surely as the sun comes up every day. All I could do was leave my luggage at the hotel and hop the next military flight out."

"Ironic, isn't it?" said Bob. "You were selling them loans and I was buying their drugs."

"The financial aid we provided enabled them to modernize. What did your drug buying do for them?"

"It helped them repay your loans."

"I don't think so, Bob. I think it merely slowed progress."

"I strongly suspect they had a very different idea of progress."

"Well, in any case, they have modernized," I said, "but I suspect they still export drugs."

"Very much the way our Kentucky ancestors continued to make and sell whiskey, during and after the Whiskey Rebellion."

"Yes, it takes a while for these things to be brought under control."

"And then the controllers get out of control," said Bob. "Do you have any idea how much marijuana is grown and sold out of Kentucky today?"

"Oh, I suppose there will always be criminals," I said.

"Which criminals do society the most harm? Your money merchants and alcohol dealers, or the folks who are selling an herb that makes people high and lucid rather than helpless blathering idiots?"

And so we slid back into our seemingly ageless debate. Still, Bob was now nattily dressed and that was progress. In fact, he presented an impressive persona when we arrived at Herby's office.

Herby had heard of him, of course, and looked him over carefully for a while, as we got down to business, Robert and I in easy chairs and Herby behind his teak wood desk. Herby is a craggy-faced Orthodox Jew with an eye for classic quality.

He got his secretary to make plane and car rental reservations while we talked. I gave Bob my personal American Express card for now, till one for him came through.

"What I have in mind," I told Herby, "is for Bob to call you from Rehoboth Beach with the details of what needs to be done and how much it will cost. I'd like you to send the money directly to him so he can pay as the work gets done."

Herby said a slow, "Oh...Kay," indicating he wasn't sure my head was screwed on straight, considering all he'd heard about my long lost crazy brother. "If you'll sign this document, Jack, it will give me power of attorney to act for you in dealing with Robert and the requested money to be sent."

Herby watched me sign and I knew from his expression that he wanted to say more, express skepticism about this whole venture, sending brother Bob on this mission. I ignored his concern. If I was making a mistake, so be it. It would not be the end of the world. And if Bob rose to the occasion and performed up to snuff, I'd have more of my big brother back, and that was really what I wanted out of all this. Even spending the rest of our lives arguing politics was far better than the ennui of loneliness.

Herby gave Bob a notebook and Bob made up a to-do list with the phone numbers and addresses he'd need. Bob didn't like to be hurried, I noticed. He wrote without hurry. Herby knew Laura's address and mentioned that her house was right on the beach, in the most fashionable area of town. "My last trip to New York, I drove down to Rehoboth Beach and paid Laura a visit," he said.

"That's news to me," I said.

"I know. I got back yesterday, John. Haven't had a chance to tell you till now. I wanted to check out the property. A great spot. But in need of constant upkeep because of the salt air. It would have made more sense to buy a house a block or two inland, but it's more glamorous to live on the beach."

"And Laura has a taste for the glamorous."

"She does. She's a beautiful woman. Even without makeup."

"Are you saying you had an affair with her, Herby?"

"Oh no no no. I called her from New York and asked about her living conditions and she invited me to come see for myself, which I did. It's your house she lives in, after all. You should take a trip there and see it for yourself, John."

"We went through a nasty divorce. I don't think she'd welcome me the way she welcomed you, Herby."

"Who knows? People change."

By the time we left Herby's office and were driving Sunset toward Pacific Coast Highway, avoiding the freeway in the late afternoon and planning to stop in Malibu for dinner, Bob showed signs of acclimating. "There is just one more detail I need to take care of, John," he said, "and that is getting my driver's license renewed."

"You don't have a current driver's license?"

"Been away a long time."

"Well, let's see if my friends at the Sheriff's Department can help us with that. I think they can arrange a temporary license."

We stopped for dinner at the Malibu Pier. I thought I would drive after that, but then I had a couple of gin martinis and decided to let Bob continue driving. He's sticking to his teetotaler routine. I'm usually more disciplined about my alcohol intake. It's the excitement of having brother Bob back that has me drinking more than usual.

"I want you to know, brother Bob, that I really appreciate having you back in my life," I said as we drove the curves of Pacific Coast Highway toward Oxnard.

"The feeling is mutual, Jack. And I'm even feeling more confident about this trip, now that I know I'll have plenty of backup."

"If you run into any snags, just call me or Herby. I realize this throws you into the swim of life a little sooner than expected."

"That's all right. I'll be okay. It's like riding a bicycle. You never forget how."

As we were connecting with the freeway at Ventura, he surprised me by saying, "Do you have full trust in your security people?"

"They're hired by the company, Bob, and I have no reason to distrust them. They come highly recommended and thoroughly vetted. Personal background checks, the whole nine yards. Why?"

"I saw one of them on the beach last night."

"You'll get used to it. They do seem to materialize out of thin air at times. But that's what they're hired to do—make sure we're protected from all angles."

"Protected from what, exactly?"

"Well, terrorists and criminals have taken to kidnapping business people, Bob. So it's mainly to make sure that doesn't happen to me. There are also thieves about, you know. Not that they'd get much out of the Padero house. But if I got kidnapped, it could cost the company millions—that's mainly why we keep the security people."

"Your company would pay a ransom?"

"If necessary. We have an insurance policy against such a contingency."

"They have you insured against kidnapping?"

"All our senior executives are insured. There are top-secret business strategies and technologies involved, you know."

"How ironic."

"What do you mean?"

"You have enough money to kick back and relax the rest of your life yet you have this kidnapping thing hanging over your head."

"Wherever I go. Which is another reason I want to send you around to inspect and keep up the properties. When I travel, the logistics can get complicated for the security people."

"Suppose you get kidnapped while I'm away," Bob said.

"Don't worry, the security around the Padero house is very, very tight. They have a laser beam marking the property's boundaries and do a daily fly-over with a helicopter. The only time I'm not under surveillance is when I meet a girlfriend at the Biltmore. They do allow me that privacy, thank God."

Chapter 8

My psychiatrist Dr. Mary Grace had warned me of a Rip Van Winkle effect coming out of incarceration but her words did not prepare me for the reality at the airport. Everywhere throughout the airport in Los Angeles were long lines of docile, obedient people the likes of which I could not recall since Cold War propaganda about life in the old Soviet Union. The government's response to the attacks of 9/11, it appeared to me, was to destroy what had been the most prosperous society on the planet and turn it into the most efficient dictatorship in history. Instead of enlisting the people's help, the government had turned the traveling public into suspects. The long-range consequences of this gave me the shivers.

When the man ahead of me in line turned and gave me a friendly nod, I indicated the line with a wave of my arm and said, "Freedom and the American way?"

He held up a hand and said with a smile, "Don't make jokes. They'll arrest you."

"Arrest me for making jokes?"

"Absolutely," he said. "It's against the law."

"I've been away a long time," I mumbled to myself.

"Where have you been?"

"Out of the country." Not entirely a lie.

"A word of advice: Don't attract attention to yourself or they'll pull you out of line and strip search you, maybe even arrest you on suspicion."

"Suspicion of what?"

He made a gesture of helplessness and turned away. I suppose he did not want to get caught conversing with someone who hadn't

humbled himself to this new political madness. Back in the early seventies, I worked on contract writing public relations garbage about
how the Communists imposed this routine on their citizens. Now our
free-marketeer corporations are imitating the Commies. Manu-
facturing the consent of the governed, it's called. We have become
silly putty in the hands of corporate public relations experts and K
Street lobbyists who translate the desires of CEO's into national law.

John had lent me luggage and helped me pack, showing me
what I was permitted in a carry-on bag and what I had to put in the
suitcase to be checked at the ticket counter. The crowd lining up to
board the plane reminded me that the last time I'd flown a
commercial airliner, it was only half full. This one, I discovered upon
boarding, looked like a complicated game of musical chairs played in a
crush of bodies and jungle of perfumes, colognes and body odors, in
aisles that had been narrowed to put in more seats, which had also
been narrowed to fit more butts for more profits. In past years,
airliners had been for the comfort and convenience of passengers.
Now they were for the corporate bottomline. Another triumph for
herd mentality.

I found myself in a window seat beside a lady whose butt was
too large to fit into her seat and spilled over the armrest into mine. In
a lifetime of being jammed into jails, prisons and psych wards, I'd
never before found myself as a stack of human flesh. My left butt
cheek rested on the seat while my right rested on my neighbor lady's
roly-poly left butt.

She was a pleasant lady and embarrassed by her out-of-control
bulk, and we soon found a better way to fit together into the two
tight seats. She deplaned when we stopped at Las Vegas, and my new
seatmate became a middle-aged businessman who brought aboard
copies of the Wall Street Journal and New York Times, and read them
both cover to cover before we landed at Baltimore. He read with the
nervous energy of someone cramming for an exam. Out of the corner
of my eye, I learned that some oil producers were now selling for
euros instead of dollars. Across the aisle and one seat forward, a

young woman had her laptop on and was getting her news from other sources. I leaned forward pretending to pick up something from the aisle in order to read a chart she'd brought up. It showed that oil production was headed down while new demand for oil was headed up. I was reminded that Jorge Hernandez had written an article predicting this a decade ago, but could not get it published.

Outside the baggage claim area, I surmised I had to catch the Hertz bus to get to the Hertz car rental. The last time I'd rented a car at an airport—how long ago?—back in the early eighties, I guess—car rentals were inside the airport.

The Chevy sports utility vehicle I was given had an onboard map display, which a young man at the agency programmed to guide me to Rehoboth Beach, complete with verbal prompts. The whole process seemed like one step forward into the twenty-first century, two steps back toward the horse and buggy, given the shrinking supply of oil and the skyrocketing demand.

It was dark now, like piloting through a tunnel of light in black outer space. I wanted to stop for a bite to eat, even thought of finding a motel between Baltimore and Rehoboth, but the verbal prompts kept coming and I kept driving, and the gizmo delivered me to the front entrance of the Boardwalk Plaza Hotel around midnight East Coast time.

I was charmed to find parrots in the lobby, their cages covered for the night. Once installed in my oceanfront room, I put on an old army-surplus jacket and went back to the lobby and, with a jaunty wave to the desk clerk, went out for a stroll on the boardwalk. No matter where I am in this world, if I am near an ocean I feel soothed.

Where the main avenue ends at the boardwalk, I decided to call Jack. He'd asked me to let him know that I had arrived safely, and it was shortly after 9 his time. I caught him in a jaunty mood. "Brother Bob! How was your trip?"

"Smooth as silk, brother Jack. What are you up to this evening?"

"I'm entertaining a lady friend. At the old Biltmore Hotel on the beach. You remember, where we had dinner the other night."

"Oh sure. Not far from the graveyard."

"I guess that's why we used to say Santa Barbara is for the newly wed and the nearly dead."

"Are you thinking of a third try at matrimony?"

"No, no, nothing like that, Bob. I'm enjoying life. For a change."

"Well, just wanted to check in. Oh, there is one thing I want to ask you. What does it mean that the dollar is sinking against the euro and other currencies?"

I heard him heave a sigh before he said, "Imports will be more expensive, while our exports will be more affordable overseas. Why? You planning a trip to Paris? If you are, bring about twice as much money as you think you'll need."

"I've been noticing that real estate is plummeting while gas prices are skyrocketing, and some oil producers will no longer take dollars, just euros and other currencies. If it now takes a buck fifty to buy a euros worth of—"

"Use that American Express card I gave you and you'll be fine. Call Laura tomorrow, let her know where you are, stop around and see the house—then you'll want to call a professional house inspector, they spot things we amateurs miss, you know."

Jack was in a hurry to sign off. He left me sitting on a fog-dampened bench, staring out at the night sea, still a bit baffled by the headlines in those papers about the falling dollar. I decided to call Hernandez, ask him the same question.

"What it means," said Hernandez, "is the rest of the world is attacking the USA economically—they can't do it militarily so they're doing it economically. But they have to be careful. If they can bring down the dollar slowly, they'll own us. But if the dollar drops off the cliff, the whole world will be in trouble. It needs to be done gradually in order to end American hegemony. The idea is to defeat the US military by sucking the financial support from it."

I told Hernandez I was on the East Coast but he ignored that and said, "What the falling dollar also means is that after the inflation will come deflation and another great depression."

to sharing that

I get strange

another high
ip. He comes
New Jersey, I
cement guy.
municipal to
nd a lot. We
likes to tell
d you'll hear
this agency
babysitting
sed to have
ke the rest

ver heard
ecause he

want to

when I

gs?"

sin, Joe

iding a cynical joke.
civil war because the big
self-destruct."

en we sit outside."

call."
vhen we talk. Where are you,

ng on a bench on a boardwalk,

tky! The Atlantic is warmer than the
."
it's still the tail-end of winter."
. Your rich brother is taking care of

anaging his properties."
, Robert. You know what can happen

o the regimen."
nd tired. I'm signing off for now, got to

ck to the hotel and call it a night, too,
wanted to ask Al Hansen about brother
lance. I fished his business card out of my
one number, relishing how luxurious it felt
, overlooking the Atlantic.
ve and breathe," said Al. "Where are you?
a strange area code and 'unknown'."
e his old cell phone. I think the area code is
n on my latest movements then got to the
calling," I said, "is to find out a little more

about these security people my brother has. You up
information?"

"What exactly do you want to know?"

"Well, for starters, who is this guy Jake Valance
vibes from him."

"Spoken like a true child of the sixties. Jake's
school jock who wasn't good enough to get a scholars
from somewhere back East, I'm not sure exactly where.
think, but I could be wrong. He's a journeyman law enfo
To hear him tell it, he's done everything from small-town
stints with a SWAT team, ATF and FBI. He's moved arou
play poker once a week with a group of cops, and Jake
stories of his adventures. Give him a snoot-full of beer an
some pretty tall tales. He's making very good money with
he works for now, but I think he's bored. Says it's like
sleeping dogs. I think he misses the slam-bang action he u
knocking down doors, collaring the bad guys. He's aging,
of us, you know, but he still lifts weights every day."

"Is he married? Where does he call home?"

"He's single and has a furnished condo in Goleta. Ne
him mention a wife. Talks about retiring to Costa Rica b
likes the *puta* there. He's something of a ladies man."

"Thanks, Al. I got an idea of who he is now."

"Why are you curious?"

"Well, since he makes his living knowing about us, I jus
know something about him."

"I may go to work for the same agency he works for
retire."

"You don't think you'd be bored... babysitting sleeping do

"I've had enough excitement for one life."

"Another question, Al. I've been remembering your cou
Gerrity."

"Have you! That's right, my cousin was a swimmer."

"He was thinking of going to Texas last I talked to him."

"He went to the University of Texas and, sad to say, got himself killed in a motorcycle accident. That was a long time ago, Bob. I think he was in his junior year when he passed. His mother, my Auntie June, never got over it. Everyone had such high expectations for Jack Gee. He was a bright guy with a big future. Did you know that his father's mother was an Irish lady named Bradford?"

"No. He never mentioned that."

"We used to wonder if there was any connection between your Bradfords and his grandmother Bradford. What do you think?"

"I have no clue. Where was his grandmother from?"

"Moved to Santa Barbara from L.A. But everybody's from somewhere else, right? Jack Gee's granddaddy was a laborer, a ditch digger. Company he worked for made him foreman. Rest of the crew was Mexican. I remember his white grandmamma from church."

"Did you notice any resemblance to my Bradford family?"

"Naw. All you white folks look alike."

We laughed.

"God, Al, I'm so sorry to hear Joe Gerrity is gone. He enlightened me about race relations when we were seniors in high school."

"How do you mean?"

"We used to go for health drinks after swimming practice and he'd talk about the history of Africans in America, about colonial times, definitions of the color black, Jim Crow laws, the fact that there probably aren't any pure Africans left among so-called African Americans, there's been so much mixing. Stuff like that."

"I suspect he got that from his Bradford grandmother. She was a history buff."

"He was one of the reasons I became involved in the counter culture movement when I went away to Stanford."

"No kidding."

"He left me with insights into the history of black Americans that drove me out of the classroom and into the street demonstrations."

"And then you stayed too long at the party? I don't think his Bradford grandmamma would be delighted to know that. She was a school teacher. Tell me again, what are you doing way over there on the East Coast?"

"I'm being a property manager for my brother. It's my new job."

"Ah, I'm happy for you. I know you've been through some rough times. You deserve a break. Listen, I hate to cut this short but my favorite TV show is coming on, Crime Scene Investigators. But call me tomorrow, let's stay in touch, okay?"

I went back to my hotel room and turned on the TV news. CNN's Lou Dobbs was badmouthing Barack Obama. MSNBC's Keith Olberman was portraying Obama as a savior. On the financial news channel, four or five guys were doing a rant and rave about the latest stock market drop. I dropped a milligram of Clonezepam, turned off the TV and put myself into the alpha brainwave state to do my daily meditation.

Chapter 9

After dropping Bob off at the airport, I had a date at the Biltmore with one of my young darlings, Lola. She's my favorite, a classic beauty with a quick wit, sensitivity and charisma. She could walk into a room full of the world's most rich and famous and all eyes would immediately lock onto her. She drives up from L.A. and we meet in my room at the Biltmore. We usually order dinner sent to the room. Once, we went downstairs to the superb restaurant, The Four Seasons, but drew so many stares—the older man with the ravishing young beauty—we decided it was just more comfortable to stay in the room. Correction: I decided. I didn't want to play the sugar daddy in front of local Santa Barbarians. Lola is blithely unselfconscious.

On this occasion I was feeling extra frisky for a man my age, mainly because I was happy to have brother Bob back in my life. Oh, I suppose we'll never stop arguing politics but that's okay. What really happened to my brother was quite different from what I imagined happened.

Between trysts, I told Lola a little about Bob, how we'd lived such vastly different lives, how we'd been estranged since the sixties, when I was sixteen and he was eighteen, and now we're together again, getting reacquainted. That elicited a mention of a half-sister who is about ten years older than Lola. The sister has some kind of corporate job, she said without going into specifics, and is married and doing well financially—"but not as well as me," said Lola.

"And how much do you make?" I asked.

"You tell me yours and I'll tell you mine," she said with a smirk.

We usually meet in the early evening, have sex, dine, have sex again, and then chat till we get sleepy. Or I get sleepy and Lola packs her tiny travel bag and departs around 9 or 10 o'clock. She leaves, she says, because she never wants to overstay her welcome.

She was preparing to depart this night when a call came from Bob in Rehoboth Beach. Said he just wanted to let me know he'd arrived safely and now felt more confident about traveling.

After the call, Lola sat back down on the bed and said, "You have your brother looking after your properties?"

"Yes."

"I don't mean to pry," she said, "but someone told me your brother was in a...well, a psychiatric hospital."

"He was."

"Is he okay now?"

"I'm told that as long as he takes his meds, he's fine."

"John, my dear friend, I wish you would marry again. Pardon me for saying so, but that's what I wish."

"What? You don't want me as a customer any more?"

"You know it's not that, my darling. We can still get together whenever you like. It's just that...well, I worry about you, living a bachelor's life with your brother. Is that how you intend to retire? Don't you think you'd be happier with a wife?"

"I've had two wives, Lola. Both made me happy, but temporarily, I'm afraid. Eventually my schedule, my career, the travel etcetera, nixed both marriages."

"But you no longer have that schedule. Right?"

"Right. Now, I suddenly have so much time on my hands, it's a bit scary."

"Do you like me?" She asked in a serious tone, not joking or being frivolous.

"Of course I like you, Lola. I more than like you. I adore you."

"Then how about marrying me?"

"Marry you? Don't you think our age difference would make a marriage awkward?"

"Awkward how? I have a lot of time on my hands, too, you know. I can make enough money on a few dates that I get all my bills paid and am left with nothing much to do, except more dates, more money, more time on my hands. I don't even have a boyfriend. Nor any social life, really. I read novels, watch movies and go to museums."

"Sweetheart, I never in my wildest dreams ever imagined you would propose marriage to such an old codger as me. Are you feeling all right?"

"I'm feeling fine. And you're not an old codger, John. You're a very handsome, mature man. You're wonderful. I love you. I love dating you. You're my all-time favorite date. You're the nicest man I know."

'I am flattered, my dear. But also skeptical. Are you kinky for old geezers? I mean, I know the difference between your servicing me and us being real lovers. I know we're good company for each other, darling, but why would you want to marry an old fart like me? The money?"

"The money, yes, that's definitely part of it. Money is a turn-on. But I also like you for you. I like the way you smell—except when you drink too much, that is. After you drink too much, you don't smell so good. I like the way you carry yourself. I'd like to have your child. I could see a little John Bradford running around, with that certain cocky air you have, like he owns the world. I like the way you talk to people. Just now, you gave your brother orders but without making it sound like you were being bossy. Besides, I can't do this work all my life. Someday I'll have to quit doing dates and I'd like to become a wife and a mother. I got pregnant once, long ago, in high school—when I was fifteen. I aborted. Had no idea what I would do with a kid. Hell, I was in high school and had no idea what I would do for a living. Well, I found this line of work, and I enjoy it, but now I'm looking for something else. Like marriage, children, becoming a soccer mom."

"A soccer mom! Lola, no offence intended but I cannot see you as a soccer mom. The other soccer moms would be so intimidated by your sex appeal, they'd want to stone you."

"You mean, as in banish me? How could they banish me if I were your wife? You have enough money that our child would go to the finest private school, right? I read an article about you in the Wall Street Journal that huge retirement package you got. Jesus, John, you have so much money you could buy a private school, and then who could banish me, your wife? I could help run the school. I could oversee it, make sure everyone's doing their job."

"Ah, Lola, my lovely, that's not realistic but you put me in a hell of a bind. I would love waking up every morning beside you in bed, would love interacting with you all day long, but as for overseeing a private school, my darling that's a pipe dream. And how would you deal with my aging? You're young enough to be my granddaughter. Marriage to an old fart like me would grow old fast. You'd wind up in bed with other guys, and that would kill me."

"You don't understand me at all, John. I've been in so many beds with so many guys. Been there, done that. What I need now, or soon, is something else. No more new beds and new guys. Children, schools, parent-teacher meetings, making sure we eat the best and stay healthy, stuff like that. I could go to college and develop my mind. Sex is great but what lasts is friendship."

I grabbed Lola in a big hug and pulled her down prone on the bed and began making love to her, again. She made me feel forty years younger, and it would be very easy to convince myself that we could make it in a marriage. But that would be totally delusional. I'd seen older men take trophy wives and in no instance did they end happily. Younger wives didn't comprehend who and what they had to be to complement a top executive. Yet even as these thoughts were running through my mind, Lola was responding to my ministrations. Seeing the arch in her gorgeous back, her lovely butt raised expectantly, hearing her cries of passion, feeling a powerful sex energy take me over like I was really forty years younger, it all became so intoxicating.

Afterwards, lying side by side, I said, "Montecito is full of ambitious divorcees, you know. They'd take one look at you as my wife and reach for their weapons."

"I'd charm the bitches out of their britches," she said. "I'd sit at their feet and draw out the mother in them. I'd do the lowliest job on their fund raising things. Within a year, they'd be beating down our door to help me with whatever I'd ask for help with. You'd see."

"God, Lola, you are the sweetest, most beautiful female I've ever known. Do you realize how gorgeous you are? I'm so tremendously flattered that you'd propose marriage to me. I'm overwhelmed."

"Well," she said contemplatively, "we wouldn't want to rush into marriage without having our first fight, would we."

"I can't imagine fighting with you. What would we fight about?"

"Two people get to know each other, no matter how deep their friendship, they are two different people and so they find things to fight about. Even if we didn't find anything real to fight about, one of us would have a bad day and take it out on the other, and that would cause a fight."

I laughed. "So true. But since you and I are both aware of that syndrome, how could we have a serious fight over one of us being in a bitchy mood?"

"Know what I think? What really scares you is growing old. Like, there you are a gimpy old man with a cane or a walker, and there I am still young with our brood of kids. You're so old and decrepit, and your wife and kids are so young and full of vigor. That's what really scares you, isn't it?"

"How did you know?"

"I put myself in your skin and see through your eyes and that's what I come up with."

"You're right on. Doesn't that end our fantasy of marriage?"

"Not mine. You have another good twenty years. You're healthy as a thoroughbred horse. By the time you're decrepit—let's say we have two kids—they're on their way to college."

"And I'm on my way to assisted living. Or else checking out so I don't take up any more of your precious life."

"Shit, John, by that time I'm in menopause and busy with... what's it called? Charity duties. Being a wealthy old battle-ax, running a foundation or whatever."

"What kind of foundation could you see yourself running, Lola?"

"I don't know, haven't given it any serious thought. But twenty years from now I'd know. Anyhow, I want to stay here the night with you. Okay?"

"Of course, better than okay. Whenever you leave, I crumble from joy to loneliness."

She threw an arm over my chest and said, "I was raised by my grandfather, you know."

"No, I didn't know. Where did you grow up?"

"The Valley. Canoga Park. My mother got pregnant in high school and I never knew who my father was. My mother dropped me off with her father when I was less than one year old and took off for parts unknown. Her ex raised my half-sister. My grandmother died of cancer when my mother was still in grade school. My grandfather spent his life raising girls, my mom and me. He was an electrical contractor. Made a pretty good living. And he had a sex life. He had this hooker that he saw. I caught him at it one night but never told him, never let on. I was around ten years old and was asleep when I heard him out in the hall on the phone, talking to someone. I heard him say she should come to the house. So I stayed awake and waited. An old car drove up and this young broad gets out and comes into the house and gives him a blowjob, then drives away. I watched it all. He used to tell me my greatest asset is my beauty and that I should never squander it. Take care of yourself and your beauty will take care of you, he used to say."

As we snuggled and drifted toward sleep, I said, "We'd need a pre-nuptial contract, you know."

"Absolutely."

"I don't know whether to feel I'm lucky in love or an old fool who's being conned."

"People sure can load up sex with a lot of junk," she said. "Why don't we just turn off the fear and go with what feels right."

That remark flashed memories of my teenage years when I was a pudgy kid with horn-rim glasses and brother Bob—star athlete, well built, sparkling personality—turned the heads of gorgeous girls like Lola. Once when two girls got into a hair-pulling fight over him, Bob waded through the crowd to separate them and walked away with one under each arm, saying there was enough of him for both of them. I felt a mix of pride in my older brother and burning envy. He couldn't have cared less who liked him for his philandering and who resented him. Now here I was with fabulous Lola pumping me full of the kind of confidence Bob had back then.

"What feels right?" I responded. "Easy for you to say. You're the young innocent."

"Okay, let's change roles. I'll be the perp and you be the innocent. It's me who is talking you into this."

"But I'm of sound mind and it's 'buyer beware'."

"You want to buy me? Make me your love slave? What a turn-on."

Was my heart singing from pure unadulterated love, or from the ego sensation that at last I was one up on my brother?

Chapter 10

I was up by 6 the next morning and the first thing I did was drive to Laura's address to see the house. It was located along Ocean Drive in a part of town called North Shores. It sat up on steel pilings overlooking the beach and was somewhat protected by a sand dune. I couldn't see many details with the morning sun reflecting off the ocean into my eyes, but it had a good, solid feel about it. Anyone who chose to live here would have to love the ocean as much as I do.

I went back to the hotel, showered, shaved, dressed in my sports attire and had breakfast in the hotel restaurant, called Victoria's. It seats around a hundred, I'd guess, and I was one of only four people there this morning. The waitress was a sturdy young blonde who spoke with an accent and walked with a little strut. I guessed she was from one of the former Soviet Union countries. She asked if I was on vacation and I told her no, it was a business trip. She seemed curious about this gent who was here in the bleakest month of the year, but she didn't pry. I wanted her to pry because I was fantasizing having sex with her—I'd been involuntarily celibate a long time—and she glanced at me now and then, like she knew what I was thinking. Was my fantasy tickling her fancy? Or did that intense, almost angry look in her dark blue eyes indicate she smelled I was fresh out of lockup? Should I ask if she'd like to get together later? Damn it, I said to myself, get your head back into what you came here to do.

After breakfast, I got out the cell phone and dialed Laura's number. It had been programmed as number 3 on the autodial. It was still early, not yet 8 o'clock, so I wasn't too surprised when she sounded like I'd awakened her.

"I'm Bob Bradford, John's brother."

"Oh yes, I've been expecting you. Although not this early." She had a pleasant contralto voice and spoke unhurriedly.

"Sorry, hope I didn't disturb your sleep."

"You woke me but that's all right. When would you like to come by and see the damage? How about giving me an hour to get ready?"

"Sure. I'm in no hurry. Around nine okay?"

"Make it around 10. I'm of the understanding that you're not going to do the work, you're going to hire the people to do the work, and then make sure it's done right."

"Correct."

"You know, for years I've been hearing about John's brother Bob."

"I'll bet you've heard some hair-raising things about me, eh."

"Yes, to be frank, I have. I'm...not entirely at ease with you coming by without anyone else being here."

"Well then, have someone there when I come. I wouldn't want you to be ill at ease."

I went up to my room and searched through the yellow pages for house inspectors. I called several and got answering machines before connecting with one, Joe Martino. I told him what I needed and he said he could be on it by tomorrow, and that he was licensed and insured.

I took my morning meds and sat in a straight-backed wooden chair to do my daily meditation, then drove back to Ocean Drive and pulled into her driveway, then walked under her house and looked for a front door. Near where she'd parked her Lexus was a door that appeared to lead up into the house, but it had no doorbell or knocker. On the left side of the house was a steel stairway. It brought me to a door with a button to press. I heard chimes and in a few seconds, here she was.

Laura Bradford had a thick head of brunette hair and a sly look in her eye. If I didn't know better, I'd have guessed her age at around

38. Her slim body was dressed in sweats this morning. "Hi," she said in her slow contralto voice.

"Come in, Bob. I can see the resemblance to your brother John."

Straight ahead inside the house was a treadmill being walked by another lady about Laura's age. "This is Kay. She's a neighbor. We workout together a couple of times a week." Kay nodded to me. She was wearing a Walkman with earphones as she battled the aging process.

To my right was an extra-long living room lit by skylights and a few side windows. To my left was a kitchen and dining area wrapped inside a floor-to-ceiling window overlooking the beach and sea. The view reminded me of a place I'd been to years ago about a hundred miles north of San Francisco—cold, gray, bleak, under a thick marine layer. Everywhere there were photos of their children, from baby-hood to the latest, which showed a remarkably handsome brother and sister in the blossoming of their youth. Jack Junior looked a lot like me when I was in my late teens—angular, lean, muscled. His sister resembled my mother, the same square face and broad smile, the same look of curiosity in her eyes. Dominating one wall was a photo that had been blown up, showing Laura and her two kids when they were in their teens, and another woman and her two offspring, in their twenties. It took me a moment to recognize that this second woman was John's first wife, Kelly, maiden name Fausti. Her two sons both had the swarthier skin tone and stern expression of her Italian father. I wanted to ask about this photo but Laura got down to business.

"The roof is leaking all over the place. Here over the kitchen is probably the worst leak. At the far end of the living room is another doozey. Even when it's just drizzling I have to put down pots and pans to protect the floor. See?"

Cooking pots were placed about the floor, the largest pot in the kitchen. This day was just damp enough that it was catching a slow drip, drip, drip. I'd seen the forced-air heater and air conditioner under the house. The heater was having a hard time keeping the interior reasonably dry.

"Have you had any electrical problems?" I asked.

"I keep blowing fuses. Is that what you mean?"

"That's a symptom. I have a professional house inspector lined up to give this place the once-over tomorrow, if that's okay with you."

When she smiled, her lips barely parted while her eyes gleamed with good humor. "Sure. The sooner the work gets done, the better. What I want is to sell this place and move. With both children away at college now, it's just not right for me any more."

I assumed she could not sell the place without John's signature, and I figured he'd much rather not sell, even if that meant renting it out. I said, "I don't think moving to a new place will be any problem at all but I doubt that John will agree to sell."

"Whatever. I want to get myself a place in New York City. I have friends there and I'm tired of living down here. It was fun when the kids were in prep school—they'd bring their friends here over holidays and we'd all have loads of fun—but now... oh, I stay busy but I don't know, it's just...too far off the beaten path."

"I'm sure there are lots of other people who would find living here wonderful."

"No doubt. Anyhow, are we done now? Until tomorrow when your inspector comes?"

She seemed to be hurrying me away. I'd expected to sit down and chat with her for a while longer, get acquainted. "Yes, I guess we are done for now."

"Let me know what time your inspector will be here."

"I'll do that. What time would be good for you?"

"Around mid-day."

"Done."

As I stepped out the door onto the steel landing at the top of the stairs, she hung her head out the kitchen door, her luxurious dark hair framing her face, and said, "You're not at all what I expected. I mean, you must know that a lot of wild stories circulate about you, John's brother Robert, the black sheep of the family. The crazed radical sex maniac dope-dealing criminal."

I grinned and did a brief imitation of Jay Leno adjusting the knot of his necktie. "I'm flattered by all the attention."

That fetched a coy look and a spark in her eyes. "How long are you going to be in town?"

"Oh, I suppose I'll hang around till the work on this house is done."

"Where are you staying?"

"The Boardwalk Plaza."

"Would you like to have dinner with me this evening?"

"Sure. Where?"

"Lot's of choices. The main cultural attraction is the choice of fine restaurants. Especially off season when they're not jammed."

"I've never been here before, you know."

"So how about this. I'll pick you up at your hotel around 8 and we'll go to my favorite, the Cultured Pearl."

"Fine." I couldn't resist adding, "But aren't you afraid to go out with a crazed radical sex maniac dope-dealer and black sheep of the family?"

"I'll take my chances," she said, then gave me a quick wink and closed the door.

I walked down the damp steel staircase and got back into my car and drove off like I knew where I was going and what I was going to do. I had no idea. I had expected to spend more time at Laura's house, give it an inspection, talk more about the problems, get acquainted. I found myself aimlessly driving residential streets and avenues lined with shops. I turned on the car's map of Rehoboth and figured out how to set it to show where I was now. It asked for a destination. I knew of none so I turned it off and just continued cruising, exploring empty streets. Most of the houses seemed empty too, as it was off-season. I could see that there was an affluent area not far from Laura's house, interesting little hillocks with mansions perched atop them, long uphill streets lined with expensive-looking houses tucked away under fir trees and behind shrubbery.

I found my way to Rehoboth Avenue and out to Route 1, which goes north and south along the coast here. The highway was lined with businesses, and fairly busy with traffic. A convoy of buses turned into an outlet shopping area, I noticed, and I followed the busses to find out what was happening. The busses parked and disgorged people, who fanned out in all directions, headed for surrounding stores. They were doing something ordinary to them but amazingly strange to me. I felt a weird sense of loneliness, like I was lost in a new city full of people who had no personal contact with each other. They walked silently and decorously in twos and fours and disappeared into various big brand stores. There, I knew from listening to Jorge Hernandez, they would be waited upon by clerks who didn't earn enough to support themselves, let alone support families. Of this phenomenon, Jorge had once said, "Good thing so many people in this society are uneducated and misinformed, or we'd have what the mass media calls 'unrest,' meaning violent revolution."

Soon the affluent shoppers emerged, singly or in small groups, and moved on to other stores, some carrying packages, some still intent on finding what the next store held. There were about seven women for every man, causing me to wonder what their men were doing while they prowled these sidewalks and explored these stores.

I was suddenly transported back to a small town on the north shore of the Island of Mallorca in the Mediterranean, where every morning the women—wives and daughters—shopped for the day's food, going to one store for canned goods, another for bread, another for cheese, another for pies and fancy deserts, and another for freshly butchered meats. I often sat at a café overlooking the downtown area of this small town, having my morning café and a cigar, watching these women run through this daily routine. In that time and place, I found it comforting that they had this routine and stuck to it. They each took about an hour to run through it, for they stopped and talked, laughed, whispered in each other's ears. They might have gone to the large central market about ten miles away, or driven into the city of Palma and shopped at a modern supermarket. But I soon realized that those larger, more complete, one-stop shopping venues would not provide them what they had here, in this small town, running this daily routine. They might have bought enough food in one shopping trip to last a week or more, but that would have deprived them of this daily socializing. It was something like a daily party they attended, circulating, chatting, catching up on the latest news and gossip as they sampled a bite of cheese, a sip of tea or coffee, a forkful of chocolate cake, while laughing and arguing their way around the shops lining the town's circular center.

In contrast to my here and now, where the mostly women and a few men went about the business of buying things without stopping to chat, or sample food, or whisper in each other's ears. The women of that small town in Mallorca were unappealing to me while among these Americans I spotted ladies who aroused my sexual interest. But this wasn't Sao Salvador da Bahia in Brazil where men often stopped women on the street to tell them they were aroused by their beauty—and sometimes women did the same to men. I knew I could get myself in serious trouble if I got out of my car and approached a gal here to tell her I found her desirable.

"What the hell am I going to do with myself here?" I said out loud.

I drove back out onto the highway and headed south, into a town called Dewey. It featured nightclubs and liquor stores along the highway, and summer cottages between the highway and ocean on one side, the bay on the other—a wide variety of summer vacation accommodations, from international brand motels, expensive looking condos, and funky little cottages set on the sand along narrow lanes leading to the beach, all so deserted you'd think a pandemic had swept through.

I explored some more byways, then got back onto the highway and continued south, across the state line into Maryland and then into Ocean City, a more developed summer resort, and finally came to the south end of it, at an inlet to the ocean, where I stopped for a bite to eat, then got out my cell phone and speed dialed number 1: brother John.

He sounded unexpectedly upbeat. "Hey, Bob! How's it going? How are you finding Rehoboth Beach? Have you seen Laura and the house yet?"

"Yes, and I have a house inspector coming tomorrow, but in the meantime, Jack, I am at sixes and sevens. Don't know what to do with myself here."

"How's the house look to you?"

"It has roof leaks and probably some wiring damage because of the salt air."

"Well, there you go, that's what you're there to do, get it fixed."

"I got the process started. Laura wants to move."

"Move where? I thought she loved living at the beach."

"She mentioned New York City."

"Well, I own a Park Avenue apartment but it's leased. What's she think she's going to do in New York City?"

"I don't know, Jack, but this is one lonely town in the winter months. We're planning to go out to dinner this evening."

"Good. That's probably all she needs, a little male company. She's a single woman, you know, so don't hold back."

"How was your date at the Biltmore?"

"It's been extended. Lola is with me now, here, back at our beach house. We're, eh, we're thinking of...making a more permanent arrangement."

"Are you kidding me?"

"No, but maybe I'm kidding myself. She's so much younger than me. Did you bring that laptop from the guesthouse with you, Bob?"

"Yes, I did. Why?"

"I'll send you a picture of her. At your new email address."

On the drive back to the hotel, I reminded myself that the disease of depression, it has been discovered, is physiologically based, a brain structure abnormality. I was suddenly feeling the symptoms like

I'd not felt them for years. A huge sadness descended on me like a gigantic blanket and I suddenly burst out crying. Had to pull to the side of the highway and park till the tears stopped and I could see to drive again. Something In my present situation or mindset had to change, I knew, or I'd soon be out of control, probably with misdirected anger. That's how it happens for me: first the uncontrollable crying, the gripping sadness, then anger that explodes out in all directions at everyone and no one in particular.

It occurred to me that if I spun out of control here, three thousand miles from brother John and the California of my growing-up years, I could be lost in a way I'd never imagined before. My lifeline was my little brother Jack and now he was talking about marrying again. What possible role or place would I have in his life then? Suddenly my utter and complete dependence on my brother surfaced like a monster from the deep, mocking me, threatening me. I knew next to nothing of his life and he knew the same of mine. Yet here I was three thousand miles away, supposedly in his employ. Did he intend to pay me a salary? He'd never mentioned a salary. But even if he did pay me well for this venture of looking after his properties, where would I call home? What would I do with the rest of my life? Unless I made his guesthouse my home and his every wish my command. And if he married again, what role would his insane brother have in his life? What would he want of me, other than to make myself scarce?

Such thoughts tempted me to stop at the nearest bar and knock down half a dozen shots of bourbon, which prompted the voice of Dr. Grace to resound in my mind: "Remember, Robert, you are not the disease of alcoholism. It's one thing, you are another. You are not one and the same."

And of course the one sure way to make an episode of depression life threatening is to medicate it with booze or drugs.

I went back to the hotel room and took an Ativan and lay down for a nap. I felt lost, trapped in some faraway, new, unknown, frightening space, unable to get back to myself, my own personal life.

At 6 o'clock sharp, I woke up and, remembering Jack said he'd send me a photo of his lady, turned on the laptop and went to the new email I'd established before I left on this trip. "Click on this link to see my lady love Lola Jones," he'd written. I don't know what I'd expected but certainly not the glamorous, deeply tanned girl with full lips and a super-curvaceous figure that filled my screen. She was wearing a mini that came halfway up her thighs, a blouse that bulged with firm young breasts. She was standing in profile with her face turned to the camera, so that her firm and nicely rounded butt was featured. "You naughty little sexpot, you," I said out loud. "What are you doing to my brother?" I reached for my cell phone to call him and react, but checked myself. I'd best let my first reaction cool before I said something that would destroy the new bond we were creating.

I called Hernandez, 3 o'clock his time—he'd be sitting out in the courtyard, probably, reading or working his laptop, doing astrological charts. Hernandez and I had spent years together. Became best friends. We depended on each other the way soldiers in battle depend on each other. Hernandez had my back and I had his. He was a schizophrenic with multiple personality disorder. I knew my departure form the facility weighed heavily on him, left him alone in a way he'd not been for the past seven years. I conjured up the image of him sitting in the courtyard as he does every day, weather permitting. He'd have his reading glasses perched on the end of his beaked nose, a book in his hands, his laptop on the ground beside his chair, and he'd be doing what he calls "coordinating cyclical economic events and repeating planetary patterns." He was a small man, five feet seven inches, and built wiry, tight, but when he entered a room, everyone noticed, for everyone sensed something otherworldly about him, like he carried a new dimension of reality within himself. When he answered my call, I got right to the point.

"Do you have Dr. Mary Grace's number?" I'd forgotten to get it when I left.

"Not in front of me. Why? You okay?"

"I'm not...I'm feeling a bit...depressed."

"Hang on, Bob, I'll walk inside and see if I can find her. She's usually in her office about now. Let's see. Ah ha, here she is. Dr. Grace, Bob Bradford is on the line. You have a minute to talk?"

"Hello?" said Mary Grace's slightly husky, slightly tremolos voice.

"Dr. Grace," I said, "I'm getting symptoms. A few hours ago, I cried for no reason."

"Where are you, Mr. Bradford?"

"On the East Coast."

"What are you...never mind. Have you taken your dailies?"

"Yes, plus an Ativan to relax and nap."

"Good. What are you doing on the East Coast?"

"My brother hired me to manage his properties."

"Well, that sounds good. What's going on, then? Do you know why you would be getting symptoms now?"

"No. That's why I'm calling. I'm baffled. And fearful. I don't know what to do with myself. Maybe the trigger was that my brother mentioned getting married again and that made me wonder what would become of me. He sent me a picture of his girlfriend and...well, she's a young sexpot. I have a terrible urge to drink, get drunk."

"You're looking for a way to medicate yourself in a strange new situation."

"Exactly. A situation that seems to be changing as we speak."

"But you know where drinking would take you, right?"

"I do and I never want to go there again."

"You've been taking your daily meds consistently."

"Yes."

"You see this girlfriend of your brother's as, what? Threatening to your relationship with him?"

"Yes because she's not his type. She's a playgirl. Reeking with sex appeal. And she looks young enough to be his granddaughter."

"Let's try taking another Ativan today, see if that works to get you out of your present condition."

"Okay."

"It's his relationship with this young girl that is triggering?"

"That and being alone and adrift in this strange summer resort town."

"Are you having suicidal ideations?"

"No, not yet, but I very easily could slip into having them."

"Are you where you can lay down?"

"Yes, I'm in a hotel room."

"Stretch out on the bed, Mr. Bradford. Let's do the total relaxation routine."

Whenever she laid me down like this she called me Mr. Bradford rather than Robert or Bob, to remove any hint of intimacy.

"Where exactly is this hotel you're in?"

"Rehoboth Beach. My brother has employed me to inspect his properties."

"I know Rehoboth, used to summer there. I grew up in the Washington, DC area. What hotel are you in?"

"The Boardwalk Plaza."

"Ah, I remember it well. Anyway, are you laying down now?"

"Yes."

I kept the cell phone to my ear as she stepped me through the routine of totally relaxing my body from head to toe, then whispered some previously agreed upon prompts, something like post-hypnotic suggestions. I was under her spell for about fifteen minutes and when I came out of this alpha brainwave state, I felt better. The fearful grip of depression had lifted or dissipated, and I remembered some of the sexual fantasies I'd had over the years of fucking Mary Grace. She was aware of this and kept our sessions moving, her voice stern and her demeanor strict, distancing us from any hint of romantic hanky panky.

"I feel much better now."

"What might have precipitated?"

"Being so far from familiar territory. And my brother mentioned that he may remarry, and then I saw his girlfriend. That would change my role in his life, I imagine. Maybe not, but I imagine it would. I fear it would."

"I'm concerned that he sent you on such a long trip so soon. But of course you can't expect him to provide you with the kind of care you were getting here. You've got to assert your independence, husband your individuality."

"I know that."

"Well, I'm going to make a note to speak with your brother John."

"Dr. Grace, I'm afraid that if you pressure, he'll balk. He's a busy man. I feel like I'm already an intrusion in his life."

"I promise I'll be tactful. All I want to find out is his plans for you, for your relationship. As I understand it, you two were renewing your familial ties."

"Yes, right, we were. Are."

"Good. Then this renewal is what I will explore with him. Now, Robert, are you feeling better?"

"Yes."

"Then I'll say goodbye, and we'll talk again tomorrow. All right?"

"All right."

Hernandez came back on the line. "Hey, Bobby boy, you've got to stay busy. That's indicated by you natal chart. You have an over-abundance of energy and need to absorb yourself in something you love, something or someone that enlists your passions."

"Maybe that's the nub of my problem here. I'm at sixes and sevens, waiting."

"For what?"

"I don't know—to get the work done on my brother's ex-wife's house so I can fly back to California. I'm having dinner with her this evening. Meanwhile, my brother is talking about getting married again."

"And you're wondering where that would leave you?"

"Exactly."

"Decide where you want it to take you and use the Jose Silva method, Bobby."

"Yeah, good thinking, Jorge. I'll do that."

After we said goodbye, I remembered that he'd been a PhD economics professor before his disease. It was easy to imagine him lecturing to a classroom full of college students. But there was scant chance that he'd ever return to his old profession, even with his mental problems under control. "I broke the mold," he said. "They used the phrase, 'not housebroken' to declare me ineligible to ever teach economics again. They view mixing economics and astrology as something like mixing science and witchcraft. It's not, but their belief overcomes the evidence. They feel threatened by my approach, for if it can ever be proven that our best economic forecasting tools are the cycles and recurring patterns of the outermost planets, extraterrestrial forces beyond their comprehension and control, where will that leave the so-called science of economics? So now I'm certifiably insane and they have nothing to fear. They can go on believing they're in control of the economy. End of story."

His lament reminded me of a lady who'd come into Covington suffering clinical depression, in her late fifties, married to a husband who was convinced—and had convinced her children and grandchildren—that it was her fault. If she'd suffered from a physical ailment, her family would have rallied to her aid. But they viewed her mental illness as her fault and made her life more miserable. She said she couldn't leave her husband and family because she had nowhere else to go. How could she live alone suffering from depression? Yet how could she live with a family that despised her for "faking" bouts of irrational grief and rage? About a year after she'd been released, we heard she'd taken the only way out of her dilemma: Suicide. Her case was by no means unique.

Around 8 o'clock, my room phone chirped and it was Laura's slow contralto. She was parked in front of the hotel, she said. Amazing how the pace of life has increased in the past decade. Years ago, she would have parked, come into the hotel and called from the house phone. I hurried down and got into her Lexus, with Hernandez's advice in mind. Could I immerse myself in Laura, focus my over-abundance of energy in her?

Chapter 11

It wasn't the first morning I'd awakened with Lola beside me in bed in the Biltmore Hotel, but it was the first day I'd had to deal with the notion that we might marry, have a child or two, make a new life for ourselves. I awakened with the thought that my choice was stark. Loneliness after an incredibly busy life, or the joy of Lola—and the certainty that the honeymoon would eventually end, that marriage to her would be ridiculous and end painfully. I found myself wishing I could be like my big brother was in high school—full of confident recklessness in affairs of the heart.

We showered together, always a delightfully sensuous play with Lola, and as we were getting dressed, I said, "Suppose we give it a try, living together."

"I'm up for that. I'll keep up my sexy and support myself with dates, and we'll see how we get along."

I didn't like the sound of that. "What do you mean, keep up your sexy?"

"Workout and pamper myself. That's how I keep up my sexy."

"I don't think I could handle you're going out on dates. What if you become my kept mistress instead?"

"No deal," she said. "You might keep me for a year or two and then cut me loose, and by that time I'd have lost my sexy and couldn't make the kind of income I make now."

"What kind of annual income do you make now?"

"I charge one thousand a date, as you know, and I average about three dates a week. What's that come to?"

"Well over a hundred thousand a year, my dear. Do you pay IRS taxes?"

"Hell no, I'm part of the underground economy."

"Well then, how about this. I'll pay you a salary during this trial period. You'll be my personal assistant at twelve thousand a month."

"Jesus, John, that's a lot of money."

"That's what you're making now, Lola."

"I am? Where does it go? Rent and food included in this deal?"

"Certainly."

"I could rent out my house in the Valley."

"You own a house?"

"Yes, the one my grandfather left me, free and clear. I could rent it out for this trial year and put that money into some kind of savings account for my old age."

"We could also set up a pension fund. I'd match whatever amount of your salary you decide to put into this pension fund."

"At the end of this trial year, John, I'd really like to have enough money so I could get into some other business. I mean, you know, I'd have lost my book and my sexy so I could no longer make it in this business. I've been lucky—I'm good looking—but gentlemen of means do not fancy paying for sex with girls who are, as they say, over the hill. It's a very competitive business. You have only so many moneymaking years before the wrinkles appear. After that, you've got to have some other way to support yourself, and I'm a high school dropout."

I did some quick calculations in my mind and came up with this: "At the end of our trial year, I will guarantee that you'll have a million dollars safely invested in triple A bonds, providing you with an annual income of at least fifty thousand. How's that sound?"

"Push come to shove, I guess I could open a boutique on Rodeo Drive."

"Or my financial manager could steer you into something more lucrative."

"Like what? Running my own escort service?"

"If that's what you wanted to do. There are lots of other choices."

"Okay, if you put all this in writing, let's give living together for a year a try."

"Consider it done. Now, you've never seen my home, have you."

"No, where is it?"

"It's at the beach. Follow me in your car and we'll go there now. If we happen to get separated on the freeway, I'll be waiting for you at the Padero Lane exit, just south of Carpinteria."

When we got to the beach house, Jake Valance was tail-gating her in his big black Chevy van, no doubt wondering why she was following me. The lane goes back to a circle in front of the house, and there we three parked and got out to confer.

Valance hurried to my side, his eyes wide with the obvious question. His sidekick, whose name I did not know, remained in the van with a suspicious eye on Lola, who sat in her car glancing back at the van, and then at Jake and me as we talked.

"Nothing to worry about, Jake," I said. "I'm bringing home a guest."

"A call girl?" he asked with mock surprise.

I paused a moment to cool my anger. "Her name is Lola. She's going to be my personal assistant." I suddenly realized I had no last name for her and averted my eyes. Lola was her working name. Was it also her given name? I didn't know. I got out of my car and walked to hers. "Lola, this is Jake Valance. He oversees security for this property, and for me personally."

I had to stifle a laugh at the sight of them shaking hands, she from the seat of her BMW Z sports car, and he from his ramrod straight stance as he stood looking down at her.

"Can I get out now? Or do you have dogs too?" said Lola.

"Come on in, sweetheart. Jake, we won't need you to stick around. You can get back to your regular routine."

He walked ramrod straight to the black van, got in and drove back out the lane. He was obviously not content. I suspected he'd have some questions for me later.

Inside the house, I introduced Lola to Alicia, who kept her eyes on the floor and asked if we'd like breakfast. We had a coffee and a Danish each. Lola looks vaguely Hispanic so Alicia tried some Spanish on her but Lola just returned a blank stare. Peering into her dark blue eyes, I asked, "What ethnicity are you, Lola?"

"My mother is half Anglo and half Philippine, and my father is just plain white bread—Irish, I guess. Why?"

"Your dark skin and blue eyes."

"I cultivate a tan year round."

"I can see you tan easily."

"From my mother's side."

I led Lola upstairs and opened the door to the bedroom that had been my daughter's. "You can make this your personal, private room, if you like. Or you can choose another bedroom. This one has a really fine view of the beach."

"Yes, it does," she said. "I like it. But where is your bedroom?"

"First door at the top of the stairs. Come, I'll show it to you. You can keep your things there, if you prefer."

"Oh, God, John," she said upon entering the master bedroom, "I'll stay here with you, if that's all right. This is magnificent."

"I'd much prefer that. You have your own walk-in closet here. It's the one to the right of mine." I opened the door onto what had been Laura's, with its private bathroom door at the far end of the closet.

The rest of the day was spent dealing with the details of our new arrangement. I called Herby Stein and explained the situation to him, expecting him to question my hasty decision to move a female named Lola into my house. But he hummed over the idea that I was hiring a personal assistant and seemed to approve. Didn't even ask what exactly she would be doing as my personal assistant. I suppose he guessed, and approved. I explained that she would be leasing her house in the Valley and that I had guaranteed her a million dollars invested in triple A bonds by the end of one year.

"I'll set it up," he said, "all but the leasing of her house. You'll have to go through a realtor for that, you know."

"She'll take care of that detail."

"How long do you think she'll be living with you?"

"I don't know. Either of us can break it off at any time—that's our agreement."

"Good. Men of means have been paying for mistresses since time immemorial. I do think the price in this case is a bit steep, though."

"She's worth it to me. And I can afford it."

"All right. Papers will be ready for review tomorrow."

Later this day, I got a call from Bob in Rehoboth Beach. He said he had a professional house inspector coming tomorrow, and that all was well with Laura...except that she was talking of moving to New York City. I told Bob that such a move is something she should take up with Herby Stein. She was free to live wherever she chose, at my expense, but I did not need to be involved with the details.

There was a tenor to Bob's voice that concerned me, though, for he did not sound at all happy. Not that I expected him to be gushing over spending time in Rehoboth Beach in the dead of winter, but neither did I see any reason why he should sound so unhappy. "Are you all right?" I asked.

"It's just that I suddenly seem to have a lot of time on my hands, you know. I'll be okay, don't worry."

Lola left for her house in the Valley around late-afternoon, saying she'd return in a few hours. She wanted to bring more clothes and personal items here. Tomorrow, she said, she'd call realtors and set up leasing her house. The mortgage had been paid off so all she owed were annual taxes.

As I watched her walk out to her car, I marveled that such a stunning young lady could also be so basically intelligent and practical. In my heart I already felt wedded to her but in my head I continued to have serious doubts. I consoled myself with the thought that, given the pre-nuptial agreement we planned and the fund I would set up for her, nothing extremely ruinous could happen. Worst possible scenario, we'd part after a year, maybe five or more, whenever the affair ran its course, and both of us would be better for the experience. She would bridge my transition into full retirement, and in exchange I would set her up with financial security. Best possible scenario... well, that seemed too good to even contemplate.

I wondered what Bob's reaction to the photo I'd sent him was. I'd taken it while showing her the master bedroom. I wanted to call him and ask, but decided to await his comment.

Chapter 12

Laura's favorite restaurant, the Cultured Pearl, turned out to be a maze occupying three stories of an old building on Rehoboth Avenue that had been gutted and redesigned. It had numerous areas, each with its own points of interest—bamboo partitions, ponds with gold fish, televisions on walls with moving pictures of underwater things like coral reefs busy with intricate life. Everyone seemed to know Laura. "Your usual?" asked the hostess. She led us to a table for two within a bamboo enclosure, overlooking three stories of interior. Visible from our table were two bars and any number of more private dining nooks. I'd never seen anything like it and had to battle another bout of the Rip Van Winkle effect. Still, after my conversations with Mary Grace and Jorge Hernandez, and an extra anti-depression med, the black blanket had lifted and I was feeling pretty good.

She had the filet mignon and I had the chef's sushi-sashimi special. She had some kind of rum drink and I had orange juice. "You're not a drinker?" she asked.

"No, not any more."

"I'll bet my ex, your brother, still drinks."

"He does. Without any noticeable harm."

"How long have you been...out?" she asked with a concerned look.

"About a week. Still getting adjusted to life on the outside."

"You were...in...various institutions?"

"In and out for the past three decades, really."

"Were you ever married?"

"Not officially."

"What's that mean?"

"I was common-law married several times."

"Shacked up."

"If you prefer."

"Are you in a relationship now?"

"By relationship, you mean do I have a sex partner?"

Her eyelids fluttered. "Yes."

"No, I don't have such a relationship now. And you?"

"The same. I broke up with a man I was seeing for over a year. We parted on friendly terms, just got bored with each other."

"He live in Rehoboth?"

"He lives in Washington, has a summer house here."

"You miss him?"

She heaved a big sigh and seemed to screw up her courage in order to say, "Bob, I'm a horny woman. The man I was seeing, he just didn't have the same interest in sex that I do. I'm not saying that to put the make on you, only to let you know my... present situation. Single and horny."

"That's refreshingly frank," I said with a smile.

"And you've been... away for so long, you must be horny too."

Indeed I was but I was also feeling trepidation. Laura was, after all, my ex-sister-in-law. Her two kids were my niece and nephew. John had said, "Don't hold back," but how did he really feel? I remembered times when I'd bumped into old girlfriends out with their new lovers, and how it had pushed some emotional buttons. You pump enough sperm into a woman and you feel like a farmer watching a field you've seeded, waiting for something to sprout.

I said, "What you have in front of you is an aging specimen whose last sexual escapades involved drugs, booze and two girls at a time."

That seemed to set her back on her heels, but briefly. "How long ago?"

"Let's see, given how long I've been incarcerated, first in San Quentin, then in Covington, about a decade ago. Well, I should admit to a couple of quickies while incarcerated, but they were nothing."

And so we dined with an implied sexual encounter looming, despite our advanced ages. After dinner, as she drove me back to the Boardwalk Plaza, she asked, "Do you do marijuana?"

"It's been a long time."

"I have some."

I felt a twinge of fear, knowing that marijuana had become far more potent during the past decade. My greatest fear was that, loosened up on marijuana, I might reach for the booze. It was alcohol that was the big danger for me. If the marijuana made me forget that, I could be dead within a month.

"I don't want to drink," I said.

"Neither do I—except for some fruit juice, maybe."

In the parking lot outside the hotel, she got out a little plastic baggie of grass and rolled a joint, then lit up. We shared it, staring silently at the pinkish wall in front of the parking space. The effect on me was an instant hard-on, which Laura noticed immediately. She reached over and slowly wrapped her fingers around it. "Want to come up to my room?" I said.

"Yeah," she said in her sexy contralto with a down-under look.

And so we did.

Inside the room, with lights from the boardwalk our only illumination, I said, "Take off your panties" and did her over the edge of the bed before we got fully undressed and continued our dance, which went well into the wee hours. After all these years I had a load of passion pent up, but an out-of-shape love muscle. By dawn it was spent and itchy sore, a pleasant sensation my body remembered from decades ago.

The hotel room window, with curtains parted, let in the morning sunrise over the sea, and I felt youthful inside my aging body.

"Let's order up breakfast," she said.

"Will the management be okay with this?"

I meant, will they decide the room has been rented to two people rather than one?

"No problem. They're lucky to have anyone staying here in the middle of the week this time of year."

We ordered up breakfast and then I got out my cell phone and called Joe Martino, gave him Laura's address and we hurried there to meet him.

While he went over the house, Laura and I sat staring out through her picture window at the sea, under a bright sun this morning. "The weather here can be moody," said Laura. "Sunshine for a few hours, then fog, rain, sunshine again."

Off in the distance was a ship plying its way out of the wide Delaware Bay into the ocean. I couldn't tell if it was an oil tanker or a Navy ship. It was so far away, it appeared the size of a fingernail clipping moving slower than a lazy caterpillar. We both stared at it for a long time, in a pleasant meditative trance. In this alpha brainwave state, I imagined our relationship being mellow and warm and healing for each of us. I felt an easy harmony with her and knew she felt the same with me. Best anti-depressant med I'd had in a long, long time.

It took Joe four hours to give the house a thorough going over from roof to foundation. When he'd finished, Laura and I were hungry for lunch and she was searching her refrigerator and cabinets for something to eat. He was a gregarious guy, friendly without being overbearing, so she asked if he'd like something to eat while he went over his notes. We sat around her oval kitchen table nibbling on celery and cheese dip as he gave us the run-down, recommending an entirely new roof, a complete rewiring of the whole house, and the replacement of some pipes that were old and showing corrosion. "I'd recommend replacing all the plumbing, if you can afford it," he said.

"Can you recommend contractors to do the work?" I asked.

"Oh sure. This town was going through a building boom until recently. People from Washington are suddenly not rushing over here to buy up every new house built. So there are plenty of guys in construction looking for work."

"How soon can you get estimates?"

"Before the weekend, I think."

"I'll need those to shake the money loose. Do you think work can begin by this coming Monday?"

"Maybe sooner. I'll let you know."

I'd been thinking that, once the work was underway, I'd fly back to California, but given my new romance with Laura, I changed my plans and stayed on at the Boardwalk Plaza, and for the next two weeks Laura commuted between her house and my room. The threat of depression, which had overcome me my first day here, lifted like melting snow in a warm sun. Dr. Grace preached that it was physiologically based and vulnerable to being triggered by certain situations which in turn trigger certain brain chemicals. Looking back on it a week or so later, I realized there was some homesickness involved, too, for my home had become the psychiatric facility in Camarillo, my doctor Mary Grace and my good friend Jorge Hernandez. I checked in daily with both by cell phone and felt a surge of wellbeing as I contemplated my new situation in life: on my brother John's payroll—no sum had been mentioned but I was using his credit card for everything—living high on the hog with the luxury of a new love affair to brighten my life. The winter weather in Rehoboth continued moody and changeable with chilly rains now and then, but my interior weather was as warm and sunny as July.

I remembered hearing from Mom that our father, the Harvard grad, had taken the family to Cape Cod one summer when I was five and John was three. She told a story about how I'd wandered off one late afternoon and gotten lost. She said they'd finally found me sitting on a curb in Provincetown, shivering and crying my heart out. I don't know if I had a vague recollection of this or relived it through my mother's story, but it seemed to connect with that first day in Rehoboth when I felt suddenly lost. Dr. Grace said we retain those memories from early childhood below the level of conscious awareness and they can rise up to bite us when triggered. Now, with Laura, I was triggering memories from earlier love affairs, which bolstered my macho ego and overall confidence.

Neither Laura nor I speculated aloud about where our relationship might lead, and the only odd thing was that I seemed to tell her more about myself than she told me about herself. I covered my days as a successful writer and my drug-dealing adventures, but left out the skid row experiences. She kept asking questions about my past and I knew my reputation continued to be a thing in her mind—not an entirely negative thing now, though, for I knew being with such a "bad hombre" was a turn-on for her. Danger is an aphrodisiac and we had fun with it, instigating sexual encounters at odd times of the day and night, in places where we might get caught: against the beachside of the boardwalk around noon, near the water's edge around midnight, in her car while parked in downtown Rehoboth on a crowded Saturday night, even a little hand play while having dinner at the Cultured Pearl. It was like we were looking past each other's aging physical containers into each other's essential beings.

I also kept in touch with my brother during this lull. I told him I had taken his advice, had not held back with Laura, and he seemed happy that we were having an affair. He, meanwhile, was making a new living arrangement with the girl in her early twenties who had been what he called his Biltmore rendezvous, and was now living with him in the beach house. "She's my personal assistant," he said.

"She's gorgeous as a movie star. How does she assist you?" I asked jokingly.

"The title is for tax purposes. You can't deduct a live-in mistress."

"Who is this girl, John? Where did she come from?"

"Her name is Lola Jones and she grew up in the San Fernando Valley. You know the old joke: why flip Kentucky Fried Chicken when you can make more money giving Colonial Sanders a blowjob. She became a call girl. Very successful. Makes a six-figure income. Best of all, she's very intelligent. Wants to go back to school, get a college degree."

"You sure she's not conning you?"

"I'm not sure of anything."

"And she's how old?"

"Twenty-two."

'You lucky dog, you."

"Or am I being a stupid old fool?"

"Not unless you let her steal your entire fortune."

"We've got a formal agreement, Robert. We both benefit, and either one of us can terminate at a moment's notice, no hard feelings."

"Sounds wonderful, John."

"Maybe it's having you around—I'm feeling as reckless as you were in your teens."

"Interesting. I'm feeling the kind of mellow with Laura that you must have felt—during the best of your years with her."

The town of Rehoboth had taken on such a rosy hue for me that, by the end of the second week when my brother broached a more sinister aspect of his affair, I was totally unprepared. He said, "Something is a bit out of sorts here, Robert. I'm not sure what it is, exactly, but Jake Valance, my security man, wants to restrict my movements to the point where it's becoming ridiculous."

"Restrict your movements?"

"Yes. The other day I told Jake that I was taking Lola on a trip and Jake told me that was not a good idea. He was adamant about it. Said two more executives had been snatched and were being held for ransom, and he was picking up what he called 'signals' that the terrorists were targeting people of what he called 'loose morals', so it would be best for me to stay home."

"Wow, John, that sounds a little like he has you under a subtle kind of house arrest."

"Yes it does. Especially since he doesn't come up with hard evidence of any eminent threat. Doesn't name these executives he says have been snatched. Anyhow, my old CEO wants me to make another trip to the Big Apple to confer with my replacement over some accounting procedures, which still baffle the man. I've got to be able to do that. I can put it off a week or so but it would be unthinkable to refuse. I also have a foundation to attend to, and I serve on about a dozen boards of directors and need to travel for scheduled meetings, have one coming up in a few days, but Jake talks like he'd rather I cancel and stay home. Indefinitely. He says he has no idea how long this 'code red' will last. This 'code red' he shows no hard evidence exists, mind you. I can't do that, Robert. I've got duties to fulfill."

"But this security agency works for you, doesn't it?"

"It's paid by my company to protect me, yes."

"Then who is this security guy to dictate your schedule? Have you talked this over with your CEO? Would he be the one to consult about this?"

"I seem to have gotten myself in a bind, Robert. If I press this matter to people in the company, they'll investigate and find out about Lola. That's a very personal matter that I would not like to share with them. They would immediately see it as your proverbial old fool smitten with a suspiciously under-worldly type young lady of the night. Given the famous track record of such liaisons, my reputation within the company would be greatly harmed. Doing what I'm doing with Lola is, in a sense, perceived as worse than skimming money from the shareholders. If you can believe it."

"I can believe it. We live in a puritanical society, my brother. There's a bumper sticker here, a picture of George W. Bush over the words, 'Will somebody please give this man a blowjob so he can be impeached?' He can't be impeached for lying us Into a war or plundering us, only for a sexual indiscretion."

"That's way off the mark, Robert. Nobody's plundering. Actually, even though he's unpopular right now, Bush is the best president we've ever had."

"For big corporations."

"Which is the foundation of the American economy. And the world economy, I should add. Not every Joe Sixpack understands this."

"Brother John, our ideas of what constitutes a good economy are definitely at odds, so let's stick to the security problem you're having."

"Good idea. Your forte is not economics, but I suspect you do know a thing or two about blackmail."

That stopped me. I've never been involved with blackmail. That is, beyond the personal kind that lovers and families get into. I didn't want to antagonize John by objecting to his characterization of me as knowing a thing or two about blackmail, so I evaded and told him I'd think about the situation and get back to him.

Around 10 o'clock that night, 7 o'clock West Coast time, I called Al Hansen and asked if he'd heard there was a stepped up security alert due to an increase in the kidnapping of corporate executives. He seemed to immediately know what I was referring to, for he said, "When are you coming home, Bob?"

"Why?"

"I'd rather discuss this with you in person. My cell phone is encrypted but yours isn't."

"I see. Okay, I'll be home in a day or two, as soon as I can make arrangements to fly out of here. I'll call you to let you know."

"Good."

"Not entirely. I'm having a love affair and am not eager to turn it loose."

"Whatever," said Al. "I think you need to get your butt back here. Things going down at that Padero house that don't smell right. But I don't want to say anything more about it now. Fly home and we'll talk about it."

I made reservations to fly out of Baltimore-Washington International the following morning, to arrive in LA around mid-afternoon. Laura was not happy about my sudden departure, even after I explained my suspicion that John's security people were messing with him because of his young girlfriend.

"What does he expect when he's messing around with young prostitutes," she said angrily. "That's an old habit with him, you know. He's used call girls all over the world, for years. When are you coming back?"

"Not sure."

"Well, it's been real. I hate to see you leave. I could prolong this forever."

"Really? I thought you saw me as a bad guy."

"I did. But I've come to see you as my knight in shining armor. You're a truly honest and thoroughly good man."

I was tempted to tell her I'd messed with more Lola Jones types than she or my brother could imagine, that I'd been home base and drug supplier for whole harems of them. But I held my tongue. It's not a good idea to tell your present lover too much about your past.

During my last evening there, her mood was grouchy. But she didn't want to talk about us. "When will this awful war in Iraq end?" she asked over dinner.

"When the military-industrial complex is dismantled," I replied.

Her forehead wrinkled with a perplexed frown. "What's that got to do with it? This war is breaking us financially, as a country."

"It's a magnificent profit generator for the big banks and corporations."

"You talk as though our banks and corporations are not part of us."

"They aren't. They're plundering us."

"Oh, I don't believe that for a second. Where would we be without them?"

"We'd be where we were after the Revolutionary War when banks and corporations were tightly controlled—before some rogue Chief Justice declared corporations persons."

"Bob, I love you, dear, but you're way over your pay grade here. That's ridiculous. That was two hundred years ago, for crying out loud."

She agreed with her ex-husband, my brother, when it came to pocketbook matters: Make as much money as you can, any way you can. Mentally disassociate your income from that magnificent money generator called war. Believe the patriotic propaganda. Don't rock the establishment boat. Go along to get along, you can't fight city hall.

I lowered my eyes, as though accepting her characterization of me as thinking above my pay grade. In today's America, only the opinions of the super wealthy and Ph D economists count. Everyone else should shut up and listen. This system will be toast by 2020, I figure, so why waste my breath.

My silence seemed to put a punctuation mark at the end of our affair. We went our separate ways after that dinner. She dropped me off at the hotel, saying she had things to do at home. That I might never see her again hurt, but then, what kind of future did our relationship have if we could not discuss my past, my brother's young mistress, or politics and the economy? Dr. Mary Grace had worked hard to get me to realize that my narcissism is a great hindrance to my future happiness, that the happiest in any paired relationship was the lover, not the beloved. That had not eased my feeling of isolation in what I—and Jorge Hernandez—perceive as a society shaped by the mission of corporate cartels. "The cartels have replaced the fiefdoms of medieval Europe," Jorge liked to preach, "but there's no point swimming against the current. The best we can do is adjust to the existing reality, knowing we're on the cusp of a huge transformation."

Chapter 13

Lola had been living with me for a few days when it came time for me to get ready for the trip to the Bay Area for a corporate board meeting. It would only be one overnight—I'd fly up there late Wednesday, do the board meeting Thursday and fly back Thursday night. When I told Lola about it, she assumed I wanted her to come with me. Well, I did and I didn't. It would not make the right statement to arrive at the Mark Hopkins with her on my arm, yet on the other hand it would be fun to have her there. "If you come with me, sweetheart, we'll have to make separate arrivals at the hotel. Can you live with that?"

"Oh sure. I know you can't be seen checking into your room with a chick like me. I'm too sexy to be your matronly wife. How about we take separate cabs from the airport. You get the room and call me, tell me the number and I'll come."

"Done. I'm sorry about this—I'd much rather we were together for the whole trip."

"Don't give it a second thought."

I called Jake on my cell to let him know our plan. He said, "Mr. Bradford, sir, we've got to sit down and talk this over."

"Why? It's just a trip to San Francisco."

"New developments," he said.

We sat down the next morning in the living room. I poured Jake a shot of his favorite Scotch and we talked.

"Mr. Bradford, we're worried."

"Why?"

"Red alert. There's been a sudden increase in the snatching of execs, Mr. Bradford. Globally. Head office says we should discourage you from traveling informally till this latest blows over."

"But this isn't traveling informally, it's a business trip, and an overnight within state. I'm not going outside the country."

"I know, Mr. Bradford. I'm merely telling you my orders from New York."

"From your agency or my company?"

"Both, sir. And it's not only the stepped-up alert, sir. We are concerned about the added responsibility."

"You mean Lola?"

"Yes."

"I realize she's not covered in your contract—"

"Spouses and family are, but not girlfriends."

"All right. I don't expect you to add Lola to your list of clients. She's my responsibility, not yours."

"It's also the red alert, sir. Things are getting complicated. We wish you'd cancel this trip. In time, the red alert will blow over, but for now..."

"Jake, you've got to give me specifics. You can't expect me to change my plans because of some vague red alert or kidnappings half a world away."

"Mr. Bradford, I can't give you specifics without breaching confidentiality."

"Whose confidentiality? Your job is to protect me, Jake."

"There are more than just you involved."

I thanked him for his advice. It was certainly part of his duty to advise me about the security situation globally, but there was no way I was going to cancel my trip to San Francisco—especially since he would not cite specifics.

Later that day, I got on the phone to our CEO, Jim Hurley, and put the question to him. "Did you give orders to the agency to keep me grounded here?"

"Hell no, where did you get that idea?"

"My security man, Jake Valance."

"Did he say that?"

"Not in so many words. He left me to ponder where his orders came from. Orders to restrict my travel, even inside this state."

"I'll call the head of the agency in the city here and get back to you."

He got back within fifteen minutes. "John, the agency people are saying there has been an increase in kidnappings, but outside this country. So I see no reason why your man there should prevent you from traveling inside California."

"That's curious," I said. "I'll tell him to back off, I'm making this trip and that's all there is to it."

Yet I was keenly aware that Jake Valance could spread the word I was now living with a call girl. He could tell his people in New York, who could tell my people in the company. Several years ago, a young executive with a very promising future married an African American girl around his own age. A beautiful girl, very bright, with a career of her own. Within six months that executive was history. Nothing formal. He was simply excluded, no longer part of inner-circle confidences. Yet, on the other hand, we have a black executive, Ronnie Harris, who is not excluded for his race. He's part of the inner circle. What got the younger man shunned was marrying across the color line. If word got back to New York that I was living with a 22-year-old call girl, it would be viewed as far worse than marrying across the color line. People in the company liked to say that the way you lived your life was your own private business, but if this private business became known, my honor would be down the toilet.

I called a member of the board who lived in Beverly Hills and would probably be on the same flight as me if I flew out of LAX, as I sometimes did, instead of Santa Barbara. I asked if he'd heard anything about a stepped-up security alert that should cause us not to travel. He hadn't. He asked what I was talking about. I felt foolish telling him our security people here were advising I stay home, but not giving specific reasons for the heightened caution. I pictured this gentleman seeing me with Lola on the flight up or walking through the airport in San Francisco, and felt doubly foolish. What the hell have I gotten myself into?

I called Jake by cell phone the day before I was to leave. "I want you to know that I deeply appreciate all the hard work you and your unit put in protecting me here, Jake. I'm in your debt. But I have this dilemma. If I don't make that board meeting in San Francisco, the people there will want to know why. I can't use unspecified security concerns as an excuse. That just won't wash."

"Do you plan to bring your girlfriend?"

"I'd like to bring her."

"Then please be advised that you increase the risk considerably."

"How so?"

"A man of your power and prestige traveling with a call girl like Lola, Mr. Bradford, is a very tempting target. The enemy can use that to cause a distraction and separate you, or they could grab her to get to you. You see, it means the agency has to hire extra people to get you both there and back safely. And if, God forbid, something goes wrong, is your company paying for her protection as well as your own, sir?"

"I'll make the trip alone."

"We can't stop you from making whatever trips you want to make, Mr. Bradford. But we must warn you. The red alert includes the Bay Area."

"Look, Jake, I have a duty to show up for this board meeting. And there will be others, you know. You've seen my schedule."

"Well, it certainly helps if you make such trips alone, sir. We'll keep an eye on your house while you're gone—that's routine. What we cannot do, sir, is add a traveling girlfriend without revising our agreement with your company."

"I see."

"I hope you understand."

Then came the touchy task of telling Lola we'd have to change our plan, that she'd not be going with me on this trip. She'd bought a new dress for the occasion and was looking forward to it, talking about shopping in downtown San Francisco.

"Is that the way it's always going to be? You're going to keep me here, locked away, your very own secret?"

I recapped my conversations with Jake Valance, trying to help her understand that it would put me in a very vulnerable position to be seen traveling with her on business.

"I thought you were retiring," she said.

"Well, yes, I am semi-retired, my darling, but I still have obligations to fulfill. I'm not fully out to pasture yet."

"Jack, my dear, I think you're being way too cautious. Look at that guy, Koslowski, the head of that big corporation that threw that big party on an island in Greece. He had a young, sexy wife."

"*Had* being the operative word, my love. Koslowski was the head of WorldCom. He's now in prison, you know."

"But that's because he robbed from his company, right?"

"A lot of executives charge things to their companies. Koslowski's real crime wasn't the bills he ran up, it was his sensational lifestyle and sexy young wife."

"Oh."

We were in the master bedroom having this talk. She frowned and stared out at the horizon. My heart went out to her, sitting with her knees tucked up under her chin, a forlorn expression on her pretty face as she absorbed the implications.

"I think it's time for me to look into furthering my education," she said. "I'm going to get on the phone while you're gone and see what university will have me."

"They will probably want you to complete your high school requirements."

"I'll do whatever it takes."

"Do you feel you could handle college courses without completing high school?"

"Yes. You know I'm an avid reader."

"Maybe I can call in a favor or two and get you admitted on a special basis."

"That would be nice. Funny, isn't it? There's how things are supposed to be done, how they are actually done, and who gets hassled by the law for what. A lot of it doesn't make sense to me yet, but I'm learning."

Chapter 14

The flight back to the West Coast went smoothly and I connected with the Santa Barbara airport limo service, arriving at the Padero house late Thursday afternoon. As I was getting out of the limo, Jake Valance stepped out of the house, looking as though he was not sure he would approve of who was arriving or why. "Oh," he said, "You're the brother."

"Yes. I'm Robert Bradford."

"You've been away."

"Yes."

"Welcome back, Robert."

He knew I'd been away and his tone wasn't welcoming. I was not charmed by the way he stood in the doorway with his beefy arms folded over his chest, dressed in standard police blue but without a badge, wearing an arrogant, know-it-all attitude.

I saw that behind him, at the far end of the dining area, someone else was in the house—a young lady. I took her to be my brother's girlfriend, Lola Jones. She moved toward the front entrance, wearing a white blouse and cream-colored slacks that complemented her darkly tanned skin, under raven-black hair, and most of all her voluptuous figure. Extra slim waist, sweet-backed, delightfully rounded derriere, medium-sized breasts. As she approached, I saw that her eyes were cobalt blue. She squeezed past Jake and said, "I'm Lola," extending her hand with a warm smile. "You're John's brother, right?"

"Robert, yes. Please call me Bob."

"And you're living in the guesthouse, right?

"Right."

"I'm new here, as you know."

"John sent me your photo. A beautiful addition you are."

"Thank you. Where is John?"

"He's in San Francisco attending a board meeting."

Jake, meanwhile, continued to stand in the doorway, watching and listening. Why didn't he move on, attend to his security duties? I gave him a questioning look. He stared back deadpanned, with a hint of the evil eye.

I paid and tipped the limo driver, got my two bags and started to carry them over the pine needle carpet to the guesthouse when Lola hurried to my side and said, "Can I carry your smaller bag?"

"No need to."

"By way of getting acquainted."

She took the carry-on bag out of my hand and we walked to the guesthouse together.

When we reached the front door, I glanced back to see Jake Valance had moved and was now standing in the driveway, watching us. It was as though he'd taken over as master of the house while John was away and wasn't sure, yet, whether he should approve of me or not. Or maybe he was concerned that Lola was being so friendly. I got a quick impression that Jake had a thing for Lola. I wondered if I was reading him correctly. Probably not, I thought, but time would tell.

Lola put the carry-on bag down on the floor near the coffee table in front of the couch and said, "Well, I don't want this to stir up Jake so I'll leave you now. I'm glad you're here, Bob. Let's talk later."

"Yes, let's do that."

Stir up Jake? Who the hell was he to be strutting about like he owned the place? He was in charge of security, not master of this domain.

As Lola was going out the front door, I said, "One question before you leave, Lola. What is Jake doing hanging out in John's house? Shouldn't he be with his security people?"

"I don't know. He's been inside the house since I got up this morning. John wants me to keep an eye on him, make sure he doesn't go into the master bedroom."

"Don't hesitate to call me if you need help."

"I won't. John left me your number."

I showered and napped away some jet lag before calling Al Hansen. He said he got off duty at five and asked if I could come to his house for dinner. I said I didn't have the use of any of John's cars, so would need a lift to and from his house. We made arrangements for me to be taking a walk along Padero Lane around five-thirty when Al would cruise by and pick me up. I got the impression that Al didn't feel easy about driving onto the Padero property to pick me up and asked him about this. "I'll explain later," he said.

As I climbed into his Ford SUV, his mood seemed testy. "You hear how they're using a preacher to lynch Barack Obama?" he asked. He explained how the media had somehow gotten hold of a video clip of Jeremiah Wright, the pastor at Barack Obama's church on the south-side of Chicago, and were endlessly replaying a thirty-second sound bite of Wright lambasting White American society for its bigoted insensitivity toward African Americans. I knew there was nothing unusual about such a harangue and said so. Black people routinely release the frustrations of living in a racist society by such harangues.

"They're trying to use his pastor to lynch him," Al repeated. "I knew that if a Black man ran for president, this would happen."

"I don't think it will work this time," I said.

"Why not? Worked every other time."

I'd heard the speech Obama had given defending himself from the Pastor Wright hangman's knot, and thought he'd brilliantly defined the racial situation in a way that enlisted people of all races. "Obama is looking beyond the old race wars," I said.

"Yeah but a lot of other people aren't."

"Are you a betting man, Al?"

"Sure. Why?"

"Fifty bucks says Obama becomes our next president."

"You're on."

"After that, I don't know how he'll deal with the racists. I hope we as a nation can put that behind us and start fixing what needs fixed, which is mainly the economy. We need to dismantle the corporations that are plundering us."

Al shot me a scowl. "You lost me," he said. "My bet is the powers that be won't allow him to become the Democratic candidate. No chance he'll become president. They'll get rid of him somehow."

"They'll try. I'm betting they won't succeed."

"I hope you're right but I'm betting you're wrong."

Neither of us mentioned the word assassination, although I knew it was on both our minds.

Al lived in a sprawling one-story house in the area called Ortega Ridge. Inside, his wife Molly was generating delicious odors. We sat down immediately to a dinner of fried chicken with the TV news on. CNN's Lou Dobbs was using the Pastor Wright clip to whack Obama. "See that?" said Al, as though he'd already won the bet. "Word's come down from the die-hard conservative racists and the fix is in."

"But this time, people are blogging all over the Internet, refuting what these TV script readers are saying."

"I don't own a computer so I don't know what the Internet people are saying. You think they can overcome this?"

"I think so."

"I hope you're right. Even though it will cost me fifty if you are."

Molly chimed in with some words, delivered in a soothing Southern-flavored accent. "Let's not talk politics at the dinner table. It's bad for the digestion."

"Politics don't bother my digestion," said Al.

"Well, please have mercy on mine," said Molly.

Al huffed a frustrated sigh as he clicked off the TV.

Women are so down-to-earth practical. We were now left with a view out the dining room window of the 101 far below, streams of red taillights and white headlights. "Bob," said Molly, "I hear you been gone from town a long time." Her way of politely letting me know she knew my story.

"Yes, I have. It's good to be back. Nothing like the old hometown. Where are you from, Molly?"

"Nawlins. Al and I met back during the war in Vietnam."

"New Orleans," I repeated, mispronouncing it.

"The same. Fine music and dee-licious food."

I took up my next bite of chicken and waved it at her. "Indeed, ma'am. I believe this is the most delicious fried chicken I've ever eaten."

"Molly's so into herbs and spices," said Al, "I call her the voodoo lady."

Molly gave a faux scowl and said to me, "He means that as a joke."

"No joke," said Al, "I have to jog two miles three times a week to fit into my uniform."

"I allow myself to become matronly plump," said Molly.

Al winked at me as he said, "I like her plump."

I found out that Molly worked at the County Building Department and that they owned a cabin in the mountains east of San Francisco. "Well, it's not exactly a cabin—three bedrooms and two bathrooms."

"I'd like to retire there someday," said Al.

"Not me," said Molly, "I'd suffer stimulation deficit disorder."

"Retire there when we're too old to do anything else," said Al.

"When we get that old," said Molly, "they'll lay us in the ground."

They had an easy harmony that made me smile, aware that if we'd watched the news, we'd have been in an entirely different mood.

After dinner, Al and I sat in easy chairs. Al passed me a cigar and we both puffed while Molly went about conventional housewifely duties, singing a song I couldn't identify as she loaded the dishwasher and tidied up the kitchen.

"This guy Jake Valance," said Al, "he's got some kind of wild hair. Last poker game, he was all jacked up over your brother bringing home a prostitute. Now, by itself, that's of no concern. What bothered me was that Jake seemed to think this gave him the right to judge your brother. I asked Jake, I said, 'What business is it of yours who your employer brings home? Your job is to protect the property and people.' Well, Jake got in my face and said it was a lot more complicated than I knew, and that he could not be responsible for John's whores, especially if they traveled. It was the way he said this that bothered me, Bob. Like this girlfriend gave him the right to clamp down on your brother, you know, like he was jumping on an opportunity. You get my drift?"

"I do. And it verifies my suspicions, Al."

"So how's your brother handling it?"

"I'm not sure. He's away on a business trip, expected home later tonight. I won't get to talk to him till tomorrow, I guess."

I told Al about Jake's strange master-of-the-domain behavior when I pulled up in the limo. "That's what I mean," he said. "This guy has something up his sleeve. Does he know this girl your brother brought home?"

"If he does, he's not letting on," I said. "He treats her with disdain."

"You know much about her?"

"No, not much, only that her name is Lola Jones and she's from the Valley."

"You got a name like Jones, you'd best put an unusual first name to it. I'll run a record check on her tomorrow."

"John says they've set up a one-year trial living arrangement. If it doesn't work, they part friends with Lola making some money from the deal."

"See? That's what pulls my chain, Bob. Why should Jake be concerned about this arrangement? It's not part of his job to worry about who your brother brings home. His job is to take care of the security. But he's sounding like he wants to bust your brother on a morals charge. You met this girl yet?"

"This afternoon when I got home."

"What's she like?"

"Looks sexy, talks like she's got some smarts."

"Well, she's allegedly a high-priced call girl, according to Jake, so she'd have to be sexy looking."

"John said he wanted to take her with him on this business trip he's on now, but Jake put the blocks to that. The threat seems to be that Jake could destroy John's reputation with his corporate people."

"Ah ha," said Al. "So that's it. I knew he had some kind of game going. Man, some white people would rather die than be caught having fun."

"In John's world, shacking up with a call girl young enough to be your granddaughter is a big no-no."

Al rocked back into a hearty laugh. "Not just in John's world. Still, you go where love takes you and if no one gets hurt, what's the crime? I know your brother is behaving outrageously here, but no one is getting hurt, right?"

"No, not unless Jake does something that smears John's reputation with his corporate people. Who are very sensitive about this kind of thing, believe it should be done only in the strictest secrecy."

"That's why Jake is acting like he's holding an ax over John's neck, got him by the short hairs and intends...well, I'm not sure what he intends, but I am sure it's not nice. Jake's got a mean streak a mile wide."

"You think Jake wants to use this to mug John, shake him down?"

"That and more," said Al. "He gets his jollies by hurting people."

"Seems to me he either blows the whistle on John and hurts him, or shakes him down for money and doesn't hurt him."

"I wish I could agree. But Jake is not that simple. He's full of freaky mischief. That's why, when you called, I wanted to talk to you in person about all this, Bob. Jake's a sicko. I like you and your brother. You're good people. I don't want to see that son of a bitch mess up John's life."

"John's aware of the blackmail threat. Said he thinks I know a lot more about blackmail than he does. Hell, I don't know anything about this kind of blackmail."

"See, Bob, what makes Jake a problem—I'm afraid he's got stuff in mind beyond simple blackmail. He's told stories at those poker games that would curl your toes. That son of a bitch makes the Marquis de Sade look like an altar boy."

Molly came into the living room, then, and we decided to watch a TV series. My mind was so buzzed by what Al had told me, my imagination was working overtime.

When the show ended, Molly said goodnight to me and went into the bedroom. Al turned off the TV and said, "Something I been curious about, Bob. Your mental health problem. Don't get me wrong, friend, I'm sympathetic. I know a lot of people get into trouble with drugs and booze and wind up with mental health problems. I'm just curious about yours."

"This takes us into mysterious territory, Al. After I went to Stanford, I got into the sixties Movement, you know, and street drugs. Then I took a hit to the head and suffered a concussion. That's when I stopped functioning. I became depressed. Tried to medicate myself with street drugs and booze, but mainly booze. It was the combination of being born with a proclivity for big D Depression plus the blows to the head, booze and, until recent years, doctor-prescribed drugs. By the middle eighties, I was truly insane. I could not function, spun out of control, did some things I never believed I would ever do."

"Don't confess, I'm not a priest."

"Okay, I'll skip the gory details. Got sentenced to hard time in San Quentin. My Dad, bless his heart, got me out of that hellhole and transferred to Covington in Camarillo, where my doctor was a cutting-edge thinker, doesn't take anything for granted, keeps up with the latest findings from all around the world. CAT scans showed brain damage, which other doctors considered irreversible. Dr. Grace found studies that indicated the brain is malleable, like silly putty. And so together we set about re-wiring my brain. Took half a dozen years of experimenting with medications and mental exercises, cognitive therapy and meditation. I may not be back to good as new, but damn close to it. I still take a combination of meds and I do a daily meditation. So that's my story, Al. Believe it or not."

"Oh, I believe it," said Al. "I'm looking and listening to the evidence. Are you in any danger of relapsing?"

"Always a danger. I had a little episode back East when it felt like I was relapsing. I think it was triggered by finding myself alone in a strange environment. Taught me that I had to stick to my daily meditations as well as the meds. In other words, the brain re-wiring is a work in progress."

"I can relate to brain re-wiring," said Al. "In Nam, I had a cushy job—I was never out in the jungle on patrol. But one evening, in a bar, someone threw a grenade and I was blown out of my chair and hit my head on the edge of a hardwood table. It left an indentation in my skull, man." He leaned forward and rubbed a spot on his shaved head to show me. "I was dingy for the next six months. There were moments when I went totally blank, blacked out, then I'd snap out of it and realize where I was. Those were scary. My lieutenant saw that I wasn't right and lightened up on me. Even asked if I wanted a medical discharge but I only had a few more months to do, so I stuck it out. The blackouts gradually became less and less until they were gone."

"If I could be eighteen again," I said, "I'd study brain science."

Al laughed. "If you were eighteen again, you'd be the same kid who got involved with the protests and stuck your head under some cop's billy club."

"How did you know about that?"

"I checked your records. Says you got arrested and wound up in the ER with a head wound after one of those demonstrations in San Francisco."

"They took me from jail to the hospital and dropped the charges."

"I salute your motives, but not your tactics."

"Those tactics stopped the war in Vietnam," I said.

"They stopped that one, yeah. But wars are part of human life. Wars between individuals and between nations. Being in law enforcement, I make war on bad guys every day."

I was tempted to say that he made war on poor bad guys, not the super-wealthy bad guys who rip off the whole society, but I resisted. Maybe later when we know each other better.

Al drove me back to Padero Lane around 11 o'clock, dropped me off about fifty yards from the lane back to the beach house. As I passed the area my brother had told me marked the invisible electronic fence, lights suddenly went on and a car quickly had me in its headlights from behind. It drove up beside me and a plainclothes security guard got out, shined his flashlight in my eyes and wanted to know who I was and what I was doing here.

"I'm John Bradford's brother, and I'm living in the guesthouse."

"Well, we wish you'd make your movements known to us, sir. We were not aware that you went out this evening."

"Seems to me you're over the line. Your job is to protect us, not try to control our lives."

"With all due respect, sir, we must take your mental condition into consideration in order to fulfill our duties."

"My mental condition?"

"I'm sure you know what I'm referring to."

I felt a momentary surge of rage but stayed cool. The security guy asked to see some ID so I showed him the temporary license my brother had gotten the Sheriff's Department to provide.

When I got back to the guesthouse and checked my cell phone, I had a message from Laura. I started to dial her number, then stopped. If I told her about this situation, given her moral rectitude, she'd blame John. That she could ignore the death and destruction in Iraq and Afghanistan while reacting with such anger to her ex-husband playing with a young prosty—it was more than I could handle right now.

It was too late to call Hernandez or Dr. Grace. I sat staring out at the ocean under a nearly full moon. I didn't know if the moon was waxing or waning. Hernandez would know. I lost myself in the glittering play of moonlight on the ocean's surface, rippled by a slight breeze. How many millions of human beings, going back how many thousands of years, had watched this same glittering on this same ocean as they pondered their own personal problems? I suddenly remembered something Hernandez says. "Got a dilemma? Triangulate."

Chapter 15

As things turned out, it was good that I took this trip without Lola so I could keep my focus where it belonged. The company, which shall remain nameless, as it would be a distraction to name any or all the companies I'm involved with. The company's stock had lost around 35 percent since late December and through January 2008. Its top echelon was naturally upset and the morale of its workforce had plunged. Several board members, those who were heavily invested in the company, were also upset and looking for a scapegoat to blame. The fact that the Dow and NASDAQ and other indices had plunged didn't matter to them, they believed this company should be immune to such periodic market plunges—that's why they had invested so heavily in it. I sat quietly through the airing of these dashed hopes and grievances, thinking that I would remain silent throughout this meeting. But just before we broke for lunch, the CEO said, "John Bradford, you've been too quiet. What is your take on the situation?"

I inwardly groaned. I knew some of these board members would find my take on it unconventional, but I felt obliged to be honest.

"It's been my observation over the years, gentlemen, that most of us tend to think in linear time while stocks move in cycles. During cycles of optimism, a company's stock will rise, usually in tandem with its index, as this one has with the Dow. But optimism does not last forever so eventually there is what we call a correction. Bear markets follow bull markets as surely as night follows day. This latest drop in price did not surprise me, nor does it upset me. What we all know from long experience is that new bull markets follow bear markets. What goes down in value, bounces back up eventually, unless there is some systemic reason why the company is kaput. I know of no reason why this company will not rebound. It's only a question of when the turnaround will come."

"But," said another executive, "this time we're under the gun, being investigated by various regulatory agencies, including the Securities and Exchange Commission. Doesn't that suggest to you, Mr. Bradford, that this time, this cycle, we are looking at a profit-threatening problem?"

"That depends on two things," I replied. "What's there for the SEC to find? And second, when will the turnaround come and the company's stock rebound?"

The CEO said, "Our accounting firm tells us there is really nothing out of line for the regulators to find. Maybe some minor stuff but nothing major."

"Well, then," I said, "The stock will recover when the mood changes and all stocks rebound, pushing all indices up again."

"And when," said one board member with an angry edge in his voice, "will that be, pray tell?" He was sitting directly across the long, oval table from me and the expression on his face was that of a poker player who'd just lost his stake.

The man was goading me, trying to get me to reveal something that only I knew. My net worth was greater than anyone else's in the room, so this guy across the table figured I must know something the others did not know. For an instant, I was tempted to speak my mind freely and reveal, for one thing, that the big insurers of bonds were in trouble, a fact that had so far been withheld from public disclosure. But such tidbits of information would only add to the present pessimistic mood and distract from the need to batten down the financial hatches to weather the coming economic storm. So I punted, by prattling out a cliché: "All bets are off till we find out who the next president will be."

"Don't you think the government will take steps to pump up the markets prior to November," the man across the table from me asked, "to assure the election of a Republican?"

"The public mood drives the markets. Eighty percent of the nation believes the Bush Administration has us headed in the wrong direction, according to the most recent public opinion polls. That's the mood that's changing markets and shaping the coming election."

"Mood schmood," retorted the man across the table. "Moods don't change markets, markets change moods. Dollars are fleeing to Asia and we're sinking deeper into debt to China. No wonder the public's in a bad mood."

"It seems to me," I replied, in a tightly modulated tone, "moods create the events that coincide with market ups and downs. I watch mass moods. A cycle of optimism is inevitably followed by a cycle of pessimism. The more overblown the optimism, the deeper the pessimism. What's now being called 'the subprime debacle' is just the beginning, the canary in the coal mine. It's like we've been on a great shopping spree and picked up fabulous bargains, and suddenly we're being told our credit card is over the limit, maxed out. But the national credit card was maxed out back when we all felt sublimely optimistic. We gave ourselves a big increase in our credit line because we were in such a buoyant mood, delighted with the bargains. Months ago, I saw clear evidence that the mood of optimism was moving away from developed economies to developing economies like China, India, Brazil, and I moved my investments accordingly. The mood of optimism moves like a huge mass of nitrous oxide, laughing gas. I suggest this company follow the laughing gas to weather the impending storm."

Some board members recognized my little speech as being based on Bob Prechter's 'Socionomics' theory of markets, which has its roots in the Elliott Wave Theory. Others objected to what I'd said and voiced the opinion that the board should reject my "nonsense about laughing gas balloons."

Thus we broke for lunch in something of a hubbub, with about a dozen board members clamoring to engage me further. I hated that I'd gotten myself into the position of a controversial swami. I usually keep my own analysis to myself and prattle out an acceptable cliché.

My "mass of nitrous oxide" metaphor had set off arguments among those who now gathered around me for further elucidation to refute or support. I tried to divert all this chatter by bringing up Fibronaci numbers and how they are found in the technical analysis patterns of financial charts, the patterns of seashell swirls, rabbit reproduction cycles, and so forth, but the doubters kept returning to my laughing gas quip.

As lunch was being wheeled in by the catering service, my cell phone sang and it was, who else? Lola. I excused myself from the group around me and slid off toward a corner of the large conference room for a modicum of privacy.

"I miss you," she said in a sad little girl voice.

"I miss you too, my love. How are things at the house?"

"That's why I'm calling. Jake was inside the house when I woke up this morning and he's still here, and he seems to be…I don't know, taking over. He's going around taking notes. He shows no sign of leaving. Right now, he's downstairs sitting in your favorite easy chair looking out at the ocean. Is he supposed to be doing that?"

Not wanting to alarm her, I said, "I suppose he's got some reason for being there today, inside the house. Is his presence making you uncomfortable?"

"Yes! Very! I wanted to go for a swim and get some rays but I can't stand the way he watches me. He watches every move I make. He's got some ugly stuff inside him, John."

"He's a cop, Lola. Suspicious of everyone."

"He's not suspicious, he's something else."

"I'll call him, find out why he's inside the house."

I dialed his number and listened to half a dozen rings before Jake picked up. "Yes sir, Mr. Bradford," he said.

"Lola tells me you're hanging around inside my house, Jake. What's happening?"

"We're installing a new electronic system, sir. I have to be inside your house in order to make sure it works. We're adjusting it, you see.

The helicopter is going to fly by for a final check. I need to be here for that."

"When will this final check occur?"

"Sometime between now and five o'clock."

"What exactly is this new electronic thing? Why is it being installed in my house? I know nothing of it, and that house is, after all, mine. It does not belong to your agency."

"Sir, with all due respect, the agency is charged with your security, and this device is needed to fulfill that duty. It's electronic. It doesn't put anything in your house but electronics you can't see or hear."

"What exactly does it do that wasn't being done previously, Jake?"

"It's complicated to explain, Mr. Bradford, but the way it was described to me, it expands radar surveillance beyond the present laser fence. The reason for this is the heightened alert. If someone, or some group of terrorists, invades your property to snatch you or a member of your family, we need more advanced warning. This new system increases our advanced warning capability. It's added protection for you and yours, sir."

His protection had already become overbearing, to put it mildly, but if I objected and ordered him and his new system out of my house, he could retaliate by spreading the word in New York that I have a glamorous young call girl living with me, creating a crisis of confidence—the other executives would think I'd flipped my lid, overturning security for the sake of a sex toy.

Into the lull in our conversation Jake said, "Sir, I need to ask you something."

"What?"

"How long do you plan to have this girl staying here?"

"That's none of your business, Jake."

"I'm sorry, sir, but it is. Everyone under your roof here is my business. I wouldn't be doing my job if I didn't make each and every person here my business."

I felt stymied.

Jake added, "And if you'd like to call the agency's head office in New York and check on this, I'll gladly give you the name of my supervisor and his direct number."

"That won't be necessary," I said. "But I'd like you to operate outside my house, not inside. Understood?"

"Understood. That's what I usually do—this is a special situation."

I returned to lunch and the press of people surrounding me, asking questions. Seemed every time I took a bite of the baked salmon, someone would fire another question at me. I'd chew, swallow and respond before taking another bite. Their questions all fell under the category of predicting the market's future upturn, and whether such an upturn would cause a change of mood or be the result of a changed mood, and wasn't my theory of moods fostering a dire self-fulfilling prophesy.

"It's the collective national mood," I said, "that creates self-fulfilling prophecies. When the mood turns sour, everyone looks for scapegoats. This brings the regulators and sets off squabbles. Round robins of blame finding, finger pointing, lawsuits and counter suits. The gloom-and-doomers dance and the positive thinkers sulk. This goes on till the gloom lifts and a new mood of optimism returns. Now, please excuse me, as I feel the call of nature."

With that, I got up to go to the men's room, leaving them chattering among themselves, groping through the opaque darkness of the future. Alone in the men's washroom, I called Lola.

"I'm afraid we're stuck with Jake being inside the house for now, my darling. He's rigging up some kind of new device, he says. He'll probably be there the rest of the day."

"He's not doing a damn thing, John. He's just hanging out here like he owns the place."

"I suppose he appears to be doing nothing because these electronics are operated remotely."

"I don't believe it," she said. "He's got something else on his mind."

"I'm having serous doubts myself, but there's nothing I can do till I get back tonight. Jake says he has to be there to test this new gizmo."

Lola's voice dropped an octave to a breathy whisper as she said, "What he's testing is you, John. Or us. I don't like it. Every time I go downstairs, he stares at me like he's about to pounce."

"That's worrisome. Has Bob returned from the East Coast yet?"

"No. He called to say we should expect him around 2 o'clock. Alicia took the call."

The afternoon session of the board was much less tense, as most members seemed to have settled into the realization that none of us can know the future, nor can anyone's public words of optimism overcome the collective pessimism. All we can do is be prepared to respond appropriately to whatever unfolds.

As various tactics to prop up this company's stock price were discussed, I tried to relax and slow my heart rate. It was looking like my next move would have to be sending Lola home. If we made it appear to Jake that she'd ended her visit, then he'd have nothing to smear me with, and I could call his agency and complain, get him replaced. He'd retaliate by telling key people I was living with a call girl. I'd tell them he mistook my niece from back East for a call girl and I am insulted. I'd complain that he's too intrusive, has overstepped the line and needs to be replaced by someone with more common sense and tact. I liked this plan, except that it separates me from Lola till I get rid of Jake.

When the board meeting ended around 3 o'clock, I didn't stay for dinner, as I usually do. I grabbed my overnight bag and took a taxi to the airport, hoping to catch an earlier flight than the one I'd been scheduled on. I knew this had confused whatever security guy had been assigned to accompany me on this trip. I didn't even look around to see if he'd made it to the airport with me. I managed to get a flight out around 5 o'clock, which got me back home a little after sundown.

As the limo pulled into the drive, I saw Lola's face looking out an upstairs window. She hurried down and was hugging me when I stepped out of the limo.

"Is my brother back yet?"

"He got back this afternoon but then he took a walk and he's still gone."

"Gone?"

"Yeah, I don't know where he went, and I heard Jake on his cell telling someone to locate him and keep a tight tail on him."

"Is Jake still here?

"No. He left, thank God."

As we walked toward the front entrance, I caught a quick glimpse of a darkly dressed security person lurking on the right side of the house, along the stone steps down to the swimming pool.

Inside the house, Lola threw her arms around my neck and cried, "Where the hell can we go to get away from these creeps, John? They're driving me crazy."

"I don't know, my love, but we've got to do something."

"They're hassling you because of me, aren't they?"

"I'm afraid so."

We went up to the master bedroom and curtained all the windows before making love. Assuming Bob had returned from his walk, I wanted to get his take on what was happening here but I was too tired to get dressed and walk over to the guesthouse. I did not want to tell Lola, yet, that she'd have to return to her house for a while, till we got rid of Jake. But it seemed she'd already intuited as much, for as we were falling asleep with her head on my shoulder, she said, "They haven't found a renter for my house yet. I'll move back there."

"Hopefully, we won't be separated for long," I said.

"If one of Jake's security goons follows me there, do I have your permission to hire a guy to break his legs?"

"You have someone who would do that?"

"Yes. He's the boyfriend of another working girl. He's chased away a stalker before. He'll do it again."

"I hope it doesn't come to that, Lola. If we show that our visit is over, that you've gone, they'll have no reason to keep track of you, and I'll be able to get this goon replaced."

Chapter 16

Around 8 the next morning, my cell phone awakened me. Laura calling from Rehoboth Beach.

"I miss your cute ass, Bob," she said with her deliberate enunciation and contralto voice.

"And I miss your lovely buns," I said.

"We sound like teenagers."

"Good. They have more sex energy that oldsters."

"But we oldsters have better sex."

"I think so, too. What's happening in Rehoboth Beach?"

"Martino wants to add another job. He says the existing insulation was cheap and is rotting from the salt air and will soon stink up the house if we don't replace it."

"Tell him to work up an estimate and call me. I'll take it from there."

"I'm not a happy camper here, Bob. I've been staying with a friend the past few nights because my house is such a torn-up mess. Cold, wet wind blowing through the cracks, heater working overtime. How are things there with you?"

"Complicated. I was wondering—how would you like to come here, stay here till your house is finished?"

"Are you serious? John would have a fit."

'Or maybe he'd enjoy seeing you again. And you do have old friends around here, don't you?"

"A few. My best friends moved to New Mexico and Oregon."

"Well, I shouldn't have brought it up. It's not my house. I don't have the right to invite you here. It just occurred to me that your presence here might help."

"Help what? What are you talking about?"

"I'll have to run this by my brother, but I was thinking that if you show up here and move in with me, John's security people will be distracted."

"Distracted from what?"

"I'll explain it later, Laura. Not over the phone."

"I'll bet it has to do with that young whore he brought home."

"You sound like the jealous wife."

"Which I am definitely not. But his behavior threatens the inheritance my two children are due."

"I'm sure John has all those assets well protected."

"Doesn't seem he has his sanity protected, or why else would he move in a twenty-two year old hooker? He's so nasty."

"He's lonely. Needs a mate. Which reminds me—so do I."

"Come back to Rehoboth. I need you to deal with Martino."

I was tempted to say I can deal with Martino by phone but instead, I said, "I will if I can. I'll have to talk with my brother, find out more about what's happening here. He's having a problem with his security people."

"Oh, them. They're like termites. Silent but deadly. I used to say that being unprotected was a lot better than having those security insects sneaking around. You were never sure where they were. They'd pop up at the damnedest times to scare the bee Jesus out of you."

"March is when it begins to warm up here, Laura."

"March is when the heavy rains come, too, Bob. Won't you fly east?"

"When I can."

'You know, this relationship John is having—they never turn out happily. It would be fun to arrive there just as John is realizing what a horrible mistake he's made."

"And you wouldn't have to depend on friends there for shelter while your house is being repaired."

"I'll think about it, but it would be a lot easier all around if you came here."

After Laura, I called Hernandez. He would be finished with breakfast and straightening up his room, I figured, so he'd have time to talk.

"Jorge, I was remembering how you used to say, 'Got a dilemma? Triangulate.' What exactly did you mean by that?"

"You got a dilemma?"

"It's more like my brother does. And since I am dependent on him, his dilemma is mine too."

"Well, what I was talking about is planetary oppositions. Those are what bring dilemmas into our lives, when one planet up there in the sky on one side of the Earth, and another planet is opposite on the other side of the Earth. Like, right now there's an opposition between Saturn and Uranus, pronounced You're-in-us, not Your anus. Saturn wants to maintain the old established status quo. Uranus wants to overturn the established and bring the new and radical. Depending on where this opposition occurs in someone's birth chart, it can create really difficult dilemmas. Back in the sixties, for instance, it occurred conjunct the US Neptune and square the US Mars. The nation became explosive, confused, lit with idealism. So, to resolve such a dilemma, you look for a trine angle from other planets that takes the curse off the opposition. Like, if Saturn is conjunct your Sun, you look for a planet that trines your Sun. That means makes a hundred and twenty degree angle to your Sun. A trine is like a freeway merge. It's an easy flow of energy integrating with the other energies. You focus on what the trining planet brings because that's what usually resolves dilemmas, and *voila*, you thereby triangulate."

I didn't want to tell him that most of that went over my head. I said, "Well, what I got here is my brother's security guy threatening blackmail because my brother brought a young girlfriend into his life, and his house. Moved her in."

I elaborated on the situation until Hernandez said, "Ah ha, I got it. Your brother is being influenced by Uranus's radical changes. His security person is using this, acting as the Saturnian status quo, saying, 'Either you resist this radical change or I'll bring you frustration and grief'."

"That's it. That's the situation. You have a planet for who his girlfriend is?"

"She's the Uranian change in his life. Seems to me that you, Bob, are the triangulating influence. You are the one who can resolve your brother's dilemma."

"How?"

"I don't know. You'll think of something."

"I've been thinking of John's ex. Remember? I told you about her. She lives on the East Coast. I asked her to fly out here and move into the guesthouse with me. As a distraction. Then this security guy would have John's ex as well as his new girlfriend to deal with."

"His ex is an eleventh house thing," said Jorge. "I'd have to see his chart. I don't know how moving her into that scene would work to foil his security guard's intentions."

"At least she'd distract him."

"But didn't you say his intention is to spread the word that John has taken into his home a call girl, destroying his reputation with his company? How would his ex-wife's presence dilute that threat?"

"I hear ya, Jorge."

"Give me your brother's date, time and place of birth. I'll do his chart and find out where this present Saturn-Uranus opposition falls. That may suggest how to triangulate him out of his present dilemma."

I realized I'd forgotten my brother's birthday, could not remember what day of the year he was born. I'd have to ask him. I had this in mind as I was about to get in the shower and heard the door chimes. At the front door was John. He glanced back over his shoulder toward his house before he came in. "Man, brother, am I glad to see you."

"I'm ready to help any way I can," I said.

"You were about to take a shower? Go ahead. I'll wait till you're done. Then, let's go somewhere noisy for breakfast and talk."

I took my shower and got dressed in my old jeans and a new sports shirt, and Jack drove his Jaguar to a Denny's just off the 101. It was packed with tourists and plenty noisy. We sat at a table with a view of the freeway. As we inspected the menu, I said, "You think they have you wired?"

"I wouldn't put it past them."

"How could they wire you without your knowledge?"

"I'm not an electrical engineer, Bob, I don't know, but I am aware that implants are possible. Or they could sew something into my clothing. I need to find someone who can scan me for bugs. You wouldn't believe the mind-bending feats that are possible with modern electronics."

"Do you remember a football player from high school named Al Hansen? Played right guard?"

"No, the only football player I knew was you."

"Well, Al is now with the County Sheriff's Department, nearing retirement. He might know who we get to scan you for a bug."

"Oh, yes, the black deputy. Does he have any connection to Jake Valance?"

"He plays poker with him once a week but he's definitely on our side, Jack."

"You're sure."

"I trust Al."

"Why? You haven't had any contact with him since you were in high school, have you?"

"No, but we've been talking, and we have that old teammate bond."

"Seems a very flimsy basis for trust," said John.

"Little brother, I can never explain why I trust certain people and distrust others and am rarely, if ever, wrong."

He smirked and looked away.

While we were waiting for our food to come, I hit the autodial for Al. He said he was busy at the moment and would call me back when he got a chance.

As we ate our fruit and Belgian waffles, Jack said, "You need a car, don't you. Tell you what. I'll give you a set of keys to the Jag and I'll drive the Mercedes. Now, how did you find Laura? What is Rehoboth Beach like?"

"Right now, she's sleeping at the homes of friends while the house is undergoing repairs. She's not happy about that. Otherwise, she's healthy and we had a very mellow affair."

"Mellow. That's a sixties word, isn't it?"

"I guess it is. Rehoboth Beach is very much a resort town, deserted this time of year. It reminds me of Carpinteria, you know, that mix of old and new, a family oriented tourist town."

"The reason I ask, Bob, is that I'm looking for a place to go to lose Valance. I'm sending Lola home. Temporarily. We'll get back together when we get Valance replaced. Maybe I'll fly back East and escape him till all this blows over."

"Do you think they know where we are right now, Jack?"

"Oh yes. They track my every move. They have a car in the parking lot outside this restaurant right now, or else it's prowling the street, keeping an eye on the Jag, ready to follow the Jag when we leave."

"If you flew back East, how could you lose them? They'd follow you, wouldn't they?"

"I'd need help with that, Bob, but it should be possible. I like the East Coast. Spent a lot of time in New England years ago. I'd rather go well south of there this time, though. I imagine Laura still has resentments, right?"

"Yes, some. But she's also got her own life there."

"Do you think I could find a decent house to rent in Rehoboth Beach?"

"Or a condo. Laura took me to see some condos on the beach south of Rehoboth, in the town of Bethany. A variety of types, from three-story houses to one-story flats."

"And the nearest airports are a couple of hours away. Philadelphia to the north and Baltimore to the west."

"Right. Plus Washington and New York."

Al called back and I explained that Jack wanted to get a scan to see if he was wired. Al said he could do that if we drove to the Sheriff's Department in fifteen minutes. He'd meet us there. We paid the restaurant bill with cash and got back in the Jag and headed for the Sheriff's headquarters on East Figueroa Street.

"See that white Chevy a few cars behind us?" Jack said as he drove. "That's our security. They'll wonder why I'm going to see the Sheriff. Give them something to ponder."

Al was waiting for us with an electronic wand of some kind. They recognized each other although they'd not been formally introduced before. Al used the wand to carefully scan every inch of Jack's clothing and body. No bug was found.

"Unless they're using something we don't yet know about," said Al, "you're clean, John."

Al then walked us out to the parking lot and I told him what we had in mind—Jack escaping Valance by moving to Rehoboth Beach. "The sticking point is giving his security people the slip," I said.

"And then using only cash for everything," added Al. "Use a credit card and they'll locate you in a jiffy."

"Well, then," said Jack, "how would it work for Bob to buy a condo back East and me to move into it?"

"If they're not tracking Bob, that should work," said Al. "Our department will gladly help you lose Valance and his people when ever you're ready to get out of Dodge."

Jack smiled up at Al, held out his hand and said, "Wonderful. I'm very glad you two have that old teammate bond."

As we were pulling out of the Sheriff's parking lot, we caught sight of the white Chevy about fifty yards behind us. Jack laughed as he watched it in his rearview mirror. "This plan will make it a lot easier for me to get Valance transferred," he said. "Once Lola has moved out, I'll call the security agency in New York and complain. Then, I'll give them the slip and move to the East Coast. Then I'll be in the catbird seat."

"Where you belong," I said.

Chapter 17

With Bob's help and the help of a friend of his in the Santa Barbara Sheriff's Department, we hatched a plan for me to get Valance out of my life. I went back to the beach house and, as Lola was packing her things to move back to her house in the Valley, I told her about it.

"My God, John, you need security people to protect you from security people."

"You hire a lawyer to do a job for you," I said, "then you hire a second lawyer to make sure the first one doesn't screw up or try to screw you."

"What a world you live in," she said with a grin. "And I'm becoming part of it now. Whooo."

"Have you seen any of 'em around this morning?"

"No, they're making themselves scarce today."

I helped her close her two over-stuffed suitcases. "No need to take everything, honey. We'll soon be together again."

"Will they be spying on me?"

"No. I'm going to tell Jake that we're breaking up and you're moving out, and that will end his concerns about you. I'll make sure he's aware that if his men snoop you after you leave here, they'll be vulnerable to legal action. They weren't hired to watch you. After I escape them and get settled In Rehoboth Beach, I'll call the agency and complain. I'll also suggest our company discontinue this agency and hire another. "

"How will you lose them when you fly east?"

"The details of that haven't been worked out yet, but Bob's law enforcement officer friend has promised to help. We'll come up with something. Once we're sure we're both no longer under their surveillance, I'll fly you East and we'll be together again. And eventually, we'll come back to this beach house."

"Mmmm. It will be fun living on the East Coast," she said. "I've never been there. Can we go to New York? I'd love to see New York."

"Sure. What do you say we book reservations to see a play at Lincoln Center. We can drive up there and overnight at the Hilton. I have board meetings to attend in New York, you know."

I carried her two suitcases downstairs and out to her car and we said goodbye. She was wearing designer jeans and an expensive-looking jacket of soft leather, and looked quite fetching, as usual. I could feel the eyes of our spies on us as she pulled out of the driveway and turned onto Padero, heading for the freeway entrance at Santa Claus Lane.

I then walked to the guesthouse and sat down with Bob for a cup of coffee and a chat. We needed to further develop our plan.

"When you go back to Rehoboth Beach, how long do you think it would take to find and buy a condo suitable for me?"

"You want to hire a realtor to handle this purchase for you?" he asked.

"No, I'd like you to do that. Deal with Herby Stein and keep me out of the loop. I'll tell Herby what we're up to."

Bob was silent a while. We were sitting on stools at the breakfast counter, staring out at the sea. Bob's forehead was wrinkled by a frown, his eyes narrowed to a squint. I remembered that expression from when we were teenagers and how I used to wait for my big brother's next words, and I felt a jolt of joy, strangely enough, as I realized we were, indeed, recapturing our brotherhood. I was alone no longer. Big brother was with me again. He was now officially crazy but still a comfort, still the one person in this world I could count on. And he had shown no signs of whatever psychosis had disrupted his life. He was, in fact, among the more lucid people I knew. That was another reason for my jolt of joy. What an amazing turn both our lives were taking.

"Okay," Bob finally said, "so I'm going back east and leave you here alone. Till I buy you a condo. Are you sure you'll be okay? Jake Valance will wonder why we made that trip to the Sheriff's Department, or maybe he'll know."

"This police officer, Al Hansen. You seem to be very good friends."

"The first day I was here, your maid Alicia called the sheriff to check me out. Al came. We weren't close friends in high school but we remembered each other from the football team. I think we're each the only other guy we know from those days. So we're becoming friends now. Al doesn't want to see anything bad happen to you, and he knows a thing or two about Jake Valance. Says he has a mean streak a mile wide. I think Al views him as a rogue cop and considers him very dangerous."

"Brother Bob, you've been a busy bee. Much busier with my problem than I'd realized. I want you to know that's a tremendous comfort to me."

"Your problem is my problem, brother Jack. You've taken me in—this black sheep of the family who squandered his life."

I laughed. "We sound like a couple of old monks, brother Bob and brother Jack. Makes me want to crack out the Benedictine and Brandy, made by brother monks in the Alps."

"None of that for me, Jack."

"I know. Returning to the plan, getting you back to the East Coast is no problem. They won't follow you there, they're not paid to do that. The question is, how do I get out of here undetected once we have the condo?"

"Al mentioned that he'd help," said Bob.

"Help how? What can he do?"

"I don't know. Let's get together with him and pick his brains. He and his wife had me up to their house on Ortega Ridge for dinner— how about us inviting them out to dinner at a noisy restaurant where we can talk?"

"There's Eladio's across Cabrillo from the Warf. It's usually packed with tourists for dinner."

"I'll call Al."

"Good. Now, you can't go shopping for a condo looking like a homeless person. You're going to need credentials, record of a salary, pay records, IRS statements, even an employment record indicating you've worked for my limited liability corporation for the past ten years. Herby can create all that."

"Meanwhile," said Bob, "I've been using your American Express card for everything."

"Your own card should be here. We had it sent to Herby. We need another sit-down with him."

I reached Herby's cell phone and ran the plan by him, saying we needed to lose my security guard.

"If you pay cash," said Herby, "he can't trace it. Sellers of property love cash on the barrelhead. We can spring loose the cash by accessing one of your offshore accounts, John. Your brother can deliver the cash in a suitcase. After that it will be up to the seller to explain things to the bank. Or hide it under his mattress, if he prefers. As for integrating Bob, I'll send out a paycheck today, dated February 1. How much?"

"Eight thousand."

"After that, I'll send checks on the first day of each month. I'll need an address."

"Send the first check to my Padero Lane address and we'll forward. Bob will tell you where to send them after that."

"Done," said Herby. "The other records, give me a couple of weeks to work those up.

I snapped the phone shut and said to Bob, "No need for another trip into LA. Herby's got it under control."

"My monthly salary is eight thousand?"

"Plus expenses when you're traveling. Is that enough?"

"More than enough. Jack, your wealth astounds me. How in the world did you amass such a fortune?"

"By hook and by crook," I said. "It's too complicated to tell you in a sound bite. Don't worry about it. Just accept the fact that I have a substantial amount of money at my disposal and get used to it."

"Substantial meaning...?"

"You've seen that sign in Times Square running the numbers of the national debt? Well, I own a nice piece of that, for starters. So every second that ticks off the clock in Times Square, my net worth increases. And I have other assets, mostly foreign. Whenever the dollar drops another penny against the euro, or a Chinese company buys another boatload of steel or cement...well, you get the picture. My fortune accumulates by the second."

"How did you ever...?"

"I played the game, brother Bob. During the eighties and nineties and into the first years of this, the twenty-first century, if you know the rules of the game, it's like a rigged casino. In my earlier years, I was not afraid of risk, and that paid off big. Now, I husband my assets."

"Do you ever wonder what a great depression might do to your fortune?"

"Are we back to that? There will be no great depression, Robert. We're in a recession, it may turn out to be a protracted recession, and if it goes on long enough it will be called a depression, but not a great depression. We've learned how to control the economy well enough to prevent catastrophe. You'll see—by the end of this year, 2008, we'll be in recovery and off on another run-up of profits."

"I beg to differ, brother John. I think that by the end of this year, we'll be headed into far worse than the recession we have today."

"Your expertise is not economics. Mine is. But even if we have not recovered by the end of this year, I have recession-proofed my assets and make money on the Forex no matter what currencies move up or down."

"My friend, Jorge Hernandez, was an economics professor before he suffered mental problems. I've listened to him for the past seven years in Covington, and Hernandez has a very different take on it."

"That's where you got the idea that we're doomed to suffer through another great depression."

"Right," said Bob. "You're going to say he's in a nut house so why should anyone believe what he says."

"The words out of my mouth."

"Let's remember this conversation five or six years from now, John."

"I suspect we will."

"Hernandez uses astrology combined with the usual economic projections."

"Indeed," I exclaimed, unable to contain my mirth. "Does he have a ouija board to contact the supernatural?"

"How are the wealthy going to stay afloat when the dollar collapses?"

"Bob, what we've been through is an expansion of credit. What we're going through now is a natural contraction of credit. Natural because contractions follow expansions as night follows day, and just as surely contractions are followed by new expansions."

"Hernandez is predicting a disruption in that cycle."

"So are some others, including Bob Prechter, whom I admire, but their projections are not reality. I think your friend should write a book, add to the growing number of titles predicting catastrophe. Those books are very popular. People love spook stories."

"Will you be okay if the dollar crashes to worthless?" asked Bob.

"My dear brother, I am covered every which way to Sunday. The falling dollar is a big help to our trade deficit, and it enables us to sell our products overseas. If the dollar crashes—and I seriously doubt it will—I'm covered. Any other spook stories you'd like to try on me?"

"What if the dollar crashes and brings social chaos?"

"I'll survive and so will you."

"But if our society disintegrates?"

"It will reconstitute itself."

"What if the crash of the dollar means we'll have to redesign our monetary system? Dump the Fed and return to debt-free money issued by government?"

"What if we get broad-sided by an eighteen wheeler when we go out to dinner?"

"You think the odds are roughly the same?"

"Roughly the same. But your friend from the psych ward doesn't think so, is that it?"

"He thinks we may be heading into a second American Revolution."

"What kind of medications is he on?"

"Meds to control his severe depression."

"Well, I really don't think you're crazy any more, except about the economy. Have you transferred your personal depression to a fixation on economic depression?"

"Let's drop it," said Bob. "Time will tell who's right and who's wrong about the future."

"Meanwhile, do you think it's a good time to call your friend Al and invite him and his wife to dinner?"

Bob flipped open his cell phone and autodialed. He extended the invitation to Al, who accepted, and we set the time for 8 o'clock this evening. After that, Bob listened, saying nothing much, hmmm-ing and ah-ha-ing at whatever Al was telling him.

When he got off the phone, he turned to me and said, "Al assures us that when the time comes for you to give Jake Valance and his crew the slip, he will have a few cops lined up to help."

"How might they help?"

"Detain the agency people on suspicion connected to another matter, stopping them from sticking to you like glue."

"Ah ha," I said. "I'm breathing easier."

"Do you think Valance has this guesthouse wired?"

"He says he doesn't. Says he has no listening devices in the main house either."

"I hope he's telling the truth about that."

"He should not be messing around inside either house. I'm not his agency's only client in the Santa Barbara area, understand, so he's usually busy overseeing his crew. His job is to protect us, not spy on us. I wasn't of special interest to him until I brought Lola home. She's gone back to her place now. No more sightings of Lola."

"You think that will end his blackmail threat?"

"Long enough for me to complain to his agency and get him transferred. But even then, I need a break from security people snooping into my personal life. Before Lola, I lived with it. But now, I've got to get out of that loop."

As I was about to go back to the main house and take a nap, Bob said, "Oh, Jack, forgive me but I have totally forgotten when you were born."

"November 14, 1950. Why? You going to have your friend do my astrology chart?"

"Yes. He'll need the time of birth too."

"My birth certificate says 4:45 AM. Your friend will put on his star-studded swami hat and tell my fortune?"

"And you won't believe a word of it."

"Don't even tell me what he says."

Chapter 18

Hernandez was, as expected, in the courtyard when I called to give him John's birth data. He did John's chart on his laptop in less than a minute and said, "Sun conjunct Venus in Scorpio, in the second house trine his Midheaven. Your brother is lucky with money, but he also has an opposition from Pluto to his Moon-conjunct-Jupiter, forming a T-square to his Sun-Venus. He gets his way or else. He can be, by turns, charming and dictatorial. By the Winter Solstice 2012, he'll be going through big changes, for his Mars, Uranus and Saturn will be caught in a grand cross formed by the Uranus-Pluto square up there in the sky."

"Most of that went by me, Jorge. I gather that John is in for difficult times personally rather than financially."

"Yes, except that the two so often work together, it's often impossible to know where someone's finances leaves off and his personal vulnerabilities begin. Also, given the social volatility of this period—especially between 2012 and 2016—there's no telling where someone like your brother will land. He's had to become tough psychologically because of all his natal squares and oppositions, but he's never had to deal with anything like this grand cross that will hit his Mars, Uranus and Saturn, all in areas indicating business dealings and karma, things left over from the past."

"Sounds grim."

"It's going to be difficult for the whole society—actually, the whole world. But then, without such challenges, we can't advance to real improvements. It's going to change economic and financial systems. If your brother is invested in the status quo, he'll suffer more than if he's agile enough to get with the new. With his Scorpio Sun in the second house of money, I'll bet he stays one jump ahead."

"From what he told me today, I think he's very agile and futuristic in his investments, although whenever I mention a coming great depression, he slams me for being ignorant about economics."

"Of course. That's what he's been educated to believe. How's he handling that other problem, his security people?"

"He's making it look like he's broken up with his girlfriend. Once he gets the girlfriend gone, the security guy has no way to blackmail him."

"I just pulled up his transits for today, Bob, and I must say, you're brother IS In danger from underworld or hidden sources. I say that because Mars is conjunct his natal Uranus, which is opposite his natal Mars, which in turn is being hit by transiting Pluto. His natal Pluto, meanwhile, is being opposed by transiting Neptune, conjunct his Moon and Jupiter in the fourth house of home. Yeah, right now his life is at risk, although he probably doesn't know it that Neptune moving through his fourth can mask or confuse a lot of treachery. Well, he knows about his security man. But what about his girlfriend? How honest is she?"

"Could she be in cahoots with his security man?"

"She could be, but with Neptune, nothing is definite. It could be that she's inspiring your brother, lifting his spirits on the wings of love. But he should proceed with caution in any case because all that stuff in his fourth is square his Sun and Venus in his first house. Neptune is the god of oceans and is often shrouded in fog, uncertainty. Balancing that, however, is a trine aspect from his Sun and Venus to transiting Uranus, Venus and Mercury, indicating good fortune in his area of work, daily do's. Bottom line, make sure your brother is well protected from underworld types. And tell him now is not a good time to use alcohol or drugs."

Eladio's Restaurant had a view of the statues of the dolphins that grace the entrance to Stearn's Warf, the hub of tourist traffic in Santa Barbara. I have a warm place in my heart for dolphins, having specialized in the butterfly with its dolphin kick, an imitation of this magnificent creature's powerful whiplash motion.

We arranged ourselves around a large round table by a window looking out on busy Cabrillo Boulevard and beyond that the beach. Al went quickly to the chair with its back to the window, and Molly sat beside him with her back to the view too. John sat directly across from Molly and I sat across from Al, whose size blocked much of my view.

As we were pondering the menu, Al said, "Oh, Bob, I wanted to let you and your brother know that I ran a check on Lola Jones and she's clean as a whistle. Nothing but a couple speeding tickets."

John threw me a scowl. I hadn't mentioned anything about running a check on Lola. Al caught this and said to John, "Bob told me her name. I wanted to run the check to see if she might be the type to be hooked up with Jake Valance. All signs say no. Seems she got into being a call girl as the easiest way to make a living. Went from high school to call girl with no employment record except a stint at a McDonalds when she was fifteen."

"An honest working girl," said Molly with a sardonic intonation.

I was about to repeat a joke I heard Jay Leno deliver when I bit my tongue, for Jack was saying:

"Lola is a surprisingly bright young woman. We have worked out an arrangement that benefits both of us. Besides, I'm smitten, what else can I do?"

"The world belongs to lovers," said Molly with such an exaggerated sentimental sigh it was satirical.

"You don't love me no more?" said Al with a mock tragic squeak in his voice.

"You are my all, Mr. Man, my light, my love, my life. Now shut up and let's order."

A waiter stood by, pencil poised.

I had their vegetarian special. Both Jack and Al had the filet mignon. Molly had flounder. As we ate, we discussed our latest plan: I would return to Rehoboth Beach and buy a condo, into which Jack would move with Lola, once he'd managed to escape Jake Valance and his crew. The only sticking point was how Al might engineer a bust that would take the security people off their job long enough for Jack to flee undetected.

"Well," said Al, "how long will it take you to buy a condo, Bob?"

"I'm not sure. I'll let you know when I find out."

"Once I know that, Jack and I can decide when he'll leave. Then I'll set up a bust timed to distract Jake's guys. The thing is, we've got to make sure Jake can't phone ahead after we grab him, so he can put someone on that plane with Jack when he leaves for the East Coast. Jake can't know you're plans, Jack."

"There's another possibility I just thought of," said Jack. "I have a board meeting in San Diego a couple of months from now. I'm fairly certain they only assign one man to accompany me on those in-state trips. Maybe it would be easier to give that one man the slip and leave from San Diego."

"If the timing works for that, fine," said Al. "This Thursday is our regular poker night. I'm going to go and talk like I think Jack Bradford is the worst philanderer in town, see what that brings out of Jake."

"You be careful," said Molly. "Jake may know you are friends with the Bradford boys."

"Boys?"

"Well, you know. Do you think Jake hasn't found out these gentlemen visited you at headquarters?"

"I'm going to do my best to pump Jake for what he does know. As well as what he plans. I don't expect him to tell me exactly what he plans, mind you, but he may let me know his mix of motivations. How much is he lusting for money? How much is he lusting to hurt Jack? Valance loves to hurt people. That's his main thrill in life. I think he may have done a number like this before. He does seem to have a comfortable pension fund, to hear him tell it. For one thing, he's in the process of shopping for a hotel in Costa Rica. You don't go shopping to buy a hotel there unless you have some money."

"Maybe it's a cheap hotel," I offered.

"No, it's a beach hotel. A lot of retired military are making Costa Rica their home now, you know, so prices ain't cheap."

"Are you sure Lola and Jake aren't in on this together?" I asked.

"Where in the world did you get that idea?" said Jack. "Oh, I'll bet I can guess. Your astrologer friend."

"Right," I said. "He said the planets are aligned in such a way that you should make sure you're well protected, and that Lola is being totally honest with you, not hiding anything."

Jack turned away with a derisive snort.

"Well," said Al, "she's got nothing on her record that would indicate such a thing. But she's young. There's always a first time."

Jack said, "Lola was very upset yesterday when Valance hung around inside the house. She said he gives her the creeps and it's hard for me to believe she faked that. I can't believe she's in bed with Jake."

"I can't believe it either," I said. "Jorge said the other possibility is that she's inspiring you, lifting you on the wings of love."

"See," said Jack, "that's why astrology is such junk. Either Lola is plotting with Jake or lifting me on the wings of love. Which is it?"

"Neptune," I said.

"What?"

"It's foggy, hard to read."

"Leave it unread."

"Let's stick to what we know for sure," said Al.

"And let love take its course," said Molly.

I felt foolish having brought up a suspicion of Lola. Jack was irritated with me for it, and I didn't blame him. I vowed to stop quoting Hernandez. What he'd said about Lola made sense to me but I could see why it didn't make any sense to everyone else here. Besides, my reading of Lola was that she's telling the truth, has nothing to hide.

On the way out of the restaurant, I wrapped a hand around Jack's bicep and said, "I'm sorry I mentioned the astrology reading. Please forgive me. I was way out of line. It won't happen again."

Jack flung his arm around my shoulders and said, "You're forgiven, brother. I think the longer you're out of that loony bin, the less you'll have to do with your astrologer friend."

Then he looked around for Al and Molly. "Where did our guests go?"

"I think Al is being cautious. He knows the security people are tracking you and he doesn't want us to walk out of here together."

"Hell, Bob, they've got to know we're together. They track me all day, every day, wherever I go, whatever I do. You drive. I need a drink."

When we got back to the beach house, Jack pulled down two large brandy snifters and reached for his expensive French brandy. "None for me," I said.

"Oh come on, Bob. You can treat yourself to one after-dinner brandy."

He poured both big round glasses half full and handed me one as he moved toward his favorite easy chair. I held it in my palm and sniffed It, as I'd done the other evening when we'd gone shopping. He sipped his and smacked his lips.

"So," he said, "when would you like to fly back to the East Coast?"

"Maybe I should get my permanent driver's license before I go," I said.

"Good idea. Can you do that tomorrow?"

"Sure. After that, I'm ready to go."

"How do you like Laura? She's a good lay, isn't she?"

"I think she's much more than that."

"Wouldn't it be stranger than fiction if you and she got married?"

"Her kids, your kids, would then have their uncle for a stepfather. No, I enjoy her company but I'm not about to marry her."

"It would keep the money in the family," he said with a grin. "That's what the Rothschilds did."

"And a lot of other families do."

"I want you to know that you're making your bones with me, big brother. Despite the past and the horrors you've been through, I want you to know that your days as a pauper are behind you."

"Thanks, John. I appreciate your confidence. It means the world to me. "

I wasn't excited by the idea of becoming rich, but I was about reestablishing our brotherliness. And feeling needed, doing something worthwhile. I have conjured a guardian angel for myself and have developed a strong sense of the great creator of the universe, and in this moment, sent up a silent prayer of thanks. My idea of God is that, since He knows all, He knows our desires before we do, so there's no point praying to him like he's a big Santa Claus in the sky. But I surmise from all I've learned about religions around the world and back through time that the great creator does like to be appreciated. And it makes me feel better to offer prayers of appreciation, especially by using the Polynesian Huna method of sending those prayers from the spirit of the body, feeling it in my solar plexus.

"Who could that be?" Jack said, leaning forward toward the window.

I followed his gaze and saw the lights of a small boat about a hundred yards offshore. It was too dark to see whether it was a motor yacht or a sailboat.

"Maybe Valance likes to fish," I said.

"Is that a joke? I hear Valance likes to drink beer and womanize."

Jack got up and went to his bar, reached under it and came up with binoculars. "Let's have a closer look at this craft. It's a motor sailor with a fly bridge. They've got the running lights on but the interior cabin lights out."

"They're anchored. Are they early to bed or peering back at us?"

"Let's show them we're here."

With that, he walked out the door leading to the stone steps down to his swimming pool. After about a minute, I heard a pop and the sky was suddenly lit up by a flare. John came back and picked up the binoculars again. We both watched in silence as the craft's interior lights went on, and soon it was underway. It circled away from shore and headed south.

"This thing with Valance," he said sitting back down in his easy chair, "has me suspicious of everybody."

"I think I'll go to the guesthouse and get online, see what I can find out about beach condos in the Rehoboth area."

"I've got to have a couple of drinks before I go up to my lonely bed," he said. "I miss Lola. Need to give her a call."

"Go easy on the booze," I said.

Chapter 19

I had turned off my cell phone when we went out to dinner, and now I saw that Lola had called around 9 o'clock and left a message. I called back and got her outgoing message and told her I was missing her so much it hurt. I felt like a schoolboy with his first crush, until I was struck by the fear that she was out on one of her paid dates. Our agreement was that she'd quit being a call girl, but maybe she figured that deal was off, now that I had sent her home. Maybe she'd gone out because she was bored. The thought of her with someone else hurt. Bob's wondering if she might be in league with Valance had embedded itself in me like a thorn. Intellectually, I couldn't believe that was possible, but emotionally, the possibility scared the hell out of me.

As I stared at the ocean shrouded in mist and darkness, I reasoned that if they were in league, Valance would not be threatening blackmail, he'd have a longer-range plan. During my career, I'd been "mugged," as it's called, more politely by competitive business people, and my lawyer had advised in two such instances that I pay the mugger and move on, rather than become involved in lawsuits that could drag on for years and cost more. I found myself wondering if I should buttonhole Valance and bluntly ask him how much he'd take to get the hell out of my life. I imagined the laughter of Herby Stein if I did that. Herby would look at me with those big brown eyes and say something like, "You gonna give him one drink from your well and expect him to not come back for more?"

Still, the two weeks with Lola had spoiled me and I was now lonelier than ever. She was such a delight to have around. On the cusp of sixty years of age, I was having the best sex of my life and the most joyous relationship too. The play Pygmalion came to mind and, yes, there was that in our relationship, as my intention was to enable her to become a high-class lady.

I had been in love before, of course, with each of my two wives when we were newlyweds, but in both of those cases the sex was routine, light-hearted fun. With Lola, sex was like a religious experience, a special magic that bonded us. That's how I felt and she said she felt the same, but how foolish can an old geezer be to believe such a scrumptious young beauty could possibly be so thrilled by him? No matter, I was deeply in love and totally greedy. If it was strictly a sex-for-money affair, so be it. Sex-for-money affairs had been my habit for decades. I'd enjoyed fleeting affairs with gorgeous call girls all around the world. Now, I felt, it was better to battle my loneliness by loving Lola fearlessly, totally, without regard for the long run. "In the long run we're all dead," as one famous economist said.

Meanwhile, how ironic that brother Bob was having an affair with Laura. I found myself looking forward to seeing her in Rehoboth Beach, repairing some of the damage we'd inflicted on each other when we went through that messy divorce with our lawyers battling over who would get how much and why. In the end, we'd settled for what I'd initially proposed, so the whole charade was really a huge waste of time and money, which intensified the resentment between us. It would be so nice to remove that resentment.

Around 11 o'clock as I was debating whether or not to have a third brandy, my cell phone chirped and it was Lola. "Hi, you horny old man. We finally connected."

"Where have you been?"

"Turned my phone off to do some shopping. I had to buy groceries, you know, and then I bought some new clothes. Can't wait for you to see me in this cocktail dress I found on Rodeo Drive. I hope you'll rip it off and ravish me."

"That gives me an instant erection. I can't stand being separated from you."

"I feel the same, Jack. I can't wait to get this security thing behind us."

"Any sign that Valance's people have followed you?"

"'None. I keep checking behind me and all around, looking for someone who would fit the description of a security snoop. He couldn't have kept up with me in the LA traffic anyhow. The Santa Monica was bumper to bumper for over an hour. I think it's like you said. Out of your house, I'm no longer their concern."

"I'm so tempted to ask you to drive up here."

"I can be there in an hour and a half."

"But they'd see your car."

"How about you drive down here?"

"They'd track me there. I don't want them to know where you live."

"Do they watch you around the clock?"

"If I drive out, they are electronically alerted and make it their business to find out where I'm going."

There was silence on the line and then: "Tomorrow I'm going to my gym and do a workout. Haven't had a good workout in a couple of weeks. That will ease my nerves."

We chatted on till we noticed it was well past midnight. I didn't tell her about dinner with the Hansens, because that hadn't changed our plan.

The next morning I went with Bob to the DMV. He aced both the written and driving tests, and we were out of there in less than two hours. As we were driving back to the beach house, Bob got out his cell phone and was fumbling about, trying to make a call as he drove the 101. I said, "Who are you trying to call?"

"Laura."

I took his phone, found her name listed in his autodial and connected to her, then gave the phone to Bob.

"Just wanted to let you know I'm flying back there soon, like later today or tomorrow."

I could hear Laura's loud delight sounding from the cell phone.

"No need for you to meet me at the airport, honey. I'll rent a car."

More chirping noises from Laura.

"But that would mean I'm dependent on you for wheels while I'm there, and I'll be doing a lot of driving. I'm going to be shopping for a condo for my brother."

The upshot was that Laura wanted to go with him on the search for the condo. Bob seemed uneasy with that. "I'd rather have my own set of wheels and deal with realtors alone. I'm representing you, after all, and she still harbors resentment toward you."

"I agree," I said. "Call her back later and tell her you'll definitely need a car of your own. If it turns out that we're both going to be there more than a month or two, we'll get you a car."

'Amazing."

"What?"

"How dependent on cars we are. What will happen if the price of gas keeps going up? How will food get delivered to supermarkets?"

"People will pay what they have to pay."

"But there are millions of people, John, who cannot afford to pay these high gas prices and also meet their mortgages and buy food. It's an impossibility for millions."

"Don't worry, Bob, we'll be fine. The high price of gas will get a lot of cars off the freeways. It will be easier to move around."

"John, if the bottom falls out of the economy, you won't be able to buy what you need no mater how much money you have—it won't be in stores. It won't be delivered. The country will grind to a screeching halt."

"Brother Bob, you are full of catastrophe theories. Just do what you have to do. We'll be all right."

"But suppose the dollar crashes to worthless. That happened in Germany back in the nineteen twenties."

"That's not going to happen here."

"I hope you're right, John."

"This recession we're in could be extended longer than most people expect, I'll grant you that. But, brother Robert, I have all contingencies covered. Rest easy."

"You're the one with the Ph D in economics from Harvard, John. I'll take your word for it. But with a grain of salt."

"What do you mean by that?"

"I think we could be in for some unprecedented surprises. And, you know, people stick to their habitual ways until there's a total breakdown. Only then are the needed changes made."

"What changes? We're in a contraction. Eventually it will end and we'll be into a new expansion cycle."

"I think this contraction cycle will be a lot different than anything we've known before," I said.

"Where do you get such ideas, Robert? From your astrologer friend?"

"He taught economics at UCLA until he had his breakdown."

"Well, with ideas like that, I can see why he's no longer at UCLA. Let's keep our eye on the ball, Robert. Survival of the fittest. We'll shake loose from Valance and his crew, and get that condo in Rehoboth."

"What about security there?"

"I'll opt to take care of my personal security myself. The security firm we retain won't send people to such a remote place as Sussex County, Delaware. They were reluctant to establish a unit in Santa Barbara County and its population is about four times the population of Sussex County.

"Today's economy is full of conundrums and catch 22's. Our country is sliding toward third-world status. That means more danger for people like you, John."

"Do you want to add global warming to your catastrophe list?"

"I think it's clear that unprecedented weather emergencies will coincide with unprecedented economic emergencies, which means mounting social chaos and lawlessness."

"You're a bundle of optimism, Robert. When would you like to fly out of here?"

"Think I can catch a plane this afternoon?"

"It's possible. Let's go through my travel agent here and see what we can do. Don't get me wrong, Bob. I love having you here, love how we're renewing our brotherly bonds. But, you know, we did agree not to argue politics, didn't we?"

"This nation's politics have become totally dysfunctional. It's economics and environmental problems I'm talking about."

"Those are problems for the government to deal with. Where did you get the idea that our government is dysfunctional? Do the stars say that's so?"

"Katrina, the war in Iraq, the massive amounts of money the government is throwing at corporations, neglecting our own social services and infrastructure...the list goes on."

"My dear brother, a sizeable portion of my wealth has come from what you liberals call corporate welfare. That's how the country operates. It's the reality. Stop fantasizing and get with the program."

"Grant me the serenity to accept the things I cannot change, the courage to change the things I can, and wisdom to know the difference."

"Ah, we've arrived at agreement. Remember when we were kids, how Dad used to get so frustrated with you? He'd tell you to do something a certain way and you'd immediately start trying to invent a better way."

"Yes, and you, brother John, were always content to go along to get along."

"I accepted the reality, didn't try to play God."

"I don't think it's playing God to prepare for adversity."

"I don't know whether you're an idealist or a mischief maker, Bob, but I do know that if you'd accepted reality back in the sixties, you'd be in very different circumstances today."

"If we had succeeded in changing certain things back then, the country would be in far better shape today. And we're now entering another period much like the sixties."

"That's fantasy, Robert. Stop trying to change the world and stick to our own business."

By this time we were home. We went into the house and got busy with my travel agent, who soon had Bob booked on a nonstop flight to Philadelphia leaving LAX shortly after 2 PM. He hurried over to the guesthouse to pack his bags and we were off again, this time with me driving.

As we rolled onto the 101, I glanced back through my rearview mirror and was startled to see none other than Jake Valance tailgating us in his big black Chevy van. He blinked his lights. I pulled over and stopped. He got out and stood beside my car door. "Where you going, Mr. Bradford?"

"I'm taking my brother to the airport, Jake."

"It would be best to stick to the routine and let us know."

"We're in a hurry, Jake. Now that you know, bye bye, see you later."

As I was rolling up my window, he said, "Where's your girlfriend?"

I floored it and left him gazing after us with a perplexed look.

"Did you see the expression on his face?" I asked Bob.

"Yeah. He looked confused. "

"He's going to look a lot more confused as this plays out."

"I'll keep in touch with Al Hansen while I'm away."

"Good. Al is a fine, upstanding, honorable law enforcement officer. And you know him better than I do."

Chapter 20

While waiting to fly out of LAX I called Laura and left word that I'd be arriving in Philly this evening and that I would rent a car, so there was no need for her to meet me.

On the flight to Philly, I nodded off and dreamed about Jake Valance. I don't remember the entire dream but at one point Jake appeared as a kind of mythological figure from hell. In the ancient myth, Pluto is the god of Hades, a pantheistic Satan. That's who Jake appeared to be in my dream. He wore an evil smile, and seemed to be telling me that our conflict with him was by no means over and he was convinced his would be the final victory. I guess this dream was stimulated by my growing fear of what he might do.

Al had warned that Jake likes to hurt people. During my stay in San Quentin I'd dealt with goons who liked to hurt people. Most could be turned away by a convincing counter threat, but a few had the suicidal mindset of an Islamic terrorist—in order to deliver pain to another, they were ready to die. Was Jake of that makeup? I didn't think so, but could I be sure? Assuming our plan works and a month or two from now Jake is transferred or loses his job, what should we expect? I made a mental note to run that question by Al Hansen.

Laura was waiting for me at the baggage claim. Having told her I planned to rent a car at the airport, I was a little frustrated that she'd insisted on meeting me. Yet her unflappable cool, her coy brown eyes, her willowy-slim figure and graceful movements charmed me, as always.

I knew she was not enthralled by the news that John planned to move to Rehoboth and bring his young girlfriend here. As we drove south on I-95 and then Route 1 through Delaware, I wanted to call Al and tell him about my dream and ask about Jake, but Laura was as frisky and primed for lovemaking as a teenager and I certainly did not want to sour that mood.

Laura resembled the lady in the Cadillac commercial who says the best test of a car is, "When you turn it on, does it return the favor?" She had that same cool intensity and coy gleam. As I drove Route 1 south through Delaware, she delivered an artful blowjob. It had been a couple of decades since I'd had an orgasm while driving an interstate. She looked at me as if to say, Now aren't you glad I met you at the airport?

"Yes," I said aloud, "I can rent a car in Rehoboth."

There were times I felt I could marry this lady and live happily ever after. But our implied agreement was that marriage would threaten this lovely, exciting romance we were having. It would also be difficult to explain to her two grown children, too. We were too old to start our own family, but not too old for a passionate affair.

We dropped my luggage at the Boardwalk Plaza and I suggested we go out for dinner at the Nantucket Restaurant in Bethany. I wanted to check out the condos on both sides of Route 1 just north of Bethany, where a thin strip of sandy land separates the ocean and Rehoboth Bay. Even though it was dark by the time we got there, I detoured off the main highway to check out a development that faced the bay.

"Are you sure you want to move to New York City?" I asked her.

"You think living here is better?"

"I think I can be happy anywhere with you."

"There's a lot more to see and do in Manhattan."

"Manhattan has wonderful attractions but, hey, imagine the sunset from here. Isn't it magnificent?"

"If I was going to live here," she said, "I'd rather live on the ocean side and get the sunrise."

"Why?"

"It's so much more...dramatic!"

"And vulnerable to hurricanes."

"That too. It's not expected to be here much longer, with the oceans rising because of global warming. That's part of its drama. It's intensely tragic...doomed."

"On this side of the road, you can build a dock and keep a boat."

"I didn't know you're a boat enthusiast, Bob. You're keeping secrets from me."

I started to say that my brother and I had done a lot of sailing when we were kids, but checked that and said, "I did a lot of sailing growing up."

"I love living near the sea. I don't know about sailing on it."

We spotted one three-story house built on steel pilings that had a dock and a yacht tied up to it, and got out of the car and made love standing up against one of the pilings. "That did improve the view from here," she said as she was pulling up her panties and slacks. "You're such a stud! Where do you get all this sex energy?"

I almost blurted out that it came from a decade of incarceration—the newly released prisoner syndrome—but checked that and said, "It comes from how nicely you stroke my macho vanity."

"That's good. I intend to keep stroking."

Over dinner at the Nantucket, I decided to bring up buying property here. It would not have been a lie if I'd told her that I was also interested in buying for us, now that I had income. But I felt it would be better to let her know what her ex-husband had in mind now, rather than wait till later when her mood might not be so mellow and agreeable.

"John wants me to buy him a condo on the water here," I said.

'You're kidding!"

"No, he's got a problem with his security people in Santa Barbara and wants to absent himself from them for a while."

"What kind of problem?" She was frowning now, not delighted with the prospect of John—plus a girlfriend, she probably surmised—living so close.

I didn't want to bluntly tell her that John's security guard was blackmailing him because he was shacking up with a girl young enough to be his granddaughter, so I said, "It's complicated and changing day by day. I'll tell you all about it when the dust settles. But I can see that having your ex so close does not enchant you."

"It certainly does not. He's overbearing."

"I suspect he'll move back to the Padero Lane house when his present problem blows over."

"We could live somewhere else while he's here, then," she said. "Proximity to him is poisonous for me, Bob. It's like he's an unlucky charm, if you know what I mean. Life with your brother wrecked me. I very much like having three thousand miles separating us. But I need to be on the East Coast now so my children have someplace nearby to come home to on breaks."

"Living in Bethany, he'd be twenty miles away from you in Rehoboth. You'd never have to see him."

"Just knowing he's so close would make me sick."

"That bad, is it?"

"Worse. I love you dearly, Bob, but your brother is a monster. He is so obsessed with business, he doesn't even contact his children. Which is a good thing—they witnessed some of the horrible fights we had and have no interest in ever seeing him again."

"I shouldn't have brought it up. It could have waited till later."

"It's already spoiled our night. The very thought of John being anywhere near me...how serious is he about you buying him a condo here?"

"Very serious."

"Why doesn't he buy on Cape Cod if he wants to be on the Atlantic? He learned to love that area when he went to Harvard. Why would he want to move here?"

I sure had stuck my foot in it. I was silent for quite a while before I ventured this: "He's still got to travel for board meetings and there are two or three airports within easy driving distance from here."

"Atlantic City is much better for air travel," she said.

"My impression is—and this is my impression, not what he told me— he'd like to make it up to you and your children."

"Please convey to him that all is forgiven but we do not want to revisit the past by having him anywhere near us."

"It's my fault," I said. "I suggested this area."

"Can you suggest another? How about the Outer Banks of North Carolina, or one of those beach communities in South Carolina, or even Florida. The Gulf Coast. Anywhere but here."

"If he wasn't committed to attending board meetings, he could go to Asia or Africa or anywhere else in the world. But about half his board meetings are in the New York area. He can drive up to those from here, and he enjoys driving."

"How long do you think he might live here?"

"I don't know. Six months, maybe."

"Well, let me sleep on it. I had two cocktails before dinner, you know. Maybe in the morning I'll feel different. Six months I can survive, I guess. Will you promise to be here, with me, while John is here?"

"I'll stick to you like glue, Laura."

"Can you see us living together?"

"As in marriage?"

"No, shacking up. No strings attached."

"Any idea when the work on your house will be finished?"

"Martino says it will take about a month for everything to get done."

"A month! That seems like a long time for what they're doing."

"I agree. That's why I need you to talk to Martino, intercede on behalf of 'the little woman'."

"I'll do that."

"Oh, god damn it, Bob, I am just so fucking mad about you, I'll do anything to keep you near me. I'll even tolerate John. For a limited time."

"It's possible that John and his new girlfriend could live in Bethany and you'd never see them or have any contact with them."

"Ah, yes, his new girlfriend. I'd almost forgotten. Well, I really cherish having a continent between us. The thing I resent most about him is that he needs to get his way. It's his way or the highway. I can't imagine him living this close and not intruding on our lives. He has half ownership of the house I live in, and they are his children as well as mine. Years ago when we lived in California, he'd come flying in for a two-day weekend, and even before finding out what was happening in our lives, he'd become overbearing. When the kids were little, they wanted to play with him, show him things they'd done, win his love and approval, but he'd be jet-lagged and want only to drink himself senseless and sleep till it was time to rush off to the airport and fly away to whatever Timbuktu he'd come from. The kids would look forward joyfully to his arrival, only to be left feeling sorry for themselves by the time he left. When he wasn't demanding they get perfect grades in school, he was neglecting them. If he's living nearby and doesn't want to see them, that will hurt. If he does want to see them, that will hurt even more because he's so narcissistic, so absorbed by his career, he leeches love and energy from us and leaves us wrecked."

What could I say to that? We both sat silently staring out the window at the traffic on Route 1. As she finished an after-dinner drink, I tried to change the mood by asking, "How do you keep your girlish figure?"

She gave that down-under look, eyes gleaming, slightly smiling, and said, "Lusting for you."

By the time we got back to the hotel room, she was exhausted. She shed her clothes and dropped them in a pile beside the bed, and fell asleep immediately. I got into bed beside her and lay staring at the ceiling. I was jet lagged on West Cost Time, needed to contact Al Hansen, and didn't want to disturb her. She might awaken as quickly as she'd fallen asleep, and I didn't want to upset her by telling her how John's war with Valance involved Lola. So I got up, found paper and pen and wrote a note: "Gone for a walk on the boardwalk."

Dressed in a new trench coat—a "high-end brand" as John put it—I left the hotel and headed south along the boardwalk. It felt good to stretch out briskly and I was soon at the end of the boardwalk, a desolate area compared to the center of town. Desolate suited my mood. I sat down on a sea-dampened bench and dialed Al.

"You caught me playing poker," he said. "I'll have to call you back."

I then called John. "How was your trip?" he said.

"Easy. I'm getting used to civilian life."

"Living among normal people now, eh."

"And they are crazier than the inmates I left."

"You're incorrigible, Bob, but you're improving. How is Laura?"

"We had a wonderful evening—until I told her."

"Told her what?"

"That you are planning to move here. If I'd also told her about Lola, I might not be alive now."

"She's still carrying a grudge?"

"A whopper of a grudge."

He asked if I'd heard anything from Al and I told him about my call, and that we'd speak tomorrow.

"I went online and checked out the real estate scene in Rehoboth," he said, "and it looks good. I think I'll enjoy owning something on the ocean there. And it's an easy drive up to Manhattan or over to Washington, DC. I'm going to ship my car cross-country when I come. Would you like me to also ship the Jag?"

"Hold off on that, Jack. I'm not planning to live here forever."

"Neither am I. Would you rather rent a car there?"

"Otherwise I have to borrow Laura's."

"You two are becoming two peas in a pod."

"Yeah, we are getting along nicely. Most of the time. What's the latest on your security situation?"

"Valance seems to be making himself scarce. I had a quiet dinner at home, cooked by Alicia. And now I'm catching up on my email and checking out properties In the Rehoboth area. But, hey, I just spotted that yacht. The same one is back again, anchored just offshore."

"You going to send up another flare?"

"No, not this time. Intellectually, I don't think it's connected to Valance. Emotionally, I'm prone to paranoia."

"You sure it's the same yacht?"

"Absolutely. Same single-mast motor sailor."

"Why would it come back there again, after you chased it away with the flare?"

"That's the question."

"Why don't you call the agency's number and ask about it. Have your security people find out who is on that boat?"

"Even as you spoke, Bob, I saw one of the security people down by the pool. He, or maybe she, seems to be sitting there, watching the yacht. I'll walk down to the pool and ask."

"How about doing that while we're still connected, Jack? I'm as curious as you are."

"All right. Here I go. I'm in the bedroom so it will take me a minute to get down there. Hang on. I'll send you some pictures."

I adjusted my phone to receive the picture and soon saw a blurry video movement, as John made his way to the pool, then the image of a female security guard, sitting in a deck chair. She wore a police visor cap and a dark uniform under a Navy jacket. Her butt filled the deck chair. She didn't bother to move as they made light conversation. I wondered about that. Then Jack said, "Who's in that boat?" And swung his phone camera to show it.

"Who knows?" said the security lady. "Does it concern you?"

"I thought it would be of concern to you," said Jack.

"It's just anchored there. It's not doing anything."

"It's the second time its anchored here. Would you be so kind as to check out who is aboard that boat, and why they decided to anchor in front of my house?"

"We can do that," she said, "but it will take time to get our people there."

"Suppose it posed some kind of threat?"

"Our electronics would tell us if it was a threat."

"But your electronics can't tell us who's on that boat?"

"No."

"Or where it came from?"

"No."

"Please get your people to find out who is on that yacht and report back to me as soon as possible."

"Yes, Sir. I'll get right on it."

The video ended. As Jack was making his way back up to his bedroom, he said, "Jake spends a whole day in this house to install some kind of electronics, if we are to believe him, but this guard can't get her ass out of that chair and check on this boat. Am I missing something, Bob?"

"Who does she think she's guarding by sitting in a deck chair beside your pool?"

"That's the question. They routinely come and go, keep on the move. I have no idea why she's stationed herself there tonight. Nor why she has to be prodded to check out that boat."

I suddenly became aware of flashing lights behind me. I turned and saw a police car in the street that dead-ends at the boardwalk. A cop got out, walked up wooden steps onto the boardwalk and strolled toward me. "Seems I have a visitor," I told Jack. "I'll call you back later."

I stood up and said, "Good evening, Officer." In such an encounter as this, the danger was I'd explode at having my privacy intruded upon by a cop. I was alone, sitting on a bench, gazing out to sea.

"Good evening," he said. "Out late?"

"Just taking a walk."

"Are you from out of town?"

"Yes."

"Where are you staying?

"The Plaza."

"Please show me your driver's license," he said with stiff formality.

I patted my pockets. "I left it in my hotel room. Is there a problem, Officer?"

"I hope not. Why are you sitting here?"

"I was making a couple of phone calls."

"Why come here to do that?"

"I wanted to take a walk. Is there a law against walking at night?"

"Come with me. I'll drive you to the Boardwalk Plaza."

"No thanks, I'll walk back."

"I need to check to make sure you are registered there."

"Why? I'm out taking a walk. What crime have I committed?"

"Sir, please don't make me have to call for backup."

"What the hell kind of town is this, when a middle aged man can't go out for a walk at night without being hassled by police?"

"Sir, we're a very security-conscious town. We mean no disrespect. We just need to know who you are and why you're here."

By this time, I was hyperventilating, having great difficulty maintaining a civil tone. When someone in a uniform politely calls me sir, I feel the danger of violence. I forced myself to shut up and go with him to his car and get in. I half-expected him to drive me to the nearest police station, slap handcuffs on me, and throw me in the drunk tank—until I remembered I was wearing the "high-end" trench coat. I wish I'd left the outrageously high price tag dangling from it so he could see that too.

Back in the lobby of the Boardwalk Plaza, the night clerk's eyes bulged when in walked one of the hotel's guests accompanied by a cop.

"Do you recognize this gentleman?" asked the cop.

"Yes. He's Robert Bradford."

"Registered at this hotel?"

"Checked in earlier today."

If this cop insisted on coming up to my room to see my driver's license, I might lose my control. But he didn't. "Sorry for the inconvenience, sir," he said. "Have a wonderful vacation in Rehoboth

Beach. I hope you understand our caution. We are security-conscious. That's why we're such a pleasant town."

I knew he intended his remark to ease whatever fears I might have of being attacked or robbed by some night prowler hiding under the boardwalk or wherever. But I could not stop myself from saying, "This is an America I do not recognize."

The cop looked puzzled, then decided to ignore my remark. "Have a good night, sir." And was gone out the front door.

What pulled my chain was that, if I'd been who I was before my brother took me in, this cop could have thrown me in jail as a vagrant or worse. Once back in the system with my record available to these locals, there's no telling what might have become of me. They'd have viewed me as a dangerous psychotic with a criminal record. It wouldn't matter that my record was drug-related with no harm to other citizens or society. With the prison system now operated for profit by corporations, the more bodies they throw in jail, the more profits the prison corporations make. Plus they then order inmates to take pharmaceuticals, enriching the big drug companies. To my lights, this was doing society a lot more harm than smoking dope or robbing convenience stores.

I went back up to my room, thinking of moving out of the country and wondering if Laura would like to live elsewhere too. I thought of cities we might move to—Paris, Copenhagen, Tokyo, Bangkok, Rio de Janeiro. But that was unrealistic. She wouldn't want to be that far away from her two children. Come to think of it, I would not want to be that far away from my brother, and from my support group, Hernandez and Dr Grace. By the time I was in bed snuggled to her, with my legs under her butt, the urge to flee the country had left me and I was aware that I'd again beat up on myself with my imagination.

Tomorrow, I decided, I'll call Jorge and Mary Grace and tell them about this incident, and the feelings it had stirred in me, and my final realization.

Chapter 21

I worked at my laptop till around midnight when I saw lights on the water below. It was a Coast Guard patrol boat arriving to check out the yacht. I stood at my window and watched the pantomime. The patrol boat pulled up to the port side of the yacht and a couple of figures emerged from its cabin. They talked with the Coast Guard briefly, then the patrol boat moved away and turned back toward the Santa Barbara Harbor. Down by the swimming pool, the lady security guard was still there, standing up now as she watched, a cell phone clapped to her ear. When the yacht's cabin lights went out again, she turned and climbed the stone steps toward the front door.

I was down at the door when she arrived. "They're a couple from Laguna Beach," she said. "They plan to go fishing tomorrow."

"Did you contact Jake Valance about this?"

"No, sir. This is his night off. I contacted his backup."

That she addressed me respectfully as sir was reassuring. "All right, Miss. Thank you for responding to my concerns."

"No problem. Will there be anything else, sir?"

"Not tonight. Where will you go from here?"

"Sir, my orders are to stay on your property tonight."

"That's odd. Don't you usually make the rounds of other properties?"

"Yes, but there's a red alert tonight, sir, so my orders are to stay on your property."

"Only my property is threatened?"

"Ah, no, sir, no, that's...other people are assigned to other properties tonight."

"What happened to cause this red alert?"

"I don't really know, sir. I'm just obeying orders."

We said good night then, and I went back to the bedroom, but was not feeling easy with this new situation. I started to dial Bob's number but realized it was the wee hours of the morning where he is and stopped. I missed Lola, yet was glad she was not here now, for my feelings of insecurity would be worse if she were.

Two days from now, Saturday, I had another board meeting, this one in Silicon Valley. It would be a brief affair, probably last only a couple of hours. I went into the bathroom to brush my teeth and get ready for bed, but on a sudden impulse, I got out my dopp kit and threw toiletries into it. I got fully dressed again and went downstairs, and quietly slipped out the front door, went to the garage, and backed out the Mercedes. I knew the laser beam would alert the security people but I intended to lose them by getting on the freeway before they could react.

Once on the freeway, I wondered where the hell I should go. I drove south as far as Ventura, then got off the southbound and reentered going north, and drove to the Biltmore. It was a test run, I decided, to see how Jake and his gang would respond. If I'd given them the slip—and it appeared that I had—how would they do?

My favorite room was available and I slept soundly, secure that I would not be disturbed by either security guards or my own paranoia, if indeed it was paranoia and not reality-based fear.

The next morning, while having breakfast alone in the hotel dining room, my cell phone sounded and it was Bob. I put the earpiece on so my hands were free and ate breakfast as we conversed.

"I had a sit-down with the contractor here, Tony Martino, and we went over the house together. He showed me what's been done and what remains to be done. Construction in this town has ground to a halt, you know—"

"It's ground to a halt all across the country," I said.

"—so these workers are taking their good old time, boondoggling this job."

"That's the least of our worries."

"Okay, just wanted you to know. Now I'm beginning the search for a condo. Laura would like to chauffeur me around for this but I'm insisting on doing it alone."

"She's a woman of leisure, and horny."

"Only one car rental in this town, but that's okay. I won't be dependent on Laura. She knows I'm going house hunting, and why, it's just that she'd rather we spend all day together."

"What does she usually do all day?"

"Exercises, shops for health foods, plays bridge, attends civic and philanthropic committee meetings and I don't know what else. She's very social, you know. I think she wants to keep me separated from her busy social life here."

"So what's the problem? She'll do her thing, you do yours."

"Brother John, your ex-wife wants my companionship but she would much rather you not move here."

"Please assure her that I will not intrude on her life."

There was a long pause, as though Bob was sorting through what else to tell me, or perhaps weighing what not to tell me.

"The other thing is, I damn near got arrested here last night."

"What?"

"A cop hassled me as I was finishing talking to you. I'd gone out for a walk, didn't bring any ID with me. I thought you'd appreciate the irony of why he said he hassled me. Security. This is a very security-conscious town," he said.

"Maybe we can use that to our advantage," I said. "Once Lola and I are there, maybe the local gendarmes will keep an eye out for Jake Valance. In case he happens to track us there."

"I never thought of that."

"Have you heard from Al Hansen?"

"Not yet. If he doesn't call by six today, I'll call him after nine our time, six your time."

"Other than all that, Bob, how are you doing? Are you feeling more at ease as a civilian? Any mental or emotional problems?"

"No, Jack, I think I'm getting through my Rip Van Winkle period. I almost went around the bend last night when that cop had me, but I managed to hold my mud. What amazes me is how distrustful this country has become. That's new. There was nowhere near all this concern over security a decade ago. Now it seems that everyone is spying and being spied upon, policing and being policed."

"Well, we've had nine-eleven and we're at war with the terrorists, you know."

"How do the rulers of this country expect to enlist the loyalty of the population by making people take off their shoes at airports? Seems counter-productive to me."

"It's the economic down cycle, Bob. Fear is creating distrust."

"That sounds like something my friend Jorge would say, and then give astrological reasons for it."

"It's the national mood, Bob. The stars have nothing to do with it."

"Jorge would say it's planetary patterns which bring the mood."

As we talked, I was looking around for signs that the agency people had tracked me to the Biltmore but could see none. On the way to the restaurant earlier, I'd checked the parking lot and saw no agency vehicles.

I told Bob how I decided to leave my house late last night as a test run to see if I could lose Jake's guys. "Looks like I've succeeded," I said.

"Way to go, brother! I'll be eager to hear Jake's reaction."

"Get that condo bought as soon as you can, Bob, so I can get out of here and bring Lola."

"Will do."

After breakfast, I drove home to find Jake standing in my front door, hands folded over his chest, looking perturbed. I parked in my garage and took my time walking to the front entrance.

"Where have you been?" he asked.

"None of your business," I said.

"You're wrong. It is my business."

"Your job is to protect my property."

"And your person."

"Standing in my doorway is not part of your duties, Jake."

"I was searching your house, afraid that you might have had an accident or something. By the way, where's your girlfriend?"

"She's not here, as you can see. Now, I'm sure you have other duties to attend to."

"You have a board meeting in Silicon Valley tomorrow. Again I urge you to cancel, but if you insist on attending, we need to know how you'll travel and where you'll stay."

"I'll let you know. Get out of my doorway."

He moved with insinuating slowness. I felt an urge to shove him, hurry him along. I soothed my emotions with the thought that I had indeed succeeded in losing him last night.

"Why was one of your guards stationed by my swimming pool all night?

"We changed our routine. We do that every now and then. When conditions warrant."

"What conditions warranted the change last night?"

"I'm not at liberty to divulge that, Mr. Bradford."

"You're supposed to be providing me security and you can't tell me what dangers exist?"

"Company policy. Suspected threats would needlessly upset our clients."

I shook my head and went into the house, closed the front door. Alicia was vacuuming the living room and dining area. As I headed upstairs, we made eye contact and I could see that she was upset. I went to her and motioned for her to turn off the machine. "What's wrong, Alicia?"

"Your policeman, he ask me questions all morning. He's angry. I don't do nothing to make him angry. Mr. Bradford, I must leave and get another job."

"Oh, Alicia, please don't leave. I'll tell Jake he must never question you again. That's terrible. He has no right to question you."

I had to speed up my escape from Valance, join Bob in Rehoboth. It would be only his newly issued American Express card we'd use. No trace of me. I'll call to the security agency today, tell them I am fed up with Jake Valance, that he needs to be replaced. I'll tell them that a niece was visiting me and that he insulted her by calling her a hooker.

Last night's spontaneous departure had demonstrated that if I move unexpectedly, I can give Jake and his crew the slip. With Lola gone now, he no longer has what he needs to blackmail me. Even so, he was turning up the screws. My next move? I'll get Herby to withdraw cash, pack what I need, leave around 3 AM, pick up Lola and we'll drive across the country to Rehoboth Beach without leaving a paper trail. We'll make it a leisurely trip, stop at all the major tourist sites from the Grand Canyon to Yellowstone. I'll ask Al Hansen to keep an eye on Jake as we disappear from his radar screen. Eventually we'll move into a new house on the Atlantic Coast and start a new life.

Chapter 22

Enterprise car rental, true to their TV commercial, picked me up at the Boardwalk Plaza and drove me to their office on Route 1 in Rehoboth Beach. The young lady behind the counter said they had a special—instead of a mid-size Chevy, for the same price I could drive away in a Chrysler 300. That would make a statement to the realtors, I figured, so I went for it. Trying to figure out how to operate the climate control on this splendiferous Detroit product reminded me of how long I'd been away.

I drove down Route 1 to Bethany and visited four realty offices before I met someone I felt compatible with. Her name was Kathy. Thirty-five years old with a trim figure and a quick, bright smile. What sold me on making her my buyer's agent was when she said, "Not all the condos here are listed for sale, but if you make a decent offer on an unlisted unit, you may be able to name your price."

When I said, "I'll be paying cash rather than financing," her eyes widened and she grinned. "In that case, you can steal whatever unit you like. Within reason, that is."

"What are the boundaries of reason?" I asked. I'd never bought real estate before.

"Last unlisted sale we made was for thirty percent below asking. I don't think an offer less than that would be taken seriously."

"Sounds like property prices are dropping like a rock." I'd gotten this from a TV news show.

"Prices are holding up better around here than elsewhere in the country," said Kathy. "But these summer homes—which is what

199

most units are here, vacation homes—many owners are trimming their expenses. It's definitely a buyer's market."

"Okay," I said like I knew what I was doing, "let's go shopping."

Feeling the released prisoner, I wanted to fuck every decent looking female that crossed my path. Kathy was especially fetching. I felt like I did back in the sixties when my loyalty was to my own selfish libido, not any particular partner. Of course I knew that at age 60, the released prisoner syndrome was absurd and even dangerous, and I did not want to hurt Laura or embarrass myself. Kathy and I flirted with light-hearted banter, avoiding serious intensity. She was using her feminine wiles to sell. The closest we came to crossing the line was when I asked if she liked older men, and she came back with, "Don't get your hopes up."

By the end of our first day, we'd seen a dozen or more condos that roughly fit what I was looking for—at least four bedrooms and plenty of floor space, enclosed garage and a real fireplace. John and I had grown up with a father who'd loved his fireplace, and the temperature could go down to the teens at night here.

The next day, I went back with Kathy to the three I liked best, and finally settled on one. Its front door faced Sandpiper Lane—seemed all the streets here had been named by realtors. Sandpiper ran parallel to the ocean, inside a gated community. The house was elevated on steel pilings and had three floors, reached by either stairs or an elevator. A balcony on the second floor provided a wide-angle view of the broad beach and sea, and there was a high sand dune that gave the house some protection from full-moon high tides. The dune was topped with newly planted sprouts and was environmentally protected, a sign said, an attempt to restore this beach to its original condition—even while icebergs are melting and ocean levels rising. If most environmental scientists are correct, sooner or later this narrow spit of land will be ocean bottom. But then, don't we always survive or die at the whim of a seemingly capricious Nature?

"This one is not officially listed," Kathy said, "but the owner gave our office the key in case we ran into someone willing to meet his asking price, and he's not likely to budge."

"He's an exception?"

"Right. He owns it free and clear, can rent it out in season."

"What's his price?"

She made a comic face, did an exaggerated swallow, and said, "Two million even."

I wondered how large a suitcase would be needed to deliver two million in cash. "How long would escrow be?"

"How long would you like it to be?"

"The shorter the better."

"I'll suggest two weeks. If the owner has no qualms about that, it's done."

"Will the owner have any qualms about being paid in cash?"

"I seriously doubt it. If he does, I believe we can come up with a process to get him paid with a check. He and his wife are in their early eighties now and have another home in Florida, where they plan to live year round. They no longer want to drive up here for the summer months."

For so many years of my life I'd felt a couple thousand was serious get-ahead money. Now, with flying coast to coast and staying in an expensive old hotel, eating out, I was going through a couple of thousand in a couple of days, and talking a couple of million to buy this condo. Not many years ago, it seemed to me, million-dollar real estate was rare. Now, it seemed, a lot of people were paying multi millions.

Hernandez had told me that what a dollar bought in 1800, it would still buy in 1900, but that since 1950 the dollar has devalued by more than 1,000 percent. And because owning real estate provides a tax advantage, a house bought in 1959 for $14,000 now costs around $215,000. "What follows inflation," Jorge has said, "is deflation, meaning depression. They are cooking the frog slowly," he says, the frog being American society. Drop a frog in boiling water and it will leap out, but drop the frog In cold water and heat it slowly, and it will peacefully cook till its meat drops off.

I thought about how my brother told me he was invulnerable to depression because his wealth was invested in a variety of foreign currencies, and how Hernandez was predicting the dollar would collapse and eventually take all paper fiat currencies down with it. If Jorge is right, brother John is the frog cooking slowly.

When we were kids, our family used to play the board game Monopoly in which one winner would end up owning everything. Brother John won more than anyone else in the family. I guess that was a harbinger of his financial success as an adult. Yet I couldn't discount Jorge's prediction that we'd be in the dumpster of another great depression by 2015, seven years from now. Seven years is how long I'd been in Covington, isolated from normal life. I am the only person I know—aside from Jorge—who is aware of how prices had inflated during those seven years. On the other hand, brother John seems to have the mythical Midas touch, as witness how his Padero Lane house has increased in value way beyond the average inflation of real estate.

As Kathy drove us back to her office, I put through a call to John. "I found a condo, just over a protective dune from the ocean." I described it. "What do you think?"

"Make an offer, Bob. I'll get Herby to set up a cash delivery. How much do you think we can get it for?"

"Asking a firm two million even."

"Is that all? Properties are cheaper there, eh."

"Nothing is as expensive as southern California."

I explained that this condo sat on a narrow spit of land between ocean and bay, and was thus vulnerable.

"We'll insure against flooding," said John. "Let's meet the asking price and get on with life. Herby will find a way to make it deductible and I am really anxious to get as far away from here as possible, as soon as possible. How long will escrow take?"

"We're pointing for two weeks."

"Good. Another matter. I called the security agency's head-quarters in New York and spoke with an executive there, told him my complaint about Jake, that he called my beautiful young niece a hooker, and that he's dictatorial and surly and overbearing. I was told they'd replace him immediately."

"Wow, brother, you're moving fast."

"I have to be. Valance is tightening the screws. Have you heard from Al Hansen yet?"

"No. Called yesterday and he said he could not talk, that I should call him today, after he's off duty."

"Well, right now I'm road weary. I had a board meeting in Silicon Valley and drove to it. A lot of driving for one day. Didn't spot any security people. I think I confused them by driving around the airport as though I were going to fly up, before I hit the highway for Monterey. Reminded me of playing bumper cars at Santa Claus Lane when we were kids."

Jack was speaking loudly over the road noise and I suspected that Kathy heard a word or two, for she glanced at me with a questioning expression. I said, "Gotta go now, Jack. I'll call you later today."

"My partner," I said to Kathy.

"Oh," she said. "You two will feel right at home down here." She'd jumped to the conclusion that we were a gay couple.

Back at the hotel room, I found a note from Laura. She'd apparently stopped by, for it was written on hotel stationary and stuck under my door. "Missed you all day. What would you like to do for dinner? Call when you get in."

Less than a month ago, I was dining on institutional food, wearing thrift store clothes and locked out of ordinary life. Now I'm operating as though I'd stepped into my brother's shoes. The stark contrast between then and now hit me as I sat on the edge of the hotel bed and pondered Laura's note. Here I was living the millionaire's life, about to buy a two-million-dollar condo on the beach. It was like I had suddenly become King Midas' princely son.

When I went into Covington Psychiatric Hospital, the prognosis was that I would probably be there the rest of my life. I'd been into and out of so many psych wards by then, no one in authority believed I could survive on the outside. I didn't believe I could either. I had no control over when or where depression would engulf me and render me incapable of functioning. What had happened? I have the impression that my concussion healed itself, like a broken bone. It was previously believed that brain damage was permanent. That changed in recent years when it was scientifically demonstrated that brains are a lot more malleable than previously imagined. My long stay in Covington—a private institution where the care is up to date and intelligent—gave my brain the chance it needed to recover. Dr. Grace and I experimented with Lexapro, Cymbalta and other anti-depressants to find out which worked the best, and I helped this process by kicking my addiction to booze, avoiding processed food, and sticking to a regimen of daily meditation. Dr. Grace and Hernandez, to me, were angels in human form. The three of us had come to know each other profoundly. Certainly no one knew me as well as those two. Then came brother John and here I am, behaving like the son of King Midas. Can it last? Or is it a dream I'll be rudely awakened from? A couple of nights ago when the cop hassled me, I almost lost it.

I'd put myself in the alpha brainwave state and was meditating, bathing my body in relaxation, when my cell phone sounded—I had it set to play "When the Saints Come Marching In."

"Okay," Al's voice boomed, "I'm still on duty but I can talk now."

"Great, Al. What's the latest?"

"At our last poker game, Thursday night, I told Jake Valance I was disgusted with the Bradford brothers, mainly because John had brought his insane brother Robert home, then brought home that call girl, and God only knows what could come of that. Drugs? Orgies? Jake rose to the bait like a hungry shark. For the past two days I've been undercover with the son of a bitch. Have him conned. He's even offered to cut me in for my cooperation."

"What do you mean, cut you in?"

"I'm getting to that. This guy is definitely running a blackmail scam on John. We read him absolutely right, except for one thing—he plans to grab John while he's away on a trip and hold him till he pays."

"Pays how much?"

"Valance figures he can easily get ten million out of John. He's willing to give me one million of that ten if I help him pull this off by diverting law enforcement. He thinks we're in this together now. What appeals to him most is that he would deal only with John. Most kidnappings of corporate execs, the kidnappers demand ransom from the company. But Jake would be dealing only with John. That was his plan."

"Was?"

"Seems early this morning he got a call from his boss saying they are going to transfer him. That shook Jake. He's into his plan B. He's now talking of quitting and nabbing your brother and his girlfriend, taking them away, holding them both till John pays."

"Did he buy it that John has broken up with Lola?"

"No. See, your brother has been using his cell and Jake has been able to monitor some of his calls. Not all, but enough to know that John hasn't really broken up with Lola. He knows John is trying to take him out and he's not going for it. He wants to nab Lola along with John but he's not figured out exactly how to set it up yet. He's working on it. I hate to think what he'd do to her. Like I said, he makes the Marquis de Sade look like an altar boy."

"Do you have enough to arrest him?"

"No. I've been wired while talking to him, understand, but there's been no crime committed. Jake could say he was trash talking, putting me on, never really intended to kidnap anybody. If we want to get Jake put away, we've got to stay with this till he makes a move on John and Lola, and then collar him."

"John wants to flee. Disappear himself from Jake."

"Don't tell me any more. First thing you two have to do is buy encrypted cell phones. Go online and check 'em out. You can afford the best and I highly recommend you get the best. As it is, Jake has an electronics whiz as part of his unit in Santa Barbara, see. This guy—he's from Germany and his name is Manfred—definitely doesn't like spying on John and drags his heels. I met him yesterday. He looks at Jake like a deer caught in headlights. Knows something sinister is up but hasn't quite figured out what. He'll turn on Jake in a New York second, if it comes to that. But of course Jake keeps Manfred in the dark about what he plans. What you and your brother have to do is buy encrypted phones. Manfred will be happy you did. Till then, assume he can hear what you say on your phone."

"You sure have been busy."

"You better believe it. I had to set all this up with the department first, understand, and I know a couple of deputies are suspicious that I'm playing both sides of the street. The old timers know I would never do that, but I don't want to prolong this, Bob. You say John wants to flee?"

"As soon as possible. I'm buying a condo for him."

"Careful what you say. Don't say where you are."

"It's to get John gone from California without Jake and his guys tracking him. Can you divert those guys, hold them on suspicion?"

"Watch what you say. That's a remote possibility. Seems John has been giving these security guys problems the past few days. He's stopped cooperating with them and they're having trouble figuring out his moves."

"That's good to hear."

"The department wants to either nail Jake or get him the hell out of our jurisdiction. The news that his company plans to transfer him has him on the hot griddle. If Manfred has been monitoring this, Jake may already know where John plans to go."

"Ouch."

"I'm not saying he knows for sure. Manfred may be off duty. But maybe he does."

"What if you arrest on suspicion? Would that change his mind?"

"I'm not going to do that, Bob. We couldn't hold him. It wouldn't stop him. We've either got to go along with Jake till he makes a move on John, then bust him, or else get him gone from our jurisdiction. And frankly, it would be lot easier to get him gone. He's crafty, knows police procedures. There's a chance he could lose us if he nabs your brother. I doubt he completely trusts me and I'm sure he has no intentions of ever paying me that ten percent."

"But if he quits his agency and comes here—what then?"

"Then it's your problem, son. I can alert law enforcement where you are. But that's about all I can do. He's not committed a crime in California so I couldn't extradite."

"Well, my brother by another mother, I really appreciate what you've done. I owe ya."

"Hey, we grew up together, we're old teammates. It's a personal thing—I don't want to see anything bad happen to the Bradford brothers."

Then he added, "First thing you gotta do, though, is buy those encrypted cell phones. Let me know when you've got them. I'll feel a lot better then. I'll try to find out if Jake knows for sure where you are. I'm going to see if I can chat up Manfred when he's off duty and surfing. He's a surfing fanatic. If I can get him to talk, I'll let you know."

"Thanks so much for everything, Al."

"Watch your brother's back and get an encrypted phone as soon as you can."

I wanted to call Jack immediately but was stopped by the realization that Jake, using Manfred, might pick up the call. I thought of emailing him, but emails are easier to snoop than phone calls. So what I did was go online and buy two encrypted Nokia cell phones and have them both overnight Federal Expressed to each of us. I'd have bought a third for Lola but did not know her address. When my brother gets delivery, I'm sure he'll put two and two together and know why I bought them.

Laura called around 6 o'clock from her car to say she was on her way here to pick me up for dinner in about half an hour. I checked my mood. I seemed to be breezing along without any hint of the dark storm of depression looming, despite all the excitement. Not too high, not too low. Grooving as the princely son of King Midas.

Since I had a few minutes before Laura would arrive, I called Dr. Mary Grace, and told her a greatly reduced version of what was happening. She called my depression *The Monster*, and asked if I felt it was creeping up on me. I said it threatened when the cop hassled me for walking the boardwalk late at night. She wanted to know all about that, but I had to put off going into it now, I said, because I was about to go out to dinner with my lady friend. Ah ha, she said, a loving mate can be the best medicine, if she understands your disease. I deferred telling Dr. Grace that I wasn't sure if Laura and I would ever feel truly mated, as her reality was far removed from the horrors of mental illness. I signed off by saying I was having a fun affair, nothing more.

I did a quick Silva Mind Method imaging of myself cool, calm, unthreatened by a relapse, and felt ready to meet Laura.

Chapter 23

When I got home from the long day of driving up to Silicon Valley, attending that board meeting and driving home again, it was after midnight and I was exhausted, but I forced myself to go for a brief walk around the property to see which security people might be here tonight. I could find no trace of any of them. I suppose Valance's explanation—if he's still here—would be that they had returned to their regular routine. It was too much to even hope that he'd departed for his next assignment and I'd seen the last of him.

I slept late the next morning. When I came downstairs around 10, Alicia handed me a package and said, "Fed Ex delivery." It was an encrypted cell phone. Sent by my brother, I discovered in a gift note. I was about to call and ask him what this was all about when it dawned on me—regular cell phone conversations can be plucked out of the ether by those with the know-how. Chances are, Valance had connections to people with the know-how. I silently thanked my brother for his thoughtfulness. I also realized, in a flash, that I'd been using encrypted cell phones for company business for years, yet when it came to my own personal business, I'd been using regular wireless. This oneness identification with the company must change as I transition into retirement. The company is well protected. I'm not. I'm reminded how brother Bob must have felt sitting on a curb in downtown San Francisco, alone and unprotected.

I sat down and went through the instructions and finally got the new cell phone working and called Bob. First words out of his mouth were, "Are you on your new phone?"

"Yes, I am, thanks."

"Al told me Valance has a tech guy who can monitor regular cell phone conversations. Doesn't know how much of ours he's picked up. That is, Al doesn't know if Valance knows that I'm in Rehoboth and that you plan to come here too. Depending on what Valance knows, we may have a new set of problems."

"Maybe the best thing for me to do now is hire a new security guard to protect me from my old security guard. Like with lawyers. You hire one lawyer to do the job and a second lawyer to make sure the first doesn't cheat you."

"Jesus, John, what a country this has become."

"It's been that way forever, Robert, and it's all around the world...although, I agree, it has definitely gotten worse, at least for you and me. I spoke with my CEO yesterday afternoon—he'd been told about my call to the security agency headquarters and was concerned, wanted to know more. He'd been told that I'd moved my brother out of an insane asylum and into my home, and that I'd also moved a hooker in as well. I told him that the young lady was a niece, a university student visiting California, and that Valance had called her a hooker out of some twisted, perverse perception of his own. I told him you'd been in a private psychiatric facility but were fine now, and I was helping you get back on your feet. I told him your problem had been alcoholism—Jim Hurly understands alcoholism—but you were now completely recovered."

"No one completely recovers. I'm in remission. But why would any of this be your CEO's business?"

"Because Valance told his people about you and Lola. Someone at the agency called Jim to pass on the nasty rumors. Years ago, he would have shrugged them off. In today's social climate, he felt he needed to check them out. What I said put his mind at ease."

"What did you tell him about Valance?"

"I told him Valance invented these false rumors and that I had to get rid of him because he had become overbearing and intrusive. I did not go into all the gory details. Didn't want to upset Jim. He's got a security detail assigned to his home in Connecticut. I wanted to minimize the whole sordid flap and move on. Now, tell me, what did Al have to say?"

"He verified that we'd read Jake's motives correctly. Al gained his confidence and Jake told him his plan to hold you hostage and demand ten million dollars. He offered Al ten percent."

"Why the hell doesn't Al arrest the bastard?"

"Can't arrest him till he commits a crime."

"Isn't conspiracy to commit a crime enough?"

"Jake could deny it. He has to kidnap you for there to be a crime. Al says the Sheriff's Department would rather see Jake gone from their jurisdiction, so they are hoping his transfer will be the end of it."

"Do you think transferring Jake will be the end of it?"

"I don't know. I doubt it."

"So do I. Anyhow, I don't have another board meeting for a couple of months, so I want to use that time to move out of here. You say the condo is in a gated community?"

"The gate faces the highway. No one can drive in from that direction without a key. But there's no protection from the beach side. The beach is public so anyone can walk to the house from the beach."

"When you were there, did you see anyone on the beach"

"Not a soul. This is the most deserted month of the year. Most of the houses along the beach are empty, waiting for summer. Few people live here year round."

"I'm going to bring Lola, and I'm assuming we'll all three live there, right?"

That caused Bob to stammer a bit. Turns out he and Laura have talked about living together, and she hates the idea of me being within a hundred miles of her. That she was still unforgiving felt like a kick in the gut. Was there nowhere I could go to find convivial company in my semi-retirement? I'll be traveling now and then for board meetings—what will Lola do while I'm away? Of course, without Jake draped around my neck, I can take Lola with me on my travels, although that would be pushing my luck—if any business associates spotted us together, I'd have more explaining to do. My niece story will take me only so far.

I began to wonder if, in my quest to end the loneliness, I'd jumped from the frying pan into the fire. I'd spent most of a lifetime building a sterling business reputation, giving no one any reason to question my character or doubt my word. Now here I was caught in a web of lies and half-truths, all because I wanted to be with a younger woman who'd made her living as a high-class call girl. And there was Bob. I'd come to see him as less crazy than a lot of the people I knew, people I now feared could destroy my reputation with a whisper campaign launched by Valance.

In the old days, there'd been business tycoons who'd lived more bohemian than the most outrageous artists, and nobody had batted an eye. A man's personal business was just that, nobody else's business. Since the Clinton-Lewinsky affair in the White House, followed by a rash of revelations about numerous Republican politicians whose behavior had been even trashier, on top of the panic of nine-eleven, there had arisen this puritanical urge to judge everyone's morality. In the mood of this time, the early months of 2008, with the real estate market's collapse and collateral damage to other sectors of the financial community, the economy sinking into what could become a protracted recession, people were resorting to a holier-than-thou attitude. It was like everyone lived in a glass house and threw stones at the glass houses of everyone else, thinking this would save their own glass house. For these idiots to destroy my reputation because of Bob's mental problems and Lola's age and previous occupation struck me as insane. Yet it's the weapon Jake Valance holds over my head.

Bob and I had both been silent while these thoughts rushed through my mind. Here we were on a secure connection, and silent. "Bob," I said, "I feel tempted to kill that son of a bitch."

"Jake?"

"Who else? Do you know where we could hire a professional to do the job?"

"Are you serious, Jack?"

"I'm giving it serious consideration. I am bone-weary of him threatening me. It seems I cannot turn to law enforcement people for help—unless or until Valance commits the crime, and that could be too late. If I stay here, I fear he'll do me harm, and if I move, he may follow and do me harm. Know anyone we could pay to end that?"

"Let me sleep on it, John."

"Do you understand how I feel?"

"Oh yes."

"I either wait for this bastard to make his move—and then it may be too late—or I take preemptive action and get rid of the threat."

"I'll sleep on it. And I'd like to find out the latest from Al. He may have learned things since we last spoke."

I said goodbye to Bob and simultaneously decided to change my will so that in the event of my untimely demise, he would be provided for.

I was about to call Herby Stein's office number and leave a message on his machine to get the ball rolling. This was Sunday so he'd be home. I won't bother him at home. As I started to dial his office number to leave a message he'd get Monday, the door chimes sounded. I was upstairs in my bedroom. I moved to the front window and looked down. The big black Chevy van was parked in the driveway. I caught a glimpse of Jake Valance's crew cut hair. He was standing at my front door. My heart raced as I pondered what to do. My father used to say, "When in doubt, procrastinate."

I went back to the bedroom, checked my old cell phone for the number of the Sheriff's Department and called on the encrypted phone.

"Is Officer Al Hansen there?"

"He's not in the office right now. Can I take a message?" asked a female voice.

"This is John Bradford. I've been having a nasty disagreement with the head of security assigned to protect my property, and I'm feeling threatened by this guy, and he's just come to my front door.

Unexpectedly. I don't feel safe answering the door. Would you please send someone out here to help resolve this?"

She seemed to know something about my situation, for her tone suddenly took on urgency. "Yes, sir, Mr. Bradford, we'll get someone there as soon as possible. I believe Al Hansen may be in your area as we speak and if he is, we'll dispatch him."

"Thank you."

"What's this person at your front door doing, exactly?"

"Waiting for me to open the door."

"But you're fearful of doing that?"

"I have reason to believe he means to do me harm. I don't want him showing up like this. He's been transferred and has no business here. I don't have anything to say to him and no longer believe anything he tells me."

"Okay, hang on. We just located Deputy Hansen and he's on his way. Would you like to stay on the line till he arrives?"

"Yes, I would."

Chapter 24

Sunday afternoon, as Laura and I were inspecting the work done on her house so far, and I was making notes concerning what had been missed or needed to be redone, I got a call from John, using his new encrypted phone. As we talked, I strolled away from Laura. She surmised who was on the line when I asked if he was using his new encrypted phone and shot me a glowering glance.

The upshot of our talk was that John was feeling at the end of his rope and talking about hiring someone to kill Jake Valance. He asked if I knew who he might get to do the job. I empathized with how he was feeling but it irked me that he thought I might know a profes-sional killer or two, just as he'd previously assumed I knew something about blackmail. Well, I'd known guys in San Quentin who had no qualms about killing anyone, but after seven years in Covington, I had no connection to such people.

I told Jack I'd sleep on it and get back to him tomorrow. It dazed me when my brother mentioned hiring a professional killer. Was he serious? Or was he momentarily over the edge? There had to be another way to remove Valance as a threat. A contract killer could come back to haunt us.

By the time this call ended, I was under Laura's house, leaning against her Lexus. I could hear her up in the kitchen making us a light lunch. Mom used to tell us to never eat the food of an angry cook, but I would make an exception. I felt trapped between Laura's resent-ment and John's desperation, and although I could empathize with both, I felt tempted to take off walking up the road and not stop till I'd found my way back to Covington. But this is normal life, I told myself. Normal people behave like this. Hold your mud and deal with it. Demonstrate that you can function in the real world.

There are two sets of stairways up from her garage, the steel stairway outside the house that brings you up near the kitchen, and a carpeted inner stairway that leads to the living room. I opened the door to the living room and called up, "Are you making lunch?"

"Yes. Are you done talking to your brother?"

"Yes, and I want to call someone else before I come up."

"Soup and salad await you. You really don't have to hide out when you make these calls, you know."

"I don't want to bother you with all the stuff that's happening in California, honey."

"As long as it stays in California, it's no bother to me."

Didn't she know that her ex-husband was bringing it from Santa Barbara to Rehoboth Beach?

Before I dialed Al's number, I took a moment to think through what I wanted to ask him, and what I did not want to tell him—that brother John had mentioned killing Jake Valance. "Hi, Al. I'm calling on my new encrypted cell phone," I said.

"I'm glad to hear you got it, Bob. Does your brother have one too?"

"Fed-exed to him today. I just finished speaking with him. He's getting kind of overwrought about this threat from Jake. He's got me a little worried."

"It's a worrisome situation. I found out another piece of information. I think you'll be happy to hear that Valance doesn't know where you are."

"Man, that's a relief."

"That doesn't mean he won't find out."

"How?"

"Various ways. Are you using a credit card?"

"Yeah, I'm a co-card holder on John's American Express."

"Well, that's a giveaway. Jake can find that out without much trouble and figure out that John must be headed to where your credit card charges are."

"I don't want to tell John that. He's already upset."

"What kind of upset?"

"He sees no end to this, no way to get rid of Jake as a threat."

"Well, Jake will soon be moving on. He's been reassigned to New Orleans. He's complaining that he'll have to put things in storage because he doesn't want to move all his stuff to New Orleans. He's got to fly down there and get himself an apartment, and he's not happy about that either, because New Orleans is still mostly a toxic junk pile left by Hurricane Katrina. All the money the federal government is spending to rebuild Iraq and Afghanistan, you'd think they'd spend some to rebuild New Orleans."

I thought of what Jorge Hernandez had explained about modern war and said, "Those so-called wars are just another form of corporate welfare. Getting back to business, once Jake's in New Orleans, you think he'll forget about John?"

"Hard to predict. He's got that ten million dollars in mind and seems to believe he can pull it off. Anyhow, his company will probably give him a week or two to make the move and get resettled. So he's not out of our hair yet."

"Do you know when he leaves?"

"No, but he's already been replaced here. The security company sent a new guy in to take charge. I haven't met him yet. I'll kind of miss old Jake and his horror stories on poker night. Made a teenage daughter give him a blowjob while he had his gun stuck down the father's throat, pulled the trigger when he came. More gruesome than primetime TV, Jake's stories."

"Why the hell isn't he doing hard time in prison, Al?"

"He should be, that's for sure. He's a rogue cop that's gotten away with murder. In my book, that's the worst kind of criminal there is. Hold on a minute."

I heard Al's car radio blast out something but could not decipher it from the blur of background noise.

"Got a call that someone is at your brother's front door. It must be Jake. This may be show time. I'll call you later."

"Could you leave your phone on?" I asked, but too late, he'd hung up. I dialed John but got an outgoing message. Had he turned off his phone? Gone away? Or did my call get diverted because he was on the line with someone else? All I could do was wait for a call back.

Laura had made something like a Greek salad, lots of olives and several kinds of cheese, and warmed a can of vegetable soup. As we ate, I stared out at the ocean lost in thought. "Are you your brother's keeper?" she asked in her slow contralto.

"We've become each other's keepers."

"You are so very different from him, I wish I could pry you away."

"We are very different. He's a huge success in life and I'm a total failure."

"I don't believe that for a minute."

"Well, it's true. And I'm learning the meaning of that old saying, blood is thicker than water."

"I wouldn't know. I'm an only child. What's going on out there?"

The phrase "out there" triggered memories. Inside lockups, everyone wants to know what's going on "out there." I broke out in a sweat and my hand trembled as I spooned the soup. Laura became suddenly concerned. "Are you okay, sweetheart?"

"I'm worried about Jack. Would you please drive me back to the hotel? I need to make a few calls."

"I will if you insist, but you can make them from here."

"Laura, I know how you feel about Jack and don't want to bother you with his problems by making the calls from here."

"Is there some kind of emergency out there?"

I was tempted to blurt out that life "out there" seemed to be nothing but emergencies, compared to Covington and its drug-mellowed crazies. I said, "That's what I need to find out."

"Bob, honey, I'm sorry about John, but I don't want him to come between us. Whatever it is you're upset about, I want to be with you and help any way I can."

That momentarily confused me, given what she'd told me at the Nantucket, but before I could respond, my phone chirped and it was Al.

"What's happening?" I said.

"The EM's are coming. Jake hit him with a tire iron. I took Jake down with a shot to the knee. I got him cuffed and I'm taking him in as soon as the medics get here. I'm not sure how bad John's head wound is, Bob. He's knocked out cold but breathing. I'll call you in an hour or so, after the dust settles."

What irony, I thought as I clapped the phone shut. I get a concussion when a cop hits me for being homeless, and now a crook hits John for being a multimillionaire and may have given him a concussion.

"Can you share with me?" said Laura.

"John's been injured. Not yet sure how serious. I'll give it an hour and call Cottage Hospital in Santa Barbara. That's most likely where they'll take him."

I got up and paced. Laura got up and cleared the table, loaded the dishwasher.

"Was he in an auto accident?" she asked.

"No. Someone came into his house and—"

How could I explain all this to her? Knowing how much she still despised John, I really didn't want to tell her anything. She was staring at me with an expression of keen concern, but what was she feeling inwardly? Was she secretly happy that this man she hated had suffered? What was I doing here, caught between love for my wounded brother and love for this ex-wife who hates him so? What kind of Gordian knot of loves is this?

"And what?" said Laura.

"Huh?"

"You said someone came into his house. What happened?"

"He hit John on the head with a tire iron. He's on his way to the hospital now. I'll need to go back there and take care of him."

"Who hit him? Who did you learn this from?"

"An officer with the Sheriff's Department, Al Hanson. Al arrested John's security guard. Now he can charge him with a crime. But how long a sentence will he get?"

Laura was staring at me, wide eyed and open mouthed. She didn't know these people. I felt a new charge of love for this pretty, tender, sensitive face, this woman who was, without being aware of it, helping me make the Rip Van Winkle transition. I wrapped her in my arms and held her. I'd tell her the whole story now. There was no reason to withhold anything. If it made her secretly happy to learn of John's misfortune, we'd deal with it later.

Jake Valance

Jake had found Santa Barbara very much to his liking. And why not? It seemed to have more millionaires per acre than anywhere else he'd been. If he could figure out a way to shake a few million loose from a client or two, his own life would be greatly enhanced.

The only irksome thing about his new duty was John Bradford's attitude. The man was such a snob. And, Jake had to admit to himself, intimidating. Everyone seemed to admire him for his wealth and intelligence. As Jake got to know more about the man, he decided Bradford was lacking in street smarts. Why else would he live like a recluse? When he was home at his house on Padero Lane, he rarely went out to socialize. Jake could count on one hand the times Bradford had gone to parties. He didn't seem to have any men friends in town. He didn't even play golf. He holed up in that huge, splendiferous house of his and stuck to a Spartan routine. Went out to jog every morning, worked out in his home gym, then spent hours on his laptop, husbanding his investments.

It was when Jake learned from his staff that Bradford had dates with call girls that his juices began to flow. Bradford kept a room at the Santa Barbara Biltmore Hotel for these trysts. One of his men told him that Bradford's favorite girl was a 22-year-old beauty who kept her skin tanned and wore clothes that were expensive and sexy. This, thought Jake, was something he'd have to look into.

One late afternoon when he knew Bradford had a date, he stationed himself in the Biltmore parking lot so he could check out this girl for himself. He watched her arrive in her BMW two-seater and strut her stuff through the hotel's front entrance, her blouse stretched by her perfect tits and her mid-thigh skirt riding high on her derriere. "Damn," he said to himself as he sat in his car, "that bitch is an instant hard-on." And, he thought to himself, she could be a super highway to a piece of Bradford's millions. He fantasized partnering up with this whore, using her to make a killing. He imagined her fawning over him when he enlisted her help to shake down Bradford. Taking a john for a quick million—that's sure to get this whore's juices flowing. If he found her compatible, maybe he'd bring her to Costa Rica after they scored.

Bradford had made it known to Jake that his security duties did not extend past the hotel's entrance. "I'm certainly in no danger inside the Biltmore," John had told him, "so you keep your people outside. Understood?" So after the whore disappeared into the hotel, Jake drove his Chevy Malibu out of the parking lot and cruised awhile, pleasant scenarios playing in his mind.

Then one morning, John Bradford drove to Camarillo and picked up his brother, who was being discharged from a nut house there. A private, very expensive nut house. This brother, Robert, looked like a homeless person who'd been panhandling—until John took him shopping and bought him new clothes. Jake was so intrigued by this new development that he personally tracked the pair when they left the house on Padero Lane, for he was curious to find out more. When other members of his unit monitored the brothers, Jake kept in close communication and wanted to know all the details, where they went, what they did. Between this bodacious, super-sexy bitch and this scarecrow-skinny, nut-house brother, Jake figured he would find the key to his very own treasure island.

One day Bradford informed Jake that he was about to see his brother off at LAX. He didn't say where the brother was going or why. Jake was curious but didn't ask. The agency was not obliged to protect the brother when he left John's house.

The day after that—even before Jake had had a chance to learn her name—Bradford suddenly arrived home with his favorite call girl following in her car. Jake happened to be cruising nearby and when he got the word that the girl was following Bradford home, he stomped on it and was there to greet them when they arrived. Bradford introduced her as Lola and said she was going to be his personal assistant.

That was outlandish enough but the next thing Jake knew, the girl was living in Bradford's house.

This aroused Jake with passions stronger than he'd felt in a long, long time, for Bradford had suddenly overstepped the line and, like a deer peeking out through woodsy foliage, was ripe for the kill, with his luscious girlfriend ripe for the plucking. Jake knew from his years in the New York metro area that any corporate executive who flaunts his relationship with a prostitute is in big trouble with his peers. Jake figured he now had this arrogant son of a bitch by the balls. All he needed was some hard evidence.

He scrapped the idea of partnering up with this whore, for the time being, and bought a small digital camera and waited for the right opportunity, which arose one sunny afternoon when he cruised by the Bradford house, intending to stop by and just say hello. When he turned off the engine of the Chevy van, he heard laughter coming from the pool area, down stone steps along the right side of the house. From the top of this set of flat stones down to the pool, he saw Bradford and the girl in the pool, rubbing their nude bodies together. He quickly pulled the camera out of his pocket and snapped a photo. He knew that shot wouldn't show much. His camera didn't have a telescopic lens and the pool was forty or fifty yards away. He wouldn't know how effective the shot was till he cropped and enlarged it on his computer.

Jake stayed out of their sight around the corner of the house, sneaking a peek every now and then. Presently, the pair emerged from the pool, naked, and stood drying themselves with large towels. Jake snapped another photo, catching both in nude profile. He got back in the van and drove on. He knew that second shot, cropped and enlarged on his computer, would clearly show John Bradford consorting with a naked young beauty beside his home swimming pool with the beach and sea in the background.

He asked around, trying to figure out what Bradford was worth. No one seemed to know precisely. "He's a multimillionaire," was the word on the street. "Don't let his simple lifestyle fool you," one elderly gent told Jake, "John Bradford is probably the wealthiest man in Santa Barbara." Jake decided that ten million would set him up for life, and be chump change to Bradford.

Jake found himself daydreaming of living in Costa Rica. He'd found that country his favorite place to vacation. He'd bought a small bungalow there. It had fabulous beaches, delicious food, modern hotels and houses to rent or buy, retired cops and military guys to play poker with, and gorgeous girls willing to do anything for a few dollars. If he could get about ten million of Bradford's fortune, he reasoned, he could buy a beachfront hotel for income and status in the community, retire to a luxurious beach house in his mid-forties, and live happily ever after—a lot happier than if he went on working till he was a decrepit old sixty-five. Jake's new sex fantasy became doing Bradford's girlfriend Lola while Bradford, bound and gagged, watched. First he would make Lola give him a tongue bath from the bottom of his feet, up his legs and over his chest and back, into the crack of his ass, lick his balls and then put her mouth over his cock. She would work it slowly, very slowly, making it last, building up the tension magnificently, and then he would stand her in front of Bradford's face while he fucked her from behind standing up, and finally he would pull out and come in Bradford's face, right in his wide-open, shocked eyes.

The question was, how to go about persuading John Bradford that he had to pay ten million dollars, or be exposed to his colleagues, who would shun him for his gross impropriety. Jake wanted to go about collecting this tribute as suavely as Bradford went about disdaining him.

As things developed, Bradford was sharp enough to read the writing on the wall. That became clear by his radical change of attitude. The man now knew he was vulnerable and his change of attitude was so ego boosting to Jake that he was tempted to move himself into the man's house and get the ball rolling as soon as possible.

Maybe he could live out his favorite fantasy by just letting John Bradford know he had no other choice, for the man was definitely quick on the uptake. When Bradford left for a trip and Jake stationed himself in the house, hoping to get acquainted with Lola, it didn't work. Lola looked at him like he was dog shit on the living room carpet, and avoided him all day. When Bradford arrived home—with sweat breaking out on his forehead and hands shaking—he ordered Jake out of his house and off his property. Then, as suddenly as she'd arrived, Lola disappeared, moved out, and was there no longer. Bradford's brother was gone, too, off on another trip. Okay, Jake decided, this was a chance to develop his plan in more detail.

A member of his weekly poker group, a big black dude named Al Hansen, asked him out for a drink after the last game, which had ended early, around eleven when Jake had pocketed everyone's weekly stake in Texas Hold 'Em. They'd gone to a noisy bar in downtown Santa Barbara, and hoisted a few. African Americans were not among Jake's favorite people, but Al was different. And he worked for the county sheriff's department, which meant he could be useful.

As they kicked back with vodka highballs and eyeballed the local ladies in the bar, Jake brought up the subject of John Bradford. "You know him?"

"Yeah, I know him," said Al, turning away with a look of distaste.

"What's your make?"

"He flaunts it, his money and his girlfriend. And why did he take his crazy brother out of the nuthouse and bring him home? I think he's a moral degenerate. Is he going to get his brother to help him keep his bitch well fucked? If I had my druthers I'd kick his ass. He's just another Santa Barbara trust fund baby. If it weren't for the fortune he inherited, he'd be pathetic. I don't like anything about the Bradfords."

"Man, Al, you're big enough that if you kicked his ass, it sure would stay kicked."

"Why you ask? You got kicking his ass in mind?"

"Something like that. You know he moved his crazy brother into his guesthouse, right?"

"Yeah. I know Bob Bradford. We graduated high school together."

"Do you know anything about that prostitute he moved into his house?"

"I don't even know her name."

"Her name's Lola. What I'm getting at, partner, is a man in John Bradford's position just doesn't do a thing like that, move a whore into his house, unless he's asking for trouble. If his corporate friends found out about it, what do you think they'd do?"

Al's face lit up in a big toothy smile and he said, "Man, they'd fry his ass. They'd ostracize him, take away everything they could from him."

"What if we were to save Bradford from such a fate?"

"What you got in mind?"

"Well, his people back in New York ain't gonna find out anything about this bitch unless someone tells them, and that someone is me, because it's my job to keep tabs on the man."

Al grins and says, "Looks like you got him by the short hairs, partner. Go for it."

"I'd like to but I need help. Interested?"

"What's the deal?"

"I get ten million out of him for keeping his secret, and you get ten percent for helping me. It's not something I can do alone."

"Right," said Al. "You can't just walk up to him and hold out your hand and say pay or else."

"Right. What I'll need to do, I figure, is get him off by himself. Just me and him and this Lola bitch. Well, he's sent her away now and I don't know if she'll be back. I suspect she'll be back because they were really tight, but maybe it'll just be me and him."

"You don't think you could find out where Lola went?"

"Sure I could, but he's the one with the money and I don't want to spread myself too thin. I got to keep my eye on the ball. With the money I get out of Bradford, I can buy bitches like her by the dozen."

"But if she's no longer living with him, what's your leverage?"

"I got photos of them together in the nude by his pool."

"Okay, second question. Where you going to deposit ten million in cash without answering a lot of questions? And do you really think you can take ten million from Bradford and let him go? Hell, he'll sic the law on your ass bigtime."

"See, Al, that's where you earn your ten percent. You're the law around here. You get my drift?

"Not yet, but keep talking."

"Say I grab Bradford and take him away for, like, a vacation. I'll need time alone with him to get him to come up with the cash. If you can divert local law enforcement when I return him, send 'em down the wrong trail, whatever it takes, I have connections south of the border that will enable me to convert that cash to legit securities. So, what do you think Bradford will do when I return him ten million lighter?"

"He'll call my office and charge you with kidnapping and extortion. He'll call the FBI, too. He'll get photos of you from your employer and insist that we all launch a massive manhunt."

"Ah, but suppose you can make Bradford's vacation look like it has no connection to me and the ten million?"

"Then he could have a hard time making his case," said Al. "He'd have to get the cash out of a secret account outside this country, an account the Feds can't access the records of. You'd make sure of that, right, Jake?"

"Right. See? All you gotta do is make sure Bradford doesn't come up with the kind of evidence that would start a manhunt. You get what I'm saying?"

"While you do what? Where you gonna go with the ten million? How am I gonna collect my payoff?"

"I go into retirement. Best you not even know where. After a month or two, maybe four or six, I send you one million cash by personal courier."

"How long after?"

"Once we know Bradford can't sic the cops on me. How long will that be?"

"You play it right, Jake, and Bradford won't have much, if anything, to bring to law enforcement. Why do you need me?"

"In case he tries to bring something, anything. I need you to do whatever it takes to nullify that evidence. If he files a complaint, then you need to dig up that he's been away on vacation and may be trying to run an insurance fraud. Whatever he tries, you put the blocks to it."

Al said he was very interested but he'd have to think about it. He'd have to know more specifics of Jake's plan before he could figure out his end. Jake said that made sense to him and suggested they go out for a drink again tomorrow night.

The next night, at another bar, Jake told Al his plan A was to nab Bradford on one of his trips, hold him till he produced the ten million in cash. Maybe Jake would resign from the agency before Bradford is snatched, or resign because Bradford's disappearance had occurred on his watch. Either way, Bradford's company would not be involved—no ransom from them would be demanded. It would be strictly a personal affair. Jake would tell Bradford, "Ten million or your life, sucker," take the cash and disappear into retirement. Jake said he knew a security guy back in New York who'd pulled off a caper just like this and was God-only-knows, living high on the hog. A gentleman of means isn't inclined to scream about losing a small portion of his fortune, Jake said, especially when he has a record of messing around with young girls. If Lola comes back to Bradford's house, then they take this "vacation" together, which makes it impossible for Bradford to raise a ruckus. "What's he gonna say? That he and his missy went off for a vacation and he came back ten million lighter? I can hear the laughter already."

Jake said that if it goes down this way, Al's main job will be to find evidence that the security unit had used due diligence and that it was Bradford's lack of cooperation that got him snatched. Since he wouldn't tell them where he was going, they could not go there with him and protect him. Al said he loved this idea and they high-fived to seal the deal.

But at 6 o'clock the next morning, Jake was awakened by his landline phone's loud ringing, and his boss back in New York telling him that Bradford had called to complain and demand that Jake be removed from service in Santa Barbara, or he'd have his company switch to another security firm. As Bradford's corporation was their best account, Jake was told he was being transferred to New Orleans. "We know this isn't really your fault, Jake," his boss had cooed, "but we have no choice. We can't afford to lose this account."

Jake was shocked and furious, and blurted out that Bradford had moved his insane brother and a young prostitute into his house, and Jake had told Bradford the agency was not under any obligation to protect either of them, and that's why Bradford got on his high horse and called New York. His boss said it didn't matter why Bradford wanted Jake gone, they couldn't afford to lose the account. His replacement was on his way and would take over the unit tomorrow. Goodbye.

For about an hour Jake sat, stunned, staring out his bedroom window at the tops of palm trees, wondering what to do next. He couldn't just walk away from this golden opportunity—yet what choice did he have? For now, keeping his job was priority number one. But this wasn't the end of it, he vowed. He'd figure out something. Either he'd offer Bradford the deal, your money or your life, before he left town, or he'd go to this new assignment and work out a new plan, one he could do long distance.

Jake didn't have much to pack. He'd rented the condo furnished. His company would send a letter explaining that he'd broken the lease because he'd been transferred. For a while, he felt sorry for himself as he packed. "I'm nothing but a god-damned lonely itinerant cop, no home, no family, nothing but my clothes and car." He had lost track of his brothers and sisters. His mother had died while he was in Newark but he'd not taken time off to attend to her burial. What was the point? They'll put her in the ground and forget about her, he reasoned, and they'll do the same to me when my time comes.

He took his time carrying his clothes and other personal possessions down from his second floor condo and loading them into his personal Chevy Malibu. Although he worked out at Gold's Gym, he also kept a personal set of dumbbells at home and when he stacked them behind the front seat, the car sagged on its springs. He was so angry, he contemplated using the agency van to move to New Orleans. He could later tell them he thought that was permissible, given the circumstances. But then he'd have to drive back here to get his car. Four trips. He took the set of dumbbells out of his car and left them on the front lawn. He then drove to the parking lot where the agency van was kept, parked his loaded car, got behind the wheel of the van, and headed for Bradford's house. He stopped along the way to down a couple of Tequilas. He wasn't sure what he was going to say or do when he got to Bradford's house but he could not leave town without paying that snotty son of a bitch one last visit.

He knew Bradford was home but the man refused to answer his door, adding further insult. Jake yelled through the door a few times, trying to get a peep out of Bradford. Nothing. Well, he thought, he could not leave it like this. He went to the van and got out the tire iron and pried open Bradford's front door, knowing as he did so that it was setting off security alarms, bringing the nearest cop to the scene. He had only a few minutes before he'd have to get the hell gone. Bradford wasn't downstairs so Jake hurried upstairs and, finding the door to the master bedroom locked, pried it open with the tire iron.

Bradford stood in the middle of the room holding a chair, ready to use it as a weapon. Jake laughed. He faked a sudden move toward Bradford and that got the chair flung at him. He sidestepped the flying chair and came at Bradford with the tire iron. "Give me ten million dollars in cash, you cocksucker, or I'll take your head off," he bellowed. He found Bradford surprisingly nimble—or had he had one too many Tequilas? Bradford managed to duck and dodge Jake's first few swings of the tire iron, but eventually he connected with Bradford's head and knocked him unconscious with one blow. He had the tire iron raised above his head in preparation for venting his rage with more blows when, simultaneously, his right knee buckled and he heard an explosion.

Looking up from the floor, he found Al Hansen leaning over John Bradford, testing for a pulse and speaking to someone by cell phone. "Send an ambulance," Al said calmly. "John's alive but unconscious." Then he glanced at Jake and added, "Send two ambulances, one for the perp."

Chapter 25

I could feel that we were moving and caught sight through a window of passing trees, heard traffic noise, but I had temporarily lost all recollection of the confrontation with Valance. One of the medics waved a hand in front of my face and asked me how many fingers I saw, and I could not focus well enough to be sure. I knew I was bleeding profusely, for they were using towels to soak up the blood. I was well aware of that. But for the first few hours in the emergency room I wasn't sure where I was, nor exactly what had happened.

I began to come back to my senses when Dr. Ray Rici arrived. I know Ray from social occasions and was glad to see a familiar face. He asked me what seemed like an endless string of questions, mainly trying to gauge how serious the blow had been. Gradually, I recalled the battle with Valance, piece by piece, and tried my best to give Ray cogent answers. He said his concern was brain damage. I felt as though I couldn't think straight, couldn't put a logical string of thoughts together, and that was frightening. Ray soothed my fears by saying a period of disorientation was to be expected in such a case as mine.

I guess Ray or one of the nurses gave me a knock-out shot because the next thing I knew I was staring out a hospital window at a bright sunny day and Ray was back, asking more questions, and telling me that a CAT scan had showed a clot of blood between the inside of my skull and the brain casing. I reached up to feel my head, not sure what part of my skull he was talking about, and he gently guided my arm back down to my side and said that they were going to keep me relaxed and do another CAT scan soon. If the clot didn't dissipate, he said, he'd have to operate to remove it.

Imagining surgeons opening my skull to remove that blood clot had me feeling helpless and hopeless, and reminded me of the tales brother Bob had told about the after-effects of his head traumas. Dad had been a good, church-going Catholic who'd tried to raise his sons in that tradition but Bob had rebelled early, around age 12, and I had drifted away from the Church when I went away to Harvard. I was tempted to ring for the nurse and request a priest, but the idea of becoming a deathbed convert made me feel even more hopeless. Did I really believe in a Heaven and Hell? No, not really. What did I believe in? Medical technology. If Dr. Rici and his staff can't bring me through this alive, what do I face? Oblivion? Nothingness? But if that's the larger truth—that death is the end of every bit of us—why do so many human beings believe in some kind of after-life? Are so many billions of humans just misinformed and stupid? These thoughts thrashing around in my brain brought back the memory of when I was six years old and my big brother held my hand as I walked out to the end of the high diving board and jumped. If Dr. Rici's procedures don't work, will Bob be here to hold my hand as I face the great abyss?

By the second morning, I was coming out of this addled state and could clearly remember the battle with Valance. I remembered that he'd broken down my front door, and I had locked the bedroom door and looked around for a weapon to defend myself with, but all I could find was a heavy antique chair. I'd picked it up and prepared to throw it if he broke into my bedroom, and he did, and I threw the chair but to no avail. He then chased me around the room swinging his tire iron. I managed to make him miss his first few swings but eventually he connected with the top left side of my head and I went out like a light. Ray Rici told me a sheriff's deputy had arrived and brought Valance down with a shot to the leg before he could deliver another blow with his tire iron, and that Valance was now in jail awaiting arraignment.

I said, "What do you think he'll be charged with?"

"Attempted murder, I guess," said Ray. "From what the sheriff's deputy told me, this guy was definitely trying to kill you."

By the second day I was fully aware that brain damage was Ray's overriding concern, and aware of being put through another CAT scan—they told me it was the fourth. I don't remember the others. I wanted to stand up and move around, even get dressed and leave the hospital and go home. Ray and his staff gently discouraged this and kept me prone on the bed. They turned on the little TV set over the bed to distract me and I watched little figures moving about inside a glass box, disconnected from reality.

I think it was late the second day when Robert arrived. When I saw his face hovering above me, I had an instant flashback to another memory of us as kids—we'd been surfing at Jalama Beach and I'd gotten slammed on the sandy bottom by an extra large wave and momentarily stunned. Bob had hauled me out of the surf and onto the beach, and was staring down at me, mouth open, eyes wide. He'd asked if I was okay and I sat up and said, "Sure. What's the problem?" I got to my feet and grabbed my surfboard and was forcing myself to head out to catch another wave. Bob laughed and went with me. As we paddled out he must have seen that I was not quite right, for he said, "Hey Jack, let's go home." We'd shoved our boards into the back of Mom's station wagon and by the time we got back to town, I was feeling fine. Over dinner, Bob told the story of how I'd caught this monster of a wave and he'd had to fish me out of the surf when it rode me instead of me riding it.

"For a conservative executive," he said, "you sure are reckless. If Al Hansen hadn't gotten there in time, you'd be worm food, brother."

"You're much too kind, Robert."

"I damn near lost the only family I have left. How are you feeling?"

"I've been better. Would you do me a favor and call Lola? I'm sure she's wondering why she can't reach me."

"I'll need her number."

"Get the staff to give you my cell phone. It's on my autodials."

The next day Lola arrived. She burst into the room as frisky as a young colt and smothered me with hugs and kisses. Her touch was healing. Her cheeks and hair smelled of wind and sunshine. Her presence was so exhilarating, I wanted to get up and dance. Then I saw Bob's hand. He was standing behind Lola, holding his hand up like a traffic cop, telling me to stop. I lay back down. Lola made jokes about my head bandage, saying I might be mistaken for a Muslim terrorist. The two of them pulled chairs close to my bed and we made light conversation for a while, then I suddenly felt exhausted and needed to close my eyes and sleep. I had a quick dream of Lola, pressing her gorgeous body against mine and me asking her what in the hell she saw in an old geezer like me, and her saying, or indicating, she didn't know, she just loved me, wanted to have sex, and me feeling that she would eventually meet someone else who attracted her and leave me. In the dream that didn't bother me. While she was with me, I told her, I would thoroughly enjoy her. She turned her body this way and that, striking poses, indicating she was turned on by my admiration of her beauty.

When I woke up half an hour later, Bob and Lola were gone. But my cell phone was on the table beside my bed. I called her. She was driving the 101 going home. I said, "Why didn't you stay a little longer, honey? Sorry I conked out on you."

"You need to rest, my love, and I have a possible renter coming to look at the house. I need to be there."

"Now that Valance is in jail, you can move back to my house any time, my dear. And I want you to come with me when I fly back East to see this condo Robert is buying. On the beach, for us, you and me."

"I need to get my house rented, put my stuff in storage, and then pack my clothes and come to you, and this time never leave. Don't want to be dashing back and forth, you know. Once I'm totally moved out of my house, I'm totally with you, lover. Are you ready for that?"

"More than you'll ever know. My only fear is that you'll make yourself scarce, now that I'm a wounded wreck."

"Not a chance. You're stuck with me till you throw me out."

And so it went, this love chat. I'd never talked this way with any of my wives or girlfriends. But this time, I was determined to give a relationship—this relationship—everything I had. Nothing to lose and a world of joy to gain.

On the third day, Ray came in with a big bright smile and told me there would be no need for surgery, for the blood clot had dissipated. I felt a whole world better by this time, was now sitting up in bed, walking to the bathroom instead of using the bedpan. Ray said I was not entirely out of the woods yet, that we'd need to do extensive follow-ups. I said I needed to fly back East and see my new condo. I told him Bob had just bought a condo on the beach in Bethany and he perked up and told me how he'd grown up in Baltimore and used to go to Bethany for summer vacations. He said he would dismiss me but added, "Go back East if you feel up to it, but don't exert yourself and do keep in touch with me, let me know how you're feeling, especially if you're having odd feelings, disorientation, anything out of the ordinary. Head traumas must be taken seriously. Don't try to do too much. A good time to call me is around six in the evening. If the need arises, I'll get you admitted to Johns Hopkins in Baltimore."

The next day, late afternoon, I was wheel-chaired out of my room and down to the entrance, where Bob met me in the Mercedes. I stood up and looked around at the lengthening shadows, the palm trees swaying in the breeze, the traffic coming and going, people walking here and there, and it all struck me as such a wonder, all these signs of ordinary life, that I shed a tear or two as I climbed into the passenger side and we drove away.

Bob said, "I got both doors replaced."

"Wonderful."

"And I'm ready to fly out of here whenever you are. But, you know, I want to be sure you're up to it. Don't rush things, John. We have the rest of our lives, you know."

He sounded tentative, like he'd been sternly talked to by Dr. Ray Rici. I said, "Big brother, I'm more ready to enjoy life than I've ever been before."

After I'd almost lost my life on that solo sail to Hawaii, I devoted myself to building the company. After this last scrape with death, I was ready to devote myself to love. Loving life, loving Lola, loving Bob. It occurred to me that, for the past three or four decades, I had not loved myself, really. I'd loved my work and the fruits of my labor—the growth of our company, the recognition of my business associates—and I'd stuck to an exercise regimen, kept myself in pretty good shape. I'd enjoyed the sexual favors of beautiful women around the world, but I had never really loved myself, my own physical being. I'd spent most of my life feeling that my big brother occupied his body with joy and grace while I existed inside my physical container like a prisoner waiting for release. That was a mindset I was determined to change. After all, it was the only body I'll ever have this life, and Lola loves it, so why shouldn't I? The next instant, I was doubting Lola's love and then chiding myself for that doubt. If she walks like she loves me, talks like she loves me, and makes love like she loves me, who am I to doubt that she loves me?

Chapter 26

Cottage Hospital kept John for almost a week. They were worried, they said, because the imaging showed a blood clot between his skull and his brain, and that would require brain surgery if it didn't move on and dissipate. It finally did disappear from their imaging screens, and so he was released. I picked him up at the hospital. That was two days ago. He was anxious to see the condo in Bethany so we booked a flight to BWI and here we were, about 30,000 feet above the surface of the earth, with John having a scotch on the rocks and me having freshly-squeezed orange juice. We were in first class but close enough together in seats that seemed to return me to feelings I had when we were teens and used to sit side by side debating loudly, shouting out our points at neutral space rather than at each other, with our parents sitting at either end of the table. Now we spoke in quiet, calm voices. Unlike our teenage selves, we were now able to discuss our political differences without becoming loud and angry. Was that a change in him, or a change in me? Maybe it's because, now that our parents are dead, we no longer act as surrogates for our conservative father and liberal mother. I didn't know for sure.

Dad used to encourage us to engage in "thrust-and-parry" dialogs at the dinner table, with me usually doing the thrusting and John doing the parrying. I would accuse the establishment of taking action that undermined the working class, and John would justify such action as logical and necessary for the greater good. When Fidel Castro's rebels overthrew a Cuban government subservient to the US big money interests, among the reactions taken by the US government was a trade embargo. I would thrust out the argument that this was a self-defeating move because it harmed the Cuban people and made them more supportive of Castro's government. The economic embargo was imposed after the US government had tried to overthrow the Castro regime by various other means, including the Bay of Pigs invasion. John's parry was that the US had been forced to impose this economic embargo, for otherwise other third world countries would follow Castro's example. This would frustrate and anger me, for my allegiance was always to the working people and I could not understand why the US government would harm working people. We were a democracy, weren't we? As a democracy, we were dedicated to the improvement of the working class, weren't we? John would parry that of course we were a democracy, but that the only way to improve the lives of working people was to back the capitalists who invested in productivity. Without such investments, how could the poor have jobs and pull themselves out of poverty? This further enraged me because my perspective was that American capitalists were running the world like mafia dons. Which in turn enraged John because he perceived mafia dons as criminal and the dons of American capitalism as heroic—among the latter being our father, owner of a factory in Ventura that enabled us to grow up rich and privileged.

Now here we were some forty years later, sitting side by side in the first class section of an airliner bound for Baltimore, ages 58 and 60, having essentially the same debate. The details were different, for these were different times, but the essential difference between our two perspectives was the same as it had always been. Since we'd last engaged in such thrust-and-parry debates, I'd become a wretchedly impoverished loony—if it hadn't been for our father's money and influence, I'd still be in San Quentin, or more likely I'd have died there. And little brother John had obtained a Ph D in economics from Harvard and climbed the proverbial corporate ladder to seemingly inexhaustible wealth and power. Yet we had a strange kind of sentimental attachment to the dinner-table debates of our youth, apparently, for we both settled into this present one with the same gusto—but without the rancor and anger of our youth. We quietly and calmly discussed the monetary system like a couple of economics professors sifting through a basketful of theories, in search of one that was universally valid.

I said that Aristotle was right 2,300 years ago when he defined money as a means of exchanging goods and services, and warned that making money reproduce itself for the super rich instead of spread real wealth to all society was ruinous usury. Therefore, I thrust at John, the Federal Reserve System was the core reason why the American Empire was deteriorating and collapsing, after having been extant only since the Reagan Administration, less than 30 years, and despite the US having the mightiest military the world had ever seen. The creation of the Fed, I said, had privatized control of US money without the public knowing. Most Americans believe the government issues our money, when in fact it's the bankers of the Fed, a small, private company of money merchants, who control our money—and thus our government had bestowed this absolute and absolutely corrupting power upon them. The Fed lends money to the government, which socks the taxpayers with the bill at ever-compounding interest. A steady inflation of the dollar has been the finder of interest, enabling the system to go on repaying the bankers of the Fed, as they slowly but surely vampire American society. Jesus had kicked the moneychangers out of the temple, and the US Government had brought them back in.

John parried by saying I'd flunk any university economics course with that notion. The creation of the Fed back in 1913, he said, brought good orderliness to a monetary system that had been chaotic. Moreover, he said, the Fed has become the prototype of every modern central bank in the world, the IMF and World Bank, and the Bank of International Settlements. The Fed was such a success, he said, that when the Nixon Administration ended the gold standard, the dollar replaced gold as the basis of all national currencies. That the creation of the Fed had privatized US money was a huge benefit all around. Do you want politicians controlling our money? They are focused on winning their next elections, and have no knowledge of monetary systems. All they know about money is that they need more of it to mount and win their next campaign to stay in power.

I countered that bankers are now big corporations, which, by law, are obliged to generate as much profit as possible for their shareholders. This profit becomes the national debt, which has reached something like $9 trillion dollars out of a total debt of $54 trillion and growing daily. Adding up all this debt—mortgages, credit cards, cars, etc.—to this ballooning federal government debt, there is no way it can be repaid, because collective income is no longer enough to repay collective debt. Thus, the creation of the Fed has led us to the rapidly sinking dollar, which very well could become totally worthless, as happened in Germany in 1923.

John saw the downturn of the dollar as a magnificent profit opportunity, which I would be well advised to capitalize on, now that I had income—the $80,000 per year he had agreed to pay me for managing his real estate holdings. Instead of forever trying to destroy the established order, he said, I should go with the flow and profit from conditions beyond my control. There was nothing any single individual can do to reverse these macroeconomic trends, so why not profit from them?

I said I couldn't do that because it squeezes too many people between rising prices and shrinking incomes. I couldn't live with myself if I profited from the pain and misery of my countrymen.

Human societies, he said, can be compared to the societies of other primates. It's the alpha males who decide when the herd should move to greener pastures, he said. That's why democracy doesn't work. The people, the herd, are not capable of making such decisions. They follow where the alpha males lead. Our human aristocracy is comparable to those primate alphas, he said.

It seemed to me, I said, that he was conflating aristocracy, plutocracy and oligarchy. I proposed that we could be moving toward a second revolution that may topple the plutocrats and overthrow this system which is still based on beliefs rooted in medieval times.

This would dramatically change society as we now know it, opening up more and better democracy.

John parried by saying society is a kind of organism whose primary motive is to survive, so the new leaders put in power by my precious revolution would soon learn that they must assume the same old roles as those they replaced. In other words, the same old drama repasts. Only the actors, costumes and settings change.

I pointed out that more money is now made by making money reproduce itself than by investing in the production of useful products and services. We must change the system, I said, not just replace the actors in the same old roles. I quoted my friend Dr. Jorge Hernandez—we are now moving into a time of horrendous radical change, very much like the change that swept through the Americas shortly after Columbus ran aground in the Bahamas. Indians before Columbus had cities larger and more advanced than European cities, and these were decimated by pandemics of diseases brought from Europe. Natives of the Americas had no immunity to such disease and died by the hundreds of millions. Which in turn led to millions of Europeans migrating to the Americas to build an imitation medieval Europe here. And now that is about to undergo changes as horrendous as those in the early 1500s. All because the wealthy horde money rather than use it to create real tangible wealth for everyone, because the wealthy don't understand the difference between money and real wealth, and thus they erode the foundation of their own wealth.

John dismissed that by saying it came from an economist who was a certified nut, a lifetime resident of a psychiatric hospital. Should we take this loony seriously? Certainly not.

What happens when your employees stop working for your company, I asked. "We don't have employees," he said. "We have subsidiaries. Our subsidiaries have employees."

"Suppose you wake up one morning to discover that your subsidiaries' employees can no longer make ends meet financially by working, and quit."

"Suppose the Moon turns to green cheese and lands in Wisconsin," said John. "You would have done well in the old Soviet Union, Robert."

I thought, but didn't say: As well as you're doing in the new Sovietized corporate empire, John? I wanted to say that he had not parried my thrust about the wealthy destroying the foundations of their wealth, but we were both weary now. We napped.

When I awoke we were preparing to land at Baltimore. What struck me as I thought about this debate we'd just had was that we'd gone through our youthful thrust-and-parry routine with a new tolerance for the other's point of view. And with John's quip about the Moon turning to green cheese, he had defaulted.

It also struck me that it didn't matter which of us was the most accurate in our economic analysis, there was, as John said, nothing either of us could do about the overall conditions we found ourselves in, except adapt—not by becoming self-sustaining on our own land, but by playing the macroeconomy for our own benefit. I had lived most of my life seeking change. John had lived most of his life adapting. I had become a loony. He had become a success. I'd fought the establishment while he'd become the establishment. To even contemplate marrying a girl as young as Lola—forget that she's also a prostitute—was moving John into treacherous new waters. Meanwhile, with my newfound income, I was contemplating investing to make my nest egg grow and provide me with the financial security I'd wasted in my youth, even while a little voice in the back of my mind kept asking, What if all forms of paper money become obsolete?

Well, we would soon convert two million dollars in paper money into the condo in Bethany and move into it, and bring Lola there. John assumed I'd move in with him and Lola, while Laura assumed we would get a place together. But I needed my aloneness. I couldn't do my daily meditations with regularity if I were living with either John and Lola or with Laura. I needed my daily rituals like an addict needs his fix. I also felt that, push come to shove, it would be nice to own a row boat and fishing gear.

When we landed at BWI, we rented a car. John insisted on a Cadillac Escalade. I drove and he stared out the window at the passing sights. It was late afternoon and we were both hungry, so we stopped at Hemingway's Restaurant just off a causeway over a part of the Chesapeake Bay. John had his usual martini and we both ordered steaks, filet mignons, cooked medium rare. I said, "Do you think it's a good idea to drink alcohol so soon after your head injury?"

"My doctor didn't say not to."

Typical of my little brother. He'll trust the expert rather than tune into his own intuition.

While we were waiting for the food to come, I told him that after my two head injuries, alcohol affected me differently. "Ah, Bob, you were born reckless," he retorted. "I'm much more self-disciplined than you." Then he gazed out at the waters of the bay and changed the subject. "Wouldn't it be nice to get a sailboat? Looks like good sailing out there on this bay."

"Wait till you see Delaware Bay. You can sail around it and then go out to sea and cruise up and down the coast. You can dock close enough to your condo to walk home."

"I haven't done any sailing since the seventies," he said. "Let's buy something around forty feet long and do it. Where can we go for overnighters?"

"Across the Delaware Bay to Cape May, New Jersey. Down the Delmarva Peninsula to the mouth of the Chesapeake. Up the Jersey coast to New York City, if you like."

"Wonderful. I look forward to sailing to board meetings. What fun."

"With Lola?"

"Sure, and with you, too. And Laura, if she'll come."

"Laura says she doesn't want to see hide nor hair of you."

"So you've told me. Well, maybe she'll change her mind when she sees my turban," he said, indicating the big white bandage wrapped around his shaved head. "No one can hold a grudge forever.

By the way, what's the latest on Jake Valance? Did Al Hansen say how long a prison term he's looking at?"

"Al said he could be charged with a felony or a misdemeanor. Best possible outcome, he'll be put away for a long stretch on a felony, attempted murder. Worst possible scenario, he'll get the charge reduced and walk."

"What can we do to make sure he gets a long stretch? He did try to kill me, after all."

"Call the Santa Barbara DA's office. You've got to let them know where you are. You'll have to testify. Al says it looks like there will be a jury trial."

"Well, Al witnessed the attack personally and saved my life. If he hadn't arrived in time to bring Jake down with a shot to the leg, I'd be dead. Jake was totally berserk. They tested him and his alcohol count was over the top. What more is needed to charge him with a felony and put him away for life?"

"Al said the agency Valance worked for has hired a defense lawyer. They don't want him charged with a felony. That would besmirch their reputation. I suspect they're going to cook up a cover story of some kind in an attempt to hold it to a misdemeanor."

"Incredible. The man tried to kill me. Al saw it."

"The DA's people took a statement from you, didn't they?"

"Yes, while I was in the hospital, still disoriented."

"So it's your word and Al's word and evidence from the crime scene. Given your standing in the community and reputation, John, I don't see how Jake can squirm out of a felony."

"But there's a possibility he can. Is that what you're saying?"

"That's what Al said, not me."

"If the son of a bitch gets off with a misdemeanor, Robert, I'll have a mission for you."

I knew what he meant. He'd want me to hire a pro to kill Valance. I did not want this mission. But I held my tongue and changed the subject.

"When will Lola arrive?" I asked.

"She wants to have her home in the Valley rented out, her furniture in storage, before she comes here. She's working on that now. You know, Bob, I'm going to put her through college, make a lady out of her. The only thing that concerns me is that she wants to have a child or two. Even if she gets pregnant soon, I'll be in my late seventies when the kid is going off to college."

"Are you bragging or complaining?"

"Neither. I'm amazed that she's really serious."

Chapter 27

I don't know how I would have coped without Bob when I got out of the hospital. He flew back to Santa Barbara and drove me home, took care of me, and showed me photos of the condo he was buying on the East Coast. The two doors Valance had splintered had been replaced, and the blood on the master bedroom rug thoroughly cleansed, thanks to Bob.

He wondered if I'd prefer to stay put in the Padero Lane house. No, I definitely felt the need to get out, fumigate all remnants of Jake Valance. Bob insisted that I rest for at least two more days.

Before we left, I called Herby Stein, told him a condensed version of what had recently befallen me and asked if he'd gotten my message about changing my will to include brother Robert. "Yes, I did," he said, "and the changes are in process now. Would you like to be more specific about what you want to bequeath your brother? Or would you like us to just cut him in across the board for, say, ten percent?"

"More than ten percent," I said. "If he'd not fallen on such ill fortune, he would have inherited half our father's estate. Can you set it up so he gets fifty percent of the net earned from this point forward? What do you estimate that would come to?"

"Oh, a million or two a year, depending."

"Good. Can we establish a fund to shelter eighty percent of his investment income, risk twenty percent?"

"Consider it done," said Herby.

I was happy that Herby didn't question my decision, as others would surely have done, based on the supposition that anyone who had spent so much of his life in jails and insane asylums was not right for such an inheritance. Herby had met Bob and had been dealing with him by phone regarding the refurbishing of Laura's beach house, and knows, he said, that the man is clear minded and able.

I did not tell Bob about this. It may turn out that he passes before I do. Even if I pass before he does, I wanted this inheritance to come as a surprise. Besides, brother Bob's focus, I knew by this time, is on personal relationships, not money. Personal relationships are my weak suit while money is Bob's weak suit, so we balance each other. I've come to regard him as my own personal human resources department.

The security people were apparently undergoing a restructuring and, I was happy to note, none of them were aboard the plane when it took off from Los Angeles. I made it a point to walk the aisle of first class and get a good look at all the other passengers, and none remotely resembled a security guard. Without Jake's leadership, I surmised, the Santa Barbara unit was temporarily at sixes and sevens. This, oddly enough, gave me a new sense of security.

During the flight, Bob and I got into the kind of debate that had been so much a part of our lives growing up. I was surprised by how interested my big brother was in economics. He'd been passionately interested in politics back in the mid-sixties when he left for Stanford, but not economics. He'd planned to major in literature, and take some creative writing courses. Now, as we flew to Baltimore, he was talking like he'd taken lectures from a Soviet economist. Some of his notions made me smile, and I made a note to buy him Dr. Milton Friedman's famous book at my first opportunity. But even though his ideas were kind of wacky, it was a huge comfort having him with me again. There was a kind of déjà vu quality to our new relationship, as though we were picking up our old teenage debates like they'd happened only yesterday. With one important difference---no more anger. We talked quietly as we flew east, like two professors coolly exploring various theories.

I've received feelers from several universities to lecture in economics. If that's the way I chose to spend my retirement years, I wondered if it would work to bring my brother into a class to reproduce this debate we'd just had. It would reveal why free-market capitalism fits human nature. We're competitive primates, after all. Competitive with each other and with other species for the Earth's bounties.

It was late afternoon when we landed and rented an SUV and began the drive to Rehoboth Beach. The flat landscape with its estuaries brought back memories of my Harvard days when I used to vacation on Cape Cod. I'd acquired a love of swampy estuaries back then, so different from the West Coast's hills and cliffs. I remembered that my first impression of the Atlantic Ocean was that the Pacific was misnamed—the Atlantic seemed much more pacific than the Pacific. This made me all the more eager to see the beach house. The deal was still in escrow, Bob told me, but we could close as soon as the cash arrived. All I had to do now was call my banker in the Cayman Islands and it would be on its way by personal courier, in a company plane, with security features in place to make sure the courier didn't get any wild ideas and try to abscond with the money. Meanwhile, I would take a room at the hotel Bob had been staying in, the Board-walk Plaza. By this time next week, we'd be buying furniture for the new condo and Lola would be on her way there as soon as she found a renter for her house in the Valley. I hoped Lola would arrive before we went shopping for furniture, for I wanted her to be happy with the choices.

Best of all, I was free from Jake Valance, who was in the Santa Barbara County Jail awaiting trial. The only anxiety in that regard is the possibility he might get off with a misdemeanor, so that instead of being put away for life or a very long stretch, he might get out in a few years. I'd have to testify at his trial, and trust that the Santa Barbara DA does his job.

As we made the drive, Bob pointed out a restaurant that had a view of the Chesapeake Bay. It was named Hemingway's, after the famous author. I suggested we stop, and over dinner, I mentioned that if per chance Jake did get out in a few years, I would need brother Bob to find someone who would kill the bastard for a fee. I would not tolerate that threat again. But I could see that this idea did not sit easily with Bob, for he took several deep breaths and averted his eyes. I might have pressed the issue, but given his reaction, I let it go and hoped Valance would be put away for so many years, it would never be necessary.

Gazing out at the bay, I saw several sailboats and immediately wanted to get myself one. Not a trans-ocean power boat as long as a football field, just something we would have fun with. That's what life with Lola needs, I reasoned. It will give us something we can do together. Bob's eyes lit up at the idea too, and I imagined the three of us—or maybe four, if Laura comes along—sailing the summer months away. I'd done quite a lot of sailing in earlier years, and had quit only because I'd almost lost my life on that solo venture to Hawaii. Now that Valance had almost taken my life, getting back into sailing struck me as the thing to do.

It was dark by the time we got to the hotel in Rehoboth Beach. After we checked in, we took a stroll on the boardwalk. The air was brisk, even chilly, and wet with sea mist. After the long trip, it was good to stretch our legs and remember how, when we were grade school age, we used to walk several miles from Montecito to the Santa Barbara Harbor to look at the boats and watch the fishermen come in and unload their catches. Back then, the harbor scene was so informal that we'd sometimes be invited to snack on freshly caught shrimp or crab, even lobster or abalone. We remembered how Dad had bought us a small sailboat when I was ten and Bob was twelve, and how we loved to rush down to the harbor on Saturday mornings and spend the day on the briny. Mom would pack us lunches and we'd imagine we were Spanish explorers bound for the Far East, or pirates set on raiding big, expensive yachts. On one of those Saturdays, we got caught by an unusually strong riptide and didn't get back to the harbor till after dark. Mom was not delighted by that.

"And do you remember the time," Bob said, "when we sailed up the coast and surprised those nude sunbathers?"

"Nude and drugged," I added.

"Or drunk," said Bob.

"And when we first headed toward their beach, they couldn't see that we were just little kids, and they grabbed their bathing suits and clothes and covered up. It was a private beach, wasn't it?"

"Yeah, it was on Hollister Ranch. All beaches in California are public by law, but you can't get onto Hollister Ranch beaches unless you own property there. Those nude sunbathers had come there by boat. We saw their inflatable on the beach."

"How old were we when we borrowed our neighbor's thirty-footer and sailed to Anacapa Island and camped out?"

"I was fifteen, I think, which would make you thirteen. We caught flounder, dug a hole for the fire, cooked them and stuffed ourselves."

While walking back toward the hotel, I got a sudden urge to throw my arm around Bob's shoulder, as we'd often done when we were kids. I wanted to tell him that I loved him, that I was overjoyed he was here, that his presence had lifted me out of my loneliness. I didn't act on this impulse, though, and it bothered me that I didn't feel free to act on it. What held me back? A lifetime of restraining myself from such outbursts of brotherly affection, I suppose. I was wondering how I could break out of those restraints when Bob said:

"I've got to call Laura when we get back to the hotel. She's left three messages since we landed."

"If you want to sleep with her tonight, I'll stay in my room and make myself scarce."

"No need for that, Jack. I've made up my mind—if she's gong to be testy about your being here, she can make herself scarce. I love having sex with her and enjoy her company, but I will not allow her resentment to drive a wedge between us. I value our brotherhood too much for that."

Again I wanted to respond by reaching an arm around his shoulders and giving him a hug, but again I resisted. "You don't know how glad I am that we're together again after so many years."

He grinned and said, "You can't be half as happy as I am about it. You're giving me a new lease on life."

"Ditto," I said.

When we got back, the hotel dining room was still open so I suggested we have a nightcap. Bob had freshly squeezed orange juice and I had a French brandy. We sat side by side in wicker chairs, staring out through French doors at the dimly lit boardwalk and beyond that the sea, dark except for the surprisingly bright foamy breakers tossing onto the beach. Bob got out his cell phone and called Laura. I smiled to myself as I heard his end of the conversation. "Yes, we're having a drink at Victoria's before turning in... No no, I'm having orange juice...You what?...sneak into my room around midnight? I'm up for that, honey...No, John and I have separate rooms... Oh, you don't want to do us both tonight," he said with a wink at me. "Don't you think it's time to let bygones be bygones?... Tomorrow? Well, tomorrow I'm going to show him the condo he's buying. Want to come along?...Okay, suit yourself. Sneak into my room tonight and sneak out before breakfast."

He clapped his cell phone shut and said, "I hope you're okay with me having this affair with your ex, John."

"I'm charmed by it. If this were my first wife, Kelly, she'd insist on having sex with both of us. Are you and Laura going to make the big commitment?"

"I don't think so," he said. "It has me caught between her old resentment and my new-found brotherhood, and blood is thicker than water, as they say. But I can't help thinking that if she sees you with that bandage around your head, she'll lose her resentment, or at least some of it. I told her what you survived."

"How did she react?"

"The expression on her face said she was frightened for you."

"Perhaps her expression hid more negative feelings."

"Maybe. I think she's trapped in her resentment. It's an old habit. I think she really wants to let it go and get to know who you are now.

The question is, can she escape this prison, this old habit of hatred she's locked herself into?"

Memories of weekends with Laura and the kids flashed through my mind like a series of old photos. "She has plenty of reason to be resentful," I said. "I was doing a lot of traveling back then. I'd fly home for the weekend only because this was expected of me. That's what everyone did—when the weekend came, you flew home to your family on Friday, if you could possibly manage it, and then flew back to wherever you'd been on Monday. That was crazy making. Extreme jet lag. Sometimes I was flying home from cities in the Far East or Africa, and part of me would still be in those exotic places, planning my next business move. Laura would want to focus my attention on domestic details when I wanted only to sleep. I just couldn't make the transition quickly enough, especially when things abroad had not gone well that week. I was too often groggy and grouchy. I remember once I took the family out to a Japanese restaurant in Santa Barbara and found myself ordering in Japanese. I knew very little Japanese, but the waiter knew none at all. Laura had to elbow me in the ribs to snap me out of my trance and get me to order in English. But the worst of it was, I would sometimes get into a rage— mainly because I was coming home full of frustration. I'd dump my frustration on her, when all she wanted was a civil conversation. By the time the kids were in junior high, I wished I could hire a surrogate husband to handle my domestic duties so I could stay focused on business."

Bob thought about this for a moment, then asked, "Was there ever a time when you and Laura were happy?"

"Oh yes, when we first met, courted and married. When each of the children was born—those were joyous occasions. Back when I was working my way up the corporate ladder, before I became involved in so many overseas negotiations. It was those deals that expanded the company tenfold, you see, so they were crucial and put a lot of pressure on me and everyone else involved. We needed the Clinton Administration to back NAFTA or a lot of our expansion would collapse. Things got very complicated. A lot of pieces had to be put in place to make it work."

"What do you tell people like me who see the globalization of the economy as a bonanza for corporate profits but a disaster for people?"

"We show you the production figures and tell you these huge numbers would not be possible without globalization. We're the model for emerging economies. That's what we tell you."

"The corporations are successful but people are suffering."

"You talk as though corporations aren't part of society."

"The mission of big corporations—the global empire—is at odds with the needs of the people."

"Bob, don't fret. All that is about to change. American economic domination is a thing of the past. With oil now selling for over a hundred dollars a barrel and the trade deficit now more than six percent of gross domestic product, the mortgage market in crisis and the rise of emerging nations like China, India, Brazil, Venezuela, Russia and a half dozen others, the US military fighting a rear-guard action, our economic domination lasted about three decades. American society is about to sink into a sea of debt, the likes of which we've never had to deal with before. Invest wisely and you personally will profit from this change."

"But that's what I've been saying, John. The big corporations have destroyed American society and stuck working class taxpayers with the bill at ever-compounding interest."

"I agree that we're in decline but not for the reasons you gave."

For a fleeting moment, I wanted to totally agree with him. Yes, most of American society had suffered, and that had never happened before in a boom cycle. President George W. did a magnificent job of maximizing corporate profits, yet something had gone wrong and I wasn't sure what it was. I felt suddenly tired. My head ached. "I'm exhausted," I said. "I'm turning in. See you tomorrow."

I downed the last of my brandy and stood up, felt a momentary vertigo, shook that off and walked away.

As I was leaving the dining area and entering the hotel lobby, I saw Laura come through the front entrance. I quickly ducked behind a potted palm, watched her get in the elevator. The next thing I knew, Bob was standing behind me, saying, "Who are you hiding from?"

"I'll tell you about it tomorrow," I said, and walked to the elevator. He followed and we went up together in silence, me to the third floor, him to the fourth. He was looking perplexed when I got off. "Are you okay?" he called after me. The elevator doors closed before I could reply. I hoped I could reach Dr. Ray Rici at home, around 8 o'clock his time.

Chapter 28

Laura was the first thing I saw when I stepped off the elevator on the fourth floor. She was about to get back on the elevator and go down to the desk to find out where I was. "I've been trying to call you," she said, "You're not in your room. Is your phone off?"

"Yeah."

"I came up to your room but you weren't there and I didn't have a key."

As we walked down the hall to the room, I said, "I'm worried about John. He's in a weird mood. Could be from the head trauma."

Inside the room, I found I had seven messages on my cell. Four of them were from Al Hansen.

"What's up, Al?"

"Are you sitting down?"

I sat on the side of the bed and said, "I am now."

"Jake Valance has escaped."

"Tell me you're joking. How could that be?"

"Remember I told you about this ex-cop Valance palled around with, Harold Zarkowski?"

"No, I don't think you ever mentioned him."

"Maybe not. Anyhow, Jake was arraigned on attempted murder, a felony. The DA didn't want to plea bargain, which means Jake was looking at a long stretch. That made him desperate. Zarkowski was part of our poker group and he and Valance were drinking buddies. Seems Valance complained of a toothache, and Zarkowski got himself assigned to take him to the dentist, which meant shackling his hands and ankles and driving him a few miles in a van. A second guard is required to go along on such trips but for some as-yet unexplained reason, there was no second guard. Long story short, Zarkowski was found in a roadside ditch with his face bloodied. He said Valance attacked him, unlocked his shackles and stole the van."

"When did this happen?"

"This morning around 9 o'clock our time."

"And Valance is now at large?"

"Seems Valance dumped the van in a canyon out near Red Rock. Looks like he had someone pick him up there. We're bringing in anyone who had anything to do with Valance, including his agency people here, girlfriends, bartenders. They even questioned me for about an hour."

"You said he and Zarkowski were drinking buddies?"

"Yeah, and Harold has some explaining to do. Nobody believes his story. Interrogators have been having at Harold all day. It's pretty clear he was in cahoots with Jake—you just don't take a prisoner like Valance to the dentist's office alone. Harold isn't the brightest penny in the bucket, you know, so my suspicion is that Jake offered him a cut of the ten million he imagines he'll get out of your brother. Question is, does Harold know Jake's next move. I seriously doubt it. Jake knew Harold would be top suspect so if he told him anything, it was bullshit. Put yourself in Jake's shoes and what would you do? He needs to get some travel money and change his appearance. My guess is he'll rob someone. We know he likes to target prostitutes and gays. I wouldn't be surprised if he's cruising Santa Monica Boulevard as we speak. If he had someone he trusted, he might have access to cash, but I never knew Jake to trust anyone."

"What's the chance he knows where John is?"

"Maybe he doesn't know yet but the chances are that he'll find out. Jake's not without resources. Are you and John together?"

"Yes, we just got here this evening."

"Tell me the name of that town again?"

"Rehoboth Beach."

"Spell that, will you."

I did and added, "It means *room for everyone* in the original native language."

"I'm going to alert the police there, have them keep an eye on you two. Exactly where are you?"

"The Boardwalk Plaza Hotel?"

"Both of you?"

"Yup. And I was just telling someone here that I'm concerned about John because he seems to be having mood swings, which may be due to the head trauma."

"You've been using your credit card, right?"

"Right."

"Can you move out of that hotel and pay cash for whatever you do?"

I explained that we were about to close on the purchase of a condo for cash, that the cash was on its way by courier.

"What I'd like you to do," said Al, "is move your butts to another town, preferably a big city, and pay with the credit card for a hotel there, then check out of that and use cash for everything thereafter. Can you do that without using an ATM?"

"We can when the cash gets here. How about we do it tomorrow first thing?"

"That will work. Stay put till I call you tomorrow with the latest. Who knows what the situation will be by then? I'd like to see you delay closing the deal on this condo. Can you put off closing till we recapture Valance?"

"How long do you think that will take?"

Al let loose a long sigh that whistled through the phone. "I wish I knew. He won't be easy. My hunch is, he'll get himself new ID and maybe a disguise before he travels. But that's only a hunch. I could be wrong.

"I'd like to withhold this news from John as long as possible. He's still vulnerable."

"Well, if John calls anyone here, he'll probably find out. It's the big news locally."

"He'll probably call Dr. Ray Rici, his neurologist."

"I know Dr. Rici. I'll see if I can get to him before John calls him. What about John's girlfriend, Lola Jones?"

"She's planning to fly here as soon as she rents out her house."

"You got an address for her?"

"I'll have to get that from John."

"Can you do that right now and get back to me?"

"I'll try."

John's room phone rang about a dozen times before he picked up with a sleepy, "Yeah?"

"It's me. Can you give me Lola's address and phone number?"

"Why do you want that, Bob?"

"Law enforcement people in Santa Barbara want it. They want to question her about Valance before she leaves for the East Coast."

"Oh, all right. Just a sec."

He gave it to me and I said, "Thanks. I'll call Al Hansen with this."

"Can you let me sleep now?"

After I relayed the info to Al, Laura wanted to know what was going on. I gave her a quick summary, spare on the particulars. We forgot about lovemaking and just snuggled. Before we fell asleep, she said, "What if you move John to Atlantic City? Is that a big enough city? You'd still be on the ocean."

"I was thinking Washington."

"Rooms are hard to get there, you know, and they want a photo ID. In Atlantic City, you can finagle a desk clerk to skip the photo ID."

"Atlantic City it is, then. But I'd like to avoid moving, if possible. We'll see what develops."

Chapter 29

I called Ray before I got undressed for bed. I told him where I was and how, on the flight here, I'd had moments of disorientation and, just before turning in, some vertigo. He asked me to take the sleeping pill he'd prescribed and get a good night's sleep. "The more bed rest," he said, "the better. Would you take that med before we get off the phone, John?"

"Sure." I found the sleeping pills, took one, and told him I was off to dreamland.

He said, "Good. Now I have some bad news. Seems the guy who attacked you has escaped from the county jail. Don't let this upset you. They'll find him. People just don't escape from jail without getting caught, you know. So don't be worried, you're three thousand miles away. Sleep soundly."

It took about twenty minutes for the sleeping pill to take effect, during which time my imagination raced, and I felt like my heart would leap out of my rib cage. Then, gradually, my anxiety subsided and I could do nothing but crawl into bed and fall instantly to sleep.

The next thing I was aware of was my room phone's jangling ring. It rang and rang. I was not about to answer it. I needed to sleep, not wake up to a desk clerk asking an inane question, or whatever. When the ringing would not cease, I finally forced myself to pick up. It was Bob, calling to get Lola's address and phone number.

Strangely enough, I'd forgotten what Ray had told me about Valance escaping from the county jail and fell back to sleep the moment I returned the phone to its cradle. My usual routine is to sleep about six hours a night and catch a siesta after lunch. On this pill, I slept ten hours, till 10 o'clock the next day. First thing I did when

I awakened was pull back the curtains and gaze out at the Atlantic. Then I ordered coffee and a croissant from room service, and staggered into the bathroom for a shower. Room service arrived while I was still toweling off so I had the delivery girl put it on the table and sign for me.

In my bathrobe, I had breakfast staring out at the sharply defined horizon. It was a delightfully bright sunny day, which lifted my mood and had me smiling at thoughts of Lola. What a pleasure it will be when she gets here and we can gaze at this crystal clear horizon together.

As I was finishing breakfast, I heard a very light knock at my door and figured it was the hotel maid, so I called out, "Please come later."

The baritone of Bob replied. "Got to talk to you now, Jack."

He came in wearing a snappy sports jacket and slacks, and said, "What say we take a ferryboat ride. Like our ancestors. Remember? I told you about our ancestors who, back in the sixteen hundreds, ran a ferryboat service on the Chesapeake? Well, today I'd like to take you across the Delaware Bay to New Jersey. You'll enjoy it."

It was then that I recalled Ray telling me that Jake Valance had escaped. "Strange," I mused aloud. "I forgot all about it till now."

"Forgot what?"

"That Valance has escaped, is on the loose. Unless they've caught him. Let's call the Sheriff's Department and find out."

Bob kind of fell into an easy chair like his legs had suddenly given out. "Al Hansen will call when there's news."

I yawned and stretched, still subdued by the sleeping pill. "How long do you think it will take to catch him?"

"I don't know. But in the meantime, let's go to Atlantic City, see the sights, maybe do some gambling."

"I want to see the condo," I protested. "Casinos bore me."

Bob stared into middle space a while then said, "Okay. Let's see the condo, then have lunch and catch the ferry to Cape May."

"I can't do that, Bob. I need to be here this evening when the cash is delivered."

He stood, put his hands in his pockets and, after gazing out at the sea a moment, said, "Al wants us to move out of his hotel and use only cash. Till they catch Jake."

I felt like the coffee and the sleeping pill had suddenly clashed in my stomach. "Are you saying Jake knows where we are? That he may come after me here?"

"I don't think so, John, but Al would like us to err on the side of caution."

"The courier is on his way here from the Cayman Islands and expecting to deliver to me here, at this hotel. I was expecting to see the condo today, take delivery of the cash this evening, close on the purchase tomorrow morning."

Bob paced the room for a time, hands in pockets, head lowered, frowning. "How about this. You call your company headquarters and tell them where you are, and that the guy who tried to kill you has escaped, and that you need protection here. Will they get the security agency to assign someone to protect you here?"

"If I insist. But I'd much rather provide for my own protection here. Valance wants money, not corporate secrets. Let's move into the condo as soon as possible."

"Okay. It will be a lot easier to protect you there. Only access to the house is from the beach, and it's a desolate beach this time of year. Anyone on that beach stands out like a sore thumb."

"Done," I said. "Let's get to it. Is Laura with you?"

"She went home this morning."

As we walked to the elevator, I asked, "Is she still resentful?"

"Given Valance's escape, I think she's more worried than resentful."

On the ride down to the lobby, I said, "I've got to confess—I'm so mad about Lola, nothing else matters."

"Is she an early riser?" asked Bob.

"Now that she's not doing dates, she is, yes. You drive and I'll call her."

By the time we'd driven south to Bethany, I had tried half a dozen times to reach Lola without success. I left messages, assumed she'd call back when she could. She was probably handling the details of renting out her house.

Chapter 30

At Kathy's real estate office, we transferred to her Lincoln for the ride to the condo. I'd mentioned to John that Kathy thought we were a gay couple. We didn't disabuse her of this misconception. I caught her looking at the wrapped bandage on John's head, but she didn't ask about it and we didn't volunteer information. John's attention was on the landscape of dunes and beach and sea. As we approached the entrance to the gated community, he turned to me with a smile and said, "It's beautiful here. Pristine. Surprisingly pristine."

The condo still contained the owners' furniture and as we roamed from room to room, floor to floor, I could see the delight growing in my brother. "Can we include this furniture in the purchase?" he asked Kathy.

"I don't think the owners have any plans to move it to Florida so they may be happy to let you have it."

We made arrangements with Kathy to deliver the cash tomorrow to a local lawyer's office, where the escrow was being handled. By this time it was mid-afternoon. Kathy took us to an upscale vegetarian restaurant where we had sandwiches and health-food drinks.

Before we got into the Escalade for the drive back to Rehoboth, I called Al Hansen. "What's the latest?"

"Seems the son of a bitch may have snatched Lola," said Al. "We had the Los Angeles Police in Canoga Park go to her house when we couldn't reach her by phone. Report came back that her car was parked in the driveway but nobody was home. Very few places in that area you can walk to."

"Any sign of Valance?"

"None. As an ex-cop, he knows the search routine. Staying one step ahead of us, I'm afraid. How's John?"

I turned my head away from Kathy and John to say, "Was doing pretty good, till this…"

"When's the last time he spoke with Lola Jones?"

"Yesterday."

"And when's the last time he saw her?"

"Yesterday. She drove up from the Valley to overnight with John before we left on this trip."

"Then it's too soon to declare her missing."

"But it doesn't look good if her car's still there."

"She could turn up any minute. Maybe she went shopping with a friend. If you two will throw away your credit cards and use cash only and move out of the hotel—are you still there?"

"We're planning to be out of the hotel and into the condo this evening, nothing but cash."

"If Valance did snatch Lola and plans to use her as bait, he won't be able to fly her there. We've got the airports around here covered. He'll have to drive. That gives you a few days to cover your tracks."

"So we're still talking if?"

"Right. Nothing certain yet. What kind of security system does this condo have?"

"I'll make sure we have the best available."

"Our department has alerted the Rehoboth Beach police and the Delaware State Police."

"You think it would help if I stopped around and talked to them?"

"Couldn't hurt."

I noticed John was leaning my way now, listening to my end of the conversation. "Gotta run. Talk to you later."

"Al Hansen?" he asked.

"Yes."

"What's the latest?"

"They're still looking."

Kathy's curiosity was aroused. She didn't ask but looked at me with a question in her eyes. I said, "What time tomorrow would be good to deliver the payment?"

"Attorney Duncan Blanchard usually comes in around nine and leaves around six. Just call before you show and I'm sure he'll clear his schedule."

When we got back to the hotel, John laid down for a nap and I drove to the nearest state police station on Route 1. I went in the front entrance and found myself surrounded by walls and what appeared to be bullet-proof glass, behind which sat a burly African American with a name tag identifying him as Sergeant Delancy. I introduced myself and said I was here to inquire about one Jake Valance, wanted for attempted murder and other crimes. Have you been notified that he might be headed this way? As the sergeant was running a computer search, an older trooper opened a steel door into the secure area and said, "Did you say the name Valance?"

"Yes, Jake Valance."

"From this area?"

"We don't know where he's from, exactly, but the general opinion is he's from New Jersey. He may be headed here."

"Reason I ask," said the older trooper, "there was a family named Valance living on a farm near here when I was a kid. And I well remember one of them was named Jacob. Just a minute."

He disappeared behind the steel door and was gone for about five minutes. When he reappeared, he carried a file folder and introduced himself. "I'm Captain Gorman."

"I'm Robert Bradford from California."

"I investigated the mysterious disappearance of Jake's father back in the eighties. Here's the old file." He opened it and held up a mug shot of a young Jake Valance.

"That's him," I said. "He's from around here?"

Captain Gorman pointed to a steel door to my left and pressed a buzzer. I opened it and was in the station's inner sanctum. He held up the photo again and I could see that, when this mug shot was taken,

Jake must have been in his late teens. He wore a tight tee shirt that showed off his muscles and an angry scowl.

"This mug shot was taken when he was a senior in high school. He grew up on a farm that's now under a housing development. The thing is, when this guy was sixteen, his father disappeared. Foul play was suspected but we were unable to find a body or any evidence of wrongdoing. Jacob was the youngest of five children. Lived with his mother on the farm till he moved on to take a police job in New Jersey. We lost track of him after that. When his mother passed on about ten years later, he was the only one of her children who did not show up for the funeral. I remember that because I went to the funeral and was looking for him. A lot of people suspected foul play— Jacob had a notorious temper. We all thought it was curious that even his brothers and sisters had lost track of him."

"How long after his father disappeared did he leave town?" I wondered.

"A couple of years, maybe three. Word has it that the father was extremely abusive. Heavy drinker, routinely beat his wife and kids. They were not a happy clan."

"Did you ever find out what happened to the father?"

"No. Our files are computerized now, but we've kept this moldy old paper file because so many hereabouts are still curious. No one who knew old man Valance believes he moved away. One other item. Jacob got himself charged with attempted rape by the girl he took to the senior prom, a couple years after the father disappeared. Here's a photo of her taken when she went to the emergency room."

I looked at the photo of a young girl with wavy blond hair down to her shoulders and a battered face—a black eye, split lip and a purple bruise on her left cheek.

"Today, he'd face much more serious charges, but back then he walked after being court-ordered to pay the girl's medical bills plus a couple of hundred for damages."

"Did he make good on it?"

"Sold some old farm machinery to come up with the cash. Next thing we knew, he was gone, never to be heard from again, until you walked in. What's the story?"

When I told him how Jake had attacked my brother, Captain Gorman shook his head and said, "The tiger don't change his stripes. I'm sure a lot of longtime residents around here would recognize him today. Besides being a major bad ass, he was a star football player. Attracted a lot of attention, both positive and negative."

"He's looking at attempted murder. Escaped from the Santa Barbara County Jail."

"A telex we got this morning says he may come this way to blackmail or even kill John Bradford. Your relative?"

"My brother. That's who he tried to kill. That's why he was in jail."

"What was Jacob's motive?"

"What he has in mind is extorting my brother for ten million dollars. But his game was discovered and he was transferred out of town by the security agency he works for. That's when he broke into my brother's house. He'd been drinking. Our guess is, he forgot about blackmailing John and tried to kill him out of sheer rage and frustration."

"I see. I believe he killed his father even though we could never prove it. I'm not surprised to hear he tried to kill someone else. God only knows what else he's gotten away with. You and your brother plan to be in this area for long?"

"We're buying a condo in Bethany. Valance caused my brother a severe head trauma. He came here to get away from Valance and wants to see him securely behind bars before he returns to California."

Captain Gorman sat down in a wooden desk chair and rubbed his chin, looked thoughtful. "You didn't know Valance was originally from here?"

"No."

"Do you have a recent photo of him?"

"Let's call the Santa Barbara Sheriff's Department. I think they're planning to fax a mug shot to you."

"Let's do that."

I had the number on the business card Al Hansen had given me.

We put through the call and within minutes the fax machine in Captain Gorman's office printed out a police shot of Jake, front and profile.

"Yeah, that's our boy," said Captain Gorman. "He's aged but I'd certainly recognize him if I met him on the street. Came from a rough and troubled background, that family he grew up in."

I thanked the captain for his time and headed back to the hotel. As I drove, I called Dr. Grace and gave her an abbreviated version of the situation I was in—Al urging us to leave Rehoboth, John insisting on moving into the condo, Valance escaped from jail, Lola not answering her phone. Dr. Grace asked if I had any symptoms of depression and I said no, I was upset and anxious but not feeling threatened by the debilitating monster. She said she thought it was good that I was now forced to take care of my younger brother in his time of need. "When you were children, did you look out for John? Were you protective of him?"

"Yes, I was."

"So you've come full circle in your relationship with him?"

"This is different, Dr. Grace. This guy tried to kill him."

"But the police are alerted, aren't they?"

"Yes, but this guy is an ex-cop. He escaped from jail and has managed to stay a step ahead of the police. And we found out that he was originally from this area, southern Delaware. We have reason to suspect he'll come here and make another attempt to blackmail John, or try to kill him. This guy Valance is unpredictable and not entirely rational. Now it's possible that he may have kidnapped John's girlfriend. He may have taken her hostage."

"Oh my. You are in a pressure cooker, aren't you."

"Yes. But I'm holding up. In fact, all this excitement and danger seems to be helping me. Isn't that odd?"

"The last time you called from there, you were feeling lost and disoriented. So, yes, I'd say the challenge you're facing seems to be helping you. But do stick with your daily meds and meditations, Robert."

"I will."

"As for what you're dealing with, police work is not my area of expertise. It's odd but sometimes a crisis like this will help a depressive. Keep me up to date. I need to know you're functioning, Bob."

I found it curious that Mary Grace could call me Mr. Bradford, Robert or Bob, depending on her mood, the situation, or my mental state. "I'm functioning better than I have in many years," told her. "Seems the more responsibility I have, the better I function."

"I'm so glad to hear that, Bob. But don't forget to take your daily meds and do your daily meditation. That's important. And call me anytime. You can reach me at home on my cell, you know."

Chapter 31

I woke up from a long nap in the late afternoon and tried again to call Lola, and again got nothing. Not even her answering service, which was worrisome. She has no landline. Her cell phone is her office.

I wasn't sure I could reach Ray Rici this time of day but I called anyway and, happily, connected with him. "I'm eating a quick lunch in the hospital cafeteria," he said. "How are you doing?"

I told him I'd not felt any disorientation or vertigo today but that I was upset and worried because I could not reach my friend, Lola Jones. There was such a long silence on the line after that, I feared we'd lost our connection. "Hello?" I said.

'Yes, I'm here, John. I think you need to call the Sheriff's Department and speak to someone there about Lola Jones. Keep in touch with me, though, and be sure to let me know about any out of the ordinary feelings."

I dialed information and got a number for the Sheriff's Department, and asked if I could speak with Officer Al Hansen. Again I got a strange lull in the conversation but the lady at the other end gave me Hansen's cell phone number. "I'm not sure where he is at the moment but this number should find him."

I dialed the number and got Al Hansen's deep voice, told him I'd been trying to call Lola and asked if he knew any reason why I couldn't even connect with her answering service.

"Apparently your brother didn't tell you."

"Tell me what?"

"Are you sitting down?"

"Yes, why?"

"I have disturbing information. I won't sugar coat it. I'm in Ms. Jones' house as we speak, John. It's a crime scene. We're dusting for fingerprints and searching for whatever we might find here. When she didn't answer her front door, we had a locksmith get us in."

"What's going on?" My heart was racing now.

"When Jake Valance escaped, I called the Canoga Park Police to check on Lola Jones. I asked them to go by her house and check on her."

"Where is she?"

"That's what we're trying to find out. Apparently, she packed a suitcase before she left."

With heart racing and head throbbing I said, "Do you think Valance...?"

"We don't know but we must assume the possibility."

"Have you spoken with Dr. Rici?" I asked.

"Yes, I wanted to alert him because I knew this would come as a shock to you."

"Thanks for your thoughtfulness, Al."

"Are you and your brother making arrangements to move to another location?"

"We're planning to move into a condo."

"He told me about it. Okay. When do you think you'll be there?"

"Very soon. Tonight maybe, or definitely by tomorrow."

"And you've stopped using credit cards?"

"We have."

"Good. The police in your area have been alerted and are on the lookout for Valance. You may also want to retain a security guard for your condo."

I felt dissipated after that call. I lay back down on the bed and stared up at the ceiling and wondered what in the world I would do if, God forbid, Jake Valance...

But the thought was too horrifying. On a wild impulse I autodialed Jake's old number but got only a message that service had been discontinued.

There was a light knock at my door. It was Bob. I pulled him into the room and told him that Lola had...no one knew what had become of her. "Do you think that son of a bitch got to her?" I asked.

"Take it easy, John. We don't know."

"Nobody knows where she is. Nobody knows where he is. I'm ready to tell the son of a bitch he can have all the money he wants, just give me back Lola and get out of my life."

Bob told me he'd just come from visiting the Delaware State Police and had learned—"Hold onto to yourself, brother"—that Jake Valance was from this area, had grown up here, was suspected of killing his father when he was a teenager. The good news, Bob said, was that the Delaware State Police now have a mug shot of Valance and will send copies around to local police departments. "When is the courier due to arrive?" Bob asked.

"Around nine, I think. I'll check and make sure."

I autodialed my contact in Miami, who represented my banker in the Caymans, and assured him we were on an encrypted line. "Delivery is scheduled to be made at nine this evening at the Boardwalk Plaza Hotel in Rehoboth Beach," he said, "and our courier is on schedule, carrying two leather satchels."

I relayed this message to Bob.

"The people at the front desk tell me they can keep the bags in the hotel safe," said Bob. "But I think it would be a good idea to get ourselves a security guard."

"All right. Let's hire someone. Privately, not through the company."

"I'll see what I can find."

Bob sat in an easy chair by the window, a telephone book in his lap, and made a series of calls. I stared out at the glistening sea under bright sunlight, remembering how Mom used to say she welcomed overcast days, a relief from the intense sun. I felt a kind of lump of gloom in the pit of my stomach. A month or two ago, I was facing loneliness with stoicism. Now, the thought of going on without Lola was debilitating. That goddamned Jake Valance could come out of the woodwork at any moment, I feared, and here I was helpless. I needed to arm myself.

"I found a security company in Philadelphia who will send someone down here pronto," said Bob.

That news barely registered. "Where can I buy a gun?" I said.

"Cool it, John. We have an experienced bodyguard on the way. Should take him a couple of hours to drive down from Philadelphia. He'll post himself outside your door. The local police are informed about Valance. Hopefully, we'll be able to move into the condo tomorrow, after we close escrow. The bodyguard will be there with us. You're safe. Nothing more we can do now. Kick back and rest."

"I want a gun. If Jake Valance shows, I want to personally blow his brains out."

"The bodyguard is armed. You shoot anyone, you'll be in trouble with the law."

"Christ, Robert, I'm in trouble with my life. Trouble with the law would be a relief. If I lose Lola…"

I put my head in my hands and wept, cried like I hadn't cried since I was a child. Bob put an arm around my shoulders and murmured soothing words.

After I'd recovered from that outburst, Bob said, "Al Hansen figures that if—worst scenario—Jake has Lola, he can't fly here. He'll have to drive. Take him at least half a day to steal a car, then, even if he floors it all the way and doesn't overnight at motels, it will take him at least two and a half days to drive three thousand miles. Stopping to eat, it will be more like three days. If, that is, he's planning to come here. He may have forgotten about you and be trying only to stay out of jail. He may not have Lola. There might be another explanation for why she's not home."

"Jake escaped from jail and now Lola's missing. What are the odds there's no connection?"

"Let's get something to eat and await the courier," said Bob. "Sitting here torturing ourselves with imagined scenarios isn't going to help."

"I'm not hungry."

"It will calm your nerves."

"Well, I'll have a drink or two."

"I would insist you not drink, John, but I know from experience that when you're used to calming yourself with alcohol, nothing else will do. So, okay, it' s pushing five o'clock. Let's pass the time in the dining room downstairs and be ready to greet the courier around six. We'll put the money in the hotel safe overnight."

Chapter 32

Awaiting delivery of cash in a bag made me feel like I was back in the Bay Area, twenty years ago, doing a drug deal. Before we left John's room, I stood in front of a mirror, fingering the very conventional Brooks Brothers suit jacket and slacks I was wearing, assuring myself that I'd left that life behind, that it was now 2008, not 1988. I kept pausing to take a deep breath, glancing at John, noticing the harried, haunted expression on his face. He seemed to be feeling the mix of fear and bravado I used to feel.

Years ago in Brazil, a lady folk healer had put me through a ritual cleansing of my aura—"to get rid of the criminals who are traveling with you," she said. Her belief was that souls of the dead latch onto living people who are doing things they enjoyed doing when they were alive. "We must rid you of the criminal souls," she'd said, "or they will lead you into trouble, maybe get you killed." What kind of "invisibles" could have latched onto John? Maybe the kind who would love to consort with the likes of Lola Jones.

On the way to Victoria's Restaurant downstairs, we stopped at the desk. A pretty young lady with her hair up in a bun and a coy glint in her eye was on duty. She smiled at me as I approached, then glanced behind me at John and her smile disappeared. "How can I help you?" she said.

"My friend is expecting a delivery of valuables in an hour or so, and I've been told the hotel safe is large and very secure. May I have a look at it? I want to be sure it's large enough to contain what we're expecting."

"Actually, we have two safes but I don't have access to either one. I'll call the manager. He's at home right now. I think he may want to come in and show you."

"Thank you. We'll be in the dining room."

Brother John was into his second gin martini when a gentleman approached our table and said, "I'm the manager. You wanted to speak with me?"

"Yes," said John in his more commanding voice. "We need to inspect your largest safe, if you'll be so kind as to show it to us. We need to be sure it's large enough. We're expecting a delivery of valuables."

"Certainly." The manager held out his hand and said, "My name is Alex Tamborn. Please, follow me."

We shook his hand and followed. He led us out of the dining room by a back door and then down a stairway into a basement, through a wine cellar area to a heavy oak door, which he opened. Inside was a room with walls that looked to me like they could withstand a strong earthquake. At the far end was a safe built into this thick cement wall. Alex Tamborn put his body between us and the combination dial while he worked it. The safe door swung open to reveal a space large enough to hold half a dozen people.

"Will this be enough room?" he asked.

"Indeed it will," said John. "We'll need you here when delivery comes to secure two satchels in your safe."

"I'll be in my office," he said.

We thanked him and went up to John's room to await a ring from the desk clerk. I knew he wanted a third martini but steadfastly refused to let him call room service. "Lay down and relax," I said.

I had two messages from Laura. I called her and told her that I'd not be able to make it this evening, too much was happening.

"Tell me what's going on?"

"I can't right now. Later."

The bedside clock's big red numbers read 6:16 when the phone rang. John listened a moment and said, "We'll be right down."

We spotted the courier immediately when we stepped off the elevator. He was around 40, balding, wearing a slightly rumpled suit and standing in front of one of the birdcages, talking to a sleepy parrot. As we approached, he turned and looked us both up and down, then pulled a wallet from his suit jacket pocket, opened it, checked a photo in it, looked closely at John, rechecked the photo, and said, "Mr. Bradford?"

"Yes?"

"Your delivery is here. Just a minute while I bring it from the car."

He walked out the front entrance of the hotel. We stood in the lobby watching him remove two bags from a Ford Expedition. He lugged the two bags into the lobby and set them down gently by John's feet. He produced some documents and held them out to John. "Two million in a variety of denominations, from ones, fives, tens and twenties to thousand dollar bills."

"That's why there's so much bulk?" asked John.

"If you'd specifically requested all the money in one thousand dollar bills, it wouldn't be so bulky." It sounded like this courier was chiding John for not specifying the entire two million in thousand dollar bills only. I wondered how bulky two thousand packages of one thousand dollar bills would be.

"If you'll please sign on the dotted line, sir, I'll be on my way."

John scan-read the document while I went to the desk to get a pen. He signed. The man departed.

John opened one satchel and pulled out a packet of bills. They were all one thousand dollar bills. "We could go up to the room and count them," he said.

"Looks like that would take all night. Let's get them in the safe."

John nodded and stuffed the packet back in the satchel, just as Alex Tamborn appeared without being summoned and said, "Right this way, gentlemen," and was leading us toward the back of the hotel when, as though materializing out of thin air, the figure of a large man with dark curly hair and bushy sideburns blocked our way.

It took me a moment to recognize the face encircled in that hairdo—Jake Valance.

"I'll handle those two," he said to the manager, indicating John and me while shoving a handgun into the manager's ribs.

Alex Tamborn raised his arms and pressed his back against the wall of the narrow hallway we were in and turned pale.

"Follow me," Jake said to John and me. Each of us carried one bag. I had a momentary urge to drop my bag and grab Valance from behind, wrap his throat in a jujitsu arm lock and squeeze the life out of him. But my rational mind prevailed, for I knew I could not subdue him before he could shoot.

He led the three of us to a door to the parking lot and held it open with his left hand, his gun close to his body in his right hand. He then led us to a car and opened the trunk.

Inside was Lola, bound and gagged. She peered up at us with a forlorn look in her eyes. "She's a beauty," said Valance. "And she'll be all yours when I am safely away."

Then he closed the trunk lid and opened a back door. "Put the bags in here," he said. We did, setting them gently on the back seat. Jake had so stunned us by his surprise that we were moving like mechanical toys.

"I don't know how much is in these bags. I want ten million from you, Mr. Bradford. If the count is short of that, you'll hear further from me. If not, I'll release the girl."

With that, he got behind the wheel and almost ran us down backing out of the parking place, and was gone. The car had no license plate. It was a powder blue Lincoln Continental.

Alex Tamborn hurried toward the door we'd just come out of, saying, "I'll call the police. Did you get the license number?"

"There was no license plate on the car," I said, as I noticed that John had slumped to the ground and was sitting with his back against another car's rear tire with his head between his knees. "It was a powder blue Lincoln Continental."

"Certainly," he said, and stopped in his tracks. "I can use my cell phone," he said as though he'd just remembered he had one. "I'm dialing 911."

I lifted brother John up by the armpits and got a shoulder under him and began walking him back into the hotel. "You need to call Dr. Rici," I said, "and I need to call Al Hansen."

By the time we got out of the elevator on John's floor, he was walking unassisted. His white-turban bandaged head was lowered as he plodded down the hall toward his room, his face ashen. I assumed he was mainly upset by the theft of the money and the mystery of how Jake Valance had managed to be here, having just escaped from jail a day ago. But the first words out of John's mouth were, "Will I ever see my lovely Lola again? Will he kill her?"

I felt embarrassed that I'd thought of the money before I'd thought of Lola's plight.

I insisted he lay down on his bed. Then I autodialed Al and he picked up on the third ring. "You'll never believe what just happened here," I said. "Jake Valance showed up with Lola Jones in the trunk of a car and drove away with two million dollars cash."

"You can't be serious," he said. "How could he get from one coast to the other so fast? Especially with a hostage?"

"He said that if the bags he took didn't have ten million in them, he'd be back. He wants ten."

There was a long pause before Al said, "I'm flying out there. Can you meet me at the airport? Baltimore or Philadelphia?"

"Either one. When?"

"I'll call as soon as I have a reservation."

"Al, you don't have to do this. We appreciate everything you've already done."

"I do have to do this, Bob. I'm the only one around here that knows what Jake Valance is capable of, and I fucked up. I should have insisted they put the bastard in solitary and not let him out for any reason. Any reason. I'm going to ask the Sheriff to let me head up this investigation and do whatever has to be done. If he doesn't agree, too bad. I'll take it over anyway. As soon as I make plane reservations, I'll try to find out how Jake got himself and his hostage there so fast. He must have flown, but how? Talk to you soon."

Since John was in no condition to call Dr. Rici, I picked up his phone, found Rici listed and hit the autodial. I told him what had just happened, that John had been robbed of two million in cash, and that he was in a state of shock, or so it appeared to me. Then I handed the phone to John and he listlessly conversed with his neurologist, mostly grunting yes or no or hemming and hawing. "He wants me to go to the nearest hospital and get an MRI," said John after he'd hung up.

"Okay, let's go."

"No, Bob. My head's okay. It's my heart that's broken. Look what I brought into the life of my precious Lola."

"You can't blame yourself, John."

"If I weren't such a pussy and had kept a gun in my house, I could have killed that scumbag Valance and none of this would have happened."

"Brother John, I appreciate how you feel, but none of this is your fault. Al Hansen is coming. He knows how to deal with guys like Valance. Besides, the local police have a description of the car, maybe they'll spot it and stop it and end this nightmare."

But even as I said that, I thought to myself that if Valance were clever enough to escape from jail and get himself here so fast, find out about that delivery of money and intercept it, any cop who stopped him would probably wind up a funeral.

I went through brother John's carry-on bag and found Ambien CR and gave him one with a glass of water. He swallowed it without comment.

As I was about to leave, his room phone rang. I picked it up and it was the bodyguard from Philadelphia calling from the lobby. I went down there and we sat facing each other in leather chairs while I told him the situation. He was a big Irishman, the size of an NFL linebacker, named Pat O'Donnell. I said there was a lot more background to fill in but let's do that tomorrow. I was bone tired. He said he'd post himself in the hall outside John's room and be there all night. If anything untoward arose, he had my room number and cell phone number.

As I headed back to the elevator with Pat O'Donnell, out of the corner of my eye I saw Alex the manager talking to two uniformed policemen. I saw that Alex was waving at me, trying to get my attention. I pretended I hadn't seen this and boarded the elevator. I knew the police were duty-bound to interview both John and myself so I went to John's room to await them. Pat O'Donnell spotted a chair at the far end of the hall and went to it as I went into John's room.

Two uniformed cops showed up about fifteen minutes later. John was half asleep so I did most of the talking, explaining that he'd taken an Ambien to ease the shock. Seems Al Hansen had already called their chief and filled in a lot of the details so all I had to do was remember details of the theft in the parking lot, which wasn't difficult. I told them Valance has a crew cut but was wearing a wig with fake sideburns, wearing a leather car coat style jacket, and carrying a handgun. What kind? I didn't get a good enough look at it and besides, I'm not familiar with the makes and models. What model and year was this blue Lincoln? A Continental. It looked new to me. It had no license plate, nor did it have a tag in the back window or anywhere else that I noticed. I guessed that Valance had removed the license plate to avoid identification. And what was in the two bags Valance stole? Two million in cash. That seemed to freeze both cops momentarily. I described the bags as black leather with both metal locks and leather straps. By this time, John was sound asleep. The two local policemen both looked very young, but at my age, most people look young. They were polite and efficient, and gone within half an hour.

I turned out the lights in John's room and waved to Pat O'Donnell sitting at the far end of the hall as I headed for the elevator and my own room. It was around 8 o'clock here, 5 o'clock West Coast Time—if I called Dr. Grace now, I'd have to tell her that I hadn't felt so charged with cool energy since my drug-smuggling days. I imagined she'd be holding the phone to her ear with her left shoulder as she scribbled notes furiously while I described this feeling. What did it mean when a man with serious depression is uplifted by the theft of his brother's two million dollars, by a rogue cop who'd just escaped from jail and taken my brother's beloved hostage?

Instead, I called Laura and she came to my room and we balled for an hour or more.

Chapter 33

The next morning, I decided to buy that condo anyway. With a check, since the two million in cash was gone. I also decided that I'd pay the son of a bitch the eight million more if that is what it would take to get Lola back. I felt that by moving into the condo, it could create a kind of self-fulfilling prophecy, hastening her safe return. I wished there was some way I could call Jake Valance and tell him this. *Hey, Jake, you win. Give me Lola and take the money.* After that, the law enforcement people could do whatever they wanted or could do, to bring him to justice. Right now, it was crucial that I get Lola back safe and sound. I'd recoup the ten million in two or three years. I didn't need the money, I needed Lola.

I called Bob's room and said, "I'm going down to breakfast. Want to join me?"

"I'm just waking up," he said. "I'll be down in half an hour. I'm glad to hear you sounding good this morning."

"Good? Are you crazy? I'm a wreck till I get Lola back."

When I stepped out of my room, a large, ruddy guy standing well over six feet greeted me. "Pat O'Donnell, Mr. Bradford. I'm your bodyguard from Philly. Nice to meet you."

"Likewise," I said and shook his hand.

"Wherever you're going," he said, "I'll accompany you."

"I'm going down to the restaurant for breakfast."

"I'll make myself inconspicuous," said Pat O'Donnell as he walked beside me toward the elevator.

The thought crossed my mind as I moved down the hall toward the elevator that perhaps I could get this guy to represent me to

Valance for the return of Lola. If, that is, I could locate Valance. I guess the best I can do is make myself easy for him to find.

I sat at a small table down in front with a view of the boardwalk, beach and ocean. O'Donnell sat in a far corner reading a newspaper.

As I ate breakfast and stared out at the boardwalk and the beach and sea beyond, my imagination went wild. I imagined Jake coming to the condo with Lola and me handing over the eight million more he demanded, then, with Lola safe behind me, pulling out a gigantic pistol and blowing a huge hole in the middle of Jake's forehead, watching his blood and brains fly all over the condo's living room, then calling a service to clean it up and haul away the corpse. I had half a dozen such fantasies. They seemed to agree with me, for the Denver omelet went down easily.

I paid the bill with cash and was on my way out the door to the boardwalk when Robert caught up to me. "Want to take a walk?" he said. "I'll come with you."

"No need to come with me, brother. Have some breakfast and we'll get together later."

"Well, then, don't worry about Pat O'Donnell. He'll be following you." I glanced around and saw the bodyguard standing at the corner of the hotel. He smiled and gave a small wave.

"What would you like me to tell Kathy?"

"Kathy? Oh, yes, our realtor. Tell her we've had a change of plans and will use a check to buy the house."

"A check?"

"Yes. Drawn on one of my offshore accounts. Now, go back inside and have some breakfast. Then we'll drive down to Bethany and close the deal."

When Bob didn't turn and leave, I added, "What has me stumped, Robert, is how to get hold of Jake Valance and tell him I'll do it his way—another eight million for the safe return of Lola."

He shook his head and smiled, then laughed out loud. "Jesus H. Christ, John, you amaze me. You're about to spend around twelve million dollars in a couple of days."

"On love and shelter from the storms of life, yes. If my money can't buy us peace and love, what good is it?"

"Peace and love, have you gone hippie on me?"

He threw a clowning fake punch at me in slow motion. I caught his hand and wrapped my other arm around him and said, "We'll get through this, little brother, don't worry."

"How do I get word to Valance?"

"I don't know. But Al Hansen is on his way here. Let's find out what he thinks."

Lola Jones

The night Lola was abducted by Jake Valance, she'd gone to bed early, in the same bed she'd slept in since she was in grade school, the same room in the same house in Canoga Park, a bedroom community in the San Fernando Valley. John had given her two thousand euros before he and Robert left to fly East, and she'd had to drive into downtown LA to convert them to around three thousand dollars.

Lola had been wondering why John hadn't called or returned her calls. Then his brother Robert called to tell her John was in the hospital—he'd been attacked and almost killed by that security guard, Jake Valance.

Would she like to visit him? Of course. The only reason she didn't drive straight to the hospital is that Robert said they wouldn't let her visit John because she was not immediate family. She drove her BMW two-seater to Padero Lane the next day and had lunch with Robert, and went with him to the hospital.

The sight of John with his head in a huge bandage was shocking. And it was worrisome that he didn't seem to be all there, quite. The visit was cut short when he suddenly closed his eyes and went to sleep, leaving her with a ton of things unsaid. "It's the meds," said Robert. "They want him to get as much sleep as possible."

She wasn't sure what to make of Robert. She'd heard he was crazy and had been expected to spend the rest of his life in a nut house till John got him out and moved him into the guesthouse on Padero Lane. But the Robert she'd met and was becoming acquainted with seemed very much with it. Lola had seen no indication that Robert was other than a cool dude on top of his game. He had a thick shock of white hair you could spot from one end of a supermarket to the other. He'd told her he was sixty but he looked more like forty-five or fifty.

After they left the hospital, she suggested they stop for a drink. She wanted to find out all she could about what had happened to John, and she wanted to get to know his brother better. Robert said he didn't drink but he'd be happy go with her and have a glass of orange juice. They went to a cocktail lounge in one of the big motels along the beach in Santa Barbara, and sat at a small table with a view. As they gazed out at sailboats on the sea, Robert told sailing adventure stories. The brothers loved to sail, had owned a series of boats from a small dingy to a 30-footer, which they bought as salvage and repaired themselves, then explored the offshore islands in.

"Have you done any sailing?" he asked

"No, none at all."

The extent of her boating experience was to fly to Avalon Harbor in Catalina and turn tricks on a yacht, and she was not about to mention that now.

Given the work she'd been doing, Lola had developed a knack for reading men, and figured she was pretty good at it, for she'd never been entrapped by cops—she could smell a cop a block away. The impression she got from Robert was that he was, like John, worldly and sophisticated, but that the world Robert came from was closer to hers. She sensed that, some time in his past, he'd been into drugs and working girls.

She said, "I hope you don't think I'm prying, but I'm curious about what you do for a living."

He laughed and said, "Years ago, I was a writer. Then I got involved with drugs and I also operated an escort service. Now I'm employed by my brother. I guess I'll be managing the upkeep of his properties, of which he seems to have many. And you? What's your bio?"

She swallowed her reluctance and was frank. "I've been a call girl since I was seventeen. Only other job I had was at a McDonalds when I was fifteen. Are you easy with that?"

"Sure. World's oldest profession. I'm glad to hear you worked the high end. I know the streets can be rough, even deadly."

She asked Robert what he thought of her and his brother as a couple. He smiled and became more frank than she'd expected. "At first I thought you were a cute hooker, stroking my brother's ego for the money. I was glad he had himself such a beauty, but wasn't sure where you would take him. But now, after being around you two for a while, I think you really love each other. It's a spring-winter affair, sure, but sometimes they're the best. And I know a lot of people stigmatize girls who were in the life. That's just something you'll have to deal with. It's kind of hard for other people to understand any couple who doesn't fit the usual demographic."

"I know. And I really do love him. I don't think he quite believes it yet, but I really do love him. I know a lot of people will think I'm on the make for his money. Hell, I can make enough money on my own, I don't need to prostitute myself by marrying anyone. That he's so rich is a turn on, part of why I love him. Do you find that hard to believe?"

"Not at all. I've seen it before and been involved in a few summer-autumn romances myself. We have to go where love takes us. If we don't, we spend our lives wondering how things would have worked out if we had. John has spent so much of his life being lonely," he said more seriously. "And now that he's moving into retirement, he was about to become lonelier than ever—until you two decided to live together. I'm happy for him, and wish the both of you all the best. Any long-range relationship is fragile. We all know a lot of same-age couples who wound up in nasty break-ups or divorces. Why some couples are compatible and others aren't is a profound mystery."

Lola thanked her lucky stars that her prospective brother-in-law was so understanding. She was tempted to say that if he ever wanted a little change of pace, she could fix him up with a casual girlfriend, but she knew he'd been dating John's ex-wife. Maybe later, when they knew each other better.

After two vodka gimlets, Lola said she'd better get home. She needed to check with the realtor who was handling the rental of her house, find out if anyone else wanted to see the house. That was a little white lie. The truth was, she didn't want to be seen spending too much time with John's brother, for this could undermine John's trust in her. Love was built on trust.

So they'd gone back to the house on the beach and she'd given Robert a quick peck on the cheek before she got into her BMW Z and drove back to The Valley. On the way, John called her cell and they had a nice chat. That was comforting. He sounded more alert and ready-Freddie than when she'd seen him in the hospital. He said now that Valance was behind bars, why didn't she move back into the Padero Lane house. She said she was eager to move back in with him but first she wanted to get her house in The Valley rented and get her furniture in storage. He asked why she didn't just sell the house and be done with it. She felt that would be insulting to her grandfather, "and if anything goes wrong with our relationship, it's my fall-back position."

John then reversed himself by saying, "It's really a good idea to hang onto every piece of real estate you can, Lola. It's smart. I just hope you can find a renter soon so you're not running back and forth."

Even so, she was sorely tempted to put the house up for sale and go. But real estate hadn't been selling lately and a vacant house on her street would not be a good idea. Her neighborhood was going downhill, and it might get taken over and become a crack house. She could have turned the whole rental thing over to her realtor, but wanted to make sure the new people would be right, as a way of honoring her grandfather. She didn't want to leave the remnants of her grandfather behind till she was sure of her next step.

The day John and Robert flew East, the realtor called to say she had a very promising prospect coming tomorrow from somewhere south of LA in Orange County. Before she'd hooked up with John, Lola usually got to bed around dawn. This evening she'd run the vacuum cleaner and done some dusting and straightening up in preparation of tomorrow's house showing, and been asleep by midnight. The realtor described this new prospect as an Hispanic couple with two kids. If they wanted to rent the house, she'd store her furniture, pack up and fly away to John. Lola fell asleep feeling optimistic.

The next thing she knew, the lights were on in her bedroom and someone was standing over her, towering over her. The overhead light was behind him so she could not make out his face, didn't know who it was till he said, "Get up, bitch. We're going on a trip."

But Jake Valance was in jail! She thought she was having a nightmare. But he grabbed her and roughly pulled her out of bed, stood her up and said, "Get dressed to travel." She was wondering how she could fox her way out of this when she saw he had a gun in his hand. He was leaning on a cane and holding a gun in his right hand. She slept in the nude and felt fearfully naked as she went to her clothes closet to select something to wear. "Pack a suitcase," Jake said. "We'll be gone a long time." He stood over her, occasionally poking her in the butt with the end of the cane, a couple of times slapping her with it. She pulled on panties and bra, jeans, a sweater and running shoes between pokes and slaps, and wondered if she'd come out of this alive. She threw an assortment of clothing and toiletries into her suitcase and a smaller carry-on bag.

"How did you get out of jail?" she asked.

"None of your business, bitch."

He prodded her with the cane toward the front door. It wasn't damaged so he must have picked the lock, she guessed. He pulled the door closed behind them and made sure it was locked, then pointed the cane toward the street and shoved her along the path to the sidewalk. He took her two bags and put them in the trunk, then opened the passenger side door of a big white sedan and shoved her in. Once behind the wheel, he reached into the back seat and came up with two sets of handcuffs, locked one on her wrists, the other around her ankles. As he drove, she noticed he was wearing those thin plastic gloves people in hospitals and restaurant kitchens wear.

Part of her wanted to scream and cry, kick out a window and yell for help, but instead she forced her voice to be calm as she asked, "Where are you taking me?"

"We're going to visit John Bradford," he said.

"You're going the wrong way. John's in Santa Barbara."

"He's back East. We're going to meet him there."

"Where?"

"Rehoboth Beach, Delaware."

Lola knew that Robert was buying a condo there. John wanted to get as far away from this crazy as possible—that's why he was planning to get the condo and stay there with her. She'd never been east of Las Vegas.

"I heard you got shot," she said.

"Yeah. Fortunately, he missed my kneecap. Grazed my left knee, severed a major ligament, but they did a good job at the hospital. I get around fine with the cane."

He drove her to the non-commercial part of the airport, left her sitting in the car for about half an hour. With her hands cuffed behind her back, it would have been difficult to open the door, and with her ankles cuffed, running was out of the question. She was hatching a scheme to get out of Jake's car and hide under another when he came back, unlocked the cuffs, tossed them into a little black bag and, holding her elbow, led her through a little waiting room and out onto the tarmac to a private jet, the kind Lola had seen on TV and knew was used by rock stars and corporate executives. He sat her in a seat at the rear of this plane and sat himself down beside a well-dressed man with a deeply lined face and dark hair that was graying around the temples. Soon the plane was lifting off and Lola was watching the lights of LA wink off as the morning sun rose, feeling a sense of doom like a big stone in her stomach.

Lola had been warned when she was seventeen and starting out that being a call girl could be dangerous. You could encounter guys who got off beating up girls, or you could meet guys who had other freakish things in mind, and there were killers out there. But she'd never met any of those types in her five years of dating for dough. It had been a girl named Nancy Klinder who'd invited Lola into the business. Nancy, who called herself various other names when she was with johns, told Lola she'd been asked to bring another girl with her, and would Lola like to come. "What would I have to do?" asked Lola. "Make him feel like a king. Suck his cock and fuck him. Do whatever he wants you to do. When we get there, just follow my lead and you'll do fine." Nancy drove them to a downtown hotel and they went up to a room, and two guys were there. They were in town on business, they said. The four of them had a drink together and Lola watched the way Nancy moved provocatively, and did likewise. She would learn that half the gig was vamping. Get the john aroused by moving and talking sexy, and you could be out of there with a handful of cash in less than an hour. On their way out of the hotel, Nancy gave a bellhop ten percent of what they'd made, and Lola came home with nine hundred dollars. It sure beat flipping burgers. Until now.

She was deathly afraid of Jake Valance. Had been since she first laid eyes on him in John's house. He radiated a combination of lust and barely-contained rage that made her skin crawl. Maybe she'd been prescient, she decided, for here she now was, his prisoner. She knew what he meant when he said they were going to see John Bradford— would John pay whatever ransom Jake asked? Lola knew John was anxious to get into the condo, and anxious for her to rent out her house and join them there. Jake had tried to kill John. How did he get out of jail? How did he find out where she lived? How did he manage to have this plane at his disposal? In the back of her mind she knew—but was reluctant to bring this knowledge to full consciousness—that this son of a bitch was after more than a ransom, that he was planning to rob and kill John, and was using her to accomplish this. What kind of cruel twist of fate was this? Just when she was on the verge of "happily ever after," this happens.

She strained her ears to hear what Jake and the stranger were talking about. At first, they kept their voices low, but after their second cocktail, she could catch a word or phrase now and then. After their third drink, she could pick up more. At one point, craggy face said that Jake had saved his life way back when and he was happy to be able to return the favor. She learned that craggy face was on his way to

Washington, while Jake was on his way to the man's summer home in Rehoboth Beach. If she ever got out of this alive, she figured, every tidbit of information she could pick up would be helpful.

By the time they landed at the part of the Baltimore airport for private planes, what she had picked up were impressions, mainly the impression that craggy face was somehow involved in raising campaign contributions for politicians, and that he was willing to lend Jake some cash now, provided, he made clear, that Jake repay the money before the month was out. Putting overheard tidbits together, she surmised that Jake had done this man a life-saving favor some years ago, when Jake was living in New York, and the man was now repaying the favor.

After they got off the plane, Jake took her by the elbow and led her through what looked like a waiting room to the outside, where they caught a taxi and were driven to a parking lot. The taxi drove them around and around the parking lot—Jake told the cabbie he was looking for his car. Finally, Jake said, "Here it is," paid the cabbie and they got out. Lola stood with her two bags at her feet while Jake went to the door of a powder-blue Lincoln, unlocked the driver's door and got in. He then popped open the trunk lid from a remote inside the car, got out and put Lola's bags into the trunk, then led her to the passenger seat, and away they drove. She was relieved that he did not put her in the cuffs again. But of course there was no need for that now, she realized, for how could she run away? She was in a strange new landscape, didn't know a soul here, had no money in her jeans, didn't even have her makeup on.

"Don't shit your pants, Lola," he said as he drove over a long bridge. "You do what I say and you'll be okay. I'm going to use you to pry some money out of Bradford, that's all. When that's done, I'll let you go."

Coming from an escaped convict who'd tried to kill John, Jake's words were of little comfort. But if Lola had learned one thing for sure from The Life it was that men can be controlled by sexual desire. Get their little man aroused and you have them in your power. As one of her girlfriends liked to say, "Stimulate the brains between their legs and their heads turn to mush." Lola decided to try the only weapon she had. She adjusted herself in the seat so that her breasts jutted out more prominently under her sweater. She tried to will her nipples to harden but, given how she felt, that didn't work. Nonetheless, she soon noticed Jake's eye glancing her way, roaming over her body. Now, if he would only stop some place where there were people and drop his pants, she could jump out of the car and call for help, plead for protection.

The four-lane highway turned into a two lane and Jake slowed from 80 to 60. Gas stations and restaurants became fewer and farther between, and Lola saw fewer and fewer people till they were totally out in the country with nothing but rolling farmland and barns. Finally they came to a town with a sign proclaiming it to be Lewes, and further down a four-lane highway lined with stores, another sign said, Rehoboth Beach. Jake turned onto some back streets and they arrived at a house under tall trees. He pulled into the driveway of this two-story house and stopped, fished a remote control out of the glove compartment and opened the garage door, drove the car in, closed the garage door, and said, "Home."

A door from the garage brought them into a kitchen, and Jake immediately opened the refrigerator. "You hungry?" She was but said nothing. He found a couple of steaks in the freezer and put them in a microwave to thaw. He got out two plates, forks and steak knives. She eyed the steak knives, wondering if she could use one to stab this monster. They had sharp blades but their ends were rounded rather than pointed. She'd have to slash rather than stab.

The next thing she knew, he had both hands on her and was bending her over the kitchen counter. He pulled down her jeans and panties, and rammed his penis into her dry vagina. She'd learned to relax her vagina when she wasn't ready so that it expanded enough to save her from too much pain. She'd also learned to conduct a man to climax by the sounds she made. As Jake shoved, she let out little cries that grew gradually louder and more insistent, and the rape ended almost as quickly as it had started.

"I need a shower," she said as she pulled up her panties and jeans.

"Be my guest," he said.

She wandered into the interior of the house, found a bathroom, undressed and got under the shower. She began by cleaning her vagina, and ended with a shampoo. She felt weary but knew she could not lay down in one of the bedrooms and sleep. As she emerged from the bathroom, she glanced down the hall to her right and saw what looked like a back door. Even if it wasn't locked, where would she go if she left this house? It was cold outside, raw and drizzly. Her jacket was in the kitchen.

After she and Jake ate the steaks he cooked, he said, "I've got to go out and buy something." He then sat her in a straight-backed chair in front of a television set, turned it on and asked, "What would you like to watch?" She didn't reply. He surfed the channels and found an Oprah show rerun. Then he went back to the kitchen and carried in the little black bag containing the hand and ankle cuffs. He cuffed her hands in front of her, then put one clamp around the leg of the chair and the other around her right ankle. He stood back and looked at her a moment and said, "That won't work." He unlocked the ankle cuffs and made her lay down on the floor, then lifted a heavy couch and put a cuff around its leg, and the other around her ankle. He unlocked the handcuffs and redid them so her hands were behind her back. "There," he said.

After he left, she worked her way up so she could sit on the couch. She watched Oprah without thinking about what was happening on the show. Her thoughts were racing with schemes to escape. She remembered that John and Robert planned to stay in a hotel here called the Boardwalk Plaza and reasoned that if she could get out of this house before Jake returned, she could find that hotel. She tried to lift the couch to free her tethered ankle, but on the floor with her hands cuffed behind her back, that didn't work. She tried to squirm her way toward a telephone on a table at the far end of the couch, but was too firmly tethered to the couch leg. In her frustration, she yelled out, "Nine one one." Finally, she relaxed and dozed.

She was awakened by Jake returning through the kitchen and looked up to see him wearing a wig. It gave him a big head of curly hair and sideburns. By this time, it was late afternoon. Jake went to the living room bar and fixed himself a drink, bourbon on the rocks. "Want a drink?" he asked her.

She shook her head no. "But I need to go to the bathroom," she said.

He unlocked the cuffs.

Inside the bathroom, she inspected her face in the mirror. She could see the panic in the dark blue eyes that stared back at her. Vamping Jake had backfired. This guy did not have normal male emotions. Instead of warming toward her, he'd raped her. She saw a small window at the far end of the bathroom and went to it, unlocked it, lifted the lower half up. But it didn't provide enough space for her to squirm her body through it, so she closed it. She sat on the commode and peed and moved her bowels. She remembered that her grandfather liked to say, "A good shit can bring a positive change of attitude." Maybe tonight when Jake goes to sleep, she thought, she could find a door or window that would enable her to escape.

When she went back to the living room, Jake was sitting on the couch with his pants and underwear around his ankles, his legs extended. "Come here," he said. "Get down on your knees and blow me."

As she obeyed, she remembered a romance novel she'd once read, in which the heroine goes through one hellacious series of travails before she is saved by the man she loves and lives happily ever after. She would not live happily ever after, she thought, unless she could cut off Jake's dick and shove it up his ass, then dump his body into a waste disposal grinder or a wood chipper. She glanced up to see Jake sipping his drink and staring at the TV. She lifted her mouth off his erection and said, "You really into this?"

"Keep at it," he ordered.

As she continued, she thought of John. She knew he had trouble believing she was really in love with him, but she was, really was. He was no Adonis but she'd had enough well-built guys to know that pretty muscles were no substitute for brains and personality. She loved the way John looked in the nude, how his butt flexed when he walked. He had a flat stomach and beefy shoulders she loved to lay her head on. Above all, he radiated an energy that embraced her, understood her, adored her, protected her. She remembered the first time she met him, how he didn't just wham-bam-thank-you-ma'am and kick her out of the hotel room. He played with her, joked with her. She knew her youth and curvaceous body turned him on—he made that abundantly evident. And she loved how he behaved when he was aroused. He could be foxy, gentle or rough, dominant or submissive. He was sexually adventurous and so was she. Months before she'd propositioned John, she knew he was a man she could make a life with. If she ever got out of this trap she was in, she decided, she must find ways to assure John that she really truly devoutly loved him—beyond her prosty skills, beyond his worries about aging, beyond even her own precious self, for she would lay down her life for that man. That's how much she wanted him to love her.

Her jaw ached by the time Jake came. And by this time, it was dark. He led her into one of the bedrooms on the second floor and shackled her to a four-poster bed with an old fashioned canopy on top. She slept for a few hours then awoke and lay there thinking, dreaming, worrying, scheming. "You manifest what you imagine," one of the girls had once told her. The girl was talking about walking into a hotel room to meet a john—if you imagine having fun, you'll have fun. If you imagine a bummer, it will be a bummer. She passionately imagined escaping, being saved by John, squirming out of the cuffs and jumping out this second floor window and running, running, running. But which way? Downhill, she decided, for that's where the ocean must be, and John's hotel is on the ocean.

The next morning Jake adjusted her restraints so she could sit up in bed with her head on pillows. He turned on the TV and left without a word. He'd tuned in CNN and so she was aware, without focusing on it, of the news flickering by, then repeating and repeating. Hillary Clinton and Barack Obama were contending for the Democratic Party nomination. Some politician named John McCain had already sewed up the Republican Party nomination. The script readers of CNN let it be known that they admired McCain and Clinton, and lambasted Obama. Lola found herself growing more and more sympathetic toward Obama. For one thing, he radiated the same kind of energy that John did. As she continued to watch, Lola learned that the talking heads had tried to use Obama's pastor as a rope to lynch him with, and Obama had given a speech about race that wowed his admirers and stymied his detractors. Lola wondered if she'd live to see who'd win the election in November.

Jake returned and unlocked her cuffs, led her downstairs, and told her to fix herself a meal. She ate a bowl of cereal and a naval orange. He then returned her to the bed, the shackles, and CNN. This became their routine, broken only when Jake decided to rape her. Once when he was flat-backing her, he raised his hand as though to hit her in the face and said, "Move your ass, bitch." She learned that no matter what position he put her in, if she bumped and wiggled, it got him off faster. When he was done, he'd pull up his pants and shackle her to the bed again, and leave without a word.

She'd lost count of how many hours or days passed before he told her to get dressed, they were going for a ride. She put on fresh panties and bra and the same old jeans and sweater, and he took her into the garage, opened the car trunk and told her to get in. He cuffed her hands behind her back and put the ankle cuffs on, and then tore off a strip of duck tape and put it over her mouth. He seemed to be in an agitated state, excited, tense, even anxious. She'd never seen Jake anxious before and wondered what that meant. Had something gone wrong with whatever he'd planned? Was he going to release her or kill her?

She bumped along in the trunk as he drove. The smallest pothole was jarring. Then the car soon stopped and was motionless for what seemed a very long time. Finally she heard voices and the trunk flew open and peering down at her was John. Robert was by his side and another man was behind them. Jake stood to one side with his hand on the trunk lid. At the sight of John, Lola tried to scream but only a murmur escaped the duck tape. She heard Jake tell John that he would get her back when he, Jake, got ten million dollars.

Then Jake slammed down the truck lid and drove. When he opened it again, she was back in the garage. He ripped off the duck tape and unlocked the cuffs and they went into the house. Jake carried two large leather bags into a first-floor bedroom, then came back to the kitchen and said, "You hungry?" He was now smiling and looking pleased with himself. What was in those two bags? It had to be cash. Had John made a cash down payment to get her back? A down payment till he could come up with the rest of the ten million Jake demanded? If he did wind up paying all that money to save her life, how could he love her? How can you love someone who—even unintentionally winds up enabling someone else to rob you of ten million dollars?

She'd become keenly aware of a rack of knives hanging in the kitchen, some with very sharp points. She fantasized killing Jake with one, grabbing those two bags and finding her way to the hotel, returning them to John. If the bags do indeed contain cash, she thought, maybe Jake will feel flush enough to relax and allow her more freedom, and she'll find a way to grab a knife and shove it into his heart. Then she'll dial 911 and take off carrying the bags, walking downhill toward the ocean, find the Boardwalk Plaza Hotel and John.

The police would come and find Jake's body and eventually find out who had killed him and why. She'd be questioned but when the police learned the whole story, they'd let her go. Above all, killing Jake and recovering that money would show John how much she loved him. How could he doubt her love after that? They'd return to California, to the house on Padero Lane and she'd go to college, get a degree, maybe a post-graduate degree or two, and in a few years she'd be the head of a foundation John would create. Then she would look back on this mess she was in now and see it as like a romance novel or a psycho thriller movie. Maybe she'd even write a book about it.

"Too bad we can't go out to eat," Jake said, as he slapped two thick pieces of steak down on the kitchen counter. "Can't even go outside and cook these on charcoal. But it won't be long now."

"What won't be long?" she asked.

"Before your john pays my asking price."

"Didn't you get enough in those two bags?"

"No, but he wants you back. He'll pay."

"What will you do when you get all the money you want?"

"Shut up and make a salad," he said, "while I cook the steaks."

She thought of reaching down the back of her jeans and running a finger over her rectum then using that shitty finger to make Jake a salad that would make him sick. As though he read her mind, he said, "And wash your hands before you make the salad."

Chapter 34

By noon, John had emailed his bank in the Caymans and they had wired a check to a bank in Bethany, and we were ready to close on the condo at the office of Attorney Duncan Blanchard. The bodyguard Pat O'Donnell sat in the back seat of the Escalade as we drove to Bethany. When we went into the bank in Bethany, he kept a courteous distance. In the lawyer's office, he sat in the waiting room, thumbing through magazines.

I sat across a large conference table from John during this ritual. John wasn't entirely pleased. Blanchard's duty to this process apparently consisted of telling John where to sign his name and where to put his initials as they flipped through the thick document. John was expecting a lot more information from the attorney, and did not see why so many papers were needed when there was no mortgage involved. At one point, John asked Blanchard, "Isn't there a paper in this pile that vouches for the condition of the property?"

"No, we're an old fashioned buyer-beware state," said Blanchard.

I said, "I can have our man Tony Martino inspect it before you finalize the deal."

"That's all right," said John, "I'm anxious to get this done with and behind us. Then we can get the house inspected and see to whatever repairs might be needed."

He made a separate arrangement to buy the previous owner's furniture, saving himself a lot of shopping. Kathy saw to getting the utilities turned on.

As we walked outside and got back into the Escalade—with the bodyguard in the back seat—John said, "These real estate people and attorneys would be in noncompliance in California and other parts of the world. Mr. Blanchard seems to have made a juicy fee for no legal advice whatsoever. On the other hand, Delaware does have laws friendly to corporations. We're incorporated here, you know. What say we check out of the hotel and get moved in?"

"Now?"

"After we have lunch."

"I'd like to take out an hour or two to make some calls and do my meditation," I said.

"Fine. Just so we're moved in before sundown. Do you think Valance knows what we're doing? Will he know where we are when we move into this house? Does our new security person here know what the situation is?"

O'Donnell said, "I've talked to the police and the hotel manager. They've filled me in. Anything else I should know?"

"Do you know the who?"

"I understand there is a thug named Jake Valance who is threatening your life."

"Correct."

"He's holding a hostage and no one knows where he is at the moment."

"Correct."

"So my job is to make sure he doesn't get to you."

"If he found us at the hotel," I said, "I suspect he'll be able to find the house."

John said, "And we have no way of contacting him. Have to wait for him to contact."

"He probably has your old cell phone number," said Bob. "And you can leave your new cell number with the hotel desk in case he calls them to contact you."

"Perhaps," O'Donnell interjected, "it would be a good idea for me to go through the house before you move in."

"Good idea. Let's detour to the house now and drop you off. You'll then be there when we arrive with our things late this afternoon or early evening."

I hung a U turn and drove back to the development. A guard was on duty at the gate. That was odd because there were so few residents here in the dead of winter. He explained that he was here to greet us, give us the card key and show us how to use it. We made introductions all around and dropped O'Donnell off at the condo with the second set of house keys, then continued to Rehoboth.

Bob said, "I don't understand why you wanted to separate yourself from your bodyguard, John."

"I want to make myself easy for Jake Valance to contact. I don't think he'll try to harm me—until I pay the ransom. That's when I'll need all the bodyguards I can get. Which reminds me, when Al Hansen gets here, maybe he'll handle this transaction, making sure Lola is uninjured and getting the cash to Valance."

"I wouldn't count on it," I said.

"Why not?"

"He's in law enforcement. He'll want to catch Jake and return him to the Santa Barbara County Jail. He may not like the idea of you meeting Jake's demands. He may want to set up a sting."

"You're right. I don't know what I'm thinking. Maybe I did suffer some brain damage."

"You're anxious about Lola."

"She's become the light of my life. I'll do anything to get her back."

He gazed out at the sand dunes whizzing by as we drove Route 1 just south of Dewey Beach. "There seems to be something about these magnificent sand dunes that tugs at the soul," he said. "They give me a déjà vu feeling, like I've lived here before but can't remember when. But maybe that's my memory playing tricks on me. I've driven by lots of sand dunes before, on Cape Cod, the Outer Banks of North Carolina, Thailand, India, Africa, and near Apalachicola, Florida."

"And that stretch between Mexicali and San Felipe where we used to go when we were kids. Remember?"

"Oh, yes. The mouth of the Colorado River. Dad used to love to drive down to San Felipe to go deep-sea fishing. We used to rent those three-wheeler ATMs and go motoring all over those dunes. What fun we had."

"During the seventies, I used to go down to San Felipe to make arrangements to fly dope over the border."

John smiled at that, then said, "What puzzles me, Bob, is this: You come from the same privileged background as me, yet you're lucky you aren't dead or doing hard time in prison. Why did you choose a life of crime?"

"I didn't choose it. It was the only way I had to generate income and get off skid row. My behavior changed radically after the second head trauma. I couldn't write, couldn't string two sentences together that made sense. I'd fly off the handle at the slightest provocation, and I'd sink into crippling depressions for days or weeks. That's when I got into serious drug dealing and began drinking heavily, too. Trying to medicate myself."

"And now you're worried about me."

"Let's say I'm keeping a close eye on you."

"I'm not feeling the least bit depressed, I assure you. What I'm feeling is anxious to get into that condo and get Lola back, no matter what it costs. Then I want to buy a sailboat, a forty footer, so we can all go out on the briny like we did when we were kids and just enjoy life."

It seemed to me John had just described a change in his personality. I said, "You spent most of your life as a workaholic."

"What are you implying? Brain damage?"

"If Valance hadn't attacked you, would you be here now? Would you be willing to pay the ransom for Lola? Would you want to buy a sailboat, kick back and enjoy life?"

John was silent for a time. "I tend to think it's Lola, and having my big brother back in my life—that's what's changed me. When we were growing up, I so much wanted to emulate you, Robert. You had so many girlfriends, so much fun, everybody admired you. You cut such a dashing figure at parties. Me, I was a bookworm full of secret fantasies."

"Then you became the big success in life, the man of extraordinary wealth and power."

"Strange, isn't it, how our paths have crisscrossed."

"I'm not sure what you mean."

"Well, now my life is in danger the way yours used to be, and you have an income that puts you among the most affluent."

"You're paying me eighty thousand a year, if I understand the deal correctly. That's a middle class income these days, isn't it?"

"I have surprises in store for you, Bob."

"What does that mean?"

"When the time comes, you'll not be disappointed."

"Are you cutting your derelict brother in for some of your fortune?"

"I'll say no more."

John has the Midas touch but money goes through my fingers like water. I didn't want the burden of a lot of money. Jorge Hernandez has convinced me that the world's system of fiat currencies will eventually crash, and I didn't want to get so hooked on money as a status prop that I'd be bereft if or when the system crashes. In my ideal world, no one has too much, no one too little.

When I got back to my hotel room, I tried to call Al Hansen but his phone was off. I then called Dr. Mary Grace and had a half hour session with her. She was concerned that I am so caught up in my brother's life that I may be neglecting my own. "The problem is," I told her, "that my life is now so entwined with John's. Whatever happens to him impacts my life as though it happened to me."

"Be that as it may, you need to establish your own life, Robert. You're a separate individual. Are you doing your daily meditations?"

"Yes, although I've missed a day or two."

"Robert, it's of primary importance that you use the Silva Method to seed the causal plane. Bathing your brain in alpha waves daily is a must, Robert."

"I know. And when things settle down a bit, I'll not miss any days. I value my meditations."

"Are you taking your medications?"

"Yes. Medications and meditations."

Then I called Jorge Hernandez. He was sitting in the courtyard, as usual. I pictured him with a book in his lap and his laptop by his feet, his reading glasses halfway down his nose, a distant look in his eye whenever he stopped reading to capture a fleeting thought.

"You know something, Jorge? This world has surely turned upside down when a guy like you is locked away as crazy while people on the outside are behaving like psychopaths. I'm acquiring a new sense of what's sane and what's insane."

"Your secret is safe with me," he said. "Just don't blab it around or they're liable to lock you up again."

"Are you sticking to your prediction? That we're moving into a great depression?"

"Yes, I am. This spring and early summer may fool people. It may seem that we've avoided the worst. But by late summer and climaxing around Election Day, things will get ugly, for that's when the Saturn-Uranus opposition will make its first exact hit."

"Do you see any connection between the mental disease of depression and economic depression?"

"I've thought a lot about that. If we see society as an entity, yes. Like an individual suffering from the disease, a society manifests the same symptoms. Alternating outbursts of self-destructive violence and crippling self-loathing."

"Do you think that suffering from the disease makes you pessimistic about the economy?"

"When I've been trapped in my disease, I've tended to see society as rollicking happily on without me. Strange as it may seem, Bob, I can analyze individuals and nations whether I'm suffering or not. I can see from history that this coming planetary pattern is going to bring depression. First on the causal plane, the mood will turn gloomy, and that will manifest in our material reality as events bringing more gloom. Most people mistake the string of events for the cause, when in reality it's the sequence of planetary patterns that precipitate the events."

"Who would you like to see become our next president?"

"Obama, he's the one with the potential. He can rally the masses and change the game, and that's what it will take to navigate our way through the coming decade. I think we'll need to change our monetary system to survive as a society. And that will be as difficult and dangerous as JFK ending racial segregation. If Obama fulfills his potential, he could become another FDR."

"And if he doesn't fulfill his potential?"

"Things will get worse than they have to get, then desperation will overcome ideology and dictate practical solutions."

"You've convinced me, professor." I gave him a quick summary of my debate with John on the flight here.

"Well, your brother is among the few Ph D economists with such a keen appreciation of economic cycles. Most economists are linear thinkers, trapped in econometrics. Some seem to think history began when the Bush Administration took office."

"My brother tells me that I am now among the affluent few. He's put me on his payroll and hinted he may have added me to his will."

"Hold that hint, Bob. If he hasn't yet, he will. Why not? He needs you."

"But me and money aren't on friendly terms."

"Convert the money to hard assets, especially real estate, and you'll be fine. Land, terra firma, is the essence of real wealth."

"But owning things gets in the way of my personal happiness."

"Poor baby."

I didn't go into detail about the latest episode with Jake. I'd told him in a previous call that Jake had escaped and may have kidnapped Lola. Something stopped me from telling him that Jake had shown up here, with Lola in his trunk, and stolen the two million John had planned to use to buy the condo. Jorge seems to view life on earth from a perspective way out in space, from Polaris or the Galactic Center of the Milky Way.

For the last five minutes of the call, he told me the history of Pluto's past conjunctions with the Galactic Center. "It adds up to the fact that we have entered another period of huge transformations," he said, "much like the two decades following Columbus' discovery of the Western Hemisphere, and the years leading up to the Revolutionary War. Now that we're so dependent on oil—for fuels, plastics, fertilizer, you name it—if the next president doesn't take radical action, life as we know it could be relegated to the dustbin of history."

"That's enough, Jorge. You're threatening my depression."

When I got off the phone with Jorge, I saw I had a message from Al. I dialed him again. "I hate to spring this on you so suddenly, Bob, but can you meet me at the Baltimore airport around 11 tonight?"

"Sure. John and I are moving our personal things into his new condo later today. We should have that done by dinnertime. Then I'll drive over to BWI. Listen, I have news."

I then told him how Jake had showed up with Lola in the trunk of a Lincoln, took two million in cash from John, and disappeared. Local law enforcement had every major route into and out of this little town covered but no word that they've spotted the light blue Lincoln Jake was driving. I mentioned that Jake wants another eight million in cash to return Lola, and that John is ready to pay it.

"In a town that size, the police should be able to find that car. Maybe he's hiding right under ya'all's noses. I've done some research into Valance. He grew up in that area."

"Yes, I learned that, too, from the state police here. They suspect he may have murdered his father."

"I didn't know that. What evidence do they base that on?"

"They don't have any hard evidence, just the strong suspicion."

"Do you know any psychics?"

That took me aback. A cop asking about psychics? "Let me think about it."

"Okay, see you tonight."

Chapter 35

Bob and I had dinner at the hotel restaurant and by 7 o'clock had loaded the Escalade with our luggage, ready to drive to the condo and move in when—wonder of wonders—who should I see walking toward us but Lola. She was staggering toward us on an uneven sidewalk, lugging the two big leather bags Jake had taken. I rushed to her and wrapped my arms around her and kissed her all over the face, and said, "My God, Lola. Are you okay? How did you escape?"

All she could do for the first ten minutes was sob and cling to me. Bob picked up the two bags and carried them to the car, did a quick inspection of their contents, and gave me the thumbs-up sign. The money appeared to be there.

The next logical move was to call the police and report this latest development, but Lola insisted we not do that. "Please, please, not yet," she cried. "Can you do that later? They'll want to question me and I'm falling apart. I'm totally wrecked."

"Well," Bob put in, "can you take us to where Jake is?"

"Yeah, but not right now. I'm just too beat. That slime ball put me through hell."

We were standing outside the front entrance, inspecting Lola from head to toe for signs of brutality. "The damages are psychological," she said. "You just loaded up your car. Where are you going?"

"To the condo, my darling. I closed on it this morning."

"Can we go there now? I need to rest and clean myself up before I talk to anyone else."

Bob drove and Lola and I sat in the back seat, where we could cling to each other. She sobbed for about fifteen minutes. I held her tightly in my arms and rocked her gently. Finally, she stopped sobbing, straightened her back and whispered, "I stabbed him, John."

"Stabbed?"

"Jake."

"Did you kill him?"

"Yeah. He wasn't moving when I left. I stabbed him with a little cheese knife. In the back, down near his waist."

"How did you manage that, Lola?"

"I spotted this sharp little knife in a rack with a lot of other knives. It was small enough so I could palm it, you know? It has a little blade about four inches long. Jake took me upstairs and shackled me to the bed and was on top of me, going to rape me again when I slammed this little blade into his back. He goes, like, 'Ahhhhh,' and then rolls off the bed. I got the key out of his pocket and unlocked myself. Then I got dressed, grabbed those two bags and started walking. They're heavy. I thought I'd give out before I got here. I wasn't sure where the hotel is. I had to kind of feel my way to it. You'd told me it was on the ocean so I kept going downhill till I spotted a big pink building. Bob had told us it was pink, so I figured that must be it. That's how I got here."

"You said he was going to rape you again. How many times did he rape you, darling?"

"I lost count. He had my hands and ankles in handcuffs most of the time. He'd unlock me to eat but most of the time he kept me locked down. He raped me whenever he felt like it."

"We've got to get you to a hospital, my love."

"Not tonight, John. I can't go through that yet. I know I should for the police report and all, but please, I can't do that right now. Please hold me and tell me you love me. I'll do all these official things tomorrow, okay?"

For the rest of the ride, she sat with her back pressed to me, my arms around her, staring out at the passing scene. It was twilight, the sun sinking over Rehoboth Bay. I kept silent but was a fireworks of emotions inside. That she had killed Jake Valance stirred both joy and dread. Joy that he's gone, dread at what problems her act might bring. This was surely more excitement than this small town had seen in a long time, so it was going to stir a hornet's nest of media attention, I feared.

Unless we didn't report it. But how could we not report it when the police are involved now, searching for Valance?

"How far from the hotel were you?" I asked.

"Hard to tell. Less than a mile, I think. We were in a house, two stories, on a quiet street, lots of trees. If I hadn't been dragging those two big bags, I think I could have walked it in ten minutes or less. I lost my watch so I wasn't keeping track of time. Not many people around. Only a couple of cars passed me while I was walking. One lady stopped and rolled down her window and offered me a ride but I told her no thanks. I didn't want to complicate this any more than it already is. My hands are sore and my legs feel like rubber. Hell, I'm sore all over, really. But he stole those bags of money from you and I've returned them, John. That counts for something?"

"I was ready to give Jake whatever money he demanded for your return."

"You were? That's nuts, John. That son of a bitch would take every cent you have, if he could."

"You are far more valuable to me than money, darling."

"Oh John, that's so sweet—I'm about to bawl like a baby all over again."

"You're the most precious thing in my life, Lola."

She went through another bout of sobbing and by the time she'd dried her eyes again, we'd arrived at the address on Sandpiper Lane. Bob used a card key to open the gate. O'Donnell the bodyguard was waiting in the house.

All this security suddenly seemed superfluous, now that Valance was dead. I imagined his body rotting beside the bed where he'd held my darling captive and raped her. Raped her. I felt an urge to get Lola to guide me back to that house so I could beat Valance's corpse with a tire iron. I wanted to batter his soul as it made its way to hell.

Bob had told me that he was going to take off for the Baltimore airport this night to pick up Al Hansen when his flight got in around eleven. I led Lola upstairs and helped her lay down on a couch in the living room, with a view of the ocean through a floor-to-ceiling window. Pat O'Donnell kept his distance while I made her comfortable. I thanked him and told him we had no further need of his service. This news momentarily startled him, then he said, "Okay. I'll need a lift back to the hotel to pick up my car."

I said Bob can drop him off at the hotel so he can drive back to Philadelphia tonight, and shoved two hundred dollar bills into his hand as a gratuity.

Back downstairs unloading the Escalade, I said, "Bring Al here, Bob. No point in his staying in a hotel."

"Okay."

"And will you drop our bodyguard off at the hotel on your way?"

"Sure. You letting him go?"

"Yes. Listen. There's one thing that worries me, really worries me. What do you think Al will want to do about this, what Lola just told us?"

"I don't know. The state and local police know Lola was in the trunk of that car. Now that we have her back, the question Is, where is the corpse? How do we find the house?"

"What if we just don't mention anything to the police?"

"The desk clerk at the Boardwalk Plaza had a clear view of her when we were loading the car and she appeared. I wouldn't be surprised if he's already called the police."

"Let's hope he didn't call the local media. I fear them more than the cops."

"I don't think this town has much media, just a weekly newspaper or two and a radio station."

"I'm sure there are big media outlets in the cities around here—Washington, Baltimore, Philadelphia. New York isn't that far away either."

"Let's get Al's input before we decide what to do, John. He knows this stuff a lot better than either of us."

"Does that mean telling him everything? Which brings me back to my original concern—what will he want to do about it?"

"You want to keep it quiet and get on with life. Is that it?"

"Exactly."

"I'm sure Al will understand. What we don't know is, what's he duty-bound to do? He's coming here to help us, you know. He can't help us if we withhold information."

"I wonder how it might work to set it up so he finds Valance's body. Would that complete his mission? Or would he feel obligated to find out who killed Valance?"

"You mean, have Lola take us back to the house she was in?"

"Yes. You and me and Al Hansen. No one else."

"I don't know. Al strikes me as a very dedicated law enforcement professional. We get Lola to lead him to Valance's corpse, and what?"

My mind felt like it was spinning. "Another plan. You and I go there, wrap the body in a blanket, and dump it somewhere remote. Maybe we rent a boat and tie a weight to it and dump it ten miles offshore."

"John, please. Get some sleep. I'll drop O'Donnell at the hotel and bring Al here and we'll take it from there. Okay?"

I smiled and said, "He'll be surprised to see Lola."

"I'll tell him she's back," said Bob. "He'll be more than surprised."

Chapter 36

I met Al by the Southwest Airlines luggage carousel. He was wearing a baseball cap, Nordic sweater and blue jeans, and appeared to be a foot taller and two feet wider than anyone else in the room. I smiled as I remembered he'd said that Jake Valance had asked him to work for the security agency when he retired. With such a wide face, broad nose and full African lips, Al could probably make a living as a character actor playing savage cannibals and spooky hit men, but I could not imagine him as a security guard. Other passengers did a double take when they noticed him as he stood waiting for the conveyer to deliver his luggage.

I told him the startling news as we drove out of the parking garage. "Jake Valance is dead?" he asked, incredulous.

"Lola stuck a knife in his back, so yeah, he's a rotting corpse, waiting to be found."

"And Lola brought back the two million?"

"That's right. You should have seen her staggering down the street hauling those two big leather bags. That assortment of bills weighs a lot."

"Case closed. What the hell did I fly three thousand miles for?"

"There is," I said, "the delicate question of what to do with the corpse, and what will become of Lola if she tells the police what happened."

"She could get slapped with a murder charge. Is that what you're saying?"

"Yes, and John would like to hush up the whole sordid mess. He feels Lola has suffered enough. Jake repeatedly raped her, kept her hands and feet shackled in handcuffs, duck tape over her mouth. We wanted to take her to the hospital for a rape test, but she flatly refused to go. What's the point of charging a dead man with kidnap and rape?"

Al stared ahead at the string of taillights as we drove south on I-97 toward Annapolis.

"What do you think?" I asked.

"Puts me between a rock and a hard place. Damned if I do, damned if I don't."

"Oh, you don't have to become involved either way now," I said. "You can take a vacation, if you like."

"If you all haven't told the police, what do you plan to do with the body?"

"We're undecided."

"Undecided? Whose house is the body in?"

"Don't have a name. Lola thinks it belongs to the same guy who provided the private plane for Jake's escape from the West Coast. She has no name for this guy, but she says she remembers him clearly. Thinks he's some kind of Washington hotshot."

"That rock and hard place are tightening on me, Bob. Knowing all this, if I don't go through official channels, my ass is grass. When did Lola show up?"

"Around seven."

"Four Pacific Time, eh. I was already airborne. Plane made one stop in St. Louis. I'm getting a headache. Can we stop, pick up some aspirin?"

"Sure. We're coming up on Route 50 going east. Lots of places to stop along that stretch. This thing has me in a bind, too, Al. John is talking about dumping the body somewhere remote. Even renting a boat and sinking it in the ocean. Lola wants to put it behind her without going to the police and John wants to avoid a media frenzy."

"If you leave the body, it'll stink up the neighborhood and that will bring the police. They'll see the stab wound, and want to talk to you."

"And if we dump it?"

"How will you get it out of that house without the neighbors seeing? Where is this house?"

"Lola says she can find her way back to it. Says the other houses on the street look deserted this time of year."

"Her fingerprints will be all over that house, right?"

"I assume."

"What did she do with the knife?"

"I think she left it in his back."

"More fingerprints. Well, you and I have both talked to the state police and got a line on Valance. Earliest opportunity, I'd like to talk to them in person, find out what they know, what they don't know, then decide."

"We can do that first thing tomorrow. John wants you to stay in his condo instead of the hotel."

"Not a good idea, Bob. If this thing blows up, that would implicate me as an accessory. I'd rather stay in the hotel and visit the state police tomorrow morning. By myself. That way, I'm here to bring back Valance, period. Where can I rent a car?"

"Only one car rental in town. You can get the hotel desk to call and they'll deliver. I'll show you where the state police building is as we drive into town."

"I'm here on official business, see. To bring back Valance. Sheriff will back me up. I can be of more help to your brother and Lola this way. We're coming up on a gas station. Let's stop so I can get something for this headache. Haven't had a headache in years."

After we stopped for aspirin, Al got into a better mood and as we drove on toward Rehoboth Beach, he told me stories of crimes he'd dealt with over the years. He seemed to be sorting through past experiences for a way to resolve the dilemma we'd put him in.

"There was this lap dancer, a local girl, who got abducted by a customer when she quit for the night and was going to her car in the parking lot. Drove her up into the hills above Mountain Road. We found his body in his car at the base of a canyon a week or so later. Coroner found a high alcohol blood count plus Ecstasy. We lifted her prints from his car. Otherwise we never would have connected her to him. We picked her up and she told us her story, which was that this guy raped her and then drank himself senseless. She turned on the engine, put the car in gear, got out and watched it go over the brink into the canyon. Took her till dawn to walk back to her apartment. Our department didn't want to press charges but some young upstart in the DA's office did. We withheld one piece of information—that she'd put the car over the cliff—so the DA and court knew everything except how the car got down there. We fixed her up with a pretty good count-appointed lawyer and he kept her off the stand, and the judge ruled cause of death unknown, but because of the high alcohol blood count and drug, suicide was suspected. That DA later found out from the grapevine about the piece we'd withheld and he was pissed. But, you know, sometimes you've just got to fuck the system so a victim doesn't get railroaded. I mean, you can say she should have done time for pushing him into the canyon, but put yourself in her place."

That's very much what we were looking at now, preventing victim Lola from being tried for murder. Most people would consider stabbing Valance under those circumstances justifiable homicide, but that didn't mean Lola would be found innocent by a court of law. Depended on what court of law, what state, what judge and what district attorneys were involved.

"I watched the criminal justice system deteriorate," said Al, "since they started privatizing prisons, turning them over to corporations to run for profit. They throw harmless dopers, pathetic addicts and schizophrenics in with habitual killers and rapists. Millionaire dealers walk and street dealers do time. Black kids do hard time for crack and white kids walk for powder. It's a mess."

"I know just what you mean," I said. I'd been among the dopers who'd done time.

"I know you do," he said. "I checked your record."

"Oh. I wasn't going to tell you."

"I don't blame you. But let's forget you. You're somebody else now."

"Years ago," I said, "your cousin Joe Gerrity told me about that blanked-out period of American history, following the Civil War, when black men were captured and sold into a kind of extra-legal slavery, laboring for mining and steel companies. "

"Oh, man," said Al with a groan, "let's not go there."

I shot him a look of curiosity.

"I had a grandfather who did time in that system," he said. "A world worse than chain gangs, even worse than antebellum slavery. The stories he told were so sickening... I know my cousin Joe wanted to write a book about it but I can't talk about it, it's too painful. Let's leave the past behind and find out what we can do to keep Lola out of today's criminal justice system—without costing me my job and retirement, that is."

As we drove into Rehoboth, I pointed out the state police building, so he'd know it would be easy to find tomorrow—out Rehoboth Avenue to Route 1, north on Route 1 for a few miles.

It was around 2 AM when we arrived at the Boardwalk Plaza. The young lady desk clerk took one wide-eyed look at Al Hanson and was ready to call the police when I interceded and introduced Al as an officer of the law from Santa Barbara, here on official business. Al had a reservation so she cooled out and processed him quickly. I asked that she leave a note for the person who came on in the morning to call Enterprise car rental, then said goodnight.

Chapter 37

The next morning, Lola and I found a note in the kitchen. "Our guest is staying in the hotel," it said. I recognized Bob's handwriting.

Lola and I took the Escalade while brother Bob slept in—he hadn't gotten home till the wee hours. We drove to the Boardwalk Plaza and she guided me back along the route she'd walked last night, and we found the house. It was on Dodd's Lane, a shady, subdued neighborhood with towering fir trees and lots of shrubbery.

"Where's his car?" she said. "It was in the garage when I left. Maybe the owner came back."

"The owner?"

"The guy who owns the plane we flew here in. He owns this house and the car Jake was driving."

The garage door was open and that gave us access into the kitchen. We stuck our heads inside and listened to the silence of a tightly sealed house on a very quiet street.

She then led me upstairs to the bedroom where Valance had held her captive. The shackles he'd used were on the floor beside the bed, but only a large puddle of drying blood was soaking the carpet, no body.

Lola let out a tiny yelp of a scream. "Jesus, John, where the hell did he go?"

I wrapped my arms around her. She was trembling. "Only two possibilities I can think of," I said. "Either someone took the body away, or you didn't quite kill him."

"He rolled off me and fell on the floor, didn't move."

"What did you do with the knife?"

"I left it in his back."

"But it had a very short blade, right?"

"Right."

"Maybe he pulled it out."

I got down on my hands and knees and looked under the bed. No knife. Then I got up and moved the table beside the bed, and voila, there it was. She'd described it as having a blade about four inches long. It appeared to be more like three inches, with a handle of about four inches.

"Let's get rid of this thing," I said.

"What became of him?"

"I don't know. I guess somebody took his body away. Or did you only wound him? If you wounded him..."

We looked at each other as the implications registered.

"Let's get the hell out of here," Lola yelled like she was fearful that Jake Valance would reappear at any moment.

We hurried back downstairs and out through the garage and into the Escalade. I stopped a couple of blocks away when I saw a storm drain, and tossed the knife down through its iron grid.

"The first thing I've got to do is buy a gun. If I'd had a gun when Valance attacked me, I'd have shot the son of a bitch," I said, and drove out Rehoboth Avenue and up Route 1 to the Rehoboth Shopping Mall, which was anchored by a Wal-Mart.

But this particular Wal-Mart did not sell guns. We were instructed by an elderly white-haired lady greeter to go to the Wal-Mart in Georgetown. Except for Route 1, the speed limit in southern Delaware was 45 mph, with frequent 25 mph zones. Life here was about half as fast as life on the West Coast. If I weren't so concerned with our situation and the question of what became of Jake Valance, the slower pace would be charming.

An hour later, I had purchased a Smith and Wesson forty-three caliber with two boxes of bullets and we were headed back to the condo. The clerk had wondered if I'd prefer to buy hollow-point bullets because they're much more lethal. I considered it but decided on the conventional bullets. If Valance made an appearance and I had to shoot him, I decided, I'd rather wound him so Al Hansen could bring him back alive to Santa Barbara, and I wouldn't face a murder charge. If it was necessary to shoot to kill, I figured I could put more than one bullet into him. I hadn't fired a gun in over twenty years but wasn't going to let that stop me.

When we got back to the condo, we found Bob eating a bowl of cereal. "The previous owners left this in the cupboard," he said.

Lola said, "Have you heard anything?"

"Yeah," said Bob. "Al Hansen called to say that Jake somehow drove himself to the emergency room at Beebe Hospital in Lewes."

Lola and I both sat down hard on kitchen chairs and stared at each other, as Bob continued.

"He had no ID on him and gave a phony name but one of the ER nurses had grown up with him, and thought this guy who staggered in looked familiar. He's been gone from this area for many years, so she wasn't absolutely sure. She's a friend of the state police captain and called him, asked him to come by and check. It seemed incredible to her that Jake Valance would suddenly reappear like a bad penny, she said. She had him on a gurney in one of their ER treatment areas, but by the time the state troopers got there, he'd vanished."

I automatically began scanning the beach from the kitchen area, which provided a wide-angle view.

"He's no longer driving the powder-blue Lincoln," Bob said. "He left that in front of the ER entrance. That means he probably stole a car from the hospital parking lot, or a nearby street. Until someone calls to report a stolen car, we don't know what he's driving now. But it's a good bet he's not walking. The ER nurse said the wound wasn't deep enough to kill him but it did sever a tendon or nerve, because he was using a cane when he arrived. He wouldn't get far walking."

Lola said, "I'm feeling sick."

"Would he know where we are?" I wondered out loud.

"He knew where we were staying and he knew about the money, so let's assume he knows where we are now."

Chapter 38

I'd been wakened around 9 o'clock this morning by Al Hansen calling from the Delaware State Police station on Route 1 in Lewes. "This case is nothing but surprises," he said.

"What now?"

Al told me how Jake drove himself to the local ER and then, before the troopers could arrive, had slipped away and apparently stolen a car, for the Lincoln he'd arrived in was left parked in front of the ER entrance. They called for a tow truck to haul it to the state police lot.

Lola said, "He had more than one wig."

"More than the wig he wore when he showed up at the Boardwalk Plaza that night?"

"Yes, two or three more. I'm not sure how many, but the one he preferred is dark brown with trim sideburns, almost a match for his natural hair but longer. He wore that one when he went out to a supermarket to stock up on food."

I finished the cereal and put the bowl in the sink. "Al wants us to come to the state police barracks. I told him you two were gone but I expected you would return soon. Are you ready to drive there now?"

John and Lola looked at each other for a moment, then he said, "I'd feel better if the police sent a car here. I'd hate to be spotted by Valance out on the highway. Here, we can see if he tries to approach us from the beach, and he can't drive in from the highway without a card key."

I said, "He knew about the money and where we were staying, so let's assume he knows where we are now."

I called Al and relayed John's request that the troopers send a car here. "Okay," he said, "if you all feel safer there, we'll come there. Give me the address."

"Any report of a stolen car yet?"

"Not yet. My hunch is he stole a pickup or SUV, probably ten or more years old. Less conspicuous."

"Got any hunches where he might go? What his next move might be?"

"No, but that's why I was wondering if you know a psychic we might tap. Back home, we have a psychic who is very good at locating fleeing suspects."

"I'm surprised you believe in psychics, Al."

"I have no idea how this lady can do what she does, but she's right about eight out of ten times. If you all don't know any local psychics, I'll call her. She says it doesn't matter how far away someone is. If she can get her hands on something that's personally theirs, she can track 'em down."

"There's a gal in Covington who is psychic," I remembered. "Her name is Maryanne. I don't believe she's ever worked with the police, but she can read minds. Truly. She'll be sitting at the dinner table or out in the courtyard and begin running a monologue that sounds like she's possessed or something, and the next thing you know, someone will stand up and pace about, and confront Maryanne, try to make her stop talking their thoughts. Could we fax her a photo of Valance? Or maybe someone from his security unit in Santa Barbara has something that belonged to him."

"Let's keep this to ourselves, Bob. I don't want the law enforcement people here to find out we're consulting psychics. They might think we're a couple of loonies."

"Isn't there a TV series about a psychic?"

"That's TV, not real life."

John said loud enough for Al to hear, "I can call the unit back in Santa Barbara and ask if they can find something Jake left behind."

"Good," said Al. "And if they can come up with something, some personal item, can you get them to bring it to each of our psychics? We'll try Helena first—they can find her by contacting the sheriff's department. Meanwhile, I'll tell the people here your address. I think they'll send someone down there to interview you and keep an eye out. I'm leaving to drive there now."

Jake Valance

On a street behind the hospital, Jake had spotted a beat up old pickup truck with a license plate that was so rusty and beaten it was hard to make out in daylight. He'd had no trouble crossing wires to get it going. It was low on gas so he stopped at a station on Savannah Road, filled up, then continued toward Route 1. He'd stopped at the Food Lion supermarket before he'd headed south on Route 1. He still had a thick wad of bills from a one thousand dollar note he'd lifted and gotten changed into twenties at a PNC Bank on Route 1. He bought a cooked ham, cans of soup, a bunch of bananas, some cheese and crackers, and drove south to Route 24, where he turned right and headed out toward Angola by the Bay.

He wasn't going to any of the trailer parks in Angola by the Bay. There was a dirt road before you reached the bay, a right turn that led back to what had been a farm years ago. His father's brother, Rick, had owned that farm. Uncle Rick had no wife and kids, had lived alone on that old farm since he was in his early twenties. He grew a cash crop of corn and cultivated a large garden, and canned vegetables for the winter. He rarely went into town. Was considered a hermit. The last time Jake had driven out there was about a week before he left for his first police job in New Jersey. That was 22 years ago. He'd asked Uncle Rick who he intended to leave his farm to when he passed, and the old man had said, "My ghost." What did he mean by that? "I'll be dead for years before the county knows I'm gone," he'd said. "Nobody's come back this road in more than a decade. Can't get past the cow fence. I'll lock that sucker and put my own self down and pass on peaceful."

Over the years, Jake had wondered exactly what Uncle Rick meant by put himself down. Did he intend to dig a grave and lay down in it, put a bullet through his head? Let the critters pick his bones clean? But it wasn't only this curiosity that attracted Jake to Uncle Rick's old farm. It had a large and sturdy barn on it that Jake figured would outlast the old shack Rick called a house. Having nothing much else to do during his idle hours, Rick had kept that barn spic and span.

Maybe I'll find that farm and barn still there, Jake thought, and maybe I won't. If it's been sold, he'd present himself to the new owner and decide what to do then. But considering how remote that old farm was, Jake guessed Uncle Rick may have been correct in figuring that people who work for Sussex County would never bother driving back there. No one would want to develop those few acres for tourists or retirees. It was too far from the bay for that. No small farmer would want it because agriculture had gone corporate, and no agribusiness would want it because it's too remote. And who knows? Uncle Rick may still be alive, still living as a hermit. If he was still alive, Jake guessed he'd be in his early seventies. And since he never drank or smoked, got plenty of fresh air and exercise, Jake thought he might still have his wits about him, although he'd never been what most people consider normal.

He turned down the road to Angola by the Bay and drove a few miles, then took a right turn onto the old dirt road back to Uncle Rick's farm. The dirt lane was so deeply rutted now that the stolen pickup's under carriage scraped bottom as he drove. He had to hug the right edge of the lane so that his left tires stayed on the hump in the road's middle while his right tires rode close to a barbed wire fence around one of Rick's fields. The field looked like it hadn't been worked in years. Part of Jake hoped he'd find his old uncle alive and well, while another part hoped he'd find the old place deserted. Either way would work for him.

When he reached the locked gate over the runoff gully and steel cow crossing, he knew old Rick was gone, for it was clear that no one had come back this lane in many years. The lock was so rusted, there was no turning it, even if he'd known the combination. The wooden post that attached to the swinging end of the gate was deteriorated by time and weather. All Jake had to do was give it a hefty push and it broke off at ground level and lay flat, so he could drive over it.

Around the next bend the old barn came into view, and a few yards beyond, the old shack appeared too. Jake had laughed when his uncle had called it his house, for even 22 years ago its roof had been sagging. Now it was listing toward the east, one side blown to about a thirty degree angle off vertical. But the sturdy old barn, although its boards were severely weathered, still stood tall and strong.

Jake stopped the pickup but left it running till he could open the barn door and look inside. He heard a variety of animals scurrying for cover as he pulled the barn doors open. The barn sat up on an elevation of about four feet, enough to keep its base dry enough for survival. Jake got back in the pickup and drove it up the short driveway into the barn, going slowly in case the flooring started to give way. But the flooring held. It was solid. Jake turned off the engine and got out to inspect his new digs.

An old potbelly stove sat in the middle of the barn floor, with a small stack of cut wood nearby. The four stables were reasonably clean and long empty. The haymow on the second floor looked like it housed a mess of critters. Every move Jake made stirred up dust. In a far corner, Jake spotted Rick's tools, neatly aligned on hooks or resting on the floor, among them a push broom. Jake took the broom and began sweeping. If he could move out just enough dust to breathe easy in here, fine. Then he took off his leather jacket, pulled the gun out of its right jacket pocket, and hung the jacket on a hook near the tools. He walked out of the barn and gazed around, and was happy to see that forest still surrounded the shack and barn, forest that Uncle Rick had cultivated as another cash crop. Looked like he never got to cash in on the timber, though, judging by the tangled brush on the forest floor. Amazing it hadn't spontaneously ignited and burned everything in sight.

"Okay," Jake said aloud, "I got my hideout and I know where Bradford's condo is. When I'm recovered enough, I'll pay that son of a bitch one last visit, and this time I'll either walk away with that asshole's sorry life or the ten million."

He was reluctant to venture into the old, falling-down shack. The walls might collapse on him. The roof might fall on his head. There was probably nothing useful inside anyway.

He stepped up onto the front porch and inspected the door. It looked like the doorframe was all that was holding up the shack. Open this door, he thought, and the whole wreck could keel over. He pulled gently on the door, ready to dart for safety, got it open a small crack, then checked the walls. They hadn't moved. He slowly pulled the door all the way open. Incongruously, Rick's ridiculously thick carpet seemed to have held up surprisingly well. It was pregnant with dust and littered with trash that had blown in through the cracks, and a variety of animal feces, mostly so dried it was ready to blow away. Jake wished he'd changed into his blue jeans and work shoes before he'd crawled out of the house and driven himself to the hospital. His street shoes and sports slacks would soon be ruined. Well, he was wearing his best wig. Tomorrow he'd go to Wal-Mart and buy jeans and boots and whatever else he'd need, including a better cane to help him walk without fear that his left leg would give out and land him flat on the ground. The throbbing pain of the knife wound didn't bother him half as much as the fear that his left knee kept threatening to collapse like a limp dishrag.

He continued into the house. The coats and clothes in the living room closet were so moldy, they would disintegrate at a touch. He moved back the single hallway that bisected the shack and led to the kitchen. This took him past two bedrooms. He opened the door to the one on his right and felt an electric shock of fear at the sight of the skeletal remains prone on the bed. Uncle Rick had indeed handled his own funeral. His bones appeared to be picked clean by a variety of critters and insects, but the jeans and checkered work shirt were in surprisingly good condition.

"Goodbye, Uncle Rick," he said as he closed the bedroom door and moved on toward the kitchen. He wondered why it was that both his father and Uncle Rick had lived such wretched lives. They could have done something with their lives. They chose to live the way they did, Jake thought. Why? He had no idea, and felt a momentary flush of pride

that he had escaped such a life as they'd lived. He'd gone out into the larger world and had a career, made something of himself. Before that fuckhead Bradford had busted his balls and gotten him transferred to New Orleans. Well, he wasn't going to New Orleans till he had the ten million. Then maybe he'd visit under a new alias, stay at the finest hotel, pick up a sporting girl and do the town right.

In the kitchen, nothing worked. The stove and fridge were rotted beyond repair, and the plumbing had apparently frozen, for no water came from the faucet. But in the cupboard he found pots and pans and plates and dishes that were useable. And in a drawer he found knives and forks and spoons. Through the back door he saw Rick's old outdoor pump, built over a well when Jake was a schoolboy. Rick had capped the pump with a plastic cover when he'd installed indoor pumping. Jake removed the plastic and worked the pump handle and was surprised to find water gushing from the pump's steel mouth. A lot of insects had made their homes in the pipe so he pumped harder and faster to blow them out. The anchor of any farm is a water source, his father used to say. Without a good, reliable source of drinking water, you can't live there. The first half dozen spurts of water to gush out were brown with rust and thick with spider webs and such, but as Jake kept pumping, the water cleared. He went back to the kitchen and brought out a glass, cleaned it out and filled it. He held it up to inspect its clarity, then sipped carefully. Tasted good. He drank the glassful without a pause. "Cold and clean," he said aloud.

Among the things he'd bought at the Food Lion were half a dozen cans of soup. He'd have to use the potbelly stove in the barn to boil the soup, but he was pleased, now, that he would have soup and ham for dinner. Since it was lunchtime, he walked back through the house and out to the barn, fished around in the Food Lion's plastic bags on the pickup's bed till he found bread and cheese, lunchmeat and mustard, and fixed himself a sandwich.

He decided he'd sleep on the pickup's seat this night and add blankets and an inflatable mattress to his shopping list for tomorrow. As he sat against the barn's outside wall in the winter sunshine, he felt proud of his ability to survive. He'd also bought antiseptic, gauze and duct tape to replace the hospital's bandage. He exercised his left leg by gently bending and straightening it, bending and straightening. "In a couple of weeks," he said to his knife wound, "you'll be as good as new."

Jake had one regret, though. The two photos he's shot of Bradford and his bitch were still in his digital camera, and the camera was tucked in his suitcase, which he'd had to leave behind when he struggled out of the house to the hospital. He'd never transferred the two shots to his computer, edited them and printed. He wasn't sure how definitely they'd identify Bradford and Lola Jones, it's just that it would have been nice to have prints so when he finally caught up to Bradford, he could shove them under his nose and watch the expression on his face. But they weren't necessary. He could get that money out of Bradford without the photos. He smiled to himself as he imagined the local cops going through his suitcase, finding the digital camera, flipping through the few photos he'd taken and coming to those two shots.

His friend, Harry DeVale, the ex-senator, was due to arrive at his Rehoboth house in a couple of days to spend the weekend. The photos were in a folder tucked into a side pocket of Jake's carry-on luggage. No doubt the local cops had traced the Lincoln to Harry so his house was now a crime scene, probably, in which case the cops would have found the photos. Harry would be collared for questioning. The best Jake could do at this point was call Harry, warn him.

He pulled his cell phone out of his jeans' pocket and hit Harry's number. The line was dead. He was too remote to get wireless service. Well, I'll try him tomorrow when I drive into town, Jake thought. Would the locals recognize the subjects in the pictures? Maybe. Maybe not. Even if they did recognize Bradford and the girl, would they be inclined to subject this super wealthy corporate executive to humiliation by publicizing those two photos? Not likely.

"Too late to sweat the goddamned photos," Jake said aloud. When he healed enough, he would scout Bradford's condo and eventually pay a visit, and a most memorable visit it will be, he promised himself.

Chapter 39

A young State Trooper named Sam Hoffman and Al Hansen arrived at the condo before noon in separate vehicles. I was glad I had bought the previous owner's furniture, for otherwise the place would have been bare. Ordinarily I much prefer to acquire my own furniture and have an interior decorator arrange it, but there was, I felt now, something comforting about these pieces that came with the house. The trooper sat down at the kitchen table and pulled out a notepad and pen and began questioning me. Al sat on the large, beige leather couch and commiserated with Bob. Lola went into the master bedroom to rest. And avoid the questioning. Maybe the policemen thought they'd interview her later, when she was willing. Or maybe he was acceding to our wishes to leave her out of it.

I told Sam Hoffman the story of how Jake Valance was head of our security agency's Santa Barbara unit, and how he'd become so intrusive I'd called his employer and had him transferred. Then he'd come to my house and attacked me with a tire iron, landing me in the hospital. Valance had been arrested and jailed, but had escaped from the county jail and kidnapped Lola Jones, and brought her here. He waylaid me at the Boardwalk Plaza and stole two large leather bags containing $2 million in US dollars. Lola had escaped from the house in Rehoboth where Jake had been holding her prisoner, and, well, here we were.

The trooper knew that Lola had been taken hostage by Jake and that Jake had showed up at the Boardwalk Plaza to steal the cash, which I'd intended to use to buy this condo. He did not know that Lola had stabbed Valance and I did not tell him. I said only that Lola had escaped with the two bags of money and returned it to us at the hotel.

"Do you know who stabbed Valance?" he asked.

"No, we don't," I said. "He may have backed into something sharp, for all we know."

Trooper Sam Hoffman looked away with a wry smirk at that. Al Hansen had told him about finding me bludgeoned and rushing me to the hospital, and that Jake had managed to kidnap Lola from her home in the San Fernando Valley. "Well," said the trooper, "Valance is alive and at large, so this is not a murder investigation. He grew up on a farm near Lewes, so he knows his way around this area. He was using a cell phone. We're working now to find out which phone company he used, and locate his phone with a global positioning device. Captain Gorman knew this man years ago, and says he doesn't know of any living relatives hereabouts. It's possible Valance has fled this area, gone to a city, Baltimore or Philadelphia. But until we learn where he is, we're going to assume he's in this area and may try to get at you here, in this house."

The trooper also told me that the police checked into who owns the house where Lola was imprisoned. "It's a Mr. Lawrence H. DeVale, a lobbyist in Washington, who goes by the nickname Harry. Years ago, DeVale was a Senator from Colorado. He became a lobbyist when he lost an election a couple of years ago. What we don't know is his connection to Valance. We're working on that. We figure he flew Valance and Lola to Baltimore from LA in his company's plane. We contacted the DC police and they visited DeVale in his DC home and are convinced that Valance is not there."

"Did they ask him about flying Valance and Lola across the country? Wouldn't that be grounds to pick him up and demand more information?"

"He's lawyered to the hilt, they said. And inviting guests onto his private plane is not a crime."

Bob said, "If he weren't rich and powerful, I suspect they'd have grilled him as an accessory."

"He could be dirt poor and homeless," said Trooper Hoffman. "They have nothing to hold him on. The crime happened here, not in DC."

"I thought we might install a monitor so we can see who is approaching from the highway side of the house," I said. "As you can see, we have a good view of the beach, but we could be blindsided from the front of the house."

"Good idea," said Officer Hoffman. "We've alerted the Bethany police to keep an eye out for him, and they will keep a watch on your neighborhood and house."

From the couch in the living room area, Al Hansen said, "Captain Gorman said he's going to contact people who knew Jake years ago. The farm where Jake grew up is now a housing development. Is it possible that someone who knew him way back when might have an idea where he could be hiding?"

"We're looking into that possibility now, sir. Captain Gorman knows people who knew Valance as a youngster, before he left this area."

We learned that Sam Hoffman was from Philadelphia. He had no family connections in this area, but he was a part-time assistant basketball coach at Cape Henlopin High School, where Jake had gone, and would put out the word in the high school that the police wanted any information about him they could get. "It's possible that someone in the school has a parent or relative who might know something."

"He sure is a slippery son of a bitch," said Al Hansen. "He engineered an escape from our county jail, and now he's disappeared again, from your hospital. Any word on a stolen vehicle?"

Trooper Hoffman pulled out a cell phone and made a call, inquiring about reports of stolen vehicles. "Not yet," he said.

Both Al and Trooper Hoffman suspected Valance would not relent in his mission to blackmail me. "Our number one priority now is to make sure you are protected here," said Hoffman.

When the trooper left, Bob and Al joined me at the kitchen table and the subject turned to psychics. I felt a flash of angry exasperation and said to Bob, "First you tell me about this friend you have who believes the planets influence the economy, and now you want to dig up a so-called psychic to find Valance. Please! Let's not waste time with such flimflam. God knows we're vulnerable enough as it is. Let's not lose ourselves in la-la land."

"It was my idea," said Al. "Our department works with a lady named Helena who has, on several occasions, been able to tell us where to find people we've been hunting for."

I took a deep breath to calm myself. "I apologize for my tone. If you two want to try psychics, fine. Meanwhile, I'm thinking I dismissed O'Donnell too soon. I'd feel safer if he came back and guarded this house full time."

"I don't think Jake is in any condition to approach you now, John," said Al. "According to the people in the emergency room, he'll need time to heal his wounds before he's mobile. The knife hit something in his lower back that partially incapacitates his left leg. Whether this is a temporary condition or permanent they don't yet know. They planned to use an imaging device to find out exactly what the knife hit, but he disappeared before they could do that. And let's not forget that he's also got a severed tendon in his left knee. In retrospect, I wish I'd shot him in the middle of his back."

"Isn't it possible that he could have invaded a house near the hospital and be holding someone hostage there?"

"That's possible," said Al.

"If he's that lame, he'd want to find the nearest hideout. And no stolen car has been reported, right?"

"Let's check again," said Al. He used his cell phone to call the Delaware State Police installation in Lewes to verify. "Nope," he said after a brief discussion. "No stolen vehicle reported."

Just then Lola appeared. She'd come out of the bedroom and was standing at the far end of the living room area. "Let's get the hell out of here and go back to California," she said.

When no one replied to that, she approached, saying, "You came here to get away from him and now he's here."

Bob turned to Al and said, "What do you think?"

"Seems to me," said Al, "that you all are better protected here. Get that monitor set up and you'll be able to see anyone coming from either front or back. But it's up to you, John. Where would you feel safer?"

"Lola, don't you think we're safer here?"

"I don't know. I just don't know." She ambled over and took the fourth chair around the kitchen table. "I've been listening from inside the bedroom. Maybe we should try those psychics before we decide."

"Well," I said, "we could go anywhere, really. We might go to New York City, take an apartment. Only one way in and out, guarded around the clock by doormen. For that matter, we could go to London or Paris. Or just about anywhere else in the world."

"It's beautiful here," said Lola, gazing out at the beach and sea. "And I'm exhausted. Let's try the psychics first."

"Okay," I said, "let's get the monitor set up and try the psychics before we make another move."

"I think that's a good idea," said Al. "Jake has help from at least one other person—that lobbyist in Washington, DeVale—and who knows what other resources. You all could wear yourselves out traveling and wind up in a less protected environment than you have here. Let's try our psychics."

Chapter 40

While Al called the sheriff's department, I called Covington and cleared it with Dr. Grace. Maryanne was one of her patients.

John called the security agency's headquarters in New York and asked someone there to see if anyone in their Santa Barbara unit could come up with a personal possession Jake Valance had left behind. If so, would they deliver this item to the Santa Barbara Sheriff?

We then turned our attention to other things to fill the time till we heard back. Al asked if I'd like to go for a jog on the beach. "Jake's not ready to make a move yet," he said. We put on tee shirts and shorts and, with the tide out, jogged north on the hard sand. It felt good to push against the raw, windy chill.

The local electronics company arrived later that afternoon and by sundown, a surveillance system had been set up so that we could monitor the front of the house from four overhead screens set up between the dining area and the kitchen. I called Laura and told her the latest news, and she asked me to meet her at the locked entrance to this housing development so we could go out for dinner together. Al drove back to Rehoboth to have dinner at the home of Captain Gorman. Before he left, he got John to put his phone number in his autodial. When I left around 7 o'clock, John and Lola were sitting on the couch, hugging each other and staring up at the monitor screens, and also out the kitchen window at the beach. I said, "John, if you don't want me to leave, just say the word and I'll call off my dinner with Laura."

"No," he said, "we'll be fine. Valance needs time to heal and we need some quiet time together."

Laura and I went again to the Nantucket for dinner and didn't linger, as I felt uneasy leaving John and Lola alone. Valance had demonstrated that he was full of surprises. Laura dropped me at the gate and, when I walked the steps up to the dining area in the condo, John and Lola were still on the couch, watching the beach and monitors. I replaced them as guard and they went to bed.

Al returned about two hours later. I watched on the monitor as he parked his rented car in the driveway. Even though I could see it was his car, I grabbed the gun John had bought—he'd left it on the kitchen table—just in case. I was holding it pointed at the floor when Al came up the stairs. "I hope you have that thing on safety," he growled with a frown.

"I do."

"The captain still hasn't heard anything about a stolen vehicle," said Al, "but he did get word that an old pickup truck was abandoned on a street near the hospital and now it's missing. One of the residents told a trooper who was questioning people that a rusted old Ford pickup had been left on the street, and it had been parked there so long, the neighbors assumed it had been abandoned and had called the town police about it. They said they'd had it towed, but I called the local police and they said it had not yet been towed."

"Which means Valance may be in that truck," I said.

"I couldn't get a detailed description of it. Seems it was rusted pretty badly. An abandoned junker."

Al and I established a routine to split guard duties during nights. Al sat up till 4 AM and then I took over and watched the sun rise over the ocean. We each had a guest bedroom on the top floor, each with its own bathroom.

Two days later Al got word that several sets of dumbbells had been brought to the sheriff's office. They'd been left on the lawn in front of Jake's condo in Goleta. A neighbor had seen him drop them there. A couple of dumbbells had been delivered to Maryanne in Camarillo and another set to the home of Helena.

Al spoke with Helena, who told him she got images of a skeleton on a bed in an old ramshackle house, out in the middle of nowhere, far from any town.

I called Maryanne who said she got the impression that the man we were looking for was in a barn. Both ladies got images of a rural setting, far from any town. Maryanne mentioned that she saw a large body of water nearby. Helena got images of an old fashioned, hand-operated water pump. We asked both ladies to keep trying to come up with more details.

The next day, I called Maryanne back and asked her if she'd picked up any impressions of an old pickup truck. "Now that you mention it," she said, "I do get that image, but you're leading me, so I don't know if it's valid or if I'm getting it because you suggested it. Anyway, I think the man you're looking for is wounded, somehow. I get the impression of walking with a limp, using a cane."

"Well," said Al, "that's helpful. He's twice wounded in the left leg. Wherever he is, he'll be limping or walking with crutches or a cane."

"And if he comes for us here?" I asked.

"He'll most likely come from the beach side," said Al. "Hide under either of the two houses next door, approach us that way. That's his best shot."

"If he comes from the north, he'll have a very long walk. There's no public access for several miles."

"So," said Al, "he'll probably come from the south, between midnight and dawn."

The next morning, Al left with a police photo of Jake Valance faxed from Santa Barbara, and drove around to all the supermarkets in the Rehoboth Beach area, asking checkout clerks if they'd seen anyone who looked like this. The result was negative. I mentioned that when Jake showed up at the Boardwalk Plaza to rob John, he'd been wearing a wig with sideburns. The mug shots showed him with close-cropped hair.

That evening as the four of us were having dinner in the condo, John asked Al how long he could stay, and Al said he could be here another ten days. "After that, I'm afraid I'd better go back. We'd love to catch the son of a bitch and bring him back to the Santa Barbara jail, but the fact is, he's now out of our jurisdiction."

The expression on John's face told us he was not feeling good about Al's leaving. "I wish he'd show up here," said John. "So I can blow his head off."

Al advised that, if Jake did show up here, we call 911 first and then hide, and use John's gun only as a last resort. "Wouldn't do to complicate this," said Al.

"I'm not going to let him do more harm to us," said John. "If I can kill the son of a bitch, that's what I'll do. He tried to kill me and he kidnapped and raped my lady."

"I don't think any court in the land would convict you," said Al, "but it would stir up a mess of publicity while you were proving justifiable homicide."

Publicity was the last thing John wanted. "Okay, I'll keep my head down if he shows and, If you're still here, Al, let you handle it."

"If there's any shooting to be done," said Al, "I'll do it. Bob is my backup. But if either of you shoot Valance, it will bring out an army of scandal mongers."

I said, "He may be miles away from here and not planning to show. I suspect he has all he can handle to deal with his wounds."

"Let's assume the worst, though," said Al. "If he doesn't show before I leave, I advise that you, John, hire a professional security guard and retain him till Jake Valance is found."

Jake Valance

After a week, Jake's digs in Uncle Rick's barn were tolerable, if not comfortable. He'd pulled on his gray-haired wig and gone to the Lowe's in town with his shopping list, and he'd bought more food at the biggest supermarket, the Super Fresh on Route 1. He'd stopped at the Wal-Mart to buy clothes. At all three stops, he was able to use each store's electronically powered courtesy wheelchair. He'd also found a small gun shop up the highway north of Lewes where he'd bought two boxes of 9 millimeter hollow-point bullets.

Big box stores were impersonal and the year-round population of the combined towns of Lewes and Rehoboth had grown ten or twenty fold. When he was a kid, shopping for groceries or hardware meant meeting friends and neighbors. No one said howdy to anyone else as he made his rounds today. Driving back to Uncle Rick's farm, he passed a police car parked on the roadside. The cop was busy writing out a speeding ticket and never gave the rickety old pickup a glance.

The only sour note was that he'd not been able to contact his good friend Harry. It had been Harry who'd had a contact who came up with the information that John Bradford was buying a condo for $2 million in US currency. That he could not now reach Harry by phone even when he called from town, probably meant that Harry had come to his vacation home in Rehoboth and probably been taken in for questioning. On his shopping trip, he'd thought of cruising by Harry's house to see if it was taped off as a crime scene but given how few tourists were in town during the middle of winter, decided against it. Out on the shopping strips lining Route 1, he was almost as inconspicuous as he'd be in a big city, but on the residential streets of Rehoboth, where the vacation homes were empty, an old beater like this pickup would stand out like a stripper performing in church.

By the eighth day on the old farm, Jake was walking without the cane and trying to shuffle-jog a little, on the flat path between the falling-down shack and the sturdy barn. The knife wound was no longer giving him pain but the left knee continued to plague him. Fortunately, Hansen's bullet hadn't hit the back of his knee squarely. It was a main ligament on the outside of his knee joint the bullet had pierced. He found he could walk for five or ten minutes without the cane, but needed It for longer walks.

He'd parked the pickup outside the barn to make room for his inflatable mattress, portable gas grill, and stock of foods. Now and then a single engine airplane flew over the farm and an occasional helicopter could be heard in the distance. Jake didn't think they'd notice an old pickup on a farm so he didn't worry. He'd read a couple of mystery novels he'd picked up at the supermarket and he'd marveled that the old barn's roof didn't leak in a heavy rain that arrived after midnight and lasted through most of the next day. But with healing, he'd grown restless.

For a while, he'd seriously considered giving up his quest for the ten million, at least for the time being. "I can drive to some place like Richmond, Virginia," he said to himself, "and catch a plane for somewhere like Atlanta, and from there I can fly to Mexico City and then on to Costa Rica." He thought he could lose himself in the crowds of travelers that way. Once in his Costa Rican bungalow, he could transfer his checking account out of Santa Barbara, and his pension fund to another broker and tap into either for whatever cash he'd need till he got another job in the security business. And that shouldn't be too difficult, for there were lots of wealthy Americans living abroad, and he could demonstrate his skills. Oh, but no, he could not tap into his accounts, he suddenly realized, because the law enforcement people would have them frozen. If he'd tried to kill some bozo like John Bradford's crazy brother Robert, the net would not be flung as wide and tight. John Bradford's wealth and status, and the fact that Jake had snatched Lola in California and flown her to the East Coast meant the FBI had become involved, and they'd monitor his financial accounts. "It's a good thing I have police experience," he said aloud.

So it was back to Plan A. On the night of his eighth day at the farm, he drove the old pickup out to Route 1 and south to Bethany and searched for the address. He knew it was on Sandpiper Lane, but gated communities lined the beach north of Bethany and he didn't know which one contained a Sandpiper Lane. To gain entrance to any of these fancy neighborhoods, a card key was needed, and there were no human guards on duty to ask where Sandpiper is.

He stopped for gas in Bethany and bought a map of the local area, and found Sandpiper in the second gated community north of the town center.

When he'd fled Beebe Hospital, he'd had the wits to retrieve his Glock handgun out of Harry's Lincoln before he'd hobbled away and found the old pickup. It was a G-27 9 millimeter and It might come in handy, he reasoned, because Bradford would surely have hired security people to guard his new beach house. He imagined himself stalking the house, dropping any guard or guards with a couple of 9 millimeter hollow-points, then lassoing Bradford and his bitch, and driving off in whatever set of wheels they had. He would bring them back to Uncle Rick's farm and negotiate. He'd arrange it so that Bradford put the cash in his hands and he'd made a safe getaway before releasing them. Exactly how this would go down he wasn't sure, but figured he could depend on the help of Bradford for such logistical details, for he'd convinced the man that if anything went wrong, he and his young beauty would die. Knowing that Bradford was able to have two million delivered in cash to Rehoboth Beach to buy a condo, Jake reasoned he could have ten million delivered safe and sound to buy his life and the life of his pretty young whore. Bradford would help him work out the logistics to save all their asses. There's nothing like staring death in the face to motivate a gentleman of means.

Knowing which gated community Bradford and his bitch now lived in, Jake decided his next move was to scout the territory. The following night he drove to a back street in Bethany that dead-ended at the beach, parked his pickup and, wearing a snug leather jacket and using the cane, walked north along the water's edge. When he got within about fifty yards of Bradford's condo, he turned left and walked up onto the dry sand and toward the row of beach houses, approaching slowly, with caution, peering into the darkness for any sign of residents or security guards.

A few houses south of Bradford's he found he could access the street by slipping quietly between two vacant houses. Once on the street, he kept close to shrubbery and checked the street sign, happy to see it was indeed Sandpiper. He saw lights on in the house that he now knew must be Bradford's. It was one of only three in sight with any signs of life inside this time of year. He spotted several vehicles parked under the house, one being a Cadillac Escalade. That's the one he'd commandeer when he snatched Bradford and his bitch, he decided.

He did not approach Bradford's house from the street side, figuring the man had that area guarded somehow, probably electronically. He doubled back the way he'd come onto the street and went back to the beach, then walked slowly forward. The house had a second floor deck that was lit by inside lights, and as Jake drew near, he saw a figure rise up out of a chair on the deck and turn toward the lighted house, and was shocked to recognize Al Hansen, the big deputy who'd dimed him and shot him in the back of the knee. "What the hell are you doing here?" he whispered out loud. Well, he thought, that black bastard snitch will taste the first shot I fire. Hansen walked inside the house and presently returned to the deck carrying a drink in a glass. He sat down again and this time Jake could see that he was scanning the beach, guarding this side of the house.

Jake sat down to rest under the overhang of the house next to Bradford's, peeking around the edge of a steel support under this house. There was an alleyway about fifteen feet wide separating the houses. From here he had a clear view of Al Hansen up on the deck and could also see the area under Bradford's beach house. He saw no sign of any guard on the street side of the house. That cheered him—until *suddenly floodlights lit the front side as a car drove up and parked in the driveway. Motion-activated floodlights. Good thing I didn't try to get too close when I checked out the front. The car kept its lights on and engine running. After a few minutes, a man emerged from the passenger side and the car backed out of the driveway and drove toward the gate. In the brief moment the car lights shown on the figure, Jake recognized Bradford's crazy brother Robert, as he walked toward the ground-level door, unlocked it and went in. Presently Robert walked out onto the second-floor deck and sat down beside Al Hansen. Jake could hear their voices as they chatted but not make out what they said. Jake took the Glock out of his jacket pocket and aimed it at the pair on the deck. Naw, he said to himself, that's too difficult a shot with a handgun. He'd feel more confident using a rifle, preferably one with a scope.*

Soon thereafter Jake slipped away and, sticking close to the houses, made his way south along the beach and back to his parked pickup. As he drove back to Uncle Rick's farm, he rejoiced that he'd done his due diligence in scouting the territory, for now he had a clear idea of how he would get to Bradford and his clan. What he needed, he reasoned, was a rifle that he could disassemble to carry up the beach, and reassemble when he reached his position under Bradford's next-door neighbor's house. From there he could pick off Al Hansen on the deck, and Robert Bradford, too, if he's up there with him. Then he would blow out the front door lock, or better yet he'd mount the steps leading up to the deck from the beach, and maybe, just maybe he would not have to take Bradford and his bitch anywhere. All but a few of the houses along this stretch of beach were vacant off-season. Given the surf noise, who would hear his shots? He could drag the corpses to the dune and shove sand over them for makeshift graves. He could make this house his headquarters while he awaited delivery of the ten million.

Back in the barn, he fired up the old potbellied stove, sat down with his back against a wooden pillar supporting the hay mow, and lit up a cigar. He felt good. Things were falling into place. Now that he knew he could pick off Hansen and Robert, then move into the condo with Bradford and his bitch till the money arrived, he felt confident of success. Oh, yes, there would be the unexpected, but if he convinced Bradford and the girl that one false move and they'd both die, he felt sure he could get the money. His plan was to then kill the pair of them and leave them to rot in the condo while he drove south. Probably all the way into Mexico, where he could catch a flight to Costa Rica without worrying he'd be grabbed by airport security. Once south of the border, he'd be home free.

Chapter 41

By the second week, Lola and I were both feeling more at home in the new condo. Even though it was chilly outside, we found the upstairs deck a nice place to catch some sun during mornings. Bob and Al kept watch from the deck all night long, taking turns spelling each other. Lola and I began a routine of having breakfast out on the deck and then laying down under blankets to bathe our faces in sunshine, sheltered from the wind. With both Al and Bob on the job, I felt no need to hire more security people. All of us could keep an eye on both sides of the house from anywhere near the kitchen, and on the street side by glancing at the monitors.

But it was a strange interlude, for we had no idea where Valance was. He might be lurking nearby, or he might have fled and been miles away. Bob did the food shopping and he and Lola cooked. After dinner, Al went out onto the deck to take up his guard post and Bob caught a nap before spelling Al. Lola and I went to bed and read side by side.

This morning, I watched from the deck as Lola went with Bob and Al for a jog on the hard sand near the waterline, leaving me alone in the house to watch the monitors. A warm wind was blowing from the south as I turned my head to watch the runners, then the monitors. I felt peaceful. The growl of fear from my stomach was forgotten, and I was charmed by the view of billowing clouds over the sparkling sea.

Around mid-morning, Lola went through her exercise routine. The first day she did this, I had watched. The second day, I had joined her and imitated her moves. Several times I suggested we go out, drive around, see the sights, maybe stop for a bite to eat somewhere, but Lola was not ready for that, she said, "until I know where Jake is, preferably back in jail."

I spent the afternoons keeping in touch with various business associates, letting them know where I was now, although not telling anyone the details of how I came to be here. As far as they were concerned, I'd moved here to enjoy the local ambiance.

Lola and I had hours of leisure to chat and get better acquainted. She told me about her growing-up years in The Valley and I told her tales of my growing-up years in Santa Barbara. We fantasized buying a yacht. Brother Bob brought home yachting magazines and we inspected the photos of boats forty to fifty feet long. Lola had been aboard only one luxury yacht—in Avalon Harbor where she went to turn tricks with two other girls.

Around 7 o'clock, Laura drove down from Rehoboth to pick up Bob and the two of them went out to dinner. I arranged for her to have a card key for the gate, but never caught so much as a glimpse of her when she came and went. Lola and I were content to take a vacation from sex. She was ready at any time, she said, to take care of my desires, but not feeling turned on, feeling she needed time to get over the horrors of being Jake's prisoner. We hugged a lot, though, and snuggled all night. What amazed me is how compatible we were during this lull. She said she'd been fearful that I might not love her after what she'd been through with Jake, but I absolutely adored helping her heal from that ordeal. She wondered how I felt, too, about her having been a "sex worker," as she called it, providing sexual delights for gentlemen able to meet her price. I told her I worried that she might miss the excitement of that life. She laughed and said that she'd be happy if she never turned another trick. I said I worried that she wouldn't be interested in hearing about my business life—all that dull stuff about the financial world. On the contrary, she said, she wanted to learn everything she could about investing and how to make money grow. We talked about the courses she could take in college. Perhaps she could begin taking night classes till she qualified for a regular fulltime college program. During evenings we watched TV, mostly movies we could download. And so these leisurely days of doing nothing but getting better acquainted glided by in a kind of glowing pink haze, until the night Jake showed up.

Lola and I were in bed, reading, when we heard a kind of popping sound under the thunderous roar of a heavy surf. "Did you hear something?" she said.

"Yeah. What was it?"

We got out of bed, slipped on bathrobes and padded barefoot into the living room to investigate, and saw Al out on the deck under a full moon, his gun drawn and pointed down toward the area between our house and our neighbor's. Bob came rushing in from the deck and, after a quick search of kitchen drawers, said, "Where's your gun, John?"

I pointed into the bedroom and said, "On the shelf of the walk-in closet."

The next thing I knew there was another pop and the sliding glass door onto the deck shattered. Al fell flat to the deck. For a moment I thought he'd been shot. But no, for he was shooting back now. Robert came out of our bedroom with the handgun and waved Lola and me back into the bedroom, then switched on all the outside lights and went cautiously down the steps to the main entrance.

Before I closed the bedroom door, I heard Al yell, "Back off, Bob, let me handle this. Don't you get your ass in trouble."

I dialed 911 and reported being under attack and gave our address. Lola said, "Let's at least get a knife," and ran out to the kitchen. I watched her grab one of the larger knives from a hanging magnet strip, and come scurrying back into the bedroom. "Let's hide under the bed," she said. That made me feel cowardly. I waved her under the bed, and ventured back out to the living room. Bob was halfway down the stairs to the door, with his body flattened against the wall. Al was again flat on the deck outside peering over the edge.

An eerie silence prevailed for several minutes, abruptly broken when the wood decking near Al's head shattered. Al slid away from the deck's edge, then got to his feet and ran inside to a cabinet drawer we had designated the all-purpose drawer, and pulled out a long flashlight. He slipped cautiously outside again, and carefully propped the flashlight up with a deck chair so it shown down on the space under our neighbor's house. Even with all the outside lights on, this one space remained dark. After switching on the flashlight, Al retreated. Two more shots came from down below, the second one hitting the flashlight. Almost simultaneously Bob threw open the door under the house and fired a few shots from my handgun. Al rushed down the stairs and outside, and another shot rang out. I heard scuffling, then, followed by Al's voice saying, "I got his rifle, where's his handgun?"

Before I could get down the stairs, we heard sirens and soon the area was bathed in the colorful lights of three police cars. In the area between the houses, I found Bob and Al, standing over a body that was curled into the fetal position. Jake Valance. Wounded again, but still alive. He peered up and saw me and cackled, "I almost did it, didn't I."

I leaned over him and said, "Almost did what, Jake?"

"Almost got that ten million."

Al was holding a rifle with a scope. "He damn near got me."

Bob said to Al, "You gonna handcuff him?"

"No need," said Al as three cops came rushing back the alleyway, one waving handcuffs and urging everyone else out of his way, while he bent down to secure them on Jake's wrists behind his back.

Two Bethany policemen pulled Jake to his feet, and it was then we saw his cane. He tried to hang onto it as he was raised to his feet but it fell clattering to the cement walkway.

"I got him in the other knee this time," said Al. And I saw that Jake's right pant leg was soaked with blood.

"Why didn't you shoot to kill?" asked Bob.

"I'm a cop, not an executioner," said Al. "Can't say I wasn't tempted. This way, he'll spend the rest of his life in prison, and that's a fate worse than death."

"Unless he escapes again," I said.

"We'll make sure that doesn't happen," said Al. "I'll be back in an hour or so." Then, carrying Jake's rifle, he followed the Bethany policemen out the alleyway. It was hard to see beyond the headlights but I caught a glimpse of Al, because of his huge size, helping to put Jake into the back seat of one of the police cars. Al then got into the passenger seat and the three cars drove away.

"They'll take him to a hospital," said Bob. "And this time, I'm sure they'll stick to him like crazy glue."

Lola appeared at the top of the stairs and called down, "Is he dead?"

"Not yet," I called up.

A neighbor from about seven houses down—the only other winter resident here—appeared in the driveway. "What's going on?" he asked.

Bob and I looked at each other a moment. "Someone tried to break into our house," said Bob.

"I'm damned glad to see the cops got him," said the neighbor, then turned and walked away.

"Friendly neighborhood," said Bob with a wry twist as we slowly walked the steps back up to the living room.

I couldn't resist a jibe. "Being a liberal," I said to him, "do you think that if we lived in Huey Long's ideal society where every man's a millionaire, nothing like this would happen?"

Chapter 42

We had a thank-you party for Al Hansen the night before he flew back to California. We'd see him again when he returned to testify at Jake Valance's Delaware trial. I drove him to BWI where he had a straight-through flight to LAX. We talked about getting together in Hawaii. John wants me to inspect his several properties there, and Al said, "I need a real vacation. You play golf?"

"Not since high school," I said.

"Now that you're a respectable member of society again, you need to learn golf."

"Why?"

"It's a good sport. You can go on playing it till you're too old to move. Let's play golf when we get together in Hawaii."

Just before we parted, he pulled a hundred dollar bill from his wallet and handed it to me. "You won our Obama bet." I'd forgotten all about it and refused the money. He laughingly stuffed it into my jacket pocket and beat a hasty retreat toward the inspection line, where he turned to look at me. As a wave goodbye, I mimed swinging a golf club.

The capture of Valance seemed to put Lola through a personality change. As the legal process dragged on without any definitive decision, she became more and more despondent and irritated. A couple of months after the shootout, I got up around 7 AM to find her sitting at the kitchen table, staring out at the horizon. As I approached her from behind, I said, "Good morning, Lola," and startled her. She flinched, then turned around and glared at me. "What's wrong," sweetheart?" I asked.

She gave me a tight-lipped frown and said, "Nothing. I'm just jittery." She was wearing pajamas you could almost see through, and sitting with one foot on the floor, the other on the chair. Sexy clothes were the only clothes she owned. Even with her long chestnut-brown hair uncombed, no lipstick and a grouchy demeanor, she was the kind of young woman whose presence attracts eyes and fantasies. I squelched the fantasy that arose in me. I was proud that I could do that now because for most of my life, I'd have automatically put my mojo on any girl like Lola.

The evening before, John had asked me to go out to dinner with the two of them because, he said, my being there might lighten her mood. She'd been clamming up on him since the battle with Jake. She'd become withdrawn, non-communicative. Her mind seemed a million miles away. She'd reply to his questions perfunctorily with a shrug, or an emotionless yes, no, or maybe. She hadn't been denying him sex. She had been initiating sex, but more in the spirit of relaxing him so he'd stop asking questions and go to sleep. She had no interest in pleasuring herself. This had John baffled and worried.

Last night, John asked me to go with them in an attempt to draw Lola out of her shell. We went to the Blue Coast Seafood Grill—a large restaurant with crowds of happy people loudly chattering and laughing. Lola attracted eyes when we entered, and curiosity as we'd sat as a glum threesome, two elderly gentlemen concerned about the beautiful young woman who was physically there but mentally distracted. Our attempts to bring her out of her shell were over-whelmed by the happy noise of the crowd, amplified by the walls and floor being made of tile. The only conversation we managed was about the food. Do you like yours? Yes, I like mine, do you like yours? Yes. It was a great place to go to get sloshed, laugh and shout at rock-concert decibels.

This morning, her only reply to my question was to shrug her shoulders, turn away and continue staring out at the horizon.

My single culinary accomplishment was to make an omelet of Feta cheese and herbs. I asked her if she'd like that for breakfast.

"All the fuck we do around here is eat, sleep, walk on the beach and watch TV," she snapped. "If I keep eating and eating, I'll get as fat as a stuffed pig. I need to find a gym, go for a run."

I sat down at the table across from her and stared hard at her. "Look, Lola, cut the crap. You're depressed and on edge. Why? What the hell is going on with you? Talk to me."

A tear rolled down her cheek and she turned to look behind her. "Where's John? Is he still sleeping?"

"I guess so. He's still in the bedroom."

"I feel so shitty," she said. "I know I'm making him unhappy and it's killing me."

"What's making him unhappy, sweetie, is not knowing why you're unhappy."

"I know."

For about a minute, I thought she was going to clam up again. But then she said, "I don't know what's wrong with me. I thought once we put all that crap with Jake behind us, I'd be fine."

"What thoughts are running through your mind?"

"I'm not thinking, I'm feeling. I guess I'm homesick, but that doesn't make sense. What the hell do I have to go home to? My old car and book of johns and crappy house in Canoga Park? It's been sitting there empty. I need to call the realtor and tell her where I am. Or go back there and get the place rented. No, I can't go back."

"But...?"

"But I'm bored out of my gourd here. No, not bored, I'm...I don't know, I feel stuck. On hold. Like a computer that stopped working. Don't get me wrong, Bob, I love your brother. And you. Yes, I've come to love you like a brother, like he loves you. It's just that...I don't know. I feel dead inside, and I feel angry when there's nothing to be angry about. Sometimes I want to jump John's bones and fuck him to nirvana and sometimes I get an urge to kick him in the balls."

"Maybe you're reacting to what Valance put you through."

"No. That was more than two months ago. This morning I got up early and watched the sun come up over the ocean, and it was glorious. It was a thrill to just sit here and watch the first rays of light appear over the horizon and begin to light up the sky, then the first bright red of the sun appear, till it got so bright I couldn't look at it any more."

"Then I showed up and broke the spell?"

"No, you broke a spell of self-pity. After the thrill of the sunrise, I just sunk into my own stupid pity pot, which is really crazy because what in the world do I have to feel sorry about?"

"Maybe you miss the excitement of the life you had."

"Bob, I've been doing dates since I was seventeen. Five years. The excitement has long since worn off. I'm not complaining. I made a hell of a lot more money pleasuring wealthy gents in hotel rooms than I could have made any other way. And I enjoyed it. It was good, honest work and someone had to do it. And I was good at it. My tricks called me back. A lot of girls get out their little black books and call their list of johns. I never had to do that. They called me for seconds and thirds and referred me. But no, Bob, I don't want to go back to that. There's nothing more pathetic than an over-the-hill whore. And I love John. I truly do. I know that's hard to believe—a young girl like me madly in love with a man his age and all that—but it's true, I really do adore that man and want to make a life with him."

The tears streamed down her cheeks now. She pulled Kleenex out of a box on the table and dried her eyes, suppressed the sobs. "See, it's not that I love John less, it's that I...I don't know what it is. I just feel trapped, on hold, stuck, dead inside. Sometimes I think I should see a shrink, but what would I say? My life could hardly be better and I'm miserable?"

I was tempted to suggest that she seemed to be suffering from post-traumatic stress disorder. When I told Dr. Mary Grace the tale of Jake Valance and how he'd kidnapped and raped her, that's the suspicion she had. "Watch for signs of PTSD," she'd said. "It would be good to get her into talk therapy. Know any good psychotherapists where you are?"

Hell, the only person I really know here is Laura, and when I asked her about local psychotherapists, she jumped to the mistaken conclusion that I was trying to find one for myself and said, "Bob, there's nothing wrong with you. You're wonderfully sane. Don't worry, be happy." I started to tell her that it was Lola I was worried about but held my tongue. Lola was still a sore subject with Laura. "If I catch you so much as eyeballing that bitch's ass," she'd said, "I'll get out my butcher knife." She'd said it jokingly but we both knew Lola had gotten wrapped up in her resentment toward John. I'd been after Laura to make it a foursome for dinner some evening, but that suggestion never failed to push a hot button. "I want nothing to do with John and his trophy trashy hooker," she'd said. "I don't want to be anywhere near either one of them, so stop asking if I'd like to have dinner with them. The answer is an unequivocal no."

I was tempted to mention PTSD to Lola now but resisted. I'd had enough experience with mental diseases to know an amateur's off-the-cuff diagnosis could do more harm than good. Mary Grace had mentioned it but she'd also impressed me with her dictum that every case of mental illness is unique. "No two cases of depression are identical," she'd said.

"Maybe," I said to Lola, "it's the lack of a social life here."

"I've considered that, Bob. But no, that's not it either. I've never been much for socializing. In high school, I avoided parties—the boys always wanted to grope and leer, and the other girls were uptight because I had a sexier figure than they did. I cultivated my figure from the time I was twelve, and I much preferred to read or watch a good movie than go out to a party. I don't like to get drunk and I don't like being around people who are getting drunk."

"And after you were out of high school...?" I probed.

"I enjoyed hanging out with some other call girls now and then. We'd meet up in the wee hours at a West Hollywood club that stayed open all night and we'd cat talk, you know, gossip. We could smoke reefer in this club after 3 AM so I'd have a vodka tonic and a few tokes, listen to some gossip, tell a john joke or two, and go home.

Actually, I've always hated gossip. I was the butt of some nasty rumors in high school—made up stories, total fantasies—and never wanted to listen to other girls being raked over the coals either. I didn't mind exchanging john jokes—they were done in the spirit of fun, you know. Like, 'Do you know what that kinky son of a bitch wanted me to do?' That kind of thing. Growing up, it was just my grandfather and me. He beat a path between work and home, and didn't go out to bars or parties. He saw a hooker now and then—that was the extent of his socializing. He didn't have any living relatives, even. And that became my pattern."

She seemed to feel better after telling me these things, like speaking them lightened whatever burden she'd felt. To keep this flow going, I talked about myself, hoping to draw more out of her. I said, "I was a real party animal in high school, but not in the conventional sense. I liked to dance and clown with the girls. I loved informal get-togethers where everyone got high and danced and messed around, but I hated formal socializing. Even proms. My idea of a good time at the prom was when I dated the girl with the most risqué reputation in town and we left before the prom ended, to go off by ourselves and screw. I hated weddings and funerals. Still do. I pumped iron, swam laps and turned down party invitations to get laid instead."

"What about John?"

"He's almost the opposite. While I partied, he socialized. He loved to show off his brilliant mind in conversations with brainy people. Just before I left for Stanford, while he was a junior in high school, one evening while our parents were away, he invited eight of the brainiest kids to a dinner party at our house. We stretched out the dining room table to accommodate everyone, you know, and I just sat there like a rock, stunned into silence by the conversation John and his friends were having. A subject would come up—mostly science stuff—and each would take a turn speaking. The others would listen politely till their turn came and then shoot down points made by others. It was a very formal debate type format they stuck to. No one interrupted anyone else and no one attacked anyone else personally—it was always what someone else had said that got attacked. And John also liked formal affairs, weddings and funerals. He took them seriously. I remember a couple of weddings when my mother and I sat on one side of the aisle and my dad and John on the other. Dad and John were dead serious when the bride walked down the aisle while my mom and I whispered little jokes, like, 'What's that bulge under her gown—is she hiding her ex-boyfriend, or is she pregnant?' When Dad brought business associates home to dinner, Mom could ask the most outrageous questions with a straight face. She could convince the company she was serious but of course Dad and John knew she was putting them on, and I would make no bones about It—I'd laugh out loud, especially when Dad and his guys got on the subject of money. This would upset John. He and Dad were deadly serious about the pursuit of money. John, even as a teenager, loved to sit around the table with after-dinner drinks, talking with Dad's associates about the best stock market strategies for the times. I think that was his favorite kind of socializing."

What I'd just said, I now saw, had started Lola crying again. Her mouth looked like a baby's on the brink of a tantrum. "That's the problem!" she moaned. "He can't do that with me. He can't invite his business associates here to enjoy his favorite kind of socializing." And she had a moaning cry over that thought.

I got up and went to her side of the table and put my arms around her. "Lola, sweetie, he doesn't want to do that any more. He's been there, done that, got all the trophies it's possible to get from that game. What makes him happy now is seeing you happy."

"And here's me," she sobbed, "a miserable bitch for no reason."

"Your misery is not you fault, Lola. You didn't go the mall and buy it. It's something we've got to figure out, and then get rid of."

She dabbed her eyes again and said, "Well, give me your take on it, Bob. Why am I so fucking unhappy?"

"I think it's what Jake Valance put you through, sweetie. I think you're suffering a form of post-traumatic stress."

In spite of my good intentions, I'd blurted it out. She gazed at me a beat, a look of wonder on her face. "It did start with him, didn't it?"

"With being kidnapped, yes. And repeatedly raped. That had to be a major horror."

"It was. But I got through it. I have a lot of control over my body and mind, and I used it. One thing I learned listening to other hookers, older girls who'd been raped—how to control your mind and body to survive it."

"It's one thing to survive it," I said, "another thing to separate yourself from it, the experience, the memory of it. A thing like that can embed itself in your being and eat you alive. Until you defuse its power and separate yourself from it."

"But how do I separate myself from it? If that is what's eating me, making me a miserable bitch, how do I get rid of it?"

"Let's give my shrink a call around noon. That's when she gets into her office, 9 AM West Coast Time. I'll introduce you by phone and you talk to her. Okay?"

"What should I tell her?"

"I'll tell her what I know happened to you, that you were kidnapped and repeatedly raped, and since then you've become moody and miserable. Then I'll put you on the line. Oh, but first let's run this by John. Let's not do this till he's in on it. Okay?"

"No, we can't do that."

"Why?"

"All he'll ever think of is me doing it with Jake."

"That's why we've all three got to talk to Mary Grace. We're all in this together."

Chapter 43

A couple of months into our living in the Bethany Beach condo and I was sleeping in mornings, or just laying awake lamenting my problem with Lola, unable to come up with a solution, stymied. She'd become so withdrawn, I was convinced that our affair had already run its course. She'd thought she wanted to make a life with me but the reality had convinced her otherwise. She now realized she didn't love me, had made a serious mistake, was extremely discontented and wanted out. I couldn't blame her. Look what our relationship had brought her—Jake Valance.

I seemed to be going through the kind of travail my brother described going through in his earlier years. I wondered if there could possibly be some subtle, as-yet unarticulated connection. I'm normally an optimist who counts his winnings, but now my mind locked onto a list of painful misfortunes. I was sure I'd lost Lola's love, suspected I'd also lost Robert's respect. The loss of both ex-wives and four children caused me spasms of tearful grief. How different my life would be now if only I'd invested time and energy in my wives and children as any normal husband and father would naturally do. Now Bob and Lola were my only nearest and dearest, and I could see, day by day, a chasm of estrangement opening between myself and them. Oh yes, I'd achieved the kind of business success that had made my parents proud, especially my father, but they were gone now.

Several times my brother buttonholed me for serious talks, the gist of each being that my ennui, as he called it, had more to do with the head trauma than with what happened to Lola. He said I should get another MRI. I didn't want another MRI, I wanted Lola's love the way it was before Valance kidnapped her. Bob said, "The way you're sinking into depression reminds me of me years ago."

I was tempted to blame him, tell him that he had somehow transferred his misfortunes to me. Instead I said, "My depression has nothing to do with my head, it's losing Lola that has me incapacitated."

"We want to blame our depression on some logical cause," Bob said, "because we can't imagine what else could have caused it."

"Brother Bob, I am certainly old enough to know that most so-called logic comes from the solar plexus. That's the only part of my thinking apparatus that seems to be working."

It was working overtime, coughing up scenarios that made me sick. The worst was that she'd somehow fallen for Jake Valance—despite the fact that he'd captured and raped her, or maybe, given the quirks of human nature, because he'd done so. A man's out-of-control passion can be a turn-on for a woman, I know, so maybe Jake's passion set off something in her. And since his arrest and incarceration—they were holding him in solitary confinement in a Delaware prison—she'd become inconsolable and withdrawn. That was the root of my problem, I told Bob. Lola's love had sparked my joy. Without her love, I'm a miserable wreck.

Before the night of the big shootout, she was trembling and clinging, fearful of going to a hospital and prolonging the agony. But since that night, she was incommunicado. Well, I'd backed off battling Jake myself, as I'd threatened to do. I'd vowed to personally kill the scumbag but when the battle happened, I'd taken Al Hansen's advice and stayed on the sidelines. Was that what changed Lola's attitude toward me? That I had not done what I'd vowed to do? Did she see me as a coward and Jake as so recklessly brave that he'd lay down his life to recapture her?

I had rational moments when I knew this was a sick fantasy. How could she lust for the likes of a man who had brutalized her? She'd tried to kill him! It didn't make a bit of sense, yet it kept pestering my mind, haunting my dreams, plaguing my life, and baffling me. It was following Jake's arrest that she'd gone into this withdrawal. When she'd escaped from Jake, she was scared but alive and vibrant. When Jake was finally captured, she collapsed. Cause, effect.

Then one Tuesday morning, after I'd stayed in bed till after 11 o'clock, I came out to the living room to find Lola sitting on the couch with Bob's arm around her. My immediate reaction was that she'd fallen in love with my brother—that's what had been causing her to withdraw from me. She was a young girl who didn't know her own heart when she'd propositioned me back in Santa Barbara, causing me to lose my wits and go for this stupid notion that we could—22-year-old Lola and 58-year-old me—make a life together.

"Come on over here, John," said Bob, "and sit down. We've got something to tell you."

I moved to the easy chair facing the couch and sat, falling back onto it like a half-alive lump. We're back to that, I thought—me the nerd, Bob the ladies man. I looked hard at Lola and said, "You're in love with my brother."

"No!" she exclaimed. "That hurts! I love your brother but I'm not *in love* with him."

"You're off the mark, John. What we need to do is get your permission for Lola to talk with Mary Grace. Your permission and cooperation. This won't work without your participation."

"Your psychiatrist is three thousand miles away, Bob. Can't we consult someone closer?"

"What she needs first is a good diagnostician. There's none better than Dr. Grace. I've already told Dr. Grace a lot of the story. If Lola will tell her how she's feeling, I think we'll get an accurate diagnosis."

I was momentarily distracted by Bob's phrase, "how she's feeling." A lot of people were feeling pain and anguish these days. It was the temper of the times, the national mood. Huge amounts of equity was being lost as the stock markets plunged and the dollar continued to devalue. Big banks and hedge funds were in trouble. The Fed, under "Helicopter" Ben Bernanke, was caught in a catch 22. If they lowered their funds rate, they chanced worsening ballooning inflation. If they raised rates, they chanced throwing the country into a deep and prolonged recession. As it was, the price of energy and foods were rising dangerously while incomes for many were stagnant or wiped out. Stagflation. We were collectively gripped by a mood of depression, and it was impossible not to catch this disease personally, as witness Lola now, sitting on the couch with Bob's arm around her shoulder, staring into middle space, looking sad and confused—and me, staring at the pair of them through my own personal malaise, even though my investments were now positioned to make more money than ever before. Not every problem has a financial solution, I reminded myself.

I said, "Whatever you two decide is fine with me. Bob, you have a lot more experience with emotional things than I do. If you think our best move is to call Dr. Grace, let's do it. If that doesn't work, so be it."

"I know she'll want to speak with you too, John. Are you up for that?"

"Sure, although I have no idea what I should say."

"Just be honest," he said, "and Dr. Grace will do her thing."

Bob then brewed coffee and served Danishes to Lola and me as we continued to sit in the living room, avoiding eye contact. A few minutes after noon, 9 AM West Coast Time, he dialed his cell phone. He told Dr. Grace we were having an emergency here and asked if she could schedule an hour to discuss it with us by phone. Apparently the doctor saw fit to do this immediately, for Bob then recounted how Lola had been kidnapped and repeatedly raped, how Jake Valance had been captured, and how Lola seemed to be exhibiting PTSD, at least as far as his untrained eye could discern, and how my head wound had knocked the gumption out of me.

Bob then handed the cell phone to Lola, who answered a series of questions from Dr. Grace. Lola described having a fairly happy childhood, despite the desertion of her mother, living with her grandfather, who was a kind and gentle man, and bequeathed her his house when he passed on, and the house was now sitting vacant back in Canoga Park. She told the doctor that she really did love me, that she wasn't just a gold digger, that it was hard for other people to understand this, given our age difference, but she really truly loved me dearly.

This made me sit up and pay closer attention.

Lola said she felt dead inside, although she was having emotional outbursts too, for no reason. One minute she wanted to wreck the house and kick me in the balls, and the next minute she was numb, dead, collapsed. She knew she should be happier now than she'd ever been, and she had no explanation for why she was in such a state, depressed one moment, screaming obscenities the next, and that Bob had mentioned she might be suffering from PTSD, but that didn't make much sense to her because Jake Valance was in solitary confinement now, so she should be feeling relieved.

Lola then answered a series of questions with "Yes" or "No" or "I'm not sure, maybe." Then she listened for quite a while before handing the cell phone to me. "HI, John," said Dr. Grace. "How are you feeling about Lola's state?"

"I'm totally baffled. I feel I've lost her. Was surprised to hear her tell you she loved me. Makes me feel like I've been a self-centered fool, unsympathetic to what Lola's been through. And it's all my fault—Lola would not have been put through that horror if she'd not become involved with me."

"Well, your brother Robert is right, Lola is exhibiting symptoms of PTSD. I have a connection at Johns Hopkins in Baltimore an old colleague I went to medical school with. I'm going to call him and ask for referrals in your area. You both need to speak with a professional, but let's begin with Lola. I'd like Lola to do what's called cognitive behavioral therapy as well as try a medication, which I'll prescribe. Later, we can adjust for strength as needed, or try another medication. We're each unique so not every med works the same for every patient. You'll need to give me the name of a drug store there so I can fax prescriptions. These meds are for her and just to bridge you both through this rough period. It's natural for the symptoms of PTSD to come on as a delayed reaction, hence the term 'post traumatic'. The meds will help but the talk therapy is what's most important, for that's what will enable both of you to understand what you're dealing with, and heal. I'd like you each to see different therapists at first, and later to do couple's counseling together. Are you agreeable to all this, John?"

"Yes, yes. When can we get her to a therapist?" I was focused on getting Lola help, seeing her as the cause of my bleak mood.

"Who is your neurologist," she asked.

"Dr. Rici in Santa Barbara."

"I'll call him. I think he'll set you up for another MRI at Johns Hopkins, and we can take it from there."

"Dr. Grace, if doctors can restore Lola, I'll be fine."

"Your depression and her PDST may be symbiotic."

"Oh?"

"Meanwhile, if Lola wants to talk to you about what happened, fine. But she might be fearful that going into those details could destroy your love for her, John. And the details could be horrible for you to listen to. If you can handle hearing about it, let her know. If you can't, let her talk it out with a therapist, or with Bob. It's important for her to recall it all, relive it, regurgitate it rather than let it fester. Once she's repeatedly examined it in detail, she'll come to feel like an observer rather than the victim—the horrible experience will lose its power over her. She'll become aware of what triggers the mood swings she's now having. Are you with us on this?"

"I certainly am."

"It may help to imagine her PTSD as an invisible monster. As long as she and those close to her aren't aware of this monster, it can sneak into her life and control her feelings and instigate very negative behaviors. Once we get the monster well defined and know what it's capable of, and why, we can put it in a cage, to carry on this metaphor. Lola can then control it rather than allowing it to control her. That's something of an oversimplification, John, but it conveys the idea."

"I've always thought of PTSD as something soldiers bring home from wars."

"Yes, and it's gone by different names in past times. It was called shell shock after World War Two, and other names after other wars. it's a condition brought on by shocks. Anyone can be hit by it. And of course some traumas are worse than others, so there's a kind of spectrum of severity. My guess is that Lola's kidnapping and sexual brutalizing is in the range of most severe. Our feelings about our sexuality are the most personal feelings we have. If you're agreeable to this approach, I'll proceed."

"I'm fully supportive of it," I said.

After we hung up, I noticed Bob and Lola watching me, waiting for me to react to what I'd just heard from Dr. Grace. I said, "Seems we're a household of trauma victims. Bob and I with our concussions, and now you, sweetheart, with what you've been through. Well, I hope this medical attention will help. And I want to say right now, Lola, that I will be happy to hear all the horrible details, if you care to talk them out to me. I won't judge. I'll listen to you as though what you're describing happened to me because I am one with you. Until we can see it as though it happened to someone else. So, let's be about the business of finding this monster and caging it so it can do you no more harm."

To which I got a big grin from Bob and a slight, shy smile from Lola.

"I deal with a monster called depression," said Bob. "I suspect you're dealing with the same monster, John, but we'll get to that later. Let's be thankful that paying for the medical help won't be a problem."

He was reminding me that years ago when he was suffering, he was unable to pay for medical help. It was Dad's money that finally came to his rescue. "There's no shortage of money," I said. "The government is printing truckloads of it every day."

"On orders from the Federal Reserve," Bob said.

"Let's debate that later."

Lola said, "I like the idea of talking about what I went through like it happened to someone else. I had to become someone else to deal with that scumbag."

Bob said, "It's like we've all arrived at a stopover on our journeys through life. Now we need to kick back a while and tell each other our stories."

"Neither of you would understand my story," I said.

"And neither of us think you would understand ours," said Bob. "Doesn't matter. You can suck the nourishment out of a story without understanding it."

For about a minute, we sat looking at each other like we'd just met. I was suddenly aware of how little I knew about the shaping of their lives, Bob's and Lola's, and how little they knew of the corporate world I was coming from.

"You're right, Bob. It's like we're living in three separate bubbles. Let's see if we can put these three bubbles together and form one large bubble."

That made them both smile. I stood up and held out my arms, and they stood and we all got into one big bear hug. Lola sobbed a few times and then laughed. It was the first laugh I'd heard from her since the night of the shootout.

As we broke from the hug, Bob and I stared at each other, eyeball to eyeball. The curious expression on his face expressed my feelings too. How did his return into my life come to this, this seeming transference of destinies? Me with my head scar and my life coming unhinged, he returned to the role of the big brother I looked to for help?

Chapter 44

It seemed to me that the reunion of John and myself had somehow triggered activity in the invisible realm that manifested as trouble for John—the same kind of trouble that had dogged me forty years ago. I'll eventually tell my friend Jorge about this and he'll consult his astrological charts and, no doubt, come up with an astrological explanation. I don't pretend to have any explanation for this strange overlap of destinies, as I'd come to think of it. But I was determined to see what I could do to bring us all through this rough patch—John head-banged into depression, Lola in PTSD, Laura in resentment, and me in the middle of this psychic crossfire, looking to engineer a future of happiness in a time of social and environmental upheaval. How could I do that? I felt Laura was the key.

Over dinner with Laura, I began by relating what had gone down the day before with Lola and John.

"That poor girl," said Laura. "It hadn't dented my mind till now—the horror she must have gone through with that criminal. But, you know, it's all because she was seduced by that rotten brother of yours. If he weren't such a pederast—"

"Laura, I'm getting tired of your resentment toward John. First, John is not a pederast—Lola was a 22-year-old call girl when they connected. Second, she's as much in love with him as he is with her. Right now, they're both going through hell because of what happened. Which, thirdly, was Jake Valance's doing. No one else is at fault. Understand?"

"Oh, Bob, my dear, I didn't mean for you to get on your high horse about this. It's just that I do have a lot of resentment, and with good reason."

"I know you do. And I agree you have good reason."

"But?"

"We have to get this resolved. I can't keep on commuting between you and John. And you're the one who is most harmed by your resentment."

"Yeah, yeah, I know."

"Your resentment is poisonous, too, it poisons others."

"I can't help how I feel, Bob."

"Maybe you're pinning the tail of your resentment on the wrong donkey."

"What's that supposed to mean?"

"Your marriage with John broke up. You split. End of story. There's no reason to hang onto the resentment."

"I'm not hanging onto it," she said. "It's hanging onto me."

"There are ways to get rid of such feelings. It's harming you and it's harming Lola, and it's driving a wedge between John and me. Your resentment has me commuting between you and them. That's got to end."

We were having dinner in the penthouse restaurant of an Ocean City hotel. Laura gazed out at the view: city lights to the north and south, dark ocean to the east. I had the sensation of being poised on the edge of the known peering into the dark abyss of the unknown. The known was being reunited with my brother and comfortably mated with Laura. The unknown was if we could all make a life together. If we couldn't do that, we were ships passing in the night.

Back in the sixties, I'd lived for a time in a commune where we had a saying that suddenly came back to me now: "Police the psychic space." Meaning, don't allow resentments or negative feelings of one for another to fester. Drive them into the open, talk them out. Don't allow them to act on us from the subtle space of the unmentioned.

Already the honeymoon excitement with Laura was waning. That was okay, but we now had to fit ourselves into some larger context, find exciting work to do, fun friends to hang out with. Beginning with John and Lola. Laura's resentment was like a poisonous snake in the woodpile of our little commune. It was threatening my relationship with John and, I suspected, on some subtle level we aren't fully aware of, John's relationship with Lola. I had to find a way to kill it.

After my long silence she said, "The last thing in the world I want is to lose you, Bob. And of course I understand that the resentment hurts me most of all. If I could rid myself of it, believe me I would. But my life was slashed and burned by the divorce, and the divorce was necessary to save the sanity of my children. There came a time when I had to get us all out of there. Your dear brother Jack was more absent when he was home than when he was calling home from thousands of miles away. The father my kids communicated with by telephone was a nice guy, a good father. The father he became when he landed for a weekend was something else. It was crazy making. Worse, it was heart breaking."

"John's biggest regret is the loss of his children, Laura. He devoted himself to that corporation. It was a separate reality and it took everything he had. He had nothing left for you and the kids. Nor for his first wife Kelly and her two children. They've all left him, and with good reason. He's alone now except for Lola and me."

"Does he feel regret?"

"Of course! He won't say much about it, though. You know John. He'd rather suffer in silence than lose his dignity, or what he perceives to be his dignity."

"How do you know he feels regret if he won't talk about it?"

"We're from the same gene pool. And why else would he fetch his crazy brother out of terminal incarceration? If he had his family together, why would he want me around? And Lola? If he had his life mate and grandchildren gathering at his home for holidays and such, he wouldn't need Lola. She became the answer to his loneliness. And he to her dead-end life."

"You're not crazy, Bob. You're the sanest man I've ever known."

"Thanks, but you don't know my whole story. Yet."

"Well, all I can say is, you Bradford boys sure do know how to put up a good front. Jack could be so hung over he could hardly pull himself out of bed some Monday mornings, but by 8 or 9 o'clock he'd look like a million bucks in his tailored suit and starched white shirt. Sometimes I hear you saying that you're a hopeless nut case, I just haven't noticed. I don't see you that way at all."

"I've learned to deal with my monster, my depression. As long as I stick to my routine, I'm fine."

"Your routine?"

"My meds and meds. Medications and meditations. As long as I take my daily medications and do my daily meditations, get some exercise and avoid alcohol, I'm fine. Well, I still have moments when I feel like Rip Van Winkle, but those are becoming less frequent."

"Rip Van Winkle?" she asked with her face scrunched up.

"Some day when we know each other better—after we've had a few knock down drag out fights—I'll tell you the gory details. For now, let's get back to your resentment of John and what it's doing to us, you and me, him and Lola. It's like we all live in an invisible bubble—we're keenly aware of each other, even when we have no physical contact. We bounce feelings off each other in this invisible bubble we live in, our psychic realm. How you feel about John affects all of us, but at such a subtle level, we're not aware of it."

"Oh, that's too deep for me," she said. "All I'm aware of is that I'm in love. Best honeymoon I've ever had."

"And your love brings me great joy. Being in love with you has me starting life anew. I'm no stranger to erotic love, but I'm a newcomer to the combined agape and erotic love I'm discovering with you."

"Agape?"

"The kind of love a friend feels for a friend, a man for a woman after their sexual passions are spent, a parent for a child, a child for a parent."

"But what I hear you saying is that my resentment toward John—"

"—is threatening to destroy us."

"What would you have me do? Pretend I don't feel what I feel?"

I wanted to say, Hey Laura, Lola is lonely and needs you, an older woman to show her how to become the wife of a high-powered corporate executive, because even in retirement, John is going to go on attending board meetings, doing his work, and a man's work is sacred. But instead, I opened my mouth and stalled.

She grinned coyly. "So, Mr. Smarty Pants, you don't know either."

"I know what would be best for all concerned. I just don't know how to get from here to there."

"And what would be best for all concerned?"

"For you and John to bury the hatchet and for your kids to come visit him, for you all to accept his thing with Lola, accept her into your family."

"For my kids to accept you is easy. I can hear them now. 'Mom's having a thing with Dad's crazy brother, Uncle Robert. Can you believe it?' As long as Mom's happy with you, they'll accept you, never doubt it."

"And for you to bury the hatchet with John?"

"Bury the hatchet—what a quaint saying. How does one do that, bury hurt and resentment?"

"Symbolically," I said.

"Give me a for instance."

"Well, like the American flag is a symbol. Some people worship it as being the country they love. They pour their adoration of country into this cloth symbol."

"But I have no such symbol of my resentment."

"Then you conjure one."

"How?"

"In the ancient Huna religion of Polynesia, they developed a ritual for casting out evil spirits—bad obsessions, negative thoughts, resentments. I used it to kick a drug habit. It works."

"How in the world did you become a devotee of...what it is? The ancient religion of the Polynesians?"

"It dates from a time in my life when I was importing Maui Wowie, marijuana grown in the highlands of Maui. I dealt with a group of hippies who lived out in the wilds, the north side of the island. There was a guy there who was obsessed with something—I forget what exactly but the point is, the group put him through this ritual to rid him of this obsession. We all went to what's called the Seven Sacred Falls and camped there. Each morning and evening, this guy would stand at the top of the highest falls and imagine his obsession was a thing. He symbolized it as a bag of shit lodged in his solar plexus. When the image was crystal clear and he could feel it strongly, he'd jump off the top of the falls and when he hit the water, he'd imagine this bag of shit, this obsession, being flung out of his body and disappearing into the wild blue yonder. By the end of the third day, he was free of it. We all picked up our tents and trekked back to their permanent place, a village of thatched-roof huts up in the mountains. Some years later, I was so hooked on cocaine, my nose so full I couldn't stuff any more up it, and my system so coked, another shot of the stuff only depressed me more. I went to Maui, rented a camper, drove out to Hana and camped near the Seven Sacred Falls and put myself though that ritual. It worked like magic. I came home clean as a whistle."

"So," she said, "are you suggesting we fly to Maui and I do this ritual to get rid of my resentment?"

"We could do that. John wants me to go to Hawaii soon and inspect his properties there."

"I'll pack my bags," she said.

"Or," I said, "we could go down to the beach here every morning and evening, and you could run into the cold winter surf—once you've imagined your resentment as some *thing* in your solar plexus and really want to rid yourself of it. Doesn't matter what thing you imagine it as. The shock of the cold water combined with your intention and visualization is what does it. Three days of this, morning and evening, and you're cured."

As I was speaking, she swung her chair around so that her face was to the dark sea, and she was gazing out at it pensively. Her expression was suddenly so serious, I feared I'd overstepped the line by suggesting this "savage" way of psychotherapy.

"If," I added, "you really want to get rid of your resentment. Maybe you like having it. Maybe it's become like an old friend you like having around."

"I'm trying to imagine us all getting together and making happy small talk. Your brother and Lola, you and me. What the hell would we talk about?"

"We would tell our stories. Lola could tell her story—she very much needs an older woman to tell her story to, you know. It takes another woman to truly empathize with what she's been through. John could tell his story—facing retirement alone because he'd put so much energy into his career, he'd neglected those nearest and dearest to him. You could tell your story—how you had to leave John to save your sanity and your kids, and then what happened in your life that John doesn't yet know about. Neither do I, really. Your life after John is still vague to me. And I could tell my story—how I left home at age eighteen as an Olympic hopeful with a talent for writing, became caught up in the Movement, became a brain-damaged derelict and criminal drug dealer, living in the streets, eating out of dumpsters, sleeping in cardboard boxes, lost and hopeless."

She stared at me, shocked, raised eyebrows, and such a frowning expression I thought she was about to kiss me off and have nothing more to do with me. My drug dealing past was one thing—being a pothead herself, she found that kind of sexy—but she had not known the depths of poverty to which I'd sunk, and most people blame the homeless for their misfortune and avoid them, treat them like their misfortune is a contagious disease. It's so easy to blame the victims of our many human maladies.

A bus boy arrived to clear away our dishes. Then a waiter came to ask if we'd like desert or an after-dinner drink. We declined. She continued her frowning stare. I pushed my chair away from the table and stood, ready to leave, thinking this was the last I'd ever see of Laura.

"Let's go down to the beach," she said. "I want to see how shocking it will be to run into that icy surf."

About the Author

When **John Robert Gover** was 11 months old, his father was killed in a car crash while on his way to study brain surgery in Minnesota. His mother dropped the John from his name because his father's uncle, Dr. John, had driven the fatal car. Robert grew up in Girard, an orphanage in Philadelphia, went to the University of Pittsburgh on athletic scholarship, earned a BA in economics, became a best-selling novelist by age 30, crashed and burned to homeless by age 50, recovered, and now lives with his wife Carolyn in Rehoboth Beach, Delaware, where the state bureaucracy insists on calling him John, thus resurrecting the name he would have had if his father had lived.